BRAVE NEW LAND!

Against the worst of man and nature, a small bank of courageous men and women settled on the West Texas frontier—a harsh untamed land where herds of maverick longhorn roamed free, and fame and fortune waited for men of courage and vision.

BOLD PIONEERS!

With fearless devotion to duty, Charles Justiss and his wife Angela, their family, and a few close friends forged the raw beginnings of what would become the largest cattle operation in West Texas—symbolizing the fulfillment of their dreams and hard-won ideals in the glorious new land!

TEXAS BRAVOS #3: PALO PINTO

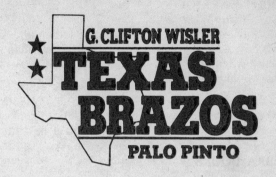

G. CLIFTON WISLER
TEXAS BRAZOS
PALO PINTO

ZEBRA BOOKS
KENSINGTON PUBLISHING CORP.

ZEBRA BOOKS

are published by

Kensington Publishing Corp.
475 Park Avenue South
New York, NY 10016

First printing: September 1987

Printed in the United States of America

*for my brother David
and his dear wife Melanie*

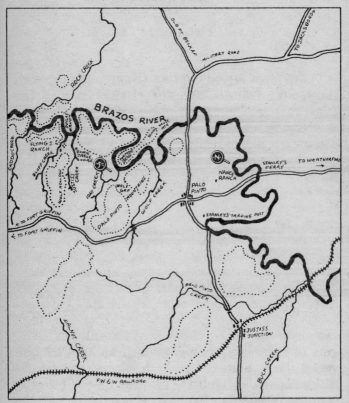

Prologue

The Brazos River cuts an uneven arc through the heart of Texas. From its headwaters in the Caprock country of the Llano Estacado, the Brazos sweeps toward the Gulf of Mexico, wrapping its waters around unyielding rocks and ridges. Not far from where the Clear Fork merges its waters with the main channel, the Brazos cuts a deep canyon. On the towering cliffs overlooking the surging waters of the river, an ancient race dwelt. How long the cliff people inhabited the land no one knows. Time and fierce enemies, or maybe the harshness of the seasons, erased them from the land, even as it swept away the Comanches who followed. Survival is always a near thing in such a hard and inhospitable land.

The first Spaniards to pass along the high canyon walls were reminded of Castille and Aragon, of ramparts and parapets from another universe. They named the high places the Castle Cliffs. The land itself they called Palo Pinto, the country of the painted stick. Perhaps it was the speckled stone native to the region that gave the place its name, or else the afternoon shadows that often painted shades of crimson and amber upon the land. No one can know, for the Spanish didn't stay.

From the time the fledgling Republic of Texas was founded in 1836, white men began venturing up the Brazos, searching out new lands and fresh opportunity. The lack of plentiful timber and the unpredictable climate proved too much for many. Others yielded their lives to Comanche war parties. Those few who built dog run cabins, planted corn, and ran cattle, fought a never-ending battle against the elements and the Comanches. It wasn't until the close of the great American Civil War when a new breed of man began to appear along the Texas frontier, that permanent dwellings rose. Desperate men, born of the fires of war and a ruined economy, found in the free-roaming longhorns a chance for wealth and power.

By 1870 vast herds of cattle were etching trails across the Indian Nations into Kansas. Northern mouths were hungry for Texas beef, and the dollars that flowed south built homes and fed children. Later, schools and churches and prosperity arrived. By the final quarter of the nineteenth century, Palo Pinto County was a wilderness no more. Market roads crossed north and south, east and west. Established ranches sent hundreds of steers to Kansas railheads.

By 1876, more than a decade had passed since Appomattox. A vengeful North had grown weary of its military occupation of Texas. Hatred gave way to political expediency, and the Republican government so long imposed on the population with its high taxes and heavy-handed laws, found itself abandoned by federal troops. A new constitution was written, and the state was returned to the hands of her people.

A new dawn greeted the ranchers and farmers

of Palo Pinto County. Quannah Parker and his Comanches had abandoned the Llano. Frontier forts which had once housed hundreds of blue-clad cavalry were garrisoned by skeleton crews. Soon post like Ft. Richardson at Jacksboro and Ft. Griffin on the Clear Fork of the Brazos would be abandoned, given back to the elements.

The heavy steel hammers of railroad crews soon resounded across the plains. From Marshall a line edged its way to Ft. Worth, already a thriving market for cattle and horses on the old Chisholm Trail. Another railroad crossed the Nations from Kansas City. Other lines linked the Gulf Coast to the state capital at Austin. There was even talk of a new railroad joining Ft. Worth with California.

For men like Charlie Justiss who'd come to Palo Pinto with little more than the shirt on his back and a will to build a future for his family, it was the birth of a new prosperity. But it was also the close of an era, for rails linking Texas to Kansas City and Chicago spelled the end of the cattle trails, and what tranquility followed the taming of the Comanche marked the doom of the open range. New population introduced new problems.

A man either grows with change or he dies with it, Charlie often told himself. He was, after all, the same man who had left the despair of his father's farm downriver to carve out a cattle empire in Palo Pinto County. When others had given way to flood or drought, Charlie had always found a way to survive. And now at a time when falling beef prices and greater competition drove other cattlemen to grief, Charlie envisioned a new future and planned accordingly.

"A wise man never forgets the past, never loses touch with his roots," Charlie told his eldest son

9

Ross. "But if he shields his eyes and refuses to see the future, it's all for naught."

And so Charlie had dispatched Ross to Austin to read the law. A younger son, Ryan, was sent to the new Agricultural and Mechanical College of Texas. When County Judge Joe Nance objected to spending tax money on a new school, to bridging creeks and the river, Charlie reluctantly accepted the reins of the opposition. In the autumn of 1876 Charlie Justiss became Palo Pinto County's first post-Reconstruction county judge.

"Who could have imagined it?" his wife Angela asked as she helped squeeze Charlie into a tailored suit. "It seems only yesterday we were crawling behind a rock and dodging Comanche lances."

"Yes," he told her as he gazed out at the cattle grazing on the far bank of Bluff Creek. "And I'm not altogether sure that I wouldn't be happier riding the trail to Kansas or chasing Stands Tall's Comanches than trying to stretch the county's taxes till they pay the county's bills."

Angela smiled and nodded her head. And yet Charlie knew she was proudest of her boys' education, of their daughter Victoria's work at the county's new schoolhouse, of roads and churches and law and order.

"No man ever tamed the land," his brother Bowie once remarked. "The women do that. We men, well, we can't help missing a bit of the wild, unfettered ways. The women, though, long for a newer, better world."

It was true. Charlie often observed the terrible emptiness of frontier cabins built by men alone. It was strange how warm a bit of gingham curtain could make a place. A dirt floor didn't matter so much come winter when children played in a corner or a soft voice sang away the evening chill.

I guess that's what we call civilization, Charlie thought. And if it swept away the Comanches, slaughtered the buffalo and fenced the range, well, nothing was had without paying a price.

I

Prosperity

Chapter 1

Springtime in Texas was the finest of seasons. There was a fresh, wonderfully sweet scent to the air. On every hillside new life sprang forth. Trees budded, and wildflowers splashed showers of color across the land. Spring was the time of rebirth, of fresh beginnings, of dreaming and wondering and building.

For Charlie Justiss, it was the best that life along the Brazos provided. The days lengthened so that there was daylight enough for all that required doing. The silence of winter was cast off by the myriad sounds of cardinals and meadowlarks. Even the mimicry of that old impostor, the mockingbird, was a welcome delight. And if April often proved a bit wet for his liking, it was so much better than hot, dry August!

Yes, spring did bring changes, Charlie thought as he rode along the river. A pair of boys from town tossed lines into the shallows just ahead, and Charlie gave them a nod. There was a time when he knew everybody in the county. Of late families seemingly arrived weekly to carve out a small farm or ranch along one of the creeks to the south. Others erected small shops in town or worked for wages hauling freight or tending livestock.

"No school?" Charlie called to them.

"No, Judge," the tallest of the two replied. "Pa's away to Weatherford, and Jim and me's got to look after the place."

Charlie laughed at the guilty-faced youngsters. His daughter Victoria would certainly have words with them. She took her duties at the school in town seriously, a bit too much so for some. Charlie'd never found fault with her, of course. Being the only daughter and eldest child in a family of eight, Charlie always felt Vicki deserved a little extra leeway. She nearly always got it.

Charlie glanced back at the boys again before continuing on. It seemed natural for them to be passing an April morning at the river. The schoolhouse with its three shelves of books was still new. Only last month Charlie had gotten the glass for windows. Not too many years back a boy of twelve would be readying himself for the long drive to Kansas. It surely must have seemed a disappointment to some that there were now plenty of men to head the steers up the trail, that instead of sharing some high adventure, boys were condemned instead to pass their spring mornings in Vicki's schoolhouse.

That's just a small change, Charlie thought to himself. The bigger ones often slipped past while you weren't looking. Like the cavalry. Wasn't it just last May that he'd stood a mile upriver and watched Captain Henry Eppler lead the last patrol from Ft. Richardson. The Comanches were

16

gone now, and the captain had wondered how long it would be before Ft. Griffin was closed as well.

"Oh, they'll leave the place open for a time," Charlie'd argued. "The country hereabouts is still unsettled. But once the buffalo are all gone and settlers arrive, that'll be the end of it."

"Ever think you'd see the day?" the captain had asked.

"Well, Henry, I quit reading palms a while back. I try to keep my eyes open and read the way the wind blows."

"What do you see?"

"Lots of changes coming."

"I suspect you're right, Charlie. For my part, I guess I'll serve so long as they want me. Catherine and the boys will have plenty of room at Griffin."

"Sorry you didn't head up to the Dakotas?"

"Custer and the Seventh mostly got themselves killed. There are those who might envy that kind of an end, but not me. I've got family. I'll serve out my enlistment."

"And afterward? Will you go back to Michigan?"

"Nothing back there for us. The boys were born here. They're Texans. Guess maybe I am, too."

"It's the meanest, hardest country you ever did see, isn't it?" Charlie'd asked. "But it does get under your skin."

"Still got your eyes on a stretch of land for me?"

"One thing for certain about this country. Somebody's always got a piece of it up for sale. Whenever you say the word, I'll find you a nice little place."

"May not be long now," Captain Eppler said,

removing his hat and wiping his forehead with a kerchief. Charlie Justiss wasn't the only man with flakes of gray in his hair.

Sometimes it seems like the world's grown old, Charlie thought, staring back at the fishermen. Was it only nine years back that Charlie'd greeted a young lieutenant on this very stretch of range? Back then Henry Eppler's eyes had been as wide and full of wonder as any of Vicki's schoolboys. Now the years had taken their toll on the cavalryman. And on me, too, Charlie confessed.

Charlie spent no more time on idle remembering that morning. He slapped the rump of his sleek Arabian stallion and headed the ebony horse along the river. It was another three miles to Stanley's Ferry, the spot where the Weatherford market road crossed the Brazos. Old Art Stanley had operated the ferry the last few years. The bridge Charlie Justiss was building would better serve the freight wagons and travelers who used that road traveling toward Ft. Griffin and the new ranches springing up in Shackleford County and beyond.

Another man might have taken that road from town, spared himself the longer route along the winding Brazos, but Charlie was partial to the river. Except for the years spent fighting Yanks with General Lee, he'd passed his whole life within a stone's throw of that river. It smelled, even tasted of home. And its slow churning waters were as much a part of spring as the songbirds.

When Charlie approached the ferry, he slowed his pace and drank in the scene. A half dozen men kept busy hammering planks onto a skeleton frame. The piers had been sunk two weeks earlier.

18

Henry Eppler had recommended Thadeus Higginbotham, a former army engineer for the job, and the grizzled old campaigner had stormed and cursed and complained for a week until the job was done correctly.

"I thought getting work out of a company of Ohio volunteers was tough," Higginbotham told Charlie afterward. "These cowboys don't seem to know a level from a square. How you'll finish the job, I don't know. It's simple carpentry, but not simple enough, I fear, for the men you've provided."

But while it was true the crew knew the hind end of a longhorn better than planes or squares, there wasn't a man among them who hadn't built a cabin or a barn. Charlie turned the men over to Marty Steele, and Higginbotham returned to Houston.

"You appear to be making progress," Charlie called as he approached the bridge. "Figure yourself to be through so you can help Wes and Billy with the roundup next week?"

"Better be, Charlie," Marty said, peeling his sweat-soaked shirt from his shoulders. "I'd about as soon drive a thousand head to Dodge single-handed as put up another of your fool bridges."

"He's just forgotten, Judge," young Andy Coonce said as he strained to lift a plank into place. "Told me the dust alone was enough to age a man ten years."

"What would you know about it, Two Bit?" Marty said, laughing as he tossed his shirt at the seventeen-year-old. "You were still wetting your mama's knee the first time Charlie and I headed to Kansas. Now get along to work with you or we'll send you back to the livery. Shoveling cow dung's more in keeping with your talents anyhow."

The older men laughed heartily, and Andy grinned.

"Was good experience," the boy declared. "Got me accustomed to the kind of company I got to keep nowadays. Some might take offense at looking at the hind end of a horse all day."

Charlie couldn't help smiling with approval. Those who couldn't join the jesting rarely survived a cattle drive, and Andy Coonce promised to be a fine hand with the horses. Since Angela's cousin, Luis Morales, had partnered up with Vicki's husband Bret Pruett, the Flying J Ranch had hired a half dozen wranglers. None of them had Luis's touch with the horses, and Charlie even now left his prize Arabians to Luis's care over at Fortune Bend.

"This Coonce boy has the touch, though," Bret had told Charlie the previous autumn. "I know he's a tad young, but so was I when you took a chance on me. The boy's got no family."

"Another stray for me to pick up, huh?" Charlie'd asked.

"Well, I don't know anyone who's got a better knack for it than you do, Charlie. You've had most of the orphans in Palo Pinto County working Flying J beeves at one time or another."

"They work cheap, and a bit harder, too. Besides, I'll not soon forget the mistake we made with young Jim Case. That boy would have taken to honest work given the chance. As it was, he wound up stealing cattle, and we ended up hanging him. A waste, that was."

"Never entirely looked at it that way," Bret had said thoughtfully. "You might be making my job

20

easier, huh?"

Charlie had nodded. It wasn't without a little pride that he'd watched his son-in-law grow into a fine county sheriff. At the time Charlie figured Bret landed the job on account of his relation to the Justiss family. Now Charlie thought Bret probably helped Charlie Justiss get reelected county judge.

There were, after all, those who thought they could do a better job. One of them sat atop his horse on the town side of the river.

"Morning, Joe," Charlie called to Joe Nance.

"Charlie," Nance answered, tipping his hat. The silver-haired rancher was among the early settlers of the county, and Charlie always judged he owed his start ranching to Joe Nance. Of late, though, Joe's Circle N spread had fallen on hard times, and Joe found himself hemmed in by small out-fits, cut off from the open range to the south and most often short on riders, funds, and patience.

"Come out to have a look at the bridge?" Charlie asked.

"That what this is?" Nance asked in turn. "Thought they were starting a stairway to the moon. Don't know how you managed to talk the people into footing the bill for all this. Art's ferry always did the job before. Taxes are high enough as is without throwing money away."

"Oh, Joe," Art Stanley said, stepping out from the ferry landing. "You know I've sometimes got wagons waiting for hours. Except when the river's way low, everybody heading east has to cross here. The county's growing. More people have stock to get to market. People pass through bound west. The bridge was needed."

"As to cost," Charlie said, splashing his way

21

into the shallows so he could address Nance better, "the county's only paid for half the lumber. Art and my brother Bowie paid the balance so their freight outfit can keep to its schedule. The crew's all off my ranch or Art's ferry. And I don't recall you objecting half so much about the bridge we built across the river on the old Beknap market road."

"Oh, the cattle markets are north, Charlie," Nance continued to argue. "Makes sense to tie us to Jacksboro, not to mention Wichita and Dodge City."

"That was before," Charlie grumbled. "They've got a railhead in Ft. Worth now. Before long they'll be crossing the county itself. No, it's the east we'll look to."

"Look to the east and spend money, eh?" Nance asked. "Taxes come hard where some of us are concerned."

"Progress has a price," Charlie said, quoting a phrase Joe Nance himself used often enough before losing the judgeship. "but as for this bridge, the county's getting a bargain. If you feel otherwise, feel free to declare for the next election."

"You can bank on that!"

Nance continued to argue against the bridge, but Charlie turned his horse away. He hadn't come to debate Joe Nance. He wanted to inspect the work. If it was moving slowly, as some said, it certainly wasn't Marty's fault. The cowboys laid plank after plank and hammered them into place. The crossbeams and rails had been finished two days before.

"I figure we'll finish in three more days," Marty whispered. "I wouldn't want the others to know I said so, but we've done a fair job once that Yank

22

Higginbotham got clear of here."

"Maybe," Charlie admitted, "But we needed him to set the piers right. I wouldn't want this bridge sinking into the mud. I've seen it happen before. Higginbotham found us the right spot to anchor the bridge. That's what he was hired for."

"Next time around Ry can do it. Angela tells me he's learning all about bridges and railroads at that college of his."

Charlie smiled at the mention of his son Ryan.

"I hope he's learning something about cattle, too. That's why I sent him there."

"Oh? And here we all thought you sent him 'cause Angela put her foot down on it."

"That, too," Charlie confessed, laughing.

He spent another hour at the bridge site before turning toward town. The Palo Pinto Stock-raisers Association held its monthly meeting that afternoon at the Brazos Hotel. Charlie didn't particularly care for the meetings. They often proved to be bitter quarrels between the big ranchers like Joe Nance who had long used the southern range for their herds and the smaller newcomers who held title to the land and resented some other outfit running stock across their acreage.

"Time was I'd round up my outfit and ride these upstarts into the Brazos," Nance often remarked. "Now they wave their deeds in your face, Charlie, and you judge them to own the range. They never bled for it! They don't have the scars to show for those years when a man deemed himself lucky not to part with his hair."

Charlie crossed the river on Art Stanley's ferry, then continued along toward town. After stopping by the courthouse long enough to fetch Bret

Pruett, he continued down the street to the hotel. The two-story structure, built by Georgia Staves the year before, boasted ten rooms, a bathhouse, and a restaurant big enough to feed, among other groups, the Palo Pinto Stock-raisers.

"Good day to you, Georgia," Charlie said as he led Bret into the restaurant.

"Welcome to the Cattlemen's Room," Georgia answered, making a broad sweeping motion with her hand as if to emphasize the status of the place. "It's not too late for dinner. The Stokelys are dining in the corner. Will you be having something?"

"Bret?" Charlie asked.

"Sure," the young sheriff said, smiling. "Just don't tell Vicki. She'll have my hide. She counts it unfair for me to hobnob about while she's eating out of a pail over at the schoolhouse."

Charlie laughed, then followed Georgia to an empty table. He waved to his neighbors, Brad and Ben Stokely, then took a seat across from Bret.

"Charlie, what do you think of all this railroad talk?" Ben called across the room.

"Time for that in a bit," Charlie answered more quietly. "I'm about to treat my son-in-law to a forbidden dinner."

"Vicki keeping you on a short leash, is she, Bret?" Brad asked.

"When she can," Bret answered, and the others in the room laughed.

Dinner passed quietly thereafter. Charlie spent most of his time eating and inquiring into the latest exploits of his namesake, Bret's oldest boy, Charles Justiss Pruett.

"Angela says he gets more like you every day,"

Bret said, grinning. "Up to some new prank every time you turn around. Now he's in school, of course, and his mama's got her eye on him. Little Charlie says it's no fun at all, this schooling."

"Yeah, I spotted a pair of boys down at the river fishing this morning," Charlie said. "Does seem a shame to pass such a fine day learning your letters."

"Don't let Vee hear you say that. She thrashes those wandering souls but good when she catches them."

"I don't see how she does it, what with four youngsters at home and the whole town to look after during the day."

"You know Vee. She loves it. If it was up to her, I think she'd have one a year like Teresa Morales. As for me, four's plenty, especially when the two youngest are scarcely a year apart."

"That's how it was with Billy and Ryan."

"Lord, I hope neither of 'em's another Billy. We'll have to shackle his feet."

Charlie laughed. Billy was twenty-one now, and he could still give the wildest hand on the ranch a run for the money. Angela would have sent him to the new ag college with Ryan except some feared Billy'd burn the place to the ground within a week.

"Remember the time Vicki tried to get him to read that English history?" Charlie'd reminded Angela. "He pranked her for a month. Never again did she offer him a book. No, sir."

Charlie might have gone on sharing stories of the family had not a group of farmers who ran stock as a sideline entered the room. J. C. Parnell,

25

the eldest and a grandfather at close to sixty, led the way. A pair of younger men, Pinkney Cooke and Lewis Frost followed. The others kept to the shadows, their fearful, mistrusting eyes testifying to the hardships of frontier life.

"You ready to get things started, Judge?" Parnell asked.

"Sure," Charlie told the older man. "Pick up a chair and gather 'round. Let's have at it."

Ben Stokely began by discussing a problem he was having with renegade buffalo hiders from the Flat, that huddle of clapboard shacks down the hill from Ft. Griffin. The heyday of buffalo hunters was well past, and many of the derelict hunters chose to skin cows instead. Others turned their hands to rustling. Even the smaller outfits had a common grievance against thieves, and for a time the meeting remained peaceful. After Bret Pruett promised to make a sweep westward toward the Flat, most of the cattlemen appeared satisfied. Then Joe Nance entered the room.

"Sorry to be late, friends," Nance apologized. "Had to have a word with my boy, Randolph. You all know he runs my outfit now."

The others nodded. Some grumbled as Nance began to recount the history of the Circle N. When Joe turned to the subject of rustlers, Charlie interrupted.

"Joe, we're glad to see you and all, but we've pretty well covered that. Bret will have a look at the western range. If there's something else . . ."

"There is!" Nance suddenly shouted. "I had a couple of hundred head grazing down at Village Bend, and somebody's run 'em down south a good fifteen miles. That's still public land, I believe."

26

"Art Stanley holds title to the river acreage," Charlie responded. "The land just below is part of the Ellis farm."

"Yes," Roger Ellis said, standing. "I had my boys chase some cows out of our cornfields. We've just finished planting, you know, and those cows were trampling the fields."

"They've always grazed there," Nance objected.

The others moaned, and Charlie walked to where Joe Nance stood.

"We've spoken of this before, Joe," Charlie whispered. "He's within his rights to protect his property."

"What right has he to that land?" Nance argued. "I've bled over this county, given it my life!"

"I've done my share of bleedin', too!" Ellis yelled, opening his shirt to reveal a wicked scar across the chest. "Yank saber did that. I've also got two holes in my legs. They were caused by a man who thought he owned all of Parker County. I've got title, Mr. Nance!"

"He does, too," Parnell agreed. "You know we've got no complaint against grazing the public range, gentlemen. Shoot, we do the same thing ourselves. We need that grass."

"Charlie, I helped you up the trail to Kansas that first time," Nance said, staring at Charlie with blazing eyes. "You remember how it was in the old days."

"Times change, though," Charlie said, sighing. "Maybe we should have bought that land when we had the chance. You can't fault these folks for wanting to ranch."

"They're choking me and my outfit."

"They're just doing the same as you and me," Charlie explained. "Trying to survive. I know in some places," Charlie went on, nodding to Ellis in particular, "the old outfits stand against the new. That solves nothing. The truth is we're all facing the same trouble."

"Which is?" Parnell asked.

"The market. Now that the Comanches are tamed, the whole of West Texas is opening up to ranching. I remember when thirty-five dollars a head was a fair market price. What'd you get last year, Brad? Fifteen? I got seventeen myself, and we were early up the trail. The profit's about gone, friends. As for trailing steers, I can smell the railroad coming. It's already in Ft. Worth, and there's talk of crossing toward El Paso. My boy Ryan's down at the new agricultural college. They talk about fencing, refining the breed."

"Fencing?" Parnell asked. "Barbed wire, you mean."

"Keeping the herds separated. It'll come once the open range is sold off. No other way to keep the cows from breeding at will. That's the future."

"Can't trail cattle across fenced range," Ben grumbled. "I'd rather tangle with rustlers."

"You've at least got water, Stokely," Parnell said, rising angrily. "I've heard how down south men with all the water fence their neighbors off. Stock can't survive without water. They have to either sell out or cut fences."

In a matter of minutes the meeting dissolved into a heated quarrel. Small farmers like Roger Ellis who ran cattle as an afterthought favored fencing the livestock off from cornfields. Most were in peril of losing the public range and its vast grazing acreage.

"Neighbors, please!" Charlie pleaded as Ben Stokely squared off with Ellis. "No one's put up so much as a fencepost yet. Let's quiet ourselves. It's almost time for spring roundup. Let's get organized for the task at hand and worry about fences if and when they appear."

Chapter 2

Talk of barbed wire and free range didn't die down quickly, though. Even on the Flying J, cowboys argued against the devil wire.

"Once the range is closed, we'll be little more than farmers ourselves," Marty Steele complained. "What's left for a wandering man to do?"

"It won't change much," Charlie responded. "We keep our stock on our own range now. In truth, it might cut down on the rustling. Now no one thinks twice if a crew drives a few hundred head across the range. Everybody moves his cows around. It's hard to spot thieves."

"Maybe," Marty said, clearly unconvinced.

Some have a tough time accepting change, Charlie thought as he left Marty brooding in the line camp. For ten years after the surrender at Appomattox Marty Steele had worn his threadbare infantry jacket. Butternut brown had long since faded into washed-out yellow, but even so the coat seemed to attest to the fact that Marty Steele had never really been defeated by anyone or anything in his entire life.

Charlie had little time to worry about Marty's

feelings or even to envision the future of the Flying J. While other ranches took on extra hands and readied themselves for the long cattle drives to Dodge City, Charlie devoted more of his time to visiting the telegraph office.

"I thought Ross was down in Austin," Wyatt Palmer, the telegraphist, commented. "When did he head to Kansas City?"

"Last week," Charlie said. "He's there to visit a friend."

"Oh?"

But though Palmer probed for more information, Charlie kept his own council. The telegrams were cryptic as well.

DOWN ONE FROM A YEAR AGO, the first message from Ross read. CAN TAKE DOZEN ROSES WILL PICK UP AT BUGLE ROSS

"You haven't gone to work for the Pinkertons or something, have you, Charlie?" Palmer asked as he delivered the message. "This some sort of code?"

"Maybe," Charlie said, pocketing the telegram. "But, of course, you wouldn't pass on a person's business even if you knew it, would you?"

Palmer shook his head and retired. Charlie Justiss wasn't a man you pressed for information. Once the telegrapher left, Charlie deciphered the message. It wasn't good news.

Down one meant the offer Jordan Talbot, the Kansas City cattle buyer, had extended was sixteen dollars, one down from the '78 price at Dodge City. A dozen meant Talbot would only buy 1,200 head. Delivery would be accepted at

Ft. Worth, the bugle in Ross's code. It was disappointing.

"We can do better at Dodge, Papa," Billy argued when Charlie passed along the message. "It's been a good year. We've got maybe three thousand steers ready for the trail."

"You remember last year?" Charlie asked. "We ended up selling three hundred head to brokers because the buyers were oversold. It could be worse with all these new ranches up above us."

"Twelve hundred, though. It's barely enough to meet expenses."

"Nonsense. It's a fair profit. What's more, we won't be paying a trail crew, and if it works, we'll be four days from shipping any time Talbot needs beef. In time we can work the price back up."

"I don't mind the trail, Papa. Truth is it's about the only excitement to be found anymore."

"We can live without that kind of excitement. You're not forgetting the year we were hit by that bandit Keeling? I'd as soon not bury any more friends."

"You've made up your mind then."

"Yes," Charlie said. "Think over who you want to take along to Ft. Worth. Doc Singer can cook and drive the wagon. You'll want Wes and Marty, of course."

"Andy Coonce to tend the horses. Might be good for Joe and Chris to come, too. It's just to Ft. Worth, so Mama won't complain too much. It might be as close as they ever come to a real trail drive."

"Feeling old, Billy?" Charlie asked, resting a hand on the young man's shoulder.

"It's hard to do a good job pranking folks when you've got such a short trail to ride."

Charlie laughed, but he saw beneath Billy's grin the same reluctance to accept change that Marty had shown wearing that old jacket.

"He's bound to have a rough time of it," Charlie told Angela. "Ross's about ready to read law, and Ry's down studying engineering. Joe and Chris will have their turn at college, too, I'm guessing. Billy, well, he's always been the wild one."

"He's his father's son," Angela said as she stroked Charlie's chest with her soft hands. "Each time I start to worry about him, though, I remember how that snake bit him on the way up here. He was close to death, but somehow he hung on."

"He survived getting his leg close to shot off back in '75, too," Charlie recalled. "There's more to Billy than meets the eye sometimes. He's good with the crew. This ranch will have need of him."

As roundup continued, Charlie passed less and less time in town. The Brazos bridge was finished, and there was no county business to conduct that Bret couldn't handle. In truth, the town was near deserted. Every able-bodied male over twelve was employed at roundup, and most everyone else was busy cooking or driving supply wagons or hawking goods at the cattle camps.

Wes Tyler and three others represented the Flying J when the open range was cleared of stock. Only three dozen Justiss cows were among the hundreds gathered in. About half had calves trailing along. Wes drove the stock across the Ft. Griffin road to the south line camp. There the calves received their brands. Of the eight bull calves, all but one were gelded and sent their way.

By the time Ross arrived at the ranch with the terms of sale, the branding was nearly finished. Billy was already collecting the steers for the drive in the box canyon out on Caddo Creek.

"Seems like a mighty small drive you're putting together," Marty observed. "Charlie, you didn't take on many new hands. You planning something different, maybe adding some acreage?"

"No," Charlie said, "though we might consider that. Land prices seem more than fair just now, and there's some good land up north along Rock Creek."

"Glad to hear it. Hey, Billy," Marty said, waving Billy to the fire, "you think we might stay on an extra week in Dodge like back in '75? You missed out on that, what with your leg all shot up. The girls were more'n friendly that year."

"Won't be going to Dodge this time around," Billy mumbled.

"Charlie?" Marty cried out. "Not Dodge? Where to?"

Charlie shook his head and sighed. He'd hoped to tell the crew later, when the work was all done and no one would object to a short trail.

"Ft. Worth," Charlie explained. "We've already sold twelve hundred steers, and we'll deliver them there."

"How many? Twelve hundred?" Marty gasped. "Why, we could still head another thousand or so along to Dodge."

"No," Ross said, breaking in. "We will be delivering five hundred more to Ft. Worth in August, and more after that, God willing. But Dodge City won't be a good place this year. Too many herds

34

will drive cattle up there. Market's down already, and it could get worse. Some may be glad to get ten dollars a head."

"Can't be!" Marty complained. "Charlie, Ft. Worth? Why, that's not enough of a trail to whet a man's thirst. I ride close to that far on a Saturday night. This is like selling steers at the slaughterhouse door. An outfit needs a trail to sharpen its edge. How else'll you weed out the bad ones?"

"Jamie Dunlap wasn't among the bad ones," Charlie mumbled. "I've been shot at, often, on that trail. I near lost Billy in '75, and before that, Bret Pruett. The Ft. Worth price is in line with last year's, and it's not near as risky. We lost what, a hundred head last year? And a man besides."

"You could have a stampede going to Ft. Worth, Charlie."

"Could, but the trail's short, and a stampede's less likely. There's only the Brazos and a bit of the Trinity to cross. It makes more sense, Marty. The last few years cattle have gone for a song at Dodge. We've had men shot up on the trail, and two years ago Mack Watley got shot to pieces in a saloon."

"Dodge isn't the only place to trail cattle to. I've heard crews take steers into Nebraska, Colorado, the Dakotas, even Wyoming."

"They take seed stock. There's no money in that, and all you really do is add to the competition. Besides, if this sale proves out, we could find ourselves supplying stock regular. It would spread the work over the whole year, too. That would mean regular work for more men."

"And none at all for some," Marty grumbled.

"Sometimes I hate for it all to end, too," Charlie confessed. "But I've seen change come enough to know it will, whether you and I like it or not. The trick is to turn with the current. Otherwise you're trampled."

Charlie intended to keep his plans quiet, but by the end of the week half the county knew. Brad Stokely was the first to speak of it to Charlie.

"I hear you're taking the short trail this year, Charlie," Brad said. "Give up on Dodge?"

"We had a tough time last year. I bet on a sure thing when I have the chance," Charlie explained.

"Ben and I haven't had much luck of late, either. We wouldn't mind contracting some steers the same way you did."

"Well, you could wire Jordan Talbot in Kansas City. He might buy your herd."

"Be even more likely if you were to wire him, Charlie. You've done some sharp business with those buyers before."

"I didn't have anything at all to do with it this time around. I sent Ross."

"But they knew who was making the deal. Send a wire?"

"I'll send a wire for you, Brad, but I can't promise anything more. Those buyers have got us by the throat. The range is overstocked, so they can sit back and wait for the price to drop."

"There's something else, too. We're pretty thin on experience, and there's talk we could end up trailing our stock to Wyoming or the Dakotas. We could use a few good men, somebody like Wes or Marty."

"You can talk to them, but I can't see Wes

36

going anywhere. Little Tim's scarcely two months old, and Alice has gotten used to having him handy."

"Anybody else? I hear the Coonce boy's handy with horses."

"I need him myself. Truth is, I've whittled the outfit down some. I'm not sure I can spare anybody for six weeks."

"You don't make it easy for your neighbors, do you?"

"You ever consider about talking to Parnell? He and some of those small operations could fill out your herd. You could pick up some good men, and with Hood Garner to ramrod the outfit . . ."

"Parnell's a farmer."

"Mostly, but he's also raising cattle."

"His boys ride like shop clerks. There's always the Flat, I suppose."

"I wouldn't wish that on a friend," Charlie said, gazing warily westward. "Henry Eppler at Ft. Griffin says half the world's refuse wanders in and out of that place. They'd as soon steal you blind as blink an eye, Brad. Might be some cavalry boys with enlistments running out."

"I don't want bluecoats."

"Well, it's your outfit, Brad. I wish you luck with it."

"Looks like we'll need more than luck," Brad said, frowning. "You will send that wire?"

"First thing tomorrow."

"I thank you for that, at least, Charlie."

"It's little enough."

Brad nodded, and Charlie couldn't help sense that the Stokelys expected more. *Doesn't he know he's the competition?* Charlie wondered. *I have to look out for the Flying J first.*

Even so, Charlie Justiss sent the wire. And he was genuinely sorry to pass the answer along to Brad Stokely.

NO NEED ADDITIONAL STOCK AT PRESENT, Talbot had wired.

"So we're banking everything on a drive to Dodge," Brad muttered. "I pray the trail's an easy one."

"Me, too," Charlie said. But he'd never known an easy cattle drive, and he doubted this year would prove the exception.

Chapter 3

Once the roundup was completed, Billy's trail crew assembled the 1,200 head destined for Ft. Worth and set off on the four day journey to the railhead. Charlie saw them off. His heart was heavy as he read the grim faces of veteran cowboys like Wes Tyler and Marty Steele. Joe and Chris rode on either side of Billy, their youthful enthusiasm a stark contrast to their elder brother's sour gaze.

The Flying J crew returned the same day Hood Garner drove the Stokely's Triple S herd across the Brazos. Charlie knew his men would as soon be heading north, too.

"Seems we ought to take a few hundred head up there anyway," Marty complained. "Gamble that many on the market."

"No," Charlie'd told his old friend. Charlie knew only too well what a gamble life was. But to survive, a gambler had to know the odds, and he never bet against a stacked deck. Besides, Ross had contracted another 500 steers for August delivery to Ft. Worth.

With the advent of summer, the cowboys silenced their grumbling and got busy. Charlie decided it was time to add a fresh coat of paint to the buildings. What was more, Marty and Billy had rounded up two dozen mustangs from the wild stretches to the north, and there were plenty of horses to be broken to the saddle.

"Work and more work," little Chris muttered. "When we're not doing lessons, Papa's got us cutting hay or working hides."

Charlie only laughed. Chris had lately turned twelve, and though even now the boy was little more than a stickbroom with a mop of blond hair attached, twelve had a way of making its arrival known.

"You'd think a man who'd already raised four boys would get used to it," Angela remarked when Charlie voiced a complaint about Chris's work habits. "This is the last one, Charlie. Once Chris is grown, we'll be but a pair of doddering old grandfolks. By that time, of course, little Charlie will be belt high."

"Seems only yesterday you were rocking Ross on your knee, dear. Now we've raised a family."

"And done a fair job of it, too."

"More you than me. All those years I was off to the war kept me from the older ones. The ranch has robbed me of the time I'd hoped to pass with Joe and Chris."

"You've found time, Charlie. They bear your brand. Anyone who's watched them ride knows that. The pranking comes of your side of the family as well. You've stirred the kettle your share, no doubting that."

Charlie nodded, then smiled broadly as Angela grasped his hands. Yes, they'd done a fair job with the youngsters. His only wish was that time would slow its pace, allow boys a few more months of being boys and delay the railroads and the barbed wire and the other changes which were bound to turn the world upside down by century's close.

Summer's arrival brought the oppressive Texas heat. The sun radiated off the hard sandstone rocks of the Brazos landscape, and the country-side seemed on fire. The work crews spent as much time wallowing in creek mud as they did painting or working stock.

"They're restless," Wes declared the same June afternoon he and Charlie broke up a wild melee down at the corral. "Trail drives gave 'em a chance to blow off some steam, let loose their free spirits. Now life's just one month's work after another."

Charlie nodded sadly. He promised himself that if the work was done by July, he'd give the whole outfit leave to spend a week down at the Flat or up in Jacksboro.

June's second week witnessed the return of Ryan Justiss. The spindle-legged youngster who'd left in August for his second term at ag college returned in the bold uniform of a cadet corporal. The frailty was gone. Instead the Ryan who dismounted was a broad-shouldered man of twenty, his bright blue eyes ablaze with newfound confidence.

"Papa, I brought a couple of friends along," Ryan said, pointing to a pair of lumbering bulls driven along by a dusty slouch of a young rider. "Brought somebody else, too."

Charlie gazed with surprise as the second rider removed his hat. Underneath was the sweat-streaked head of Bob Lee Wiley.

"Mornin', Mr. Justiss," Bob Lee said, grinning. "Been a year or two, eh?"

"Has at that," Charlie answered, wondering how it was possible that Ryan and Bob Lee could be twenty. It was only yesterday the two of them were racing ponies through the Arkansas River.

"Ry said you might have some work. There's none to be found nowadays to the south, at least none fit for a cowboy."

"You down at the ag school, Bob Lee?" Charlie asked.

"Only wanderin' through. Some of us brought stock up from Galveston. Lafe Freeman was with us. Anyway, I ran across Ry here. He was havin' his share of problems persuadin' these bulls to head north, and I offered to lend a hand."

"Don't believe a word of it, Papa," Ryan said. "Wouldn't want him to get that pretty soldierin' suit mussed up. I thought maybe we'd be in time for the cattle drive, but I'll wager your outfit's left already."

"Gone and come back," Charlie said.

"How?" Ryan asked.

"Ross contracted the steers to Jordan Talbot up in Kansas City. We took 'em to the railhead at Ft. Worth."

"No drive to Dodge?" Ryan asked in disappointment.

"Lord, work'll be harder'n ever to come by now," Bob Lee grumbled.

"Oh, I expect we can find a place for a snaggle-toothed runt like you, Bob Lee," Charlie said, laughing. "You'll find Wes at the line camp below Wolf Hollow, just above Ioni Creek. He'll accommodate you."

"Thanks, sir."

"Where you plan to put those bulls, Ryan?" Charlie asked as Bob Lee turned to leave. "I pay for these monsters?"

"They're part of my work at school," Ryan explained. "A sort of experiment. I got 'em for the summer. Saves feed for the college, and it means we can keep 'em busy, if you follow."

"Cross breed them with the longhorns, you mean?"

"Yes, Papa. Shorten the leg, cut down on the horn some. Makes better beef. The longhorn's a fine trail animal, but he's none too tender to eat. Some places in the south country have turned their whole range to Herefords."

"Winter's not so harsh there. Range cattle can survive near anything."

"Papa, you said you sent me to Bryan to get a scientific education. What good's that if you won't put it to work. In five years there'll be railroads across half the state. We won't even drive steers to Ft. Worth then. Those who've got only longhorns will be selling tallow and horn."

"All right. We'll see what your bulls produce."

"There's something more. The only way to keep the strain pure is to separate the breeding stock from range cattle."

"You mean fencing."

"It's being done elsewhere."

43

"I spoke about that to some of the neighbors not long ago."

"And?"

"Didn't get a kind reception. Some find access to the free range produces an air of freedom. Others'd find themselves fenced from water. They're fighting wars in some places over barbed wire."

"You could do it by degrees, say fence in a section out on Bluff Creek. We've got no neighbors there, and the high walls on the north keep the stock from prowling."

"That's a lot of work, and if you bring a strand of that wire in, you'll have everybody up in arms."

"It's bound to happen sooner or later, Papa. It's the only reliable way to protect the new breed."

"Sure, it is," Charlie agreed. "But is it worth going to war with your neighbors?"

"They'll follow your lead, Papa. They always do."

"Not this time," Charlie grumbled. "You haven't seen their eyes, Ryan. Joe Nance practically declared war over us bridging the market roads. Think what he'll say about fences!"

But in spite of his misgivings, Charlie gave Ryan leave to enclose 300 acres in the northwester edge of the ranch. The bulls was let loose there, and some sixty longhorn cows were driven in amongst them.

Charlie couldn't help smiling at the way Ryan took charge of the project. Maybe it was the military training that had changed the boy from wild mustang to crew boss. Or maybe, as Angela said, it was in the blood.

44

"Ry's doing a fine job out there," Charlie told her as they walked beside Bluff Creek at sundown. "He and Billy'll make a good team running the ranch."

"And to think I thought college would turn his head to other horizons."

"He belongs on horseback, that boy," Charlie argued. "I knew that from the first day he sat a colt. A natural, that Ryan."

"Like his father."

"School's been good for him, though. He's got discipline. What's more, he notices things. We might should send Billy along when Ryan heads back."

"From what I hear, they've got more than their share of young outlaws. And pranks! Ryan's got stories to curl a woman's hair. He is learning, though. And loving it."

"Can't expect a Texas college to be well-mannered and gentlemanly. That sort of man gets swallowed alive out here."

"You're talking about Emiline."

"No, anyone. A man who just says yes, sir, and doesn't think won't cope with the ups and downs of life on the Brazos. He'll perish."

"Charlie, with Ross taking his legal examinations soon, we may have both Billy and him out here to run things. What would you think about moving into town?"

"Palo Pinto?"

"You are the county judge. It would save the long rides every morning and evening. Well?"

"I like the ride."

"A county judge should abide in the county

45

seat."

"Joe Nance never did."

"His ranchhouse is closer. Besides, he didn't have grandbabies to tend."

"Ah, the truth!"

"I could help Vicki. Four little ones can prove a trial. Bret's often away, and she's teaching besides."

"I'll give it some thought."

"Do that. I wouldn't need a palace, you understand, and we could build it on the ranch itself, down in the south by the Ft. Griffin road."

"You'd want the boys with you, I suppose."

"Naturally. Joe and Chris, anyway."

"They wouldn't care for town life, and they're needed on the ranch."

"They come to town for school. When term's ended, they can go back to the ranchhouse. So can we."

"I'll have a look down where Ioni Creek begins. As I recall, there are good springs there. That's not but a couple of miles closer to town, though."

"It isn't?" Angela asked, clearly disappointed.

"No. Anyway you figure it, the Triple S blocks our approach to town."

"Oh," she said, sighing.

As the remaining weeks of summer spent themselves in waves of scalding mornings and dry, wind-swept afternoons, Charlie prowled the ranch like a hungry cougar. The site above Ioni Creek was less than ideal, and the bands of shiftless idlers haunting the road to Ft. Griffin gave him an uneasy feeling. Maybe a line camp would

46

work, but the south range was clearly not the spot for a house.

In late July the Nance and Stokely outfits returned from the long trek to Dodge City. Charlie read the despair on the face of Hood Garner, heard the panic in Randolph Nance's voice. Clearly the drives had gone worse than ever.

"Never saw anything like it, Charlie," Hood related. "We weren't a day north of the South Canadian when rustlers hit. They burned our wagons, shot down three men and made off with most of the steers. These were no Kansas renegades, either. It was an army. They were well-led, and the whole thing was planned to a T. When we went after them, they left a half dozen behind to slow our progress till the others got clear. We barely rounded up a hundred and fifty head. Most of those were run nigh to the bone, and by the time we fattened them up, most everyone in Texas had made it to market. We sold 'em for five dollars a head, and that because we had to pay the crew, what was left of it, something. If we'd had a mixed herd, we could've nudged 'em along to the Dakotas, but not even a Kansas farmer buys steers for breeding stock."

Randolph Nance's story was similar. First outlaws sliced off a hundred head. Then a thunderstorm scattered what was left over thirty miles. The Circle N got 700 beeves to market, but the price was only twelve dollars a head.

"You were the smart one, Charlie," Joe Nance declared. "You took the sure thing. As it is, I'll have a battle on my hands making out. Another year like this and I'll be broke. We haven't cleared more than a hundred dollars above operations since '74."

It was even worse for the smaller outfits. Men like J. C. Parnell who'd consigned their stock to Hood Garner or Randolph Nance had less than a hundred dollars cash to show for their efforts. Worse, there were young hands buried on the trail, and the church was draped in mourning black the last Sunday of July.

Only the pits of despair would have sent Brad and Ben Stokely riding with hats in hand to Charlie Justiss. When the brothers appeared at the door that very same Sunday, Charlie swallowed hard and tried not to frown.

"I saw Wes and Toby rounding up steers yesterday," Brad began. "You got yourself another beef contract, I'd guess."

"Five hundred head next week."

"We could sure use a slice out of that deal. I'd even split the profit with you. You'd save your stock and profit as well."

"We're overstocked as is," Charlie explained. "I usually trail three, four thousand steers. Ryan's bent on improving the strain, too. We've got longhorns running out our ears. I know you're hurting, Brad, but I've got a lot of people relying on me. We keep our crew on all year."

"We had to let most of the boys go," Ben explained. "Hood's off next week. Plans to start a place of his own down on Walnut Creek."

"Another small outfit!" Brad complained. "They'll be the ruin of us."

"Can't fault a man for wanting to be his own boss," Charlie declared. "As for business, we're slack just now, but it's like to come back. Most things do."

"May not be in time for some of us," Brad remarked. "Charlie, I'm pleading with you. If we could sell even a hundred head at twenty dollars."

"I know," Charlie mumbled. "I've found myself there before. Maybe I could loan you enough to see you through."

Ben and Brad exchanged nervous looks.

"That's the trouble we're in already," Brad said, staring at his toes. "We've borrowed the last three years. We owe more than the place is worth now. Every year we keep hoping the price'll jump back to thirty, thirty-five dollars a head. One good drive and we'd be clear. Now, well . . ."

"I'll see what I can do. Jordan Talbot might need some additional stock. I'll wire him myself first thing tomorrow."

"You wired him before," Ben said, staring off toward the cliffs to the north.

"We thank you for your time, Charlie," Brad announced, extending a worn hand toward Charlie. "I appreciate all you've tried to do. Send the wire. It can't hurt. And if you hear of anyone needing beef . . ."

"I'll let you know," Charlie promised as he shook Brad's hand. "Meanwhile, good luck to you. You've been good neighbors. I hate to see you come to grief."

"Thanks," Ben said, biting his lip as he shook Charlie's hand.

But as the brothers rode off eastward, Charlie couldn't help feeling hard times were settling over the Brazos. This was a new kind of despair, born of high hopes and trampled dreams. It was likely

49

to produce a depression in livestock prices and the usual new exodus westward, to new lands and a fresh start.

It's what I did, Charlie told himself. But he wondered how the county could survive if outfits like the Triple S and Circle N collapsed. He vowed to compose the wire carefully. After all, Jordan Talbot's slaughterhouses relied on Texas beef.

Chapter 4

Sometimes it seemed to Charlie as if all the life on earth dried up and withered away in August. Not once those first ten days did so much as a sprinkle fall earthward. Creeks shrank until they were little more than a series of muddy puddles. Springs which had always offered a cool drink in midsummer vanished overnight. Even the Brazos slowed until it was little more than a wallow.

It wasn't long before prowling longhorns clogged the river's banks, their swollen tongues aching for a drink. Wells went dry, and each ranch sent its wagons full of buckets to the river daily to fetch the lifegiving liquid from the Brazos. As stock died and children whined, Charlie searched the scriptures for some peace of mind. In time of flood, there was always a rainbow to offer hope. Drought brought only the bitter taste of despair.

"God never intended this country for white men," one bitter farmer remarked as he walked through a cornfield burned into so much withered fodder by the August heat.

For ranchers like Ben and Brad Stokely the heat and the drought spelled ruin. Six times Charlie Justiss had wired Kansas City, pleading the Stokelys' cause. Finally Jordan Talbot replied.

SORRY BUT AM OVERSTOCKED WAIT RENEWAL CONTRACT OCTOBER

"Bitter herbs," Brad remarked when Charlie passed along the telegram. "Figure the cavalry up at Fort Griffin would buy some stock? You're on good terms with that Yank captain, aren't you?"

"With hundreds of buffalo carcasses a month passing through there, I can't see anybody buying meat," Charlie answered. "Maybe you could ride up into the Nations, check at the Indian agencies?"

"We spoke to the agents up there on our way back from Dodge," Brad explained. "They've no need of beef till winter. By then I fear the banks'll call our note due. Maybe it's for the best. I feel like the world is dyin' out here."

"I know," Charlie said, gazing at the dismembered timbers that were all that remained of the tall house his brother Bowie had built on the banks of Justiss Creek. It hadn't been but a few years since the Brazos had crested thirty feet over its banks, devouring everything in sight. Now wagons splashed across the muddy riverbed in dozens of places.

"I'm glad we got those five hundred steers delivered to Fort Worth," Billy declared the day after the drovers returned. "People are hurting. The going price for a longhorn at auction seems to drop daily."

"I know," Charlie agreed. "I just wish we could have moved another thousand head. We'll bury

52

cattle if it doesn't rain soon. I don't see how the folks who don't front the river are going to survive."

"Most drove their stock north or south, west or east, as far as they had to in order to find some river."

"Maybe we ought to see about moving a few hundred head up Rock Creek. There are few settlers there."

"Not much water, either," Billy said sadly. "Ross and I rode out there before leaving for Fort Worth. Papa, what'll we do if the river itself dries up?"

"Find a way to get by somehow," Charlie said. "We always manage."

"Sure," Billy said, trying to force a smile. It wasn't much of a success.

Perhaps it was because of the desperate nature of things that Charlie decided to hold a celebration in honor of Angela's birthday. As a rule, she detested big gatherings for people outside the family, and Charlie himself enjoyed the quiet times they'd shared with the children over the more festive occasions preferred by men like Joe Nance. And yet when Charlie suggested the party to Angela, her answer surprised him.

"I think that's just what we all need," she told him. "We're all of us tired, and we haven't had everyone together since Christmas two years ago. It will give me a chance to enjoy the grandchildren. Besides, Ross is likely to go mad if we don't find some way to coax that Eliza Rogers up here from Austin."

"I know," Charlie said, smiling. "After all, he's

twenty-three years old now. Wouldn't want him turning into a grouchy old bachelor like Marty Steele."

"It will be a fine chance to bring the neighbors together, too. We haven't seen the Dunlaps three times all summer. Judith Parnell's spoken of organizing a church choir. I've been meaning to see how her grandkids are getting by in the drought. Then there's . . ."

"All right," Charlie said, grinning. "Want to have it here or in town?"

"Here. We haven't entertained in this house since Emiline and Bowie left."

"I'll see the word's gotten out. Doc can pick out some beeves for slaughtering. Will Felicidad need any help?"

"Teresa Morales will lend a hand, as will Vicki. I'm not helpless myself, you know."

"I do know, but it is *your* birthday."

"My party, too."

And so the call went out. Some argued frivolity was out of place in such hard times, but others said a gathering was just the thing to take the edge off their despair. Charlie sent his five boys riding from one end of the county to the other, inviting anyone old enough to walk. Marty Steele put a crew to work building tables. Vicki had the women in town make decorations. Sides of beef were turned on spits. Pork ribs were slow barbecued in pits, and Felicidad did wonders with cornmeal and peppers and a little rice.

By the time Angela's birthday arrived, the hillside outside the ranchhouse was covered with tables. The trees were full of brightly-decorated ribbons, and lanterns stood ready for the approaching darkness. Hector Suarez serenaded the ladies with his guitar, and Bob Lee Wiley surprised everyone by producing a fiddle. The notes were not half sour, either.

It was a strange collection of people, Charlie supposed as he stood to one side and let Angela make introductions. Eliza Rogers appeared on the arm of her father, State Senator Lawrence Rogers. Ross had lately been the senator's clerk, and the young man had taken the opportunity to meet the senator's nineteen-year-old daughter.

"Eliza only celebrated her own birthday last week," Ross was quick to point out. "Of course, she still doesn't look a day over sixteen to me."

"It's all that Eastern schooling," the senator declared.

"What's this?" Eliza complained. "I spent three years in that awful school in the Carolinas. And for what? To learn high manners and polite conversation? I learned more history talking to Ross, and I'll still wager I can outride you, Senator Lawrence Prescott Rogers, sir!"

"Watch her, boy," Senator Rogers said, grinning at Ross. "She's sassy. I'm glad she picked up her degree. I'd never gotten her back on an eastbound train."

Ross took Eliza's arm and led the young woman out to where Bob Lee and Hector were playing. Ryan was there already, dressed in his cadet's uniform and leading a golden-haired farmgirl into a waltz. Charlie smiled approvingly, then greeted guests.

Bret and Vicki arrived with a wagonload of children. Luis Morales was helping ready a pair of horses for the evening's entertainment, and Teresa was helping in the kitchen. As a result, Bret and Vicki had merged the six Morales

55

youngsters with their own four. Once the wagon stopped, six-year-old Charlie Pruett bounded out of the wagon and raced to greet his grandmother. Angela and Dona Marie Morales helped the others down, all but baby Tomas, who was safely cradled in Vicki's arms. Bret carried little Ramon in one arm and his own youngest, Tom, in the other.

"Ah, the children," Angela proclaimed, abandoning her other guests as she drew little Charlie into her skirts and kissed the child's forehead.

"Guess we won't be seeing her for a time," Alex Tuttle, Bret's deputy, remarked to Charlie. "No one'd ever know those kids had a grandma, huh?"

"I'd say something, but in truth. I'm a poor one to criticize," Charlie confessed as his granddaughter Hope wandered over and climbed up one arm.

Charlie devoted the next hour to parading one child after another through the crowd, nodding to this neighbor or that, sharing their concern over the drought or laughing at some joke. Eventually he turned Hope over to Irene Dunlap. Ma Dunlap had brought the girl into the world, and the woman's broad lap sheltered at least one or two little ones the remainder of the evening.

Charlie's brother Bowie soon arrived with his wife, Emiline, and their thirteen-year-old son, Clay. Emiline, as usual, froze the crowd as she stepped out of a carriage dressed in a satin New Orleans gown. Bowie followed, smiling as he greeted one old friend after another. Of late the couple had passed more hours in Waco and Ft. Worth than in Palo Pinto County, and Clay now studied at an academy that had once been the plantation home of a Waco cotton grower.

Charlie clasped the hand of his brother warmly.

Emiline extended a cold hand, and Charlie kissed it lightly. She'd never warmed much to Charlie or Angela, and Charlie suspected the gown was the price of her attendance.

"Joe and Chris around?" Clay asked.

Charlie couldn't help smiling. The boy tugged and pulled at his stiff waistcoat in spite of Emiline's displeasure, and Charlie nodded toward the barn. Clay was off like a hawk.

"He's really not accustomed to gatherings like this," Emiline explained. "I don't have family anymore, and, of course, Silver Hills is a small school. I did think he should come, though."

"He's family," Charlie said, catching a glimpse of Clay climbing the rails of the corral and dashing to where Joe stood saddling a spotted gelding.

"Yes, and he doesn't see much of his cousins anymore," Bowie said, sighing. "He misses the ranch, I think. Next summer he should come out here a month or so, enjoy himself."

"I thought we might travel," Emiline objected. She clearly was appalled at the notion.

"Well, there'll be time to discuss that another day," Bowie said, turning his wife away from the corral. It had taken Clay but seconds to shed his coat, cravat and shirt. The boy's pale shoulders and frail arms were a stark contrast to Joe's shaggy brown hair and leathery hide, but the two youngsters were quickly atop the gelding and headed out toward Bluff Creek.

"Where's Clay gotten to?" Emiline asked in alarm.

"You remember Alice Hart, don't you, Em?" Bowie asked, steering his wife toward Alice and Wes Tyler.

57

"It's Tyler now," Alice reminded them. "How lovely you look, Emiline! City life agrees with you."

Bowie slipped away and motioned Charlie toward an isolated table. They'd barely gotten there when they both broke into laughter.

"Think she'll forgive us, Bowie?" Charlie asked as they gazed at the young horsemen flying through the shallow creek.

"Em or Alice? Probably neither one. But that's not why I brought you over here."

"No?"

"I want to talk about a railroad."

"Oh?"

"You think there's enough public land for right-of-way should a man bring the line through here?"

"There is south of the market road. But from what I hear, the state will likely condemn anyone's holdings that lie across the route anyway. You hear something?"

"Not for full certain, Charlie, but I'd urge you to look over your resources. See if you can't pick up some of that cheap acreage south of the road. There are only two gaps through the mountains fit for this railroad, and the man who owns those sections could stand to get rich."

"I heard there was a plan to swing well south, down near Hood County."

"From Fort Worth? Never happen. West and a bit south's the best route to El Paso."

"You've done a lot of talking to somebody."

"I've gotten good at that. Don't forget. The man who builds this line will need supplies. Somebody's got to haul that freight."

"When do you think they'll start?"

"Not till winter passes. Don't pass it on, but I'll

bet you ship your steers to Kansas City from a depot in this very county by late spring."

"Next year?"

"That's my feeling. The price of land's going to soar, and the county's bound to prosper."

"It's facing hard times now."

"August is always hard. I hear it's even worse out west. Maybe we need it. There are too many longhorns on the range just now. The supply's driven down the price."

"Appears so."

"Well, that's all I had to pass along. We'd best turn to idle gossip now before somebody overhears."

"Got some gossip, do you?"

"Heard about the governor's niece? She's got six toes on her left foot, I understand."

Charlie laughed loudly, and soon others migrated to where the brothers stood. Jokes and stories were soon drowning out the music. Then Felicidad declared it time to eat, and the crowd descended on tables of pork and beef and chicken like hungry wolves.

After dinner, Charlie found himself standing beside the corral watching cowboys rope reluctant steers or ride angry bulls. Down at Bluff Creek the boys were doing their best to splash away the sweat and fatigue in water barely waist deep.

"Wish you were down there with them?" Brad Stokely asked.

"Well, I wish there was enough water in the fool creek for them to have a decent swim," Charlie replied.

"We rode across Ioni Creek coming over. It's bone dry."

"Has been before, Brad. Can't help but rain soon."

"My stock'll be dying soon."

"I know," Charlie said sadly.

Joe Dunlap and his son Jared joined them, and the talk shifted to the Hereford bulls Ryan had brought to the ranch. The Dunlaps had been living north of the Brazos ten years when Charlie arrived in Palo Pinto County. Joe and Irene were the old guard, hill people who fended for themselves and merged their lives with the land. Of a half dozen children, only Jared had reached his twentieth year.

"Ma's havin' a fine time," Joe said, pointing to where the aging midwife frolicked with the Morales brood. "Ole Jared here ought to get himself a wife before long, raise a few pups of his own. He and Ross'll be oldtimers themselves 'fore long."

"I think Ross's got himself one picked out, though," Jared said, grinning as he nodded to where Ross and Eliza Rogers walked in the dying light. "Maybe I ought to go to Austin for a time. These farmgirls are all too bony, and the ones who get raised on a ranch are bowlegged."

Charlie laughed, and the others slapped Jared on the back. Joe Nance appeared then.

"It's a fine party, Charlie," Nance said somewhat sourly. "Seems we all of us need a laugh or two just now."

"Some more than others," Brad added.

"I never thought I'd see the day a dry August could drive men to grief," Nance mumbled. "To top it off, taxes are due next month, eh, Charlie?"

"That's how the law reads," Charlie agreed.

60

"With times so hard, we might be able to spread out the county assessments, though."

"Maybe we could skip 'em altogether," Nance suggested. "A lot of money gets spent needlessly as is."

"Oh?" Charlie asked. "What would you have us do, Joe, ask Bret and Tut to work for nothing? We could quit feeding the prisoners. We still use that storeroom for a jailhouse! Maybe we could start hanging people without holding trials. Or else let 'em steal whatever they want, shoot anybody, burn a ranch now and then."

"We sure don't need to build more bridges," Nance argued. "Truth is we could walk across the Brazos just now."

"Sure," Charlie agreed. "And when this dry spell breaks, we're like as not in for a flash flood that'll make us feel like Noah."

"Taxes have to be paid," Joe Dunlap said. "It's not so much after all. As for the bridges, without 'em, we'll never settle the north half of the county."

"I don't care about the north half of the world!" Nance said bitterly. "Don't you know, you old fool, that some of us are near bankrupt?"

"That's enough!" Charlie shouted, stepping between Nance and Jared Dunlap before the young man could plant a fist in Nance's face. "This is a birthday gathering, not a boxing exhibition."

"He's right," Joe Dunlap said, patting Jared's back. "It's best we go take a walk by what's left of the creek."

"He had no call . . ." Jared complained.

"He knows it," Charlie said, turning to Nance in the hope that the old rancher might offer an apology. Nance only marched off.

"They're havin' a hard time at the Circle N," Brad explained. "If it doesn't rain soon, some of us may not last."

"Sure," Jared said, swallowing his rage. "He still has no call to say such things to my pa. We Dunlaps have bled for this country. Ole Nance there's lived off the fat of the land. When he was judge, he drew half the taxes into his own pocket. What does Charlie take? Ten dollars a month, and he spends that on lumber for bridges or telegrams to Austin!"

Charlie turned away. He was always uneasy when the talk turned to county salaries. It was well known that he himself asked for little, but most also knew that Bret Pruett's pay had doubled when Charlie started running the county.

Charlie made a quick tour of the gathering. He managed to lead Angela around the dance floor twice before Alex Tuttle cut in. Then, in as clever a maneuver as a judge could ever manage, Charlie ducked a debate between Senator Rogers and Joe Nance on the merits of barbed wire.

"Texas is a farm state, friends," the senator proclaimed. "A farmer has a right to have his field shielded from livestock."

It was all Charlie needed to hear to send him toward Bluff Creek. There, in the fading light of day, he sat on the bank and gazed at the far bank where Joe and Chris sprawled out beside their cousin Clay.

"Family," Charlie muttered as the shadows obscured the differences. The boys were three like silhouettes. Clay might lack Joe's stature, but paired with Chris, the two straw-headed boys might have passed for twins.

Charlie thought back to the warmth he'd felt

carrying Hope around the yard. Yes, family. It was the rope that bound them together, gave meaning to it all. Perhaps it gave a man the patience to withstand a drought, to survive a flood. Charlie always thought so. It took years to grow a child, and a man who'd waited that eternity wasn't shaken by two weeks, two months or even two years without rain.

Chapter 5

Drought wasn't the only problem to be faced that August, though. Even before the last guests had departed Angela's party, young Toby Hart rode to the house with ill news.

"Rustlers," the boy blurted out to his brother-in-law, Wes Tyler. "I saw 'em, Wes. Five or six anyway. They drove off maybe thirty, forty head toward the Flat."

"Where are they camped?" Wes asked as he steadied the seventeen-year-old. "How far you follow 'em?"

"Just to the market road," Toby explained. "They weren't campin' anywhere."

"As if we didn't have enough problems," Charlie growled. "Wes, you see Alice home. Marty!"

Marty Steele trotted over from the corral, and Charlie assigned him the task of readying horses.

"Charlie, you're not going out there now, are you?" Angela asked. "Bret and Tut are here. It's their job."

"She's right," Bret declared.

"You can't tackle five or six men," Charlie said

64

calmly. "Bret, you've got young ones to look after. Tut can go with us. We'll do nothing tonight except trail 'em a bit. It's best to await the sun before taking anybody on."

"Agreed," Bret said, suddenly taking command. "Alex, you see to it we haven't got a trigger-happy mob riding this range."

"I will," the deputy promised.

"I'll be up tomorrow with some of the boys from town," Bret went on to say. "Meanwhile, spread out and find their camp. Hold 'em for morning. I don't want anybody getting hung."

Bret addressed that last remark to the Stokelys in particular. It was well known that Brad and Ben had hung a pair of raiders a few years before and a third man last February. Cattle thieves found little comfort in a Texas courtroom, but some considered lynching but a notch above pure murder.

As Bret left to find Vicki and the children, Charlie and Alex Tuttle collected a party of men down at the corral. Ryan and Billy Justiss joined the two Stokely brothers. Wes and Toby trotted over, and Marty had Bob Lee Wiley and Hector Suarez saddling horses. When Luis Morales appeared, though, Charlie shook his head.

"You've got family to look after, Luis," Charlie declared. "It can't be a big bunch this time."

"I can track," Luis reminded them.

"I know, and I appreciate your offer. May need you next time. Now, though, too many men'll just get in each other's way."

Luis raised an eyebrow, but he didn't argue.

Alex Tuttle took charge once Luis left.

"Who knows this stretch the best?" the deputy asked.

"Ross," Billy answered. "He and Jared Dunlap've been over every inch of the range west of Caddo Creek."

"Jared's left for home already, and Ross has the senator to look after," Ryan pointed out. "I'd say Papa knows that country. Billy and I've been down to the Flat often enough to know the road, too."

"Not as well as Marty," Wes chimed in. "Well, Marty?"

"I've been chased over every knotty juniper and stand of prickly pear between here and Griffin," Marty admitted. "Truth is, there's just two ways to go. Use the road or cut through the hollows northwest, then head for the Clear Fork."

"Charlie?" Tut asked.

"He's right," Charlie said, "unless they turned toward town. Me, I can't see that. They've got to get those beeves somewhere and sell 'em—fast."

"I think so, too. You Stokelys come with me," Tut declared. "We'll look south of the Fort Griffin road. Marty, you and Wes take Toby and check the north side of the road. Charlie, you take those two outlaw sons of yours and go cross-country. You know the land better than me, and Ryan and Billy can outride oldtimers like me."

"My grandma outrides you, Tut," Toby said, laughing.

"Well, you just see to it you do what Wes and Marty tell you, Tobe, or else you're apt to come back with pieces missing."

"Where do we meet Bret?" Charlie asked.

"You find anything, send a rider to that stand of rocks that marks the county line. The one alongside the market road. That way we can draw everybody together again in the morning. Agreed?"

"Sure," they answered.

"Just remember one thing," Charlie said as he headed for the gate of the corral. "Don't try to do anything by yourself. Come morning, we'll take 'em together. I don't want anybody getting himself killed over thirty cows."

"Hear that?" Tut asked. "He's right. With luck, the rustlers will throw it in when they see we mean business."

"Better to hang 'em," Brad grumbled.

"I know how you boys feel," Tut told them. "That's why you're riding with me."

The riders soon split up and headed out. Charlie led his little company through boulder-strewn ravines and dry creek bottoms. Soon night swallowed the sun, and he slowed the pace. It was no country to go galloping through. Cactus and rocks, not to mention the parched and cracked earth, stood waiting to topple a horse and send its rider flying.

"Won't be much moon tonight," Billy noted. "They picked the night for it."

"Lucky for us Toby spotted 'em," Ryan said. "Otherwise we might not have noticed the stock missing at all."

Charlie nodded. He wished he'd taken time to change clothes. As it was, he peeled off his coat and stuffed his string tie in a pocket. Ryan was sweltering in his wool uniform. Only Billy had discarded his party clothes in favor of denim trousers and a cotton shirt.

As they rode along, an owl flapped its way through the branches of a white oak. A wolf howled its mournful song in the distance, and Charlie felt the breeze die. There was an eerie feel to the place, and he grew uneasy.

"We've been down this trail before, eh, Papa?" Ryan asked. "Wasn't too far from here that we fought old Stands Tall."

The young man opened up his tunic, and Charlie knew Ryan was touching the scars left by the Comanche's hatchet years before.

"I remember those wolves up above Justiss Creek," Charlie said, his eyes alert for the slightest movement through the darkness ahead. "Was like fighting an army of devils."

"They were nigh starved," Billy said, remembering. "I've seen it lots of times, animals striking out from desperation."

"Wasn't too different for the Comanches," Ryan added. "Or for these rustlers. Most of 'em would've been good range cowboys a year ago. Nobody's hiring extra help nowadays. Man's got to eat."

"Doesn't have to steal," Charlie growled. The boys let the conversation die. It was an old argument best left be.

They rode silently for better than an hour. By now the moon had risen, giving a faint light to the world. Trees could be distinguished from seven or eight yards away, and the famous Brazos haze that often haunted dusk refused to appear.

Not enough moisture to the air, Charlie thought. He lifted a canteen to his lips and sipped some water. He was glad he'd left Marty to ready the horses. Someone else might have forgotten to fill the canteens or else neglected them altogether. No need in making the ride any worse than it had to be.

"Papa, hold up," Ryan called.

Charlie drew his horse to a halt and listened. Twenty feet to the right a figure darted away. Charlie sniffed a strange scent.

"Something's dead," Ryan declared.

"A cow," Billy said, riding to where a longhorn lay split open across the belly. Charlie didn't need to look for tracks. He could already detect the low guttural growl of a cat.

"Mountain cat," Charlie whispered to the others.

"Hasn't been a cougar up here in a couple of years," Ryan argued. "Can't be. Bobcat maybe."

"No bobcat tore that steer open," Charlie said, nodding to the carcass. "This stretch is chock full of caves, perfect dens for a cat."

"Well, we'll come back later and hunt him," Billy said. "Now we've got rustlers to track."

"Oh, we're not the ones doing the tracking," Charlie declared. "He is. We've taken his kill. He's bound to take that more or less seriously."

"Papa?" Ryan asked.

"You boys back your horses on around so that you're behind me," Charlie ordered.

"Papa, you haven't been out riding the range in a long time," Billy said. "Leave this to me. I've hunted cats before, and you know it."

"Not at night," Charlie pointed out. "This isn't like any other thing you've ever been up against, boys. Leave it to me."

"Papa?" Ryan asked.

Before Charlie could speak another syllable, the cat bounded up the trunk of a fallen oak and prepared to pounce. It took Charlie but a second to ease his Winchester out of its sheath and advance a shell into the firing chamber. The cougar growled in rage, and Charlie fired. The shot slammed into the animal's side. The cat tried to jump, but Charlie's second shot tore through the big creature's throat and snatched its life away. The cougar rolled off the side of the tree and fell.

"Lord, I hated to do that," Charlie said, blinking the powder smoke from his eyes. "Aren't too many of those fellows left these days."

"He'd 'a gone on killing cattle," Billy commented as he jumped off his horse and walked cautiously toward the cat's still body. "Or else starved. It was his time, Papa."

"Maybe," Charlie admitted. "But I'd give him a few cows to keep a bit of the old ways around."

"Maybe we can bring some Comanches down from the Nations, give them a few acres and some cows if they'll agree to stage a raid once in a while," Billy said, laughing.

"Truth is I'd given Stands Tall land if he'd set aside his rifle," Charlie told them. "But he was never born to grow gray hairs and lose his teeth. A man like that was bound to fall in battle."

"Sure," Ryan agreed.

"You want me to skin him, Papa?" Billy asked as he dragged the cougar's corpse through the brush. The horses stirred uneasily, and Charlie shook his head.

"We've got other business," Charlie announced. "Little Charlie might like the claws, though."

"Papa, we'll find nobody tonight, not in this darkness," Ryan said. "Let's make camp ahead, and Billy can join us when he's got the cat skinned. Nothing's as fine as a cougar pelt. A boy who's got to live in a town ought to have something to brag on, especially now that you've built that fool bridge over the best swimming spot on the Brazos. Little Charlie's bound to grow into one of those Waco choirboys with lace on their shirts. Shoot, they've about ruined poor Clay at that school of his. Ever see a boy so white in August!"

Charlie couldn't help laughing, and he surrendered. Billy began skinning the cougar, and Charlie led the way to a small ridge sheltered by a stand of live oaks. As they led their horses to a small spring, Charlie froze. A voice carried across the hillside. Down below the embers of a campfire glowed.

"It's them," Ryan whispered as he drew alongside.

"Yes," Charlie said. "We'll camp on the opposite side of the ridge and keep watch. Tomorrow we'll round 'em up."

"Sure, Papa," Ryan agreed. They then watered their horses before leading the animals back out of sight of the rustlers. Billy appeared a half hour later, and Charlie shared the news.

"We'll stand watches in turns," Charlie told them. "Me first. Best get some rest. Tomorrow's likely to prove a long day."

Billy and Ryan nodded their agreement, then rolled out their saddle blankets and fought to find some rest.

Chapter 6

A bright August sun tore Charlie Justiss from a peaceful sleep. He sat up and rubbed the stiffness from his shoulders. It seemed that passing a night on the hard ground awoke every bruise and break that forty-six years had brought to his body.

Ryan was already readying the horses. Billy would be up on the ridge, observing the rustlers. Charlie yawned away his weariness, then prepared to stand.

"Morning," Ryan said. "Thought you might want me to ride along to the others, bring them out this way. Sure hope Bret thinks to bring along some cold biscuits, maybe a few slices of ham. I'm hungry."

"You was born hungry," Charlie said, scrambling to his feet and giving Ryan a slap on the back. "Off with you. Best walk your horse a bit before galloping. Don't want to alert those thieves."

73

"They were up and busy fixing themselves breakfast an hour ago," Ryan told his father. "If we're going to catch 'em, we'd best get to it."

Charlie nodded, and Ryan led his horse away. Charlie saddled the remaining animals, then took his rifle and climbed the ridge. Billy was huddling in the rocks, watching as a pair of buckskin-clad men nudged cattle into motion. Three other riders directed the animals westward.

"Recognize any of them?" Charlie asked.

"Buffalo hunters, the closest ones. I never saw 'em that I can recall. Others could be about anybody. Most likely they're drovers cut loose after the drive to Kansas."

Charlie nodded, then ducked as the closest rustler suddenly glanced back at the ridge.

"You see somethin', Taylor?" his companion asked.

"Thought so."

"Likely some Comanche's ghost," the first rider said, laughing. "Come on. We'd best get these beeves to Griffin before somebody finds out what we've been up to."

Somebody already has, Charlie thought as he grimly watched the rustlers. He waited with Billy in the rocks until the thieves had moved a quarter of a mile along. Only then did Charlie lead his son back down the hill to where the horses waited.

"Ry went to get the others, huh?" Billy asked as he climbed into the saddle.

"They'll be along. Our job is to keep the rustlers in sight. When the others arrive, we'll round up this whole bunch."

"You make it sound easy."

"Well, it is sometimes. Depends on how much fight's in those five. It could be they'll give it up quick. But it could go the other way, too."

"Usually does," Billy mumbled.

Charlie tried not to consider the possibilities. He knew Billy was remembering the violent clashes they'd had with raiders coming up the long trail from the Brazos to Kansas railheads. It was time Charlie wished forgotten, a nightmare of ambush and death. For the most part Palo Pinto had been immune to rustlers in recent years, but hard times often brought out both the best and worst in mankind.

Charlie and Billy Justiss trailed the rustlers some five or six miles across the hills and ravines beyond the Caddo Creek before they were joined by Bret Pruett and the others. Ryan passed over a bit of bread and some cold sausage to Charlie and Billy, and the hungry scouts gobbled the food. Then Charlie pointed out the rustlers.

"They look to know cattle," Bret observed. "Don't seem in too much of a hurry, though. What's more, they aren't any too concerned about looking ahead or behind. This is a new game with them, I'd guess."

"That's good," Brad Stokely declared. "The best way is to catch rustlers before they steal half your herd."

"Won't be too much trouble settling with 'em," Ben added, pulling a rifle out of its scabbard.

"Hold on there, you Stokelys," Bret ordered. "We'll go at this thing careful, and with luck, they'll give it up. Charlie, you take Ryan and Billy, see if you can get around ahead of them.

75

Tut, you and Marty take position on that rise between them and the road. The rest of us'll come along behind, get their attention."

"Just give us time to take position," Charlie said, waving his boys along. Marty and Tut followed as well. Bret, the Stokely brothers, Toby Hart, and Wes Tyler hung back.

"It's a fine plan," Charlie thought as he led the way southward and away from the raiders and their stolen cattle. It offered the rustlers a chance of surrender, and yet it didn't ignore the advantage of surprise should gunfire ensue.

"You think they'll make a fight on it?" Ryan asked, scratching his shoulder.

"There's not but five of them," Charlie said, "and most of them seem young for a battle. Might be they'll stand, but I'd guess not. Disappointed?"

"I've got my scars," Ryan said, laughing quietly to himself. "People start shooting, and anything can happen."

Charlie nodded. They left Tut and Marty at the rise, then swung around to cut off the small herd. By that time Bret was leading his group into the open.

"Hold up there!" Bret bellowed as his companions spread out around the flanks of the herd. "It's best you throw down your guns, raise those hands and keep awful still."

"Scatter!" a broad-shouldered rider wearing buckskins shouted. "They're after us!"

The outlaw leader kicked his horse into a gallop, but he managed to ride less than five yards before Ben Stokely shot him down. Two horsemen on the far side of the herd did manage to break into the open. Of the other two, one threw his arms up in surrender. The other galloped away toward the rise where Marty and Alex Tuttle lay waiting. A pair of Winchester bullets ended the rustler's escape.

"Think we ought to chase those two?" Billy asked as Charlie started toward the cattle.

"Let 'em go," Charlie said. "They'll be a week trying to find their way out of the briars and rattlesnakes."

Billy and Ryan breathed a sigh of relief, then followed their father along to where the thirty nervous animals stood. Bret was placing shackles on the wrists of the confused survivor of the skirmish. The Stokelys stood beside the outlaw leader, proudly boasting that death was the proper fate for such vermin. Tut and Marty brought the other corpse along.

On another day Charlie might have felt some of the hatred that filled the Stokelys' eyes, but as he approached the captive rustler, it was hard to feel anything but pity. The shackles bound the wrists of a boy of fifteen or so. His clothes were little more than tatters, and the left side of his face was swollen and bruised.

"They made me come along, mister," the boy pleaded. "Wasn't my idea. My brother Rance beat me till I said I'd go. Now he's dead, and you're goin' to hang me. Ain't you?"

"You'll have your say," Bret promised. "The judge is a reasonable man."

"What's your name?" Charlie asked. "How old are you?"

"I'm called Rame, short for Raymond Polk," the young man answered. "Turned fifteen three weeks back."

"You know it's not right to take another man's stock, don't you?" Charlie asked. "You've got the look of a cowboy to you. You would go after a man who took your cows, wouldn't you?"

"Yes, sir," Rame said, dropping his head.

Charlie frowned as he examined the would-be thief. Meals hadn't come regular of late, and the soles of the boy's boots were worn clear through.

"He doesn't even have a gun, Charlie," Marty pointed out. "Wasn't about to cause much harm, this one."

"He rode with the others," Brad reminded them.

"Wasn't my choice," the boy pleaded with wide, hollow eyes. "My eye was near closed shut from telling Rance no."

"Be a lot of work to hold a trial," Tut declared. "Seems to me a jury'd be apt to deal with him lightly on any account. We could take him to town, see he's on a wagon bound for the east."

"He'll only wind up in trouble again," Wes said, shaking his head. "Either find him work or bring him to trial."

"Nobody's hiring," Bret said, gazing at Charlie.

"No, not this time," Charlie said. "I've got more help than I can afford to pay as is, but maybe he could find some work up in Jack County, or at the stock pens in Fort Worth."

"I'll send some wires," Bret said, grinning

slightly. "You know, Charlie, he's not all that different than me when I came to live with you."

"A world of different, Bret," Charlie said. "You never stole."

So Raymond Polk, despite the Stokelys' objections, was never brought to trial. Instead Bret put him in the back of a wagon bound for Jacksboro and a job as depot hand for Art Stanley. The boy never appeared, for he stole a horse at the Trinity crossing and made off toward the Nations.

"So much for being compassionate," Charlie grumbled when Bret related the news. "Of course, he might figure we could change our minds and stretch his neck a little."

"He comes back this way, I'm liable to do just that," Bret declared.

The unsuccessful raid on the Flying J proved to be the only instance of thievery that August. Perhaps the rock bottom cattle prices made rustling a poor gamble. Rustlers were certainly the least of Charlie Justiss's worries. Except for one brief shower, the heavens continued to hold back the precious rains which would end the drought and return Palo Pinto County to its earlier prosperity.

For some, hard times led to greater despair. Rarely three days passed when Charlie wasn't visited by one of the Stokelys. Brad would ramble on about this or that, then plead for some solution to the Triple S's financial distress. Ben was quieter, but the desperation was just as clear.

"You're not considering loaning them money, are you, Papa?" Ross asked when Charlie related the story.

"I thought about it," Charlie admitted.

"Don't. They owe everybody. Art Stanley holds notes worth more than the ranch, and half the merchants in Jacksboro have unpaid tabs. Papa, they could drive five thousand head to market and not pay their debts."

"How's that possible? They've hardly been free with their money."

"Oh, Ben plays cards some, and Brad has made some bad investments. The real trouble is they've never really understood the cattle business, and they only did well the years Hood Garner got a herd through for 'em. Even then, the stock was never in as good as shape as ours. To top that off, the Stokelys never dealt straight with their outfits. They'd hire men for the drive in June, then send 'em packing come fall. There's been nobody to build their stock, at least nobody who knows cattle or cares to put in the sweat."

"They're neighbors, Ross."

"I give 'em till maybe midwinter. Then or before Art Stanley will own the Triple S."

As it happened, Art Stanley had other interests. Charlie learned to what extent when his brother Bowie invited him to lunch at the Brazos Hotel.

"You recall I told you the railroad's coming?" Bowie asked as they sat together at a corner table. "Well, there's talk the legislature's going to offer free land and grant a charter. The Fort Worth and Western Railroad, it'll be called."

"And you're going to buy into it."

"Depends on you, Charlie. See, I sold Art my half of the freight business, but Art didn't have my price in cash. I had to take this, too."

Charlie accepted a handful of papers. Each was a promissory note from Brad and Ben Stokely. Together, they amounted to close to $20,000.

"Lord, I'm not sure the Triple S is worth this much," Charlie gasped. "And Ross says there's money owed others as well."

"It wouldn't be worth it to just anybody, Charlie, but if those acres were added to the Flying J, they might prove out. It'd give you good access to town, and except for three or four small farms, the Belknap road for an eastern boundary. There's more to the offer, too."

"Oh?"

"If this deal comes through, I plan to move Em to Fort Worth. People there are more to her liking, and we can have Clay home again instead of boarded off in Waco at that high-mannered school for Waco dandies. The boy hates it, and I hardly ever see him."

"You want me to buy the house here in town?"

"That's it exactly. If you've got $25,000, the house and the Triple S are yours."

"These papers are just a promise to pay. They're no deed, Bowie."

"Look closer. If they're not paid September first, the ranch is forfeit."

"It'd be like stealing land from a neighbor."

81

"Well, you can give 'em time if you choose. Art wouldn't. I just want to sell the notes to raise capital. If I sell 'em down in Austin, the new owner isn't apt to offer any extensions."

"That hardly means it's right."

"Yes or no, Charlie? I have to know by weeks' end."

"I'll talk to Angela. She has a say in this."

"She'll love the house once Em drags all those dusty pictures of her relatives off and leaves the place in peace. It's a fine house, absolutely perfect for a county judge. Maybe that's why I ran for the office myself three times. Let me know soon as you can, though, Charlie. I've got big plans. I plan to be a vice president of the line."

"I'll speak to Angela tonight. We'll let you know tomorrow."

Charlie did just that. He expected a degree of resistance, especially where moving into Emiline's house was concerned, but Angela was actually excited.

"You know I've been wanting to be closer to Vicki and the little ones. Ross and Billy can stay at the ranch."

"What about Chris and Joe?"

"When in school, they'll be in town anyway. As for the rest of the time, they'll probably be chasing their father around his beloved ranch. I worry more about keeping you in town than those two."

And so it was hastily settled. By the time Ryan

left for the fresh college term, driving the prized Herefords between Bob Lee Wiley and Toby Hart, Angela had moved her things into the house in Palo Pinto. As for the promissory notes, Charlie deposited those in the bank vault. He was determined the Stokelys should have every last chance.

Chapter 7

Charlie didn't care much for life in town. He missed the evening sounds of the birds in the live oaks, the jabber of squirrels and the music drifting down the creek from the bunkhouse. Palo Pinto was quiet, close to dead. And the few noises that did disturb the silence were most unwelcome.

For better than two years the saloons had closed their doors at nightfall. The town's growing female population had seen to that. Once Art Stanley's freight drivers had stayed overnight at rooming houses, but Art had found it cheaper to build a barracks of sorts down by the old ferry. That way the teamsters could have a nip after sundown if they had the notion without finding themselves locked in the courthouse storeroom. A quarrel or two was not uncommon during the daylight hours, but pistol shots or shouts after dusk marked trouble.

Charlie's first encounter with the Kepp brothers came on just such an occasion. Eldon and Walter Kepp were a pair of dusty buffalo hunters, both in their late twenties and neither partial to bathing regularly. The night they stumbled into town, the Double P Saloon was locked tight. A lantern burned in the back room at the Lone Star, though, and the Kepps were soon battering down the door with broom handles. When that proved unsuccessful, they started at the windows.

"Help! Help!" Jack Duncan cried as Walter Kepp smashed the glass and climbed through the now empty window frame.

Bret Pruett and Alex Tuttle grabbed shotguns and headed for the Lone Star. They were greeted by a swaggering youngster named Tucker Fenton.

"Hold up there, Sheriff," Fenton called. "My friends just want to have a little drink. What kind of unfriendly town closes its doors so early?"

"Move aside," Bret commanded.

Quick as lightning young Fenton drew his pistol and cocked the hammer.

"It's not worth dyin' over, Sheriff," Fenton declared.

Bret leveled his shotgun, and those curious onlookers who'd ventured out onto the street quickly sought shelter. Charlie watched the whole thing from his upstairs window. He stepped back to where a gun rack stood over the fireplace and drew down a Winchester. He carefully loaded three shells, then returned to the window.

"Either fire that thing or put it up, Sheriff!" Fenton yelled. "This isn't worth you gettin' killed, you know."

"No, it isn't!" Charlie shouted as he fired the

Winchester. The bullet raised a spiral of whitish dust three inches from Fenton's toe. Even on the dimly-lit street, Fenton knew he was in trouble. His pistol lacked the range to return fire, and there were the lawmen and their shotguns to consider, too.

"All right, Sheriff," Fenton said, tossing his pistol aside. "Let's go round up Walt and Eldon. They're probably drunk enough by now anyway."

Bret and Tut collected the three wrongdoers and escorted them to the storeroom. None had the price of the bottle of whiskey drained at the Lone Star, much less the replacement cost of the window. Bret kept them locked up three nights, but by day the trio were assigned every unpleasant task to be found in order to pay off their debt. When justice was finally served, Fenton and the Kepps left Palo Pinto hurriedly, riding north.

"Good riddance," Tut said. "Drifters and malcontents! The range is full of 'em."

"Just so long as they stay out there and keep clear of town, they're just fine with me," Bret said, scratching his ear. "Of course, they can't. They won't work, so they wind up in trouble. We'll see them again."

Bret was right. Three days later toward dusk young Jack Eubanks came riding into town shouting an alarm.

"Rustlers!" the sixteen-year-old cowboy hollered. "At the Triple S! They've shot Mr. Stokely. Help!"

Bret and Tut trotted outside immediately. After

helping Jack to the Padgett House where Vicki took the boy in tow, the lawmen headed for the livery. Charlie met them there.

"The kid's shook, Charlie, but there must be quite a few of 'em," Bret explained. "They've got the house surrounded. You figure we've got time to send somebody to the Flying J, maybe bring Wes or Marty with some hands."

"Sound carries up the river," Charlie said, saddling his horse while the two lawmen did the same. "They'll likely beat us there."

"I'll bet it's those Kepps," Bret declared. "I got a poster in this morning's mail. A gang of thieves hit three ranches down south. Sounds just like Fenton and those brothers. A couple others were along. One's good with a pistol."

"Oh?"

"Shot two Texas Rangers. A kid, the poster says, with a scar over his eye."

"Then we'd better be careful."

Bret gazed at Charlie as if to tell the old campaigner that this time it wasn't his fight. But both of them knew an extra man wouldn't hurt.

Charlie followed Bret and Tut along the Belknap road perhaps three miles to where a time-worn path led to Wolf Gap and the Stokely house. Bret followed the trail a quarter mile, then started cross-country. It was a wise idea. The raiders probably had lookouts watching the trail. In the fading twilight, three horsemen would be practically invisible weaving their way through the scrub oak and boulders of the range.

"Won't be like last time, will it?" Bret whispered. "Men'll get killed."

"May be some dead already," Charlie answered.

Bret nodded. The sound of rapid firing filled the air as they drew nearer. Finally Bret signalled a halt, then dismounted.

"There's the house," Bret said, pointing to the place. A pair of rifle barrels protruded from side windows. The rifles kept the outlaws at bay, but clearly they couldn't last long. Charlie guessed there might be a dozen raiders in all. The odds were long indeed.

"I'll take the right," Charlie suggested.

"I'm left then," Tut said grimly.

"Then I've got the center," Bret declared, waving them along.

Charlie wished his companions were closer. He didn't mind being alone, fighting on his own, but Bret was as dear to him as his own sons, and Alex Tuttle had a way of growing on people.

There's a task at hand, though, Charlie told himself as he crept toward the house. The rate of fire from the house decreased, and Charlie could detect shadowy figures closing in. He was glad Jack had gotten to town. An hour later would be too late, and at least there was enough light to see the targets.

Bret fired first, hitting a bulky figure who was edging toward the front of the house. Tut opened up next, firing his Winchester rapidly so that it sounded like a whole troop of cavalry had arrived. Charlie fixed his victim in his sights, then waited for the raider to turn. Walter Kepp was unconcerned about the new danger, thinking it one of his own men grown reckless. Charlie's first shot shattered Walter's jaw, and a second bullet tore through the outlaw's chest and pierced both lungs. Walter Kepp fell dead three feet from his brother.

"Walt!" Eldon screamed, jumping to his feet. It was a fatal mistake. Bret fired, and the Kepp brothers were no more.

"They're all over the place!" a raider shouted. "Get clear."

By now the outlaws were in a wicked crossfire. A pair of men tried to reach the house and were torn apart. Three fled wildly toward Ioni Creek. They were greeted by Wes Tyler and a half dozen riders from the Flying J. All three were killed in short order.

Tucker Fenton tried to form the survivors into a half circle near the trail, but the others had seen enough. Those who could fled for their lives. Two made it. One was caught in a volley of fire and shot to pieces.

"That you, Sheriff?" Fenton called out. "We never got to finish our business, did we? Care to do it now? Personal?"

"Nothing personal about this," Bret answered. "You can throw away your gun and surrender or die as you stand."

"I could take a few with me. Rame's still hereabouts, and he's as good with a Colt as they come."

Charlie thought it was bluster until a slender figure leaped onto the porch and charged inside the Stokely place.

"Lord, no!" Ben Stokely screamed as a pistol reverberated through the front room. A rifle shot answered, and the Colt barked again. Fenton took advantage of the diversion and made a run for a pair of horses milling around the Stokelys' barn. The young killer climbed atop a saddle and turned to leave. A single shot from behind ripped through Fenton's back, and the outlaw's face contorted with pain. The frightened horse raced off toward the trail, and Fenton toppled from the saddle. For a time his left foot caught in a stirrup, and he was dragged along behind the horse. There was no pain, though. Tucker Fenton was dead.

"You in the house, come out!" Bret shouted. "They're all dead. There's no one to help you now!"

"You think not!" a voice replied. "Well, maybe I don't need any help."

A face appeared at the front window, and Charlie froze. It just wasn't possible. The gunman was the very Raymond Polk they'd caught earlier.

"You see who it is, Charlie?" Tut asked as he joined Charlie near the porch.

"Well, Brad and Ben were right for once," Charlie admitted. "He looked so young."

"Jury would've let him off anyway. Can't blame yourself. For every one gone wrong like that, a dozen'll take the right fork."

"Sure," Charlie mumbled, knowing it didn't take but one of that sort to bring a plague of death.

They tried to wait young Polk out. After all, there was no way of knowing whether the Stokelys might still be alive inside the house. Just when Charlie was at the end of his patience, Polk stepped back from the window. Minutes later the curtains erupted in flame. Soon the roof caught fire as well.

"What's he doing?" Bret cried. "Burning himself up?"

No, just the house, Charlie thought as he rushed forward. He reached the porch in time to spot Polk climb out a window on the opposite side.

"He's headed for the creek!" Charlie shouted, and the others started in pursuit. Charlie kicked open the door and raced inside. Tony Lawson, a boy Joe's age who'd been helping with the stock, lay beside the fireplace, his eyes hauntingly empty. Brad lay slumped across a counting table five feet away, his back torn apart by several bullets. Suddenly Ben stumbled into the room holding a limp shoulder.

"Come on," Charlie said, helping Ben out the door as the flames began to choke the room.

"Get Brad," Ben pleaded as they passed safely through the door. "And little Tony. Lord, Charlie, that boy never even touched a gun."

Others took charge of Ben, and Charlie led Wes Tyler back inside the blazing house. They managed to collect the bodies and escape before the roof went up like a bonfire.

"Well, Brad?" Ben whispered to his dead brother, "we fought the good fight for a time, didn't we?"

Ben collapsed. Tut went in search of a wagon while Wes and Bret treated the rancher's wounds. Charlie headed for the creek. Shots still resounded from downriver, but he spotted a single rider splashing across the Brazos. Rame Polk had escaped to kill again.

Jack Eubanks was back on his feet the next day. Together with friends and neighbors, the youngster managed to pull a few mementos from the ashes of the Stokely place. Ben lay in the downstairs suite at the Brazos Hotel. When he recovered his wits, he sent word for Charlie Justiss to drop by.

"You look better," Charlie said, smiling as he sat in a chair beside Ben's bed. "Doc Parker rode down to have a look. He says you'll be ready to chase mustangs in a month."

"Thanks for pullin' me out of there, Charlie."

"As it turns out, I might be partially responsible for 'em hitting you. The one with the Colt was that snaggle-toothed boy we caught rustling steers the morning after Angela's birthday."

"I know. I got a good look at him. You couldn't know, Charlie. I felt sorry for him myself."

"We'll see he's posted proper. Seems he killed two Texas Rangers down in Hood County."

"He's got the look. I'll give him that," Ben said, swallowing hard. "Never blinked when he shot Tony. Lord, I don't think Tony ever saw his first whisker. Now he's dead."

"Happens like that sometimes. Doesn't seem right."

"No, it doesn't. Charlie, I spoke to Art Stanley this mornin'. He says you've got the notes Brad signed."

"I do."

"You know the ranch isn't worth the value of those notes."

"It might be."

"No, not with cattle prices as they are. Shoot, the house is even burned down. The money was due the first of the month. You never said anything."

"I figured you'd make good on it if you could. If not, you'd say as much."

"That's what I'm doin' right now."

"Nonsense. You're not yourself."

"Yes, that's just what I am. Brad's dead and buried. He was the one with the business sense, what there was of it. The ranch was his dream, not mine. I can ride fair, and I work steady at a job when somebody tells me what to do. I was never a boss. It's best to make a clean break. All I ask is that you give me leave to take that chestnut mare, together with my saddle and such."

"You didn't have to ask. I wouldn't take a man's horse."

"Some would. One other thing. If you could see your way clear to let me have fifty dollars. I know Tony's ma needs that much to pay off her mortgage. It's why the boy came out to work for us. I'd say he earned it."

"Sure. Take it as a personal loan. Don't count yourself out just yet, though. September often brings rain, and the market could come back."

"Maybe once. Back when the county was swarmin' with mavericks, Brad and I could run down a few hundred head, make ourselves some real money fast. Nowadays, well, we couldn't pay the taxes on the place. I hear Colorado's a land full of opportunity. I'll head up that way, try my hand at whatever comes along."

"I wish you luck."

"You're the one who'll need it. I always did think our stretch of range fit nicely into the Flying J. Maybe we should've sold it to you earlier. Might have gone away with some cash instead of holes in my pocket and a brother dead."

"Maybe," Charlie said, sighing.

"I always thought you to be a good neighbor, Charlie Justiss. I'd like to take your hand now."

"My pleasure," Charlie said, clasping Ben's weary wrist. Afterward, when Brad turned his head away and stared out the window, Charlie took five crisp ten dollar banknotes and left them on the night table under Ben's pocket watch.

Chapter 8

As autumn broke across the land, the fearful drought gave way to more pleasant days, to spotty showers and cool evenings. The creeks and springs came back, and the cattle left the crowded river banks for better grass along the creeks. Charlie rode out among the farms and stared in disbelief at grown men gone crazy, tearing their clothes off and dancing naked in the rain.

Ben Stokely rode north the next morning, his face still drawn and pale from pain and loss. Charlie read in the New Mexico *Territorial Gazette* how Raymond Polk, aged fifteen years, had shot a widow while robbing a bank in Taos. Maybe the world really was mad. Boys shooting old women, and children working off their family's debts, getting shot in farmhouses by rustlers turned loons. Outfits like the Triple S vanished from the range. Charlie half expected the sun to come out at midnight or roses to bloom on the

95

moon.

Maybe that was why when a telegram from Bowie arrived inviting Charlie and Angela to Austin for a brief stay, Charlie jumped at the chance. Angela rarely got to travel even as far as Weatherford, and she was equally enthusiastic.

"So long as you're going, Papa," Ross said when Charlie told the boys of the planned trip, "I might come along as well. Billy can handle the ranch by himself, and I . . ."

"Have someone to see?" Charlie asked.

"You know he doesn't talk five minutes without jabbering away about that Eliza Rogers," Chris said, grinning.

Ross turned toward his younger brother with clenched fists, and the smaller Chris retreated behind their father.

"Seems to me like you could use a week away from little brothers, if nothing else," Charlie declared. "Will you want us to reserve you a room at the hotel?"

"No, I'll stay with Senator Rogers," Ross mumbled. "He's been after me to make a trip down there anyway. Shoot, their house is practically a second home by now."

"Fine," Charlie said, glad it was settled. He then spoke briefly with Billy about the ranch and received promises from Chris and Joe that if they stayed with their brother at the ranch, they'd ride into town early enough to beat the school bell.

"If not, I've given Bret leave to come out here and put shackles on you, chain you to the stove inside the schoolhouse."

Charlie could tell from the disappointment in

Joe's eyes that some fine plan had been spoiled by the threat of such punishment. The two youngsters begrudgingly nodded, and Charlie knew he could set Angela's mind at rest as to the boys' behavior during their parents' absence.

The stagecoach which carried passengers south to the state capital at Austin smelled of wet leather and stale bread. Even at the best of times the seats were damp and oily. Dust from the sandy roads hid in every crack and cranny. The storeroom jail at the courthouse was a more fit habitation.

Charlie Justiss, for his own part, would have ridden south on horseback. But with Angela and Ross along, and the autumn trail ripe with horse thieves, Charlie chose to take the coach. He sat on one end of the forward sofa, with Angela sandwiched between her husband and oldest son. Across the narrow center aisle between the seats crowded a pair of widows from Jack County, a whiskered buffalo hunter, and a young woman whose feathered hat and perfumed hair brought her virtue into question.

"Got to admit this," Ross whispered to Charlie as they prepared to board the coach. "She does improve the air some."

The scenery, too, Charlie thought as he watched Ross's eyes follow the young woman's movements. Angela seemed almost as amused.

"Maybe it's a good thing we're getting him back to Eliza Rogers," she declared. "Those eyes have been roving long enough."

97

The journey itself was miserable. The passengers placed kerchiefs over their faces to keep from choking on the dust. Even so it seemed to find its way into every particle of their being. The widows complained bitterly about the jostling ride. The buffalo hider simply leaned his head against the coach door and snored away. Charlie held Angela's hand and tried to observe the countryside through the dust thrown up by the prancing horses. Only Ross and Miss Fatima Bardley, as the feathered lady called herself, seemed even faintly amused.

"I told Miss Molly I'd not pass another winter at the Flat," Miss Bardley explained. "The cowboys down there haven't got the price of a beer, much less, well, anything else. There aren't enough soldiers to keep three old hogs in business. Do you know I had to hire myself out as a scrubwoman last spring? What's Texas come to? There was a time when it was a land of opportunity for a girl. Now it's full of wives and churches and schools!"

"Makes it hard on some, eh?" Ross asked, grinning.

The widows were not amused.

"Harlot," one of them declared. "Back when my Jed was younger . . ."

"He'd probably been by Miss Molly's," Fatima finished. "If he could spare a dollar, that is."

Charlie laughed, and the buffalo hunter even grunted.

"You know how it is, Granny," Fatima went on. "You have to get your living."

"The wages of sin shall be paid in fire and

brimstone," the second widow declared. "When Judgment Day comes, all debts will be paid.

"Not all, honey. A cowboy named Snake Fullerton owed me thirty dollars the day Hank Klepner shot him dead. I'll never see that money."

No, Charlie thought fighting back a grin. I'd say not.

As might have been expected, the Justisses arrived in Austin an hour after nightfall, hot, tired, and coated with dust. They were totally exhausted. Except for pausing to change horses and allow the passengers a chance to purchase lunch or refreshments, and to attend to their functions, the coach bounced along unchecked. As a result the weary passengers were hardly prepared for the welcome they received upon arrival in the capital.

Bowie and Emiline stood at the depot. Senator Rogers and Eliza were a few feet away, sitting more comfortably on a hard wooden bench. Emiline quickly retreated as the buffalo hunter stumbled out of the coach, and she gasped when Fatima Bardley exited. Charlie let the widows leave, too, before stepping down and assisting Angela out the narrow door.

"Well, you look to have had a long journey," Senator Rogers declared as he greeted them warmly. "I'd hoped we might make the rounds tonight, see a few friends, but you three are clearly in need of a bath and some rest."

"Yes," Angela agreed, shaking the dust from her skirts.

"Well, I'm not so sure," Ross said, taking Eliza's hands in his own and looking her over with

99

glowing eyes. "You've seen me worse, haven't you, Liza?"

"I saw you rolled in cow muck the day you fell asleep at the cowpens in Jacksboro," she reminded him. "Worse, well, maybe."

She laughed, and Ross drank it in like a man lost three months on the Llano.

"Folks, we'd best tend to your bags," a gangling young man announced, and Senator Rogers waved for the boy to follow Charlie. Between chomps on a plug of tobacco, the young man managed to introduce himself as Ab Thayer, the senator's driver and stable hand. Ab carried the three bags in hands big as bear paws. Ross's gear was loaded in the boot of Senator Rogers's carriage. A baggage handler placed the other two bags in a flat wagon.

"They're to go to the Apollo Hotel," Bowie instructed. "Charlie, I booked you the suite next to my own. Em saw to it a tub was brought in, even got you some of that scented soap, Angela."

"Thank you," Angela said, nodding to her sister-in-law. Charlie winced. That soap brought out rashes to half the hands the second year they'd driven up the Kansas trail.

"I can't tell you how glad I am you've come, Charlie. Debate on the railroad's been heated of late. Why, some fool from Houston says they ought to take the route up north through Red River Station, cross the Panhandle and join the Union Pacific at Cheyenne. Ever heard of such nonsense?"

"It would help the Panhandle folks."

"Would never get built. Who's going to travel

100

back and forth from Cheyenne? We need a link with California, and besides, the public lands are in the west."

"I can't argue with the idea. Pala Pinto wouldn't see much good in a line going north to Colorado."

"I'll need you to speak to that point, Charlie. After all, we've got a lot more taxpayers across the Fort Worth and Western route. More ranchers and farms to provide goods and passengers, too."

"You needn't persuade me, Bowie. Just now we're awfully tired, though."

"Of course," Bowie said, leading the way to a waiting carriage. Charlie bid good-bye to the senator, then pried Angela away from Eliza.

"It's time we got to the hotel, dear," Charlie declared. "I'm sure Ross will have the young lady over bright and early for breakfast, won't he?"

"If that's an invitation, we accept," Eliza responded.

"Watch her, son," Senator Rogers said, laughing and jabbing the wooden walkway with his cane to add emphasis. "She's already making the decisions, and you're not even hitched."

"Not yet," Eliza said, grinning as she put a firm grip on Ross's arm. "Give me a week."

"A month if need be," Angela said. "It's time you two were married. Ross will be an old man soon."

"Don't pay Mama too much attention," Ross spoke as he escorted Eliza to the senator's carriage. "She wants more grandkids. I'm her best prospect. Billy's not apt to let anybody rope him soon, and Ryan's down south in that cadet col-

101

lege."

"What about your sister?" Eliza asked.

"Well, it seems Vicki thinks four's about enough," Ross said, laughing.

"More than enough," Charlie said, taking Angela's hand and laughing at the two young people's pink faces. "Now, my dear, shall we go?"

"Certainly," Angela agreed with a smile.

The Apollo Hotel was a remarkable contrast to the dusty stagecoach. Charlie felt almost ashamed to enter the sparkling lobby in his dusty boots. Rich burgundy drapes adorned the windows, and a crystal chandelier hung from the ceiling. Twin staircases led the way upstairs, and a uniformed boy insisted on taking their luggage.

"I think I've gone to heaven!" Angela exclaimed when the boy opened the door and escorted them inside the suite. A canopied bed and twin wardrobes occupied the bedroom, and there was a parlor, a sitting room, and a small room off to the side complete with brass bathtub.

"It's called the Brazos Suite," Bowie explained. "I thought you'd appreciate that. We're in the Colorado Suite next door. If you need anything, let me know."

"Just some hot water for a bath," Angela said. "I think I'll never get the dust out of my hair."

"All that will pass once Texas is joined with the rest of the country," Emiline declared. "Railroads will make travel a pleasant experience. That's one of the reasons I'm so proud of Bowie's efforts to build this line to California."

"Yes, we all are," Charlie said as he handed the baggage boy a silver dollar.

"I'll see the water's brought up straight away, sir," the boy promised as he exited with a smile. "Straight away, sir."

Bowie and Emiline then excused themselves, and Charlie conducted his wife inside.

"You'll spoil the help passing out silver dollars," Angela said, grinning. "I'll bet that boy hasn't seen that much money at one time in weeks."

"I'll wager he gets our hot water up here."

"Well, I wouldn't be surprised. The truth, though, is that you've always had a soft spot for the young ones."

"I confess. I'm guilty."

"There are worse vices to life, Charlie Justiss," she said, resting a tired head on her shoulder. "Now help me unpack."

By the time Angela had filled the wardrobes with clothes, the baggage boy had returned, leading a small army of servants toting water buckets. They even located a second tub so the two weary travelers could bathe side by side.

The bath and the soft feather bed took the edge off their exhaustion, and when morning arrived, Charlie felt reborn. Angela continued to show the effects of the trip, but it didn't prevent her from joining Ross and Eliza in the hotel's restaurant for breakfast. Afterward, Eliza whisked Angela off for a tour of the shops while Ross led Charlie to a waiting carriage. It seemed Senator Rogers had invited them to an agricultural display.

"The old days when a man took a plow and a mule and made his living are passing," the senator explained as he led the way through exhibits of mass-produced horseshoes and all manner of new farm implements. It wasn't until they reached a display of barbed wire that Charlie grew impatient.

"I've seen this before," he said, sadly shaking his head. "It'll kill the open range, and that's been the salvation of Texas."

"It's dead already," Senator Rogers stated firmly. "Texas is a farm state, and the only way the farmer can protect his crops is to fence his fields. The men who will truly benefit, though, are the big ranchers like you, Charlie Justiss. Now you've probably got twenty ranches in your county who graze steers on your land. They drink from the river on your property. They get away with that because you like the feel of the unfettered range. Well, once Bowie gets his railroad built, you'll deliver cattle at a depot in Palo Pinto. You'll improve the herds so that each steer yields more beef to the slaughterhouse. The price will rise accordingly."

"All that sounds fine," Charlie confessed, "but I don't see where this wire . . ."

"It discourages cattle from wandering. It forces the small operations to acquire land or get out of the business. You won't find these two bit outfits underbidding you at market because they will face the same costs you do already."

It's caused trouble elsewhere, Senator," Ross pointed out. "Serious trouble. Men have been killed. I understand in one county last year they had two fences cut for every one left standing."

"We've fought our wars," Charlie added. "First the Yanks, then the Indians, and finally these rustling skunks who murder children and steal a man's livelihood."

"You wait and see," Senator Rogers said, pointing at the number of attentive cattlemen listening to a Pennsylvania salesman explaining the merits of the wire. "You'll have the Flying J fenced in two years' time."

"Maybe," Charlie said sadly. "But that'll be a day I mourn."

"We all will," Ross agreed.

Charlie's main purpose in coming to Austin had nothing to do with barbed wire or prophecies. The legislature was hotly debating the new railroad bill, especially since it called for the state to contribute vast amounts of public land to the railroad as an incentive. There was the additional issue of condemning right-of-way, and Texans were loathe for their state to take a man's land for any reason short of survival.

"This is survival, gentlemen," Bowie argued. "If we don't bring the cattle cars to our ranches, states like Kansas and Colorado, which lie across existing lines, will take our markets. Driving herds to railheads is dangerous, and Kansas farmers have just about closed the routes with their protective laws and vigilante tactics. Besides, as things rest now, we can only move cattle in spring and summer, when the rivers are down and the grass is high. It's the future. It is, as I said, survival."

"You're asking us to provide a pretty penny," one representative pointed out. "I know what you and your friends get, Mr. Justiss. What will the state see from this investment?"

"For one thing, much of our proposed route is

arid land. No one lives there today. Once our rails cut through, settlers will come for the cheap land, build homes and farm or ranch. They'll pay taxes and contribute to the betterment of Texas. And as the prairie is settled, there will be fewer refuges for the lawless, for rustlers that plague the cattle industry or for thieves and murderers who defy our laws and endanger our families. Towns will blossom. Schools and churches will spring up out of the wilderness. I speak of prosperity, gentlemen."

"And what do you think of this scheme, Major?" a thin-faced veteran of the Fourth Texas, Representative Tom Fulton of Navasota, asked. "Will it do as the captain says?"

"I'm no prophet," Charlie said. "I've seen the world turn a dozen times in my life. I do know we can't make a living running herds to Wyoming and the Dakotas. All we do is put more outfits in business closer to Chicago. I've got my boy, Ryan, down at the new ag college, learning about new breeds that will build a better herd. I had Ross here read for the law so he'll know the best way to conduct business. I know, and so do you, how the railroads settled Kansas. I don't see how the cattle business can survive without this line, and if it's built north through the Panhandle, it'll be more help to the Chickasaw Nation than to Texas."

A dozen representatives applauded, and one threw his hat. Several clapped politely, more out of respect than enthusiasm.

"I'd favor the line myself," Senator Rogers declared, and Charlie smiled. Eliza had gently nudged her father moments before. "Of course," the senator continued, "we'd have to agree to a deadline. We wouldn't want to pledge the land and have the railroad lay rails halfway and just flat give up."

"That's fair," Bowie agreed.

"From Fort Worth to El Paso, right?" Fulton asked. "That would mean a rail link from east to west across the state."

"That's the idea," Bowie explained. "And with Fort Worth tied to Kansas City and Chicago, the stockyards would be little more than a few days from every cattle ranch in the state."

This time the applause was louder. And as the debate continued in the days ahead, even the most suspicious began to appreciate the plan Bowie Justiss unveiled for the new railroad. The legislature voted overwhelmingly in favor of the plan, and Bowie hosted a victory party. Charlie only grudgingly agreed to come. His work was done, and he was eager to return home.

"We've got one other matter to attend to first," Angela said as he led her around the dance floor. "Look there."

Her finger pointed toward Ross and Eliza. The pair danced as if there were no other people in the room. Charlie smiled. It had been much the same way for him when he'd courted Angela.

"I'm sure they're close to declaring themselves," Charlie said. "Ross has always been a bit cautious."

"He's downright hopeless," Angela said. "Eliza's been ready since spring. She's even altered her mother's gown. It's time, Charlie. Don't you think

107

you should speak to your son?"

"He's grown, Angela. He can make up his own mind."

"You men," she growled. "You always leave the real work to the women, don't you?"

"Such as?"

"Birthing and nursing and tending and educating . . . and even arranging weddings."

Angela stalked off. Moments later she interrupted Ross and Eliza, taking both in tow long enough to communicate her feelings where engagements were concerned. Ross then set off to locate Senator Rogers. A half hour later Angela called out, and the music stopped.

"My son's got an announcement," she cried. "Ross?"

"You're all invited to my wedding," Ross said, grinning nervously at Eliza. "Miss Eliza Rogers and I are going to be married at the Capitol Christian Church day after tomorrow."

"It's about time," a voice from the back of the room called, and the assembly broke out laughing.

"The senator says after we get through the vows, everyone's to come to his house and celebrate."

"Hurrah!" Bowie called, and others echoed the call. Charlie gripped his son's wrist and smiled approvingly.

"So, did I do it all right?" Ross asked.

"Don't you think you should ask Eliza that?"

"Yes, sir," Ross answered, setting off to locate the bride-to-be.

The wedding was held on the brightest October morning anyone could remember. The sky was clear, and the sun hung like a bright yellow circle over the Travis County hills. The service was brief and solemn, sprinkled with what seemed like a thousand flowers. Charlie couldn't imagine there were that many varieties blooming in the fall.

The family had all arrived. Joe and Chris managed a prank or two, but otherwise, the event was flawless. Little Charlie and his sister Hope added a chuckle or two, and Jared Dunlap, dressed in the only suit he'd ever worn, served as best man. Eliza was supported by two dozen former classmates and a host of friends and well-wishers from the government. The governor's niece even made an appearance.

Charlie shared few of his own thoughts until afterward. As friends and relatives gathered in the expansive back lawn of Lawrence Rogers's Austin home, Charlie raised a glass and cheered the newlyweds.

"My fondest hopes to Ross and Eliza," he called out. "May theirs be a boundless future filled with endless horizons, rich dreams, and every happiness the best of hearts can find."

"Amen," Senator Rogers added.

Wine was sipped, and prayers were made. Ross and Eliza slipped quietly out the back door into a waiting carriage bound for San Antonio, and Charlie contented himself with one task completed and another well begun.

"It's time to go home," he told Angela as she

wrapped one arm around Joe and another around Chris. "I've been away from the county's business too long, and it looks as if these two scarecrows need some of their mama's tending."

"Ah, Papa," Joe said, grinning. "Dada stuffs us like a Christmas goose."

"Then why is it I feel ribs?" Charlie asked, running his fingers along Joe's chest.

"Well, you know what Ma Dunlap says, "Chris contributed. "She says the devil's work eats the fat right off your bones."

"She's probably right, too," Angela said, hugging the boys to her side. "More likely you've been sneaking another inch or two of growth on your old mama."

"Think so?" Joe asked, stretching himself taller.

Charlie laughed, then smiled at Angela. Yes, it was time to head back.

Chapter 9

As the first whisper of winter crept across the land, Charlie Justiss set off riding with Joe and Chris. The boys had been little more than babies when they'd made the long difficult trek north from Robertson County. 1879 was fast fading now. Another year had come and gone, and the Brazos remained as always, eternal, unflinching, yielding neither to the drought or to time.

Everything else continued to change. People came and went, like actors in a stage play, sprinkled into the pageant of history as if by some thoughtful playwright. The family grew. Joe and Chris seemed to reach new heights each dawning. Joe's voice now broke in mid-sentence, and Chris's flaxen hair had begun to darken to a more seasoned amber.

As for Victoria, she was a girl no longer. Her dark Spanish eyes flashed less with wonder and more with a seriousness that motherhood brought. The grandchildren were each week encountering some new milestone, discovering some marvel of life, reawakening in Charlie and Angela some half-forgotten recollection of childhood too long set aside.

"Grandparenting is a wondrous thing," Angela explained one evening as she huddled with Charlie beside the hearth. "When our own children were small, it seemed as if there was never a moment to spare for watching. There were crops to tend or Indians to fight. I was nursing Chris when Ross grew his first whiskers. I was patching trousers when Billy kissed Rebecca Longstreet the first time. It seems life holds back its rewards, and I thank God I've withstood the trials all these years so that I can enjoy the treasures little Charlie and Hope, James Patrick and Tom provide daily."

"I feel it, too," Charlie said, squeezing her hand.

"We've been here close to ten years now. It sometimes seems only yesterday we were leaving Art Stanley's old trading post. Stands Tall was burning the house only last week. Ross and the Dunlap boys were teaching the little ones to swim in Bluff Creek."

"My bones tell me it was longer than that."

"Old age is a lie, Charlie. I'm just sixteen myself, and you're that dashing young cavalier come to call at my papa's door. Your clothes are a bit dusty, and your hair won't stay down. But you've got eyes like bluebonnets, and a smile as bright as the July sun."

"I wasn't like that at all."

"Yes, you were. Have you looked at Billy lately? Except for the eyes, you've been reborn, Charlie Justiss. Put a gray uniform on that bundle of rawhide and bone, and you'd have the picture of

112

the husband I sent off to war."

"I was close to thirty."

"Can't be. You're only eighteen this very minute. Care to dance, Captain?"

"Delighted, ma'am," Charlie said, rising to his feet and taking her hand. As they turned circles in the silent room, Joe and Chris watched from the stairway. Charlie detected a trace of confusion in the boys' eyes, and he figured the both of them had likely assigned their folks to a lunatic asylum. They'd learn in time if they were lucky, Charlie decided. And if not, they were to be pitied.

Two weeks before Christmas the first snow fell. It painted a delicate white cloak across the rugged hills and rock-strewn gullies of Palo Pinto County. Children delighted in dragging sleds out of woodsheds or tossing snowballs at their elders. Charlie took the opportunity to ride the river from the new bridge at Stanley's Crossing to the canyon walls. He concluded that ride, as always, atop the majestic Castle Cliffs.

A hundred memories flooded his mind as he stood alone atop the rugged wall. Was it really ten years ago that he'd first walked those heights? Back then a Comanche burial ground stood behind him, its lifeless bundles flanked by ancient lances and war bonnets, buffalo robes and great bows. A few years back some of the scaffolds remained. Later a scrap of cloth or an arrowhead could be found. Now there was ... nothing.

Charlie glanced eastward toward Fortune Bend. The outlaws, Stone and Hayley, had rustled cattle from the seclusion of that bend. Now Luis Morales ran horses there. Across the river the charred ruins of the Stokely ranch were blanketed with snow. Brad was dead, and Ben was last seen in the foothills of the Rockies. A man could stamp the Triple S brand on the rump of a steer, but he couldn't mark the land. Not for long at any rate. Life was so brief, temporary. And even as men died and infants were born, the river flowed on.

Charlie closed his eyes. Soon the future would intrude further on his precious hills. The railroad would bring snorting locomotives and crowded cattle cars, farmers ready to break the soil and fence the range with the devilish barbed wire Lawrence Rogers put so much stock by.

Maybe Joe Nance was right. Fight change. Hold to the old ways. But in the end, Charlie knew, no man could long hold off the arm of progress, and the future had a way of burying men who stood for long, unyielding, in its path.

After all, life was change. Birth, growth, maturity, age, and finally death. He could dance with Angela, but he'd never see eighteen again. He'd already outlived his father and both his grandfathers. In truth he hadn't expected to survive the war, and he'd given himself up a dozen times on the trail to Kansas or else squaring off with old Stands Tall's Comanches.

"I know your secret," Charlie told the cliffs. "All around you has been eaten away by the years, and yet you stand tall. You know every day is a gift to be lived and celebrated. Each moment is precious, and a life well spent should have no regrets."

I have none, he thought as he started back

down the steep path leading to the ranch house. From there he would return to town, to Angela and the boys ... to the town of Palo Pinto. It was, more than anyone else's, his town. He would see it through the storms to come as he'd seen it through flood and drought. And along the way he would watch and listen, love and learn.

II

The Railroad

Chapter 1

Fort Worth was a town born of the cattle industry. Through its streets had romped the great south and central Texas herds bound northward along the Chisholm Trail. Longhorns had watered and rested on the shores of the Trinity River before embarking on the long and difficult trek to Red River Station. The first stores and saloons that huddled beside the old military post served the drovers who nudged those steers up the trail.

Cattle continued to nurture the growing town, but now they collected in the stockyards to be shipped north in boxcars to Kansas City or perhaps on to Chicago. The first rails reached the town in 1876, and two years later, thousands of cattle cars were rolling. New lines north toward Denver and south to the Gulf were already surveyed when the Fort Worth and Western received its charter.

"There was never any question," Henry Thorpe,

the New York financier and empire builder who controlled two-thirds of the line boasted to Bowie Justiss. "What else could they do? Any fool can see all Texas lacks to join the ranks of the greatest of the states is a rail network to link its diverse parts. We'll spread prosperity and population as we cut our way west to the Pacific."

"And make ourselves rich in the bargain," Bowie said, accepting a cigar from Thorpe.

"Naturally, but we're not there yet," Thorpe objected as he lit Bowie's cigar. Bowie puffed until the tip of the cigar glowed red. He then gazed around him at the rich appointments of the private railroad car that had carried Thorpe two thousand miles from Washington, D.C.

"Twenty sections per mile, Thorpe," Bowie said with a sigh. "That's over ten thousand acres for each mile of track we lay. By the time we've built the line to El Paso, we'll own more land than's in some states!"

"Oh, we'll own land," Thorpe agreed as he puffed away on his cigar. "No doubting that. We own an empire of West Texas . . . buffalo wallows and caprock, prairie dogs and ravines. The engineers are clear enough on that. I couldn't sell my bankers ten acres of that country for a dollar. Yet."

"But once the railroad is through . . . "

"Not even then. No, land isn't what will make us wealthy, my friend. That takes an idea."

"What idea?"

"The notion that West Texas land will make men rich. Cattle can graze that desolate range, and our railcars will ship them to market. A man that invests a few thousand dollars can acquire a large ranch. If he buys cattle, he can be making money almost immediately."

"That's not altogether true," Bowie pointed out. "Ranchers are having a rough time of it. Prices fall, and more competition isn't going to help."

"Well, naturally we needn't explain that to our prospective buyers. No, remember the idea of wealth. Once they're out there, they'll either make a go of it or toss in their chips. It's a gamble of sorts, but many's the fortune been made in like manner."

"And where will you find these wide-eyed buyers? Texas isn't overflowing with people out to buy West Texas land. Why would anyone buy land from us when the homestead acts give him an opportunity to stake out his own place on the prairies up in the Dakotas or Wyoming?"

"We'll find settlers. Don't you worry over that," Thorpe declared, gazing through his spectacles as a clerk in a counting house might do when examining ledgers. "You get the tracks laid. I'll bring the people."

"From where?"

"The north. The south. Europe. If necessary, I'll ship them over from Timbuktu. Don't you worry, though. They'll come."

Thorpe stroked his graying beard and chuckled to himself. There was something terribly convincing about him. His eyes lit up like the embers of a winter campfire, and Bowie couldn't help feeling reassured. Thorpe might speak of gambling, but the New Yorker's silk shirts and tailored clothes hinted he had never once left very much to chance.

"So, I suppose we should look over the surveyors' maps," Bowie said, opening a chart case and spreading out the maps on a table in the massive parlor of Thorpe's car. "You'll notice we tried to join the county seats, the major settlements. Some we had to avoid. It simply wasn't worth crossing rivers or blasting our way through a mountain."

"Might be," Thorpe objected. "This is your first railroad, isn't it, Justiss?"

"That's right," Bowie said, his back stiffening as Thorpe grinned.

"Well, we don't just make money on the state's promises, my friend. It's worth a fortune to some of these towns to be linked to our line. They can afford to pay for that."

"How so?"

"They post a bond with us. Small towns pay, say, five thousand dollars. Bigger ones ten thousand. I've gotten more in some places."

"I thought you said we wanted to attract population."

"New population," Thorpe said, laughing. "Those people already settled can pay for the passage of our rails."

"And if they won't?"

"Then we bypass them. It's a sight to see, Justiss. One day there's a fine little town. The next, people cart up their stores and houses and head for the rails. Towns just dry up and blow away. I saw it plenty in East Texas. Places set on the steamboat landings thought they didn't need us. Now they wish they'd paid the bond. West of Marshall there must be half a dozen ghost towns."

"And what use is a railroad if you don't have towns and depots?" Bowie cried. "We can't ship cattle and cotton from the empty plains. We need cattle pens and loading docks."

"We'll build them. Won't take long for some enterprising young man to buy up our interest."

"You make it sound so easy, Thorpe. It won't be. I saw railroads built in Virginia and Tennessee that bridged rivers and cut through mountains. But all that is nothing to dealing with West Texas. There's good grade all right, but you have to insure the rails against flash floods and rock slides. Rivers that seem peaceful in spring drown whole counties by summer."

"That's what I hired Burke for."

Thorpe walked to the door and opened it. A tall, square-shouldered man in his mid-fifties strode into the room. He immediately took off his hat and gazed at Bowie with cold, serious brown eyes.

"This is Angus Burke," Thorpe explained. "Burke, meet my partner, Bowie Justiss."

"Another Yank?" Burke asked, speaking in a thick New Orleans accent that seemed to mix in a touch of Scotland or perhaps Ireland.

"Texas," Bowie explained, studying Burke's face. A familiar defiance etched Burke's brow. His carefully combed reddish hair, neatly-trimmed sideburns and moustache concealed what rough, weathered hands betrayed—here was a man accustomed to hard labor and trying times.

"I knew Burke when he was just a young lieutenant fresh out of West Point," Thorpe explained. "First in his class and bound for the engineers. A hero in the Mexican War, and bound for greatness no doubt if he'd stuck to Union blue."

"You wore the gray then," Bowie said. "I was a captain of the Fourth Texas myself."

"Colonel of the Tenth Louisiana."

123

"Well, then you are a man to be counted upon," Bowie said, smiling as he took Burke's hand and shook it firmly.

"And I'm inclined to think better of this project knowing it's not all Yankee cash and New York bluster," Burke replied.

"No, but there are some hazards," Bowie said, pointing to the maps. "Terrain's far from friendly."

"Leave that to my boys," Burke declared, bending over the charts. "I worked on the Union Pacific up on the Platte. These mountains and ravines of yours are more bother than obstacle. You two decide on the route, and I'll see the tracks are laid."

"Fair enough," Thorpe declared. "We start as soon as the weather breaks. The sooner the better. Start hiring a crew. We won't receive anything from the state until we get this line heading west!"

Thorpe vanished a half hour later, leaving Bowie and Angus Burke to go over the route, at least that portion that snaked its way across Tarrant County to the Clear Fork of the Trinity River.

"That'll merit a bridge," Burke pointed out. "Once the foremen are hired, I'll take my engineers down there and start planning the trestle. Thorpe's likely to stay here in Fort Worth. What about you, Bowie Justiss?"

"I'll go where I can do the most good."

"That would be in the work camps. It never hurts a man to see the boss taking a hand in the work. But you know that, else you'd never survived the war as a captain."

"Nor you as a colonel."

Burke grinned, and Bowie knew the beginning of a successful enterprise had been made.

There was more to launching a railroad than marking maps or building bridges, though. Capital was needed. Raising funds was Henry Thorpe's specialty, and the New Yorker treated Fort Worth to a series of balls that featured a string orchestra, table after table of rich food, and the pick of Thorpe's extensive wine cellar expressed to Texas from his Manhattan estate.

Everyone of importance in the state was invited, and most came. Women put on their best gowns and adorned themselves with jewels. Practically the entire government shut down and headed north from Austin. Fine carriages discharged their passengers at the entrance to the new Cattlemen's Hotel. Onlookers might not have been surprised to see an English earl or a Russian duke in the company.

"It seems I've waited my whole life for this evening," Emiline Justiss told Bowie as he led her up the steps to the hotel. "Papa had fine parties when I was a girl, but I never saw anything to rival this, not even in Alexandria. I feel like a queen."

"You look the part," Bowie told her. Her hair was pinned atop her hair, and a golden tiara, complete with clustered diamonds, rested above her brow. A yellow silk gown traced her slim figure, and she walked with a grace that had too long been swallowed by rough boots and home-spun cloth.

"I do wish we could have brought Clay along,"

Em lamented. "He so seldom has the opportunity to share such fine company."

"He has his studies," Bowie declared. "As for the company, they're all far too old to offer much amusement to a boy closing in on fourteen."

Emiline sighed and abandoned the notion of sending for the boy. Instead she gave Bowie her hand, and they entered the hotel together. They were immediately greeted by Henry Thorpe.

"Here is my partner in this grand venture," Thorpe announced as he motioned for Bowie to come closer. "Bowie Justiss, gentlemen, and his lovely wife, Emiline."

A circle of guests greeted the Justisses warmly. Thorpe kissed Emiline's hand, then introduced a young beauty, Barbara Barr.

"I believe I know your father, Miss Barr," Bowie said, nodding politely. Carter Barr was Fort Worth's leading banker. Thorpe moved one hand over the other so as to conceal his wedding band. Clearly Miss Barr was more than a banker's daughter to be flattered with flowery talk.

Bowie was soon drawn off to one side by Senator Lawrence Rogers, though, and he had no time for the beautiful Barbara Barr.

"We passed your bill, Bowie," the senator said. "When will you lay some track? So far all I've seen of the FW & W is tall talk and partying."

"You'll see track soon enough," Bowie promised. "It takes time to survey the route, and we can hardly begin before spring arrives."

"I suppose," Senator Rogers grumbled. "I'd feel better if that Thorpe fellow wasn't running things."

"No, he's what we need," Bowie argued. "He's built lines before. I know he comes across like some fancy jackstraw from a medicine show, but he knows what he's about. Wait and see if we don't get to El Paso by summer's end."

"I hope so. For all our sakes."

"What kind of talk is that, Father?" the senator's daughter Eliza asked. Also joining the conversation was her husband, Bowie's nephew Ross.

"Married life seems to suit you, Ross," Bowie told the young man. "You've gained a pound or two. Beauties aren't supposed to be able to cook."

"Shhh," Ross pleaded. "You'll turn her head."

"Not a chance," Eliza assured them. "As it is, Ross spoils me scandalously. And the cooking, that's mostly Dada's doing."

"Then you're staying with Charlie?" Bowie asked.

"For the time being," Ross explained. "Billy has the ranch in hand, and the county has need of a lawyer."

"Oh?"

"State surveyors have come to verify boundaries. It's likely your doing, Uncle Bowie. Palo Pinto County has a fair amount of state land, and some of it's likely to be deeded over to your railroad."

"I would imagine so," Bowie said, giving Ross a polite handshake before slipping away and rejoining Emiline. She was busy recounting tales of bygone days when the Thayers of Robertson County drew high society to their home.

"All that's changed now, of course," Em said sadly. "The war put an end to southern gentility."

"Yes," Thorpe agreed, nodding sadly. "A terrible thing, war. It was always Mr. Lincoln's dream that the Union should be restored amiably. Then, when the cannons had grown silent, an assassin struck him down. Had he lived, the South might have felt a gentler touch. Many of us wished it so."

"You were in the government yourself, weren't you?" Miss Barr asked.

"Undersecretary of Commerce, my dear. My talents even then turned to the building of railroads. Our vision then was to link the Atlantic with the Pacific, to knit the nation together so that no one would ever be able to rend its flesh again. Now that we've crossed the Rockies and linked California with the north, we must strike out across the southern deserts and link the south with her sister states in the west."

"Bravo," Miss Barr cried, and the gathering applauded.

Henry Thorpe made a similar speech after dinner in the ballroom. The company responded enthusiastically.

"He's got a gift with words," Ross told Bowie afterward. "I do believe he could talk the socks off a bowlegged sow. Best watch your pocketbook, Uncle Bowie."

"I always do," Bowie answered. "Don't tell me you disapprove of the railroad?"

"No, railroads bring progress. I know Papa's a bit reluctant to see the open range die, but not me. It's brought mostly pain and death and bitterness to Texas."

"Your father and I built our futures on those cattle drives, Ross."

"That was ten years ago," Ross said, gazing about the room. "Everything's changed since then. There are no Comanches or buffalo out there. I can't recall when I last spotted a maverick longhorn. Back when the roundup involved our crew, the Stokely brothers and Joe Nance, we never had much quarreling. Now, with two dozen outfits running steers on the open range, a cow here or there means survival to some of them. Killing's sure to come of that."

"So you'd fence the land?"

"It's coming. Has to, just like the railroad."

"So why do you appear so unhappy?"

"Do I?" Ross asked. "Well, maybe it's just that I've spent too much time in Austin of late. Political speeches make me nervous. I've seen too many promises broken to put much stock in words. And this Thorpe fellow talks out of both sides of his mouth, A man who's around cyclones enough gets a feeling when to dig himself a shelter. Me, I've got that kind of feeling right now. Keep a sharp lookout, Uncle Bowie. See you don't find yourself holding any notes for this rascal."

"I'll surely keep my eyes open."

Ross's concern marred what otherwise was a magnificent evening. Emiline was rarely as over-flowing with enthusiasm. As they rode back to their temporary quarters in a rooming house on the outskirts of town, Bowie told the driver to go by way of Cherry Hill.

"What a lovely name for a place," Em said as the carriage made its way through the forested hills on the west side of town. Soon they passed the tall, stately homes of bankers and cattlemen who had chosen to reflect their new wealth in grand, turreted mansions. The carriage stopped when it arrived at the skeleton of a new house, one which would house the Bowie Justiss family.

"I can see it already," Emiline said, stepping out of the carriage so that she could stroll along the stone walkways that were already in place. "We'll plant trees and flowers. It will be such a wonderful place, Bowie. And there will be parties and balls ... with all the finest of people there to share our lives."

"Yes," Bowie said, clasping her hand. "You know, dear, I'll have to be away a lot once we start building the railroad."

"Why? I thought that's why you hired that Burke fellow, the engineer."

"He'll design bridges and mark the route. Someone will have to keep the work camps moving."

"Henry Thorpe won't be living in any work camp, passing his days with sweaty, foul-smelling Mexicans and God knows what else. It's not fair, Bowie."

"Until the house is finished, you will stay with Mrs. Taylor, of course. It won't be for such a long time. Spring's still weeks away, and the house is rising quickly. It wasn't so long ago I was off to the cattle drives for several months. I'll be back and forth much more frequently this time around."

"You promise?"

"Yes," he said, kissing her hands and pulling her close to his side. "It's a small price to pay for fame and fortune."

"I suppose. I do wish you could be on hand to watch the work on the house until it's finished."

"You'll do a much better job of overseeing that than I would, Em. I know how to put together a dog run cabin, not a castle. If you have trouble with the masons, rely on Delby Snow. He's an honest man, and a fair one. He'll get the work done the way you want it."

"I'll miss you so much," she said, holding him

tightly.

"I'm not leaving tomorrow. Besides, you'll have Clay home on weekends, and for a whole week at Easter. The time will pass quickly, and we'll be proud partners in the Fort Worth and Western Railroad."

"Yes," she said, sighing as she closed her eyes. Bowie knew she was imagining the two of them riding down the rails in a private car like Henry Thorpe's. It was a grand dream, and he hated to hasten its end. Finally, though, he urged her back toward the carriage. The days ahead held a mountain of work, and it was always best such days were started early with a fair night's rest.

Chapter 2

As the first traces of spring came to Texas, the tall house on Cherry Hill began to rise from the prairie. When he wasn't busy at the rail yards, Bowie enjoyed gazing at the mansion.

"It will be even lovelier when the cherry blossoms appear," Emiline said, closing her eyes and imagining the scene.

"Of course, they're not really cherry trees," Bowie told her. "They're peach trees. Peach Hill doesn't sound so fine, I suppose, but the blossoms will be just as nice. Truth is, I'm partial to peaches."

Soon, however, there were fewer and fewer moments for house gazing. Bowie was occupied with a thousand duties. One minute he was inspecting the delivery of railroad ties from a pair of sawmills. The next he'd be supervising the stockpiling of rails brought by flatcars from Pennsylvania mills.

"You look a bit weary, boss," Angus Burke

remarked after Bowie finished going over the company accounts.

"I'll be ready for us to get to work," Bowie declared. "If I see another boxcar full of canvas or spikes pull in, I may just go crazy."

"I know," Burke said, laughing. "But without the spikes, the rails won't do us a lick of good. If the men don't have tents to keep the rain off their beds, they'll stop working. Everything in those warehouses is needed to build a railroad. And until you stockpile at least a month's worth of supplies, there's little point to hiring men."

"Oh?"

"I've seen all sorts of things happen to supply trains. Once a mill caught fire in Pittsburgh. We were laying track right and left. Then there were no more rails. You have to plan for all sorts of disasters."

The thought sobered Bowie. He was no less thrilled when boxes of revenue bonds arrived from a New York printer.

"We have to raise funds," Thorpe explained. "As soon as we sell sections of land, we redeem the bonds. They provide us with working capital."

"I thought that's why you and I put all that money in up front."

"Oh, Justiss, you never expend your assets paying salaries or buying materials. That cash might save your neck later on. It may delay our receiving profits for a time, but in the long run, the company will be better off."

Bowie was far from convinced, and he decided to examine the accounts even more closely than before. The numbers appeared to back Thorpe's arguments, though, and he executed his plans with a thoroughness and absolute confidence that was indisputable.

By the end of February, Angus Burke had crews leveing the grade from the depot in Fort Worth to the first major obstacle, the shallow bed of the Trinity's Clear Fork. Meanwhile Bowie had hired a veteran of the Rock Island Line named Boyd Fitch to manage the three warehouses the Fort Worth and Western had bought to house supplies. On March 1, the F W & W posted notices that hiring would soon begin.

"It won't be long now before we lay the first rail," Bowie told Emiline as they watched the stonemasons complete the walls for the new house. "Once we begin, look out! We'll race across the prairie like wildfire, and we won't stop short of El Paso. By late summer you can ride the train all the way to California."

"Yes," Emiline agreed. She was clearly more interested in the progress the workmen were making on the house.

Aside from the Cherry Hill mansion, Emiline Justiss had one other passion—her son, Clayton. Thirteen-year-old Clay was the sole child who'd lived past his first winter, and the small graveyard overlooking Bluff Creek back on the Flying

J Ranch in Palo Pinto County contained the markers of brothers and sisters called away by death at an early age.

When younger, Clay had been a spindly sort of boy, always a trifle pale and more than a little clumsy. He possessed his mother's fair skin, flaxen hair and soft blue eyes. He was quiet, almost shy, and though he shared with his father a love of horses and a penchant for devilment when the opportunity arose, he was more at home in a library, his nose in a book of English history or French philosophy.

Emiline had experimented with schools. Upon arrival in Fort Worth, she had enrolled Clay in the Baldwin Academy, an institution housed in a former dairy on the banks of the West Fork of the Trinity. The school's director, a one-armed ex-Confederate named Tyrone Dillman, had studied with Judge Thayer at the Alexandria Academy. If Dillman's association with her father wasn't enough, Baldwin's policy of allowing its students weekend furloughs home surely sealed the bargain.

"I'm so delighted to have Clay in such a fine place," Em told Bowie constantly. But when Clay invited schoolmates home, her enthusiasm waned. After Clay and a younger boy, Bart Davis, escaped out Mrs. Taylor's upstairs window and took a midnight swim in the frigid waters of Polk's Pond, Emiline greeted them with an icy frown.

"It's winter still!" she shouted. "You have no sense, Clay. Haven't I buried enough children for five lifetimes? Do you have to imperil your health? And what of common decency? Have you no regard for your mother's position? To run around a pond stark naked like some heathen Indian! It's indecent!"

"We did it at night, Mama," Clay pleaded. "No one saw. We do it all the time at school. Major Dillman says the cold water is good for a body's fluids. It strengthens the heart for the ordeals to come."

"Yes, ma'am," Bart added nervously. "It's part of our training. We didn't mean any offense."

"This would never have happened at Alexandria," Emiline complained. "Boys with proper upbringing simply don't go about naked. This is your doing, young man."

Her darting eyes homed in on the Davis lad, and Clay stepped in front of his friend as if to protect the other boy.

"Mama, it was my idea. Bart only went along."

"Bowie!" she called. Bowie had heard most of the discussion, but he'd hoped, like a bad dream, it would go away. He now rolled out of bed and pulled on a robe. Still groggy, he stumbled out the door and greeted the boys. By then half the boarding house guests had gathered in the hall.

"Bowie, do you know what these two boys have been up to?" Em asked.

"I think everyone south of the Red River knows that," Bowie declared. "Let's go into the parlor and let these other folks get their rest."

She agreed, and Bowie ushered the boys into the parlor.

"Papa, can't we just go back to bed?" Clay asked when Emiline closed the door. "We didn't mean any harm, and we won't do it again."

Bowie was about to dismiss them, but Emiline spoke up.

"It appears we must look for another school," she said. "I don't believe Baldwin enrolls boys of quality. And if Major Dillman's notion of proper training is swimming naked in freezing water, then I believe he must have lost a good deal more than a limb in the late unpleasantness."

"Papa?" Clay pleaded.

"Em, you're worn out," Bowie said, squeezing her hand. "Why don't you go along back to bed? I'll speak to the boys . . . firmly. I think it would be a mistake to make any major decisions about the future tonight when we're all so tired."

"Perhaps," she agreed. Bowie kissed her forehead, and she left reluctantly.

"Papa, we're sorry we caused such a stir," Clay said, sitting on a couch and frowning. "I'm especially sorry Bart caught so much blame. He's been a good friend. His folks are dead. All he's got is an uncle all the way out in Stephens County. I thought he'd like getting away from school."

"I did," Bart whispered. "I'm sorry, too."

"Clay's mother can get excitable," Bowie explained. "Why don't you go along to bed, too, Bart? We'll see if we can't make tomorrow a better day."

Bart smiled, nodded and left the room. Clay started to follow, but Bowie held his son back.

"I think we need to talk some more, son," Bowie declared. Clay nodded, and the two of them sat together and gazed out the window at the moon.

"Papa, I'm choking to death," Clay whispered. "I can barely breathe in those britches Mama makes me wear. The uniforms at Baldwin squeeze a body so I'm inclined to believe they're designed to compress a man's bodily fluids till he's fit for nothing save book reading and hymn singing."

"It can't be that bad."

"No? You ever swim in a river in December? That's about the best thing that happens."

"You ride regularly."

"Ride?" We sit atop some old mare older than we are. Back on the ranch I rode real horses."

"Your mother frets, especially in winter. You know that, Clay."

"Sure, I do, Papa. I remember baby Katherine. I helped dig little Andrew's grave. But I can't pass my whole life sitting in a rocking chair reading poems!"

"You don't have to sneak out of windows."

"I know. I should have asked. But Bart didn't come home with me to stare at the walls. We wanted to have some fun."

"And you don't have much, do you?"

"Not like when I was on the ranch with Joe and Chris. If we weren't pranking the hands, we were racing ponies or swiping eggs from the henhouse and tossing them at each other."

"You recall I dug cactus thorns out of your bottom when that pinto colt tossed you two summers back. And what about that bull Joe teased?"

"The one that just about butted him to Kansas?"

138

"Yes," Bowie said, laughing at the recollection. Clay leaned against his father's shoulder, and Bowie gripped the boy tightly. There was more substance there than before. The boy was getting taller, and now he was adding a trace of iron to his bones.

"Papa, I'm sorry I worried Mama, but sometimes I feel like I'm being strangled. I just have to spit out the bit and run free awhile."

"I know, son. I think just now you'd best head along to bed. As for the rest, I'll speak to your mama."

Bowie passed along Clay's words, but Emiline had little use for them.

"He's not like other boys," she argued. "He's so fragile. And Bowie, if something were to happen to him, I'd just die!"

"Nothing's about to happen. Meanwhile, you're always talking about how you wish Clay had a brother. Well, think of Bart Davis as that brother. Bart's got no family in town, and I imagine he'd welcome a bit of mothering."

"I'll try," she promised. "I know I shouldn't be so hard on Clay, either. After all, he has all that wildness from our time on the ranch. He'll outgrow that in time."

Bowie nodded, but inside, he hoped not.

At any rate, there was little opportunity to worry much more about it. After spending a peaceful Sunday attending worship and afterward riding out to Cherry Hill, Bowie returned the boys to the Baldwin Academy and took to his bed early. Monday he was to help Angus Burke draw up the payroll, and afterward, they'd begin hiring the work crew.

Chapter 3

March's arrival meant the start of what Henry Thorpe was fond of calling "our grand enterprise." For Bowie, that meant hiring men to build the railroad. The F W & W had set up posters across most of north central Texas, and an ocean of men poured into the rail yards in search of employment.

"Lord, help us," Angus Burke cried, running his fingers through his bushy moustache. "What have we done?"

Bowie only laughed. He gazed among the crowd of desperate men. There were barefoot Mexican cotton pickers, former slaves who'd worked patches of played-out plantation land until their hearts broke, Cherokees and Choctaws down from the Nations, and even gangs of derelict cowboys, left jobless when railcars replaced drovers.

"I've seen worse," Bowie said as he shook his head. "They appear honest enough to me. What's more, they're hungry. A man with an appetite will do most anything for a plate of beef and beans."

"Maybe," Burke agreed. "He'll steal and lie as well."

"There's a few of them in any crowd. The work will thin out the slackers. We'll make do with what's left."

Burke nodded, then climbed atop an equipment crate and motioned for silence.

"Men, gather 'round," Burke called out. "Listen up!"

The crowd surged closer and grew quiet.

"This where we hire on?" a dusty cowboy asked.

"That depends," Burke answered. "Are you ready for work harder and meaner than anything you imagined waiting for you in hell?"

The ones in front grinned. "Yes, sir!" they cried.

"Then let me state my terms," Burke continued. "It's five dollars a week, less expenses."

"What expenses?" a tall black man asked.

"We plan to feed and clothe you, lads. We'll put canvas over your heads. A man works my line, he needs food to keep him going. For two bits a day we feed you, and for another two bits you rent a cot and a tent."

"Doesn't leave much," the cowboy grumbled. "You pay us five, then take back more'n half."

"It's a fair wage for a fair day's labor," Burke declared. "We rest on Sunday, for that's the Lord's day."

"Some of us have families," a broad-backed man with the look of a farmer called out. "How can we feed our wives and kids?"

"There'll be work for some of them," Burke explained. "Boys as young as eight and no older than fourteen can sign on as slop boys or fire-tenders. We'll need shakers, lads to hold the spikes for the sledgehammers. Woodcutters, dispatch riders ... all manner of jobs are to be had. As for the women, many's the Mary who's worked her way west as a laundress or cook."

"And the pay?" another cowboy asked.

"Depends on the task, and on how well it's done. Less than what the crew earns, but where else would you find work at all? Those that do well can expect more. But most with the will can earn their living. It beats chasing buffalo ghosts or starving, now doesn't it, friends?"

The men grumbled, and Bowie stepped up on the crate beside Burke.

"I'll up the ante," Bowie called out. "Any man or boy who signs on now and is still with us at the end of the track will receive a bonus, fifty acres of his own and a horse."

"We was promised land and a mule once before," the tall black asked. "Never saw a hair of it."

"You weren't promised by *me*," Bowie said, staring hard at the questioner. "As Mr. Burke here said, you'll get a fair wage for a fair day's effort. Any slacker can expect to be paid off and sent packing. In time we'll see who has iron in his spine. Those men will be gang bosses and foremen, with a wage to match."

"Does a black man have a chance at that?"

The crowd stirred nervously, and Burke frowned. Bowie smiled, though, and shook his head.

"Friend, I wouldn't care if a man was purple if he could hammer spikes and lay rail. I aim to get this railroad to El Paso, and the men who help me get there will share in the glory and the profits."

"We know how to work, Cap'n Justiss," someone cried out. "You point the way, give us a hammer and some room, and watch us go."

"El Paso, you say?" another asked. "Why, we'll lay track to China if you pay us."

Burke then set up tables, and eager men surged forward. Bowie left three clerks to sign on the crew. He himself walked among the men, greeting some of the cowboys by name, convincing others of his sincerity.

"First thing you do," Bowie told Boyd Fitch, "is pass out cakes of lye soap. Some of these men smell as if they haven't bathed since summer. I'll not invite sickness to my camps."

"Yes, sir," Fitch responded with a grin. "Best rename the Trinity. It's far too holy a name for what this river's apt to be when these scarecrows finish with it."

A sea of the unwashed. That's what Emiline called the two hundred vagabonds who lay in blankets that night beside the route of the Fort Worth and Western. The smell rivaled that of the cattle pens. Even after the men washed, their clothes and blankets retained the appalling odor.

"If they scrub their clothes, the cloth would likely shred into nothing," Fitch explained. "Some have little more than rags to wear as it is. I hired on two boys to run messages. One scarce had enough cloth left to his britches for decency's sake."

"It's like the war all over again," Bowie mumbled. "Ragged beggars crowding the river banks. Children left adrift, homeless and helpless."

"Do you suppose we could extend credit, sell 'em shirts, dungarees and a pair of shoes? If we bought in bulk, we could do it for a little more than two dollars."

"And if you bought shoes that would last?"

"Three, three and a half."

"Do it. Give them what time they need to pay, too."

"Yes, sir," Fitch said, smiling. "Truth is, I have the wire ready and waiting."

"What if I'd said no?"

"Well, sir, I'd most likely sent the boys to you this afternoon so you could see the need with your own eyes. I've seen you, Captain. You've got a weak spot where youngsters are concerned."

"I've buried children," Bowie said somberly. "It's a dark shadow that's fallen across humanity, this setting the little ones to fend for themselves. I pray that God will look after them, provide for their needs."

"I believe he already has," Fitch said, grinning.

Bowie and Angus Burke devoted that first week to organizing work gangs and freighting rails and spikes down the right-of-way. Burke's surveyors marked the route with long poles marked with yellow bands. Even the most illiterate of the workmen could understand that. As the work actually began, Bowie couldn't help feeling proud of the crew. Fresh air and clean clothes worked a miracle of sorts. Men shaved or trimmed their beards, and boys whose smiles had died years before tasted laughter again. Full bellies accelerated the work.

It was amazing. The Fort Worth and Western moved like an army of busy ants. Men filled the gullies and blasted through hillsides of solid rock.

Others broke up boulders and laid a solid bed. The real work was done by the rail gangs, though. Stout men anchored ties in the ground. A half dozen others groaned under the weight of each rail as they set it in place. Once the rail was securely in place, boys held spikes while men swung heavy sledges and drove the spikes into the earth.

Bowie was surprised how rapidly each man learned his task. Even the little shakers, as the spike holders were called, grew accustomed to their jobs.

Shaker is right, Bowie thought, for the clang of hammers striking steel rang out for miles. Fingers would tremble. The best of the shakers kept their eyes closed, for flinching even slightly could send the sledge slamming down on a toe or glancing off fingers. It was a risky business at best and always reserved for iron-nerved youngsters. The trust between those boys and the men who swung the hammers was enormous. And when a hammer missed its mark, the boy wasn't the only voice crying out in pain and horror.

It happened regularly. At best a finger might be crushed. More often a grim-faced child stood biting his lip as the stumps of lost fingers were bound.

"See the foreman," someone would call. "He's got tonic. Rest a day, then join the water crew."

Three out of four boys toting water buckets along the track bore the scars of bruised limbs. Most lost two or three fingers from a hand. A few lost whole arms, and one unfortunate lost a foot.

"There's no other way to do it," Burke grumbled one morning when he and Bowie carried an unconscious lad of twelve to the cook camp. "We can't afford to risk a man on the task. Maimed, he'd be no use to us."

"And what use will these boys be when they come of age?" Bowie asked.

"I know it's hard," Burke admitted, "but if they had a choice, they wouldn't be here with us. Most would starve. Death has no future at all. Some of these boys ran in gangs through the cities, stealing what they could till they got caught. Thieves lose more than fingers, Bowie. Those that aren't shot in the act find themselves locked away in some hell hole. How long do you think this one would survive in a jail? Months maybe."

The truth of those words did nothing to cheer Bowie Justiss. He couldn't help thinking about Clay and his classmates at the Baldwin Academy. Fate certainly had a strange way of choosing those it would nurture and those who would suffer. When Bowie returned to Fort Worth to supervise the loading of supply wagons, he visited his son.

"Is something wrong, Papa?" Clay asked when an older boy summoned him from the library.

"No, son," Bowie said, holding the boy's shoulders with trembling hands. "I just wanted to see you."

"Papa?"

Bowie sat with his son and spoke of the rail camps, of the terrified youngsters with closed eyes, waiting anxiously for each stroke of the sledge. Clay shuddered, but Bowie read no fear in the boy's eyes.

"Papa, Bart got a letter. He has to leave school. There's no more money. His uncle lost it in a card game. I told Bart maybe you could find him a job on the railroad. He's good with figures, and he

147

learns quickly. You wouldn't let him be a shaker, would you?"

"No, son," Bowie assured the boy. "Tell you what. I'll write Bart's uncle. Maybe we can find some money."

"I thought to ask you about that. Bart won't take it unless you let him sign a note, though."

"Maybe I should hire him on," Bowie said, grinning. "He sounds as if he has the makings of a man to be trusted."

Clay rested his head on Bowie's shoulder and matched his father's smile. Bowie touched the boy lightly on the forehead. Moments of closeness had been few and far between of late, and Bowie was grateful for each one.

Bowie wrote Marvis Davis that next week. The return letter spelled out the desperate state of the uncle's situation. The farm was lost, creditors were closing in, and Davis saw his sole chance in escaping to New Mexico.

"Luk aftr tha boy if yu can," the letter concluded. "I dun lital by hem, as he es a fin ladd. God bles yu, sir."

"If you're agreeable," Bowie told Emiline, "I'd like to adopt young Bart."

"Bowie, how can you consider such a thing? He's got no family. I saw that letter. His uncle's had no schooling to speak of. The boy himself is a bad influence on Clay."

"You'll bring him around, dear. Clay needs a brother, and our new house can clearly do with an extra scamp running about."

"You're as bad as Charlie, rounding up strays, inviting them into your home. Are you forgetting

Victoria married that Pruett boy."

"Clay's not likely to wed Bart Davis. Besides, Bret's turned out just fine. If you're opposed to adoption, then I'll have Ross draw up guardian papers. You can't find fault in that."

"No, I suppose not. It's your heart that's taken over, Bowie, and if it's too generous, well, Papa had a soft spot for widows and orphans himself."

"Good," Bowie exclaimed. "I'll tend to it."

It was a simple matter to draw up the papers and submit them to a judge. Texas was awash with orphans, and judges were only too glad to rid themselves of any they could.

"Truth is, take on any others you choose, Mr. Justiss," the judge told Bowie. "I see too many of them in here, sullen-eyed boys and girls who would cut out your heart for half a dollar. I farm out those I can to ranches hereabouts, but most run off, usually on a stolen horse. They'll hang, most of them."

Bowie nodded, then escaped before the judge could continue extolling the evils of misspent youth.

Bart was quiet during the whole business. He never said more than a word or two to anyone save Clay, and then the words told nothing.

"He feels deserted," Clay told Bowie one Saturday night when the boys were staying at Mrs. Taylor's. "His uncle never wrote much, but at least they were together in the summertime."

Bowie nodded and glanced through the open door. Bart never rested peacefully, and often the boy's arms would flail about as if in a desperate fight. Clay often seemed so much older, a man hiding in a dwarfish body.

That night was different, though. Clay stood in

149

bare feet, his chest swallowed by an oversized nightshirt. He was, after all, still a boy.

"I was thinking, Papa," Clay whispered. "You'll be busy most of the summer with the railroad, and Mama's got her new house to worry with."

"And?"

"I got a letter from Joe and Chris. Luis Morales has asked them to work some of those Arabians of his. It seems there's room for another hand."

"And you want to go?"

"Bart and me both."

"Summer's a long way off."

"I know, Papa. No point to riling Mama just yet. But you'll consider it? I'll be fourteen. Billy and Ryan were riding the trail to Kansas at that age."

"Because they had to."

"Papa, I'll choke to death if I spend the whole summer in that house."

"There won't be too many summers you can share with your mama, Clay. She'll take it hard, especially you staying . . ."

"With a Mexican? Papa, Luis's family was living in Texas long before we were. I never knew a man who could teach me half as much about horses. It will be like a great adventure for us."

"Well, I don't suppose it would hurt you to be around your cousins, though Lord knows we'll all catch fire for it."

"You will consider it then?"

"Son, I always take your wishes into account, even if it doesn't appear so."

"I know," Clay said, resting a hand on his father's back. "I never really thanked you for taking on Bart."

"No need. I'm glad you brought the matter to

150

my attention."

"Maybe before we go to Luis's ranch, we could spend some time with you in the rail camps."

"You wouldn't like that much," Bowie said grimly. "And your mama hasn't agreed to let you spend the summer with Luis."

"She will if you insist."

"We'll see."

"Thanks, Papa," Clay said, smiling as he warmly gripped his father's hands. Then the boy returned to his bed, and Bowie set off for his own room.

The visits to Ft. Worth were a welcome distraction from the trials and and tribulations of the rail camps. Miles of track were laid as the rails snaked their way westward. As promised, Bowie and Angus Burke promoted the best of the men. Slackers were sent on their way. Often bad feelings resulted, especially when black men were given leave to organize their own work gangs.

"Running a rail gang's a job for a white man!" some declared. Bowie mostly ignored such talk. But when a pair of former slaves turned gang bosses were clubbed half to death, Bowie drew the company together.

"This is my outfit," Bowie spoke. "Each one of you is a part of it as long as he does his job and sees to the welfare of the railroad. When one man falls. I expect his fellows to help him up. If one man is threatened, I expect his fellows to come to his aid. What's happened here is that some cowards clubbed a pair of my workers. I know it was no one here because you men work for the F W & W, and you'd never harm a brother. If I was to discover myself to be wrong, someone would be short their job. At least."

"Cap'n, there's a rightness to things," a dirty-faced ex-cowboy named Wording argued. "You don't expect us to work for some Mexican, do you? Or worse?"

"Isn't anything worse," another grumbled.

"I expect you to work for me," Bowie said without so much as a trace of humor. "If you can't do that, collect your pay and grab the first work train back to Fort Worth. I've got no place for anyone save one who'll work. I won't tolerate discord. It's got no place here. There's too much to do."

There continued to be a few quarrels after Bowie's speech, but as long as the food remained good and hot, the tents didn't leak in a rain, and the blacks and Mexicans kept to themselves, peace reigned over the rail camps.

Bowie was glad. Once beyond the outskirts of Fort Worth, the terrain changed. No longer did the track cross the grand prairies. The route had entered the land of cross timbers. Low ridges and crumbling creekbeds provided new challenges. The coming of spring meant more hours of daylight, and so the work day stretched itself accordingly. Tired men found Sunday alone could not restore their strength, and the work suffered. Accidents became commonplace.

"I wish we could ease the pace," Bowie told Angus Burke, "but we can't. The line's got to be through before winter comes, and the weather changes."

"I know," Burke agreed. "I'll send word that we need some fresh men. I'll add one or two newcomers to each gang."

"That should help," Bowie said. "I'll see what else we can do to improve morale. A bit more beef in the stew should help. A dollar bonus next payroll."

"Make it two."

"Agreed."

As he walked through the camps, Bowie passed along the word of the bonus. Some greeted it with a cheer. Others merely nodded and continued with their labors. Bowie observed the despair on unshaven faces, the tattered sleeves of shirts and the frayed nerves of the men who wore them. At noon he took his dinner with the water boys, sharing a prayer for their health and listening to their tales of life before the railroad. He bit his lip as one after another explained the loss of fingers.

"God bless you, boys," Bowie called as he left.

"God bless you, Cap'n," the youngsters replied.

Bowie had walked less than twenty yards when he heard a terrifying scream. A burly six and a half foot giant of a sledge man named Whitaker tossed his hammer aside and bellowed toward the heavens. Bowie raced to the giant's side and broke through a huddle of men. A boy of twelve clutched a bleeding hand as he knelt beside the tracks.

"Li'l Jay, I'm sorry," Whitaker cried, weeping freely. "Boy, I . . ."

"I flinched," the boy confessed as he gazed up at the giant. "Was my doin', Bull."

Whitaker bent over to pick the boy up, but the shaker rolled away.

"You know they can't build this railroad without you, Bull," the boy said tearfully. "I'll get

Johnny to help me to the cook's camp."

A water boy hurried to the injured boy's side, but Bowie took the injured lad instead.

"I did it, Cap'n," Whitaker said somberly. "He was a good li'l one, he was."

"It happens," Bowie said, examining the boy's hand. Three fingers of his left hand were mashed and bloody. Bowie couldn't understand how the youngster could stand, much less speak.

"You're not the first, Jay," the water boy said, wrapping a clean cloth around his friend's bloody hand. "See?"

The water boy held up two hands. Each was missing a ring finger, and the left was minus the middle digit as well.

"Come on," Bowie said, helping his maimed charge along.

"He'll be all right, Cap'n," the water boy assured Bowie. "He's bleedin' all right. See Rachel tends to the hand."

Once out of sight of the others, the shaker dropped to his knees and shook violently. Bowie admired the boy all the more for holding back his agony, but now was no moment for pretense. Bowie picked the trembling boy up in his arms and hurried toward the cook camp.

"Oh, here's another," a broad-girthed woman cried as Bowie approached.

"Where do I find Rachel?" Bowie asked.

"I can tend him," the woman argued. "Just trim the fingers and bind the wound. Nothing to it."

"Rachel," the boy whimpered.

"Down by the water barrels," the cook grumbled. "Tent with the buffalo hides stretching alongside."

Bowie hurried along. His interest in the mysterious Rachel soared. When he arrived at the tent, he discovered an ancient Choctaw woman curing a buffalo hide.

"Inside," the Indian said without looking up.

Rachel Harmer's tent resembled a small hospital. Three cots stood at one end. Each housed an injured boy. A long table occupied the center of the oversized tent. A cabinet filled with medicine bottles and ointments stood beside the door.

"You're Rachel?" Bowie asked as he spotted a slim-figured woman barely twenty years old, dressed in a simple white frock covered with an apron. She ignored him and instead examined the little bundle in Bowie's arms.

"Oh, no," Rachel said as she helped Bowie ease the boy onto the table. "Jay? Jay, can you hear me?"

"Uh," the boy mumbled.

"These railroad men ought to be shot, the lot of them," Rachel declared as she cut away the bindings and examined the wound. "This boy only joined us last week. Do you know his father sold him to a freighter? Well, needless to say I put an end to that. I was planning to send him to my sister in Waco, but he befriended this mountain of a sledge swinger."

"Bull Whitaker."

"Poor Jay. He so wanted to please someone."

"Can you save the fingers?"

"Do you care?" Rachel asked, looking Bowie's way for the first time. "Half the lads in this camp have a stump or two. Before they started coming to me, some cook just lopped them off with a cleaver."

"I care," Bowie told her.

"Then hold him still while I see what can be

done. Sometimes I can save a stub. The tips are always lost. I'm no surgeon, and I can't repair smashed tendons."

"Do you best. I'll see you're rewarded."

"Keep your money," she said angrily. "It's not for money I do this."

"I know that," Bowie said, watching her tenderly stroke young Jay's forehead before easing a chloroform-soaked rag to his nose. The boy gagged, then passed into a light sleep. Rachel then went to work, cleaning the wounds and heating a blade. With the calm, steady hands of a battlefield surgeon she removed the two last fingers of the boy's left hand. She splinted the middle finger and painted the stubs with iodine.

"He'll sleep awhile," she announced after binding the wounded hand.

"You have a surgeon's touch," Bowie told her. "You've had practice before coming here."

"My father was killed when Federal gunboats attacked Galveston."

"You couldn't have been more than a child."

"I was eight. I moved in with a doctor. I helped in his surgery, and he saw I had food and clothing. I married his son."

"Oh?"

"He wasn't much of a man," she said in disgust. "Gambled away what money we had, then got himself shot last month in Fort Worth. I had to find work."

"It looks to me like it found you. You're not on the payroll, though."

"The Indians hunt on Sundays. They bring meat. They believe I'm some sort of crazed spirit or something, I suppose. The little ones bring me a few dollars when they can. I buy cloth, and we make bandages. Medicines are harder to come by. The boys all pitch in, though. They like to think I'm their sister, I suppose."

"Aren't you?"

"Sister, mother, doctor, priest . . . you name it."

"I'll speak with Burke. From now on, you'll have anything you need."

"Anything I need?" Rachel asked, planting a hand on each hip. "I'm not the one in need here?"

"Then anything they need," Bowie corrected himself. "Of course, you're already giving them what they need most of all—a soft touch and a generous heart."

Bowie reached out his hand, but she stepped away. He swallowed hard and glanced back at young Jay.

"You said his name is Jay?" Bowie asked.

"Jay Belton. Does it make a difference that you know one of their names?"

"Don't paint me any darker than I am, Miss . . ."

"Harmer, Rachel Harmer."

"Miss Harmer, I admire what you're doing, and I want to help."

"To ease your conscience?"

"Nothing will do that. You grieve for these boys? I grieve for the circumstances that sent them out here at such a tender age. I'm past trying to alter life. I watched boys not much older race to their deaths across a dozen battlefields. Life is hard most of the time, and I seldom understand very much of it. The best I hope for anymore is to ease pain where they find it. That's why you'll have medicine or blankets or whatever you need. And it's why you'll accept them from a man you blame for bringing most of that pain

157

about."

"I will draw up a list. For them, you understand."

"Of course," Bowie said, bending over Jay Belton and straigthening his shirt. "Rest easy, son. You're in good hands."

Bowie then slipped quietly outside and left Rachel Harmer to her young charges. What was it Boyd Fitch had said about God providing? Indeed, it seemed He was.

Chapter 4

Spring began to break out across Texas. By the middle of March wildflowers blanketed the hills, and a bright sun greeted the rail gangs most mornings. Rain often fell as well, giving the men a brief break from their labors. It never lasted long, though, and the foremen would soon have their crews back on the job.

After surging westward at a steady pace, the FW & W line slowed as it reached its first major obstacle, the Clear Fork of the Trinity. Angus Burke had devoted two crews to assembling trestle for better than ten days, but the boggy riverbed swallowed beam after beam. The original crossing was moved a half dozen times before the ideal spot was finally located. Even then a bed of rocks was built around the pier beams so that floods wouldn't wash the bridge away come April.

While the bridge crews continued their labors, Bowie held up the others three days so that supplies could be brought out from Fort Worth. A

159

depot, christened Agony Springs by its builders, was constructed on the west bank of the river. A landing, water tower, two warehouses and a stable were added shortly.

As Bowie examined the work on the bridge, he couldn't help recalling the railroad bridges of Virginia and Tennessee. Near Harper's Ferry the Southern army had seemingly burned a bridge a day. What a wondrous fire trestles made! As the rails heated in the fiery embers of the bridges, they twisted into contorted iron monsters. Those rails had always symbolized the war to Bowie Justiss. Life itself seemed misshapen, wrecked beyond all recognition.

"You seem lost in thought," Burke commented as he waved two men carrying cross beams along.

"Was remembering the war," Bowie confessed. "It surely was easier burning one of these bridges than putting one together."

"Yes," Burke agreed. "I never had the heart to watch my boys destroy a railroad. I watched too many men die building them before the war. Some of these men just work for the money, but a lot more keep going because they can envision this line being here long after they're gone. It's not so great a loss to give up a finger or even a hand when you know your grandchildren will stand tall one day and recall you helped build the first line across Texas, east to west."

"You worked on railroads before. Has it always been such a difficult undertaking?"

"Oh, it's been easy this time around. When we were crossing Kansas, the cavalry was out ahead of us, clearing farms seized for the right of way.

Sometimes a man would make a stand, and the soldiers would ride him down. One time we came upon a charred farmhouse. A whole family had been inside when the troopers set it ablaze. Nary a soul escaped. There were two girls, the oldest but seven. We buried them."

"These boys ... the shakers ..."

"I know," Burke said, gazing down at the river. Both banks were swarming with weary men and exhausted boys busily scrubbing off days of dirt and sweat from their bodies and their clothes. The sight took Bowie back to the war again, to the Rapidan and Rappahannock. When brief truces broke out soldiers, Yank and Reb, would wash their clothes and bathe. Bare, it was impossible to tell the one army from the other. Days later the same soldiers were killing each other in the Wilderness.

"Did Rachel Harmer get everything she asked for?" Bowie asked, turning away.

"Anything we had on hand," Burke replied. "The medicines haven't come yet. You may have to go back to Fort Worth and hurry them along."

"Oh?"

"I'd guess Henry Thorpe will consider it a needless expense."

"Thorpe? He's not out here watching these children lose fingers. He hasn't had to listen to their feverish cries, their calls for mothers who are dead or else hundreds of miles away. He doesn't see the graves dug or carry the corpses."

"No, he learned a long time back to stay clear of the work camps."

"If the need arises, I *will* go to Fort Worth,"

Bowie promised. "Iodine and chloroform aren't half so expensive as the champagne Thorpe shares with his friends in the congress."

The following day Bowie had the rail crews across the river. Though the bridge wasn't yet completed, there was little sense in waiting on it. The route ahead was marked, and there were creeks aplenty to bridge, ravines to fill and beds to build. Another ten miles might be finished while Angus Burke bridged the Clear Fork.

Up to that point the few problems encountered had been caused by nature or temperament. That soon changed. For the first time, the weekly payroll train failed to appear on schedule. In its place came a swarm of wagons filled with shoes and clothing, hats and vanities. Wooden signs denoted which.

"Best of all, you need no money to buy!" the canvas peddlers proclaimed. "Just sign the account book and draw on your wages. This is a company store."

It seemed too good to be true, and it was. Only after selecting their purchases did many of the men discover the prices. Others failed to understand the goods must be paid for.

Already workers with families were in a bad way. Women and children traveled in oxcarts or dragged along hovels. Those women who hadn't signed on as cooks or laundresses often took on another trade. Children began to lose their color. Teeth fell out of bleeding gums, and pitiful cries haunted the midnight air.

Bowie walked among the hovels one night, passing from one nightmare scene to another. Here was another Petersburg, and yet the warehouses at Agony Springs were full of goods, and a man with a rifle could still hunt deer or rabbits a mile from camp.

"They're starving, you know," a soft voice whispered to him.

"Miss Harmer!" Bowie cried out in surprise. "And here I thought I was the only fool about this late."

"I got the blankets Mr. Burke offered. I know you were behind it, and I'm sorry I wasn't more appreciative of your offer. It's just that I've seen so much misery in these camps."

"I see it, too," Bowie told her. "The day may come when such things are in the past, but I doubt it. Men seem more than capable of creating misery for themselves."

"And for others," she added.

"Tell me, Miss Harmer . . ."

"Please, call me Rachel. Everyone does."

"All right, Rachel," Bowie said, grinning. "If you could do three things to improve this place, what would they be?"

"First, I'd have to have some money."

"Forget about the money for a minute. If you owned a gold mine, and you wanted to spend some of the profits here, what would you do?"

"Oh, let's see," she said, rubbing her chin and smiling as she envisioned the changes. "First, I'd bring in fruit and vegetables. I'd see the little ones had milk to drink and greens to make their eyes shine. There's scurvy in this camp, Captain

163

Justiss. Lemons and oranges would do us a world of good, and your trains could bring them."

"What else?" Bowie asked as he took out a notebook and scribbled a note. It wasn't easy with only the moonlight to light the page, and he wondered if he'd be able to read it that next day.

"What are you writing?" Rachel asked.

"Probably nothing. Hopefully a reminder to contract some fruit and vegetable shipments."

"You really mean that, don't you?"

"I suppose it's hard to believe a railroad man doesn't devour babies or whip old men."

"Not with some. If you're serious about food, have the cooks be more generous with the boys. Growing children need more than those men of yours. I know some boys who can barely keep their trousers up."

"We'll tend to that tomorrow, and I'll see some cows are brought over for the young ones. You think some of those three-fingered lads can still milk cows?"

"Watch them try."

"What else?"

"It may sound foolish."

"Tell me."

"These people kill themselves for a few dollars because they want to be a part of something more than themselves. They're building a railroad, and they hope that will mean towns and churches . . . and schools. We don't need a town. We carry our own along with us. As for a church, God never needed a roof to feel welcome, and in difficult times turn people to prayer."

"But a school?"

"Yes," she said, smiling. "Most of these men will break their backs if they know there's hope for their children. Even a big ox like Bull Whitaker can write his name. Most of the boys in this camp don't even know their last names. Send me some books. There are plenty of men and women in camp who would eagerly teach anyone wanting to learn."

"I'll wire my niece. She's a teacher, and she'll know what we're going to need."

"Bless you, Captain."

"I've done very little," Bowie told her. "Call it a salve for a tormented soul."

"No, it's a gift freely given. You should come down and visit young Jay Belton. His hand's healing nicely, and it'd do all the boys a world of good to know you care."

"I do, you know."

"Yes, I do know," she told him, clasping his hand. "Bless you for it."

When the payroll train arrived the next morning, Bowie turned over the paymaster to Angus Burke and rode the train back to Fort Worth. He stepped off the platform as Henry Thorpe's private car pulled into the station. In an instant Bowie headed that way.

"Well, Justiss," Thorpe called as he stepped down to the platform followed by Barbara Barr. "You remember Miss Barr?"

"Yes. How are you, Miss Barr?" Bowie asked, clearly impatient.

"Quite well, Captain Justiss," the young woman said. "I'll leave you two to your business. I've got friends waiting."

"Good day," Bowie told her.

"You will join me for dinner tonight, Barbara?" Thorpe asked.

"At eight. Don't start without me."

"Never."

Once Miss Barr left, Bowie conducted Thorpe back to the private car. They stood together as the New Yorker poured glasses of bourbon. Bowie took his and sipped it. Then he spoke.

"I understand you cancelled my order for medicines," Bowie said angrily. "Why?"

"They were never budgeted, and I judged it an unnecessary expenditure."

"Oh? How many bottles of champagne are in the budget? I noticed three tailor bills in the accounts. Were they in the budget?"

"Entertainment expenses, Justiss. The people I host buy revenue bonds or purchase land."

"And that's more important than life, is it?"

"I knew when I met you we'd be having this talk," Thorpe said, grinning as he motioned Bowie toward a chair. "You have too big a heart, my friend. The first line I built we had a tunnel collapse. Seventy men died. My engineer shot himself. What good did that do? The men were still dead. Men will die building this line as well. Thousands and thousands fell in the war. There's a price to pay for progress. You have to keep the larger vision in mind."

"Oh?"

"We'll soon link the Atlantic and Pacific by way

166

of Texas. That will mean farmers can get their products to market. It may well save the Texas cattle industry. New people will come to help the state grow. I dream on a grand scale, Justiss, but it costs money to fulfill that dream. If the line spends idly, we'll falter and collapse."

"Some cloth for bandages, a little iodine and a few bottles of chloroform won't break us, Thorpe. The men and boys who need it are dying so this railroad keeps to its schedule. You go on having your parties, but hear me now! When I send a wire ordering anything, *anything*, you see it's sent. You may know how to influence governors and romance banker's daughters, but if you know what's good for you, you'll keep my horns out of your gut. I'm a fighter from way back, and I don't mind a tangle. Truth is, I rather enjoy one."

"You'd lose this one."

"Would I? How many of these rich investors have wives and children? Which one among them would stand still for leaving a fingerless child to suffer in agony when a few dollars would buy the medicine to ease his suffering? Consider that! What's more, I'm sending schoolbooks out there. Our people will learn to read and write."

"You're crazed!"

"Maybe. It will be done, though."

"You'll bankrupt this railroad. What's more, you'll breed discontent in the work camps. They'll want more money."

"They want hope, Thorpe. I'll give it to them, and they'll lay twice the track you imagine possible."

"We'll see."

167

"Yes, we will. Watch it happen."

While in Fort Worth, Bowie saw to it crates of fruit were ordered from South Texas. Vegetables from farms were crated and shipped immediately. Vicki replied to Bowie's wire about the books, and he ordered fifty of each title she suggested from New York that very afternoon. They would arrive in three weeks.

With his immediate goals accomplished, he set off for Cherry Hill. The house was nearly complete, and he found Emiline leading a covey of ladies through the downstairs rooms.

"Bowie, what a surprise!" she exclaimed. "Is everything all right with the railroad?"

"Certainly," he said. "I've just been arranging for a school to be set up for the children."

"What a wonderful notion," one of the ladies remarked. "The poor unfortunates. I had the unpleasant experience of passing their camp last month. The stench was simply awful. Do you know they bathe in the Trinity?"

"Oh, my," the others chortled.

Bowie smiled. He was half tempted to explain his own son not so long ago took a dip in a neighboring pond. Emiline read his mind and scowled.

"Have you met the angel, Captain Justiss?" Mrs. Paulson, the wife of a local lumber mill owner, asked.

"What angel?" Emiline asked.

"That's what she's called, isn't it?" Mrs. Paulson asked. Two of her companions nodded, and she went on to explain. "It seems there's a young woman who tends the sick and looks after the

168

orphans that work for the railroad. Her name is Rebecca, I believe. The children call her the angel because she cures their fevers."

"I know another word for a single woman tending boys in such a place," Emiline declared. "We've all heard those tales of how certain nurses took advantage of our soldiers during the late unpleasantness."

"Indeed," Mrs. Paulson said, growling. "It's nothing of the sort. She's lovely, they say, the daughter of a doctor. I've heard a single word quiets the fearful, and her touch can heal."

"Do you know who they're talking about?" Emiline asked.

"Her name is Rachel Harmer," Bowie explained.

"That's right!" Mrs. Paulson agreed.

"She looks after the shakers and water boys, tends their wounds and sees they have shelter. I understand she's arranged to have a Methodist circuit rider in the camps each Sunday. A priest now journeys out from Fort Worth to conduct mass. What's more, she's just talked me into sending books out there for a school."

"You?" Emiline asked, laughing.

"Maybe she is an angel," Bowie said, sharing the laughter. "I don't know. To watch her with those poor unfortunate children is more than a man can stand. It breaks my heart. I do believe I'd build her a hospital if she'd asked."

"Oh?" Emiline asked.

"She has a way of prompting a man to listen to his conscience. It's most alarming. I knew a preacher could do it, but not even he ever got me to send books to a work camp."

"I understand she saw to the building of three orphanages between Austin and Waco," Mrs. Paulson said. "So perhaps you shouldn't feel so misused."

"Something tells me she's far from finished, though," Emiline said, giving Bowie a disapproving shake of her head. He couldn't help feeling she was probably right.

Chapter 5

Bowie returned to the work camps later in the week. He was accompanied by a boxcar full of vegetables. Two dozen cows had already been bought from a willing Parker County rancher. The fruit and the books would soon follow.

When the cooks served up greens with dinner, the men cheered loudly.

"It's difficult to believe string beans could look so good," Angus Burke commented. "I'm not all that partial to greens, but it does seem a long time since I've tasted anything but pork, beef or venison, mixed in with a bit of potato, some onion, and a few beans."

"It was like this on the trail to Kansas," Bowie recounted. "You never saw men attack vegetables in like manner. I should have thought to include them for the men. And for the boys especially. Mama always chided us about eating our greens."

"Mine, too," Burke added, laughing.

After dinner, Bowie inspected the work on the Clear Fork bridge. The trestle was finished, and men were busy pounding spikes to secure the rails. On the western side of the river track stretched on another seven miles.

"You made fair progress while I was gone," Bowie told Burke. "Built a good bridge, too, by the look of it."

"It'll hold. So, it's on to the Brazos now, isn't it?"

"One task left," Bowie said, taking a spike from a nearby crate and walking to the trestle. With the point of the spike he etched his initials.

"Mind if I do likewise?" Burke asked.

"See they all do," Bowie said, waving toward the men still hammering away on the rails. "Even the young ones. Especially the shakers. Water boys, too."

"There may not be much trestle left if you set those lads to work with knives."

"Well, you oversee things, Angus. I want them to know they've been a part of something lasting, though, that each one has contributed."

"It's a fair idea."

"Little enough reward for losing fingers and half killing yourself slaving away in the noontime sun."

When the final spike was hammered into place, Angus Burke formed the men into two lines and explained what was to happen.

"Hurrah!" the men shouted. Moments later towering Bull Whitaker appeared. Little Jay Belton clung to the giant's back.

Bowie watched with interest as Bull showed the

boy how to scratch a J and a B into the wood. The letters were a bit shaky, and Bowie wondered whether Jay might not still be in pain.

"It wasn't that at all," the boy explained when Bowie asked a half hour later. "It's just, well, I don't know my letters, Cap'n. Bull's been trying to show me, but I'm none too fast at learning things."

"You've got time," Bowie assured the youngster.

The rest of the day was devoted to signing the trestle. Afterward a celebration of sorts was held at the river. A few firecrackers were shot off, and the boys joined in a mud fight. Once the noise died down, Rachel appeared. Instantly she ordered her charges into the river, and the biggest bath in West Texas history followed.

"What is it about that woman that gives her such a hold over men?" Burke asked as the river filled with bathers.

"I don't know," Bowie confessed. "I used to think maybe it was the spark in her eyes. I guess mainly it's because she doesn't press her point."

"Could be. It's a wonder, though. If we'd had her on our side at Gettysburg, things would've been different."

"Had she been born earlier, she might've freed the slaves single-handed and put off the war. And had us all believing it was our idea."

The two men laughed heartily. But though it was said in jest, Bowie half believed it might have been true. Rachel Harmer had a truly magical touch. He was glad she had come along.

The trestle-signing at the Clear Fork marked the conclusion of the easy days for the Fort Worth and Western. The terrain quickly lost its even grade. Steep mesas and rocky ravines lay athwart the route, and each one required filling or blasting. A dozen miles out of Weatherford, the county seat, Burke's blasting team made its first mistake. Dynamite was planted improperly, and the resulting explosion sent a shower of jagged rock fragments cascading down on the waiting road gang. In an instant ten men were buried by rocks. Others rushed to the scene and dug. Soon the victims were freed, but five men and a water boy were dead. The survivors were in a bad way as well.

"Sandstone!" Burke shouted. "I hate it. It hides the other rock so well. It shouldn't've happened."

"No, but it did," Bowie said sadly. "We'll be more careful next time."

Six graves were dug atop a nearby hill. Names were neatly inscribed on simple wooden crosses, and Rachel Harmer and Father Joseph, the priest, led prayers. By late afternoon the men were back at their work.

A second accident followed. A mile west of the blast site Burke had two crews filling a series of ravines. It wasn't hard, for there were abundant rocks on a nearby ridge. Young Jay Belton was carrying a water bucket to one of the crews when the hillside suddenly broke apart. Rocks, large and small, showered down.

"Slide!" someone screamed.

The others scrambled to safety, but Jay, laden by the heavy bucket, stumbled and fell. A boulder narrowly missed his slight body, but a smaller rock hit him squarely in the ribs. Others followed. In the space of two minutes the boy's arms were covered with bruises.

"No boy should have such bad luck," Bowie declared as he lifted Jay from the dust and started toward Rachel's tent. "What sins have you committed to deserve such retribution?"

"Such what?" Jay asked as he blinked away the dust from his eyes.

"Punishment."

"I don't know, Cap'n. I guess it must be for the time I peeked through the bushes at Mary Elizabeth Lowery. Rachel says we must curb out carnal appetites. Bull didn't know what it meant, but I've got a feeling it means not to stare at naked girls."

"Something like that," Bowie said, laughing.

Jay grinned in spite of the pain.

Rachel examined the boy, announced one rib was cracked and confined him to his cot for two days.

Spirits were high in the work camps as the rails crept westward. Miles were slowly but surely devoured in spite of heavy April rains. But the pauses brought on by thunderstorms gave the men a chance to rest, and accidents decreased accordingly.

The early arrival of the payroll brought enthusiastic cheers from the weary workers. But once the paymaster subtracted monies owed the company store, many a man found himself with little more than loose change to show for the week's work.

"How can this be?" they grumbled. "Can't you take part of it next week?"

The paymaster sadly shook his head.

"I can't get my family through the week on six bits," a hulking sledge driver named Perkins complained to Bowie. "I never dreamed I'd have my bill taken from wages. Back home I paid off my accounts a bit at a time."

"I don't have much to do with all that," Bowie explained. "But if a few dollars will help, I'll loan them to you myself. You pay me back as you can."

"That wouldn't be right, Cap'n," Perkins declared. "Besides, I got into this trouble borrowing in the first place. Pa lost his farm in Tennessee borrowing against the crop. We got hail, and we lost everything."

"What will you do?"

"See Colonel Burke about hiring my eldest. John's close to twelve now. My girl Emily can help the cooks, too."

"Here," Bowie said, shoving a five dollar bill into Perkins's sweaty hand. "My own boy's just thirteen. I wouldn't have him holding spikes."

"He can work with me, Cap'n. I'm careful. It'll be all right."

"And if the spike's wet, or you're a little tired. Could you live with it if something were to happen?"

"I was in the war, too, Cap'n. I killed men, so

176

you see, I've lived with worse."

"There is no such thing," Bowie said, refusing to accept the return of the money. "If you think the boy's got to work, I'll find him work as a messenger. Can he ride?"

"Like Forrest, he can."

"Good," Bowie said, grinning. "Send him to me after supper."

But after eating, Bowie had other business. He and Angus Burke sat around a campfire, fighting off the chill of a fierce north wind when a line of shadowy riders approached from the south. Their faces were hidden by woolen scarves, but they rode with a self-assurance lacking in vagabond cowboys who came to the rail camps in search of work.

Their leader was a fresh-faced youth of fifteen or so. The boy rode out in front of his companions and gestured toward the pay train.

"Got in a bit early, eh?" the stranger observed.

"Last time it was late," Burke answered. "Evens out in the long haul, I suppose."

"Well, sir, we'd surely appreciate it if you fellows would ask the paymaster to open up his accounts for us. We're a bit short just now, and we hear he's a generous man."

"Who are you?" Burke asked. Bowie didn't ask. Instead he stepped back from the fire and moved toward a chest housing three Winchester rifles.

"Hold there, mister," the young man commanded as he flung his duster aside. He carried a Sharps carbine across his knee. The barrel was aimed squarely at Bowie's chest.

"We'd as soon avoid trouble," another rider declared. "You just find that paymaster, and we'll settle with him."

"He's gone," Bowie explained. "He had some accounts to settle in Weatherford. We'll be buying beef and pork there."

"Rame?" a round-faced thief asked.

"He's lyin'," the leader declared. "I'll bet there's a cash box here somewhere. They always keep money in a railroad camp."

"You going to go through each one of those fellows' pockets?" Burke asked, motioning toward the gangs of workers collecting around a dozen fires. "You feel up to taking on an army, just the seven of you?"

The boyish leader glanced around him. The others appeared nervous, but the boy's dark eyes burned brightly.

"Won't be wise to start any shootin'," the outlaw told Bowie. "Men will clearly die. You'll be the first."

"Maybe," Bowie said, not yielding an inch. "But not the last."

"Here," Burke called, taking a roll of banknotes from his pocket and flinging them toward riders. "Take this and be off with you."

"That's a start," the leader said, pointing toward the bills fluttering in the evening breeze. "Now you, mister."

The outlaw's carbine swung in Bowie's direction, but about that time there was a clamor behind a nearby supply wagon, and the bandits turned that way. Instantly Bowie dove for the rifle chest. Burke raced toward the nearest work gang.

"Raiders!" the engineer cried out as Bowie flung open the chest and drew out a Winchester. "Get your guns!"

"Scatter!" the fiery-eyed young outlaw shouted to his comrades. He then reared his horse high into the air and rode toward the chest Bowie Justiss was using as cover. The carbine spouted flame. One shot exploded through the trunk. A second tore into Bowie's left forearm.

"Cap'n!" a small voice cried. Behind the supply wagon appeared little Jay Belton.

"Get down, boy!" Bowie yelled as he fired his rifle. The Winchester's shell slammed into the round-faced outlaw, and the would-be thief slumped in his saddle. Bowie then turned in time to see Jay disappeared in a shower of splinters as pistols and carbines tore the supply wagon apart.

"Let's get out of here, Rame!" a nervous outlaw called. "Joe's had it, and there's got to be a dozen men comin'!"

The boyish leader signalled retreat, then fired a final shot in Bowie's direction. Bowie, his arm throbbing already, returned the favor, but the shot went wide. Angus Burke and a half dozen armed men from the work gang opened up as well, dropping a second outlaw. The others escaped.

"Let's get after 'em!" Bull Whitaker called.

Burke shook his head and then rushed to Bowie's aid. Bowie was already binding the arm with a kerchief.

"See to the boy," Bowie mumbled, fighting back pain and anger as he stumbled toward the remains of the wagon. Little Jay Belton lay half buried by splintered potatoes and molasses.

"Lord, help us," Burke said, kneeling beside the boy.

"No!" Whitaker screamed, firing his rifle into the air.

Jay cracked open an eye, grinned faintly to Bowie, then feebly freed himself from the shower of fragmented supplies. For a moment Bowie relaxed, for it appeared the boy was unhurt. But when Jay tried to stand, his left leg gave way.

"Help him," Bowie urged.

The words were wasted. Bull Whitaker had already collected the lad and was rushing toward Rachel Harmer's encampment. Bowie stumbled along afterward, his arm growing as numb as his heart.

"I'll see a guard's mounted," Burke promised.

"Send word . . . to Weatherford," Bowie muttered. "Warn . . . the paymaster."

"I'll tend to everything," Burked pledged. "You get that arm tended. It's broken sure."

Bowie nodded. He'd set broken bones, and he read all the signs. The bleeding seemed to be slowing, but a shattered arm was a serious matter indeed. As he trudged along, he felt strong arms suddenly grip his shoulders. His vision began to blur, and his knees folded under him.

"We've got you, Cap'n," someone said, and three or four men suddenly lifted him and bore him along. "Don't you worry a bit."

Bowie tried to speak, but the words wouldn't come. His head pounded, and a shroud of darkness suddenly fell. For a short time he could feel the arms of the men as they carried him. Then there was nothing but a quiet whisper of an old hymn, a gradual creeping numbness that devoured his legs. his chest, his entire being.

Burke? Bowie tried to speak. The words wouldn't come, though. Instead he closed his eyes and drifted off on a cloud.

Chapter 6

Bowie remembered little of what followed. He awoke to find himself stretched out on a cot in Rachel Harmer's tent, his arm splinted and resting on a feather pillow. He'd scarcely cracked open an eye before an ancient woman with the lined, leathery face of a Caddo Indian made her way to his side.

"Hello," Bowie said, blinking away his confusion. "I was shot, wasn't I?"

"Outlaws," she said, pointing toward the tent's door. "They left. Two are dead."

"And the boy?" Bowie asked fearfully. "Jay."

"Hurt bad," she said, shaking her head. "But he's strong."

"Still alive then?"

The woman nodded, but when Bowie attempted to rise, she put her hand firmly on his chest and prevented it.

"I'm not dying," he complained. "The arm's broken clearly enough, but I'm far from crippled. There's work to . . ."

"To what?" Rachel asked, slipping inside. "Angus Burke is taking care of things. You've lost a lot of blood. The bullet didn't want to come easy, and I'm no surgeon. You'd better keep still."

Bowie tried to rise anyway, but his stomach turned, and he grew faint. He lay back and closed his eyes. A moment later the dizziness cleared, and he looked up into Rachel's scolding eyes.

"You don't understand," he explained. "I'm in charge."

"I do understand," she objected. "You've been wounded, and for now you need rest. Angus is tending to everything."

"The thieves?"

"Bull Whitaker and his friends ran down two of them. Two were killed trying to rob the camp. The others got away."

"The leader? Young one, maybe sixteen, with a brash tongue. He stood out from the rest."

"The one they called Rame?" Rachel asked. "Raymond Polk. He got away, but we've sent word to the Parker County sheriff. Polk's wanted in New Mexico and Texas."

"For what?"

"Murder mainly. The deputy that rode in to talk to Angus said Polk's gang killed three cowboys out near Albany. New Mexico authorities have posted rewards."

"I'm glad his aim was a mite off."

"Yes," Rachel agreed, shuffling her feet. "I did my best, but I wouldn't expect too much. Your fingers may be stiff, and the arm's likely to give you pain. Sorry, but we . . ."

"You did your best. In the war, they'd likely amputated below the elbow. A bad hand's better than none at all."

"I wish there'd been something else I could do."

"There wasn't. Now tell me. How's Jay?"

Her eyes had begun to brighten. The mention of little Jay swept a dark shadow across her brow,

183

and her eyes darkened.

"Not well. He was shot in the side, and again in the hip. I don't know how he hangs on. He bled half the night, and he's so pale I've thought him dead once or twice."

"He diverted their attention. Fool of a boy rattled some pans and gave me a chance to find a rifle."

"It's how these boys are," Rachel said, sighing. "All they know of life's the hard, bitter side. But when you put them to the test, they seem to measure up. If they're foolish, it's a kind of courageous ignorance."

"Gets 'em killed."

"Sometimes. Jay liked you. It just wasn't in him to let you down."

"Let me down? That wasn't how it was."

"To him, it was. You know, boys like Jay aren't afraid of dying. They've seen death a hundred times, in all its varieties. Their only fear is being alone, abandoned, starving and unloved. I suppose that's a kind of death, too."

"Sure. I wonder how we could have let this world descend upon them?"

"We didn't choose it. Life just happens."

"I don't believe that," Bowie said, closing his eyes and imagining poor little Jay Belton lying on a like cot, his body wracked by pain.

"Well, enough talk for now. Rest. I'll have some broth brought in. Sip it slowly. Your stomach isn't apt to be any too agreeable."

"I didn't get shot there."

"Your stomach doesn't know that. When you're better, I'll take you to Jay. He'd appreciate seeing you, no doubt."

The rest of that day and most of the next Bowie

drifted in and out of consciousness. His wound festered badly, and a fever raged. Rachel feared gangrene, and Burke sent to Weatherford for a surgeon. The doctor examined Bowie's arm, drained the wound and pronounced it coming along satisfactorily.

"You can't expect the body to respond favorably to having lead introduced into the bloodstream. Just some blood poisoning was all. If it continues to fester, drain it and dab the wound with iodine."

Rachel did as instructed, and Bowie grew stronger afterward. Each time he blinked his eyes open, she was there, offering him cool lemons to suck or a bowl of broth to sip. He wondered if she ever slept. She was everywhere, changing linens and inspecting injuries. Once he was better, the old Indian instructed four hulking men from the rail gangs to move Bowie's cot into the larger tent nearby.

"So, you're better," a feeble Jay Belton mumbled when the men set Bowie's cot down beside a smaller one occupied by the youngster.

"I thought you dead for sure," Bowie answered. "That was a fool thing you did."

"Close to got you killed," the boy said, lowering his eyes.

"More likely saved me," Bowie objected. "Mr. Burke as well. No telling how many others. We fought 'em off."

"But you were shot."

"I never did have much of a head for battles, Jay. My brother Charlie's the general in our family."

"You did all right," Rachel declared as she joined them. "They haven't returned."

185

"Glad to hear that," Bowie said, reaching over with his good right hand and touching little Jay's small shoulder. "What about you, Jay? Think we ought to wait a bit before tangling with this Polk fellow again?"

"Maybe a long time," Jay said solemnly. "I'm not getting much better."

"Nonsense," Rachel cried, sitting on the edge of the boy's cot and smoothing out his hair. "Two days ago you could hardly raise your head. You can't expect to get shot all to pieces, then hop right up and start swinging a sledge! I haven't spent all this time nursing you for nothing. You're going to be fine. Unless I hear any more feeling sorry for yourself, in which case you'd best be afraid of me!"

A spark seemed to appear in Jay's eye, and Bowie warmed. What was it those women in Fort Worth had called her—the angel of the railroad? It surely appeared so. Rachel Harmer had the magical touch, and she was working miracles on Jay Belton . . . and others.

After moving amongst the boys in Rachel's canvas hospital, Bowie improved rapidly. Maybe it was watching the youngsters' silent suffering that goaded Bowie back to his feet. Or perhaps it was Rachel's tireless attention and concern. Whatever, he finally rose to his feet the fifth day after the shooting.

"It's time we get along with the business of this railroad," he announced as he pulled on a pair of trousers. Rachel located one of the boys who always hovered around her tents. She sent the lad to fetch Angus Burke.

Burke appeared with a fresh shirt and a notebook, and Bowie wearily conducted his friend

186

outside the tent.

"I suppose you already sent word of what happened," Bowie whispered. "To Fort Worth."

"I went in myself on the payroll train. I thought we should hire some guards, and afterward, I spoke with your wife. She would have come, but I told her you were in good hands, and this camp really isn't much of a place for a lady."

"And my brother?"

"He knows. Your nephew, young Pruett, rode out with some help."

"Oh?"

"Yes. In fact, the young man he left with us is waiting to see you. Are you up to seeing him?"

"I'm as close to on my feet as I'm apt to get, Angus."

Burke walked a few feet past a campfire tended by the old Indian and waved his hands. Almost immediately a slightly-built young man wearing a canvas poncho draped over his shoulders sauntered up. Bowie would have been amused by the young man's swagger had not the pair of cold, gray eyes that stared out from the newcomer's charcoal-black face hinted there was serious business at hand.

"You don't remember me, do you, Mr. Justiss?" the young black man asked.

"No," Bowie confessed.

"Well, I don't suppose I blame you much. I was more along for the ride than anything else. I had my moments, though."

"You're Titus Freeman's youngster," Bowie declared, recognizing the old trail cook's easy smile on his son's face.

"I'm Lafayette. Most call me Lafe, just as they did on the trail to Kansas."

187

"That's been years. You've grown some."

"I got older," Lafe said, laughing. "Rode with the army awhile. Ninth Cavalry out of Fort Concho."

"You were a buffalo soldier then," Burke said.

"That's right, Colonel. Survived the food and the fighting. Even the officers."

Burke scowled, but Bowie laughed.

"You're in the company of a West Point man," Bowie explained. "Me, I was a captain, but I like to think it was partly accidental. So, Lafe, what can I do for you?"

"More like the other way around," young Freeman said, leaning against a wagon and running his fingers along the handle of his holstered pistol. "I've got a band of men. All of 'em served with the Ninth, like me. They can shoot, track and ride all night if the need comes along. We hire ourselves out to folks with trouble."

"Oh?"

"We've ridden for a pair of ranches, the stage line to El Paso, even the U.S. Mail twice. We can catch this Polk fellow for you."

"We're having posters printed," Burke explained. "Reward, adding the money New Mexico is putting up with what we're offering, comes close to four thousand dollars. That ought to bring them in."

"Well, I wouldn't want to argue with you, Colonel, you bein' a West Point man and all, but no bounty man'll bring in Rame Polk. He's fast as lightning, that one. He trusts nobody, and he's mean as thunder. You want him stopped?"

"Yes," Bowie declared.

"Then hire my men. We'll keep him clear of your camps, and in time, we'll trap him and put a

188

finish to this trouble."

"For a small price?" Burke asked.

"Your brother pays his cowboys forty dollars a month. We'll take fifty, which isn't so much considerin' the hazards of our callin'. And we collect the rewards, of course."

"That doesn't sound like so much," Bowie responded.

"Can we talk a minute?" Burke asked.

Bowie nodded, and Lafe left them. Bowie sat in the back of a wagon and rested his now aching arm. Burke waited for Lafe to move along before speaking.

"You know nobody's paying a black cowboy anything near fifty dollars a month," Burke pointed out. "What's more, they'd probably do the job for half. There will be those who object to having those men around, especially armed."

"That's all true," Bowie agreed, "but they'll have twenty times a better chance of reaching Polk without causing suspicion. As for the money, they'll earn it if they keep Polk's gang away from us."

"Then you've decided. Should I send word to Thorpe?"

"I'll tell him myself. I'll be leaving for Fort Worth tomorrow."

"Tomorrow?"

"Emiline's likely cross with me already. She was against me being out here. Besides, I'm only in the way. I'm little use to you one-armed and feverish. You've run things alone nigh on a week. I'd say you can keep it going just fine."

"I'll do my best, and you won't stay gone forever."

"No, but it could be a while."

That afternoon the two men spoke again. Bowie made a few notes for Burke, then rested until supper.

"You can feed yourself today," Rachel announced as she handed him a bowl of stew. "I think I might be needed elsewhere."

She sat down beside Jay Belton, but the boy took his bowl and waved her away.

"I can feed myself, too," Jay declared, clutching a spoon awkwardly. It warmed Bowie's heart, and he could tell Rachel was almost as pleased.

"Tell me, Jay," Bowie said between bites, "do you think you can look after Rachel and the others if I go to Fort Worth tomorrow? I should look in on my wife for a time."

"Your arm will heal faster there," Rachel added. "Here someone's always likely to call on you for advice or instructions."

"You'll miss all this good stew," Jay whispered.

"I will," Bowie told her. "Rachel's Indians put my wife to shame."

"And I suppose you want to see your kids," Jay added. His lip quivered slightly, and Bowie touched the boy's pale arm.

"My son's only a little older than you are, Jay. You'd like him, I think. Maybe he'll come with me when I return. He hates living in town."

"Let him hammer spikes awhile," one of the other boys called out.

"It might do him some good at that," Bowie declared. "I've never known boys to stand as tall as you and your friends, Jay."

"I'm not so tall," Jay objected.

"You are the way I see things," Bowie told the

boy. "Back in my soldier days, I used to meet a lot of men. Every once in a while I'd come across one who was worth knowing. You're that kind of fellow, Jay Belton. Look after yourself because I figure we've got a lot more getting to know each other yet ahead."

"I will, Cap'n."

The next morning Bowie got dressed and slipped away quietly. He hoped to avoid any farewells, but Rachel, as usual, was a step ahead of him.

"You're going to your wife," she whispered. "It's best, I suppose, but the boys'll miss you. I will, too."

"And I, you," Bowie confessed. "I never knew a nurse to have a gentler touch, nor a surgeon, either."

"Thank you, Captain Justiss."

"It's me who's in your debt, Rachel. Up to now, I've enjoyed your attention and compassion. But if I was to stay, I'm afraid I'd be tempted to ask for something more. You're too fine a young woman for that."

"And if I didn't refuse you?"

"I'm married, Rachel."

"I was once myself. I know about a loveless marriage."

"Em and I have shared a lot of things, love among them. We have a son. Rachel, I'm close to old enough to be your father. I have a niece older than you are with a house full of kids. I'm too old to be the man who'd make you happy."

"Isn't that for me to decide?"

"Not in this case. I can't lie and say I don't feel

strongly where you're concerned, but I do love my wife. She's got faults, as we all do, Lord knows, but we've built a life together. There are just too many years."

Rachel nodded, then clasped his right hand. Bowie kissed her wrists, then pulled away. Slowly, deliberately he then walked to where the supply train was waiting for the return trip to Fort Worth.

Chapter 7

Bowie had expected at least a few days of rest and quiet in Fort Worth. He scarcely stepped down onto the depot platform when Boyd Fitch appeared.

"I heard about your troubles," Fitch said, fighting to catch his breath. "I'm wondering if you've got time to hear of mine."

"I'm expecting my wife," Bowie explained. "Can't it wait?"

"I don't think so," Fitch said, nervously glancing over his shoulder as if expecting some pursuing demon to appear momentarily.

"Very well," Bowie reluctantly agreed. "Make it brief, though. Emiline has little patience normally, and she barely tolerates business at all."

"She likes to spend money, though, or so I hear," Fitch mentioned. "If we have none, she'll scarce care for that."

"What are you talking about?"

"The ruin of us all," Fitch said, leading the way to a small freight office in the depot. Fitch closed and bolted the door, then took out a ledger he'd concealed in his coat and pointed to a dozen neatly written red entries.

"I don't understand," Bowie said, sitting down as his arm began to ache. "We didn't order any of this. Fancy saddles? St. Louis furs?"

"For Miss Barr," Fitch whispered. "She's doing a whole lot better than the railroad, I'd wager. There's worse. Mr. Thorpe brought in a dozen men to run the warehouses. All I do is manage the men. While they're working twelve hours to keep up with the demands of the work camps, Thorpe's cronies smoke fancy cigars and cut wages. I'm telling you, Captain, we're about to lose our whole crew. Other lines are starting construction, and if all this keeps up, the men will simply walk out."

"Whose idea was all this?"

"Mr. Thorpe said the directors voted on a reorganization."

"Directors? What directors?" Bowie asked angrily. His face was turning scarlet, and the pain in his arm throbbed.

"It's only been the last week and a half, but we've got shortages everywhere. Some of those crooks sell our lumber on the side and make a nice profit. Others sell rails to some friend, then buy 'em back at double price. Our accounts show a twenty-thousand dollar drop, and heaven knows what will come next."

"I promise to see what can be done."

"Don't wait too long, Captain. The men are downright angry. There's even been talk of fires."

"Calm them down if you can. Assure them I'll see their wages tended and these scoundrels sent packing."

"Thank you, sir. I knew you didn't know about this. If you have in mind throttling that Thorpe, just pass the word. I've got men who'd gladly join in that foofaraw, believe you me."

"I'll keep you in mind, Fitch. When you have a chance, copy those account books for me. I'll need the details to settle with Henry Thorpe. Meanwhile, do you still have the keys to the warehouses?"

"Yes, sir."

"Then keep the doors locked except to let your crews load and unload supplies for the work trains. As for Thorpe's new hirelings, settle with them as you see fit. They're not to draw a cent from the paymaster, though, nor return to their offices. Understand?"

"Yes sir!"

Fitch departed happily. Bowie left less so. His arm felt as if iron chains were now attached, and on top of that, Emiline was waiting angrily inside the station.

"We didn't know what to imagine," she complained. "I worried you might have taken fever. Clay and Bart went to search the train."

"I had a bit of business to tend," Bowie explained.

"It appears to me you've done more than enough," she said, frowning at his splinted arm. "I knew you shouldn't go out there. It's nearly gotten you killed, and even now, when you should conserve your strength and allow your wounds to heal, you busy yourself with this infernal railroad."

"It's something that merited my attention, Em.

195

Why aren't the boys in school?"

"Clay insisted on coming to greet you, and that Davis boy, well, it's impossible to pry him from Clay's coattails."

"It's good Clay's found a friend," Bowie declared. "I'd best fetch them."

"You come with me, Bowie Justiss. The carriage is waiting. The boys can find their own way."

Bowie nodded and followed her to the waiting carriage. She was right, of course, and the youngsters appeared within a few minutes. Clay wrapped an arm around his father in a rare show of affection, and Bart Davis added a good-natured smile.

"Does it hurt much, Papa?" Clay asked, examining the arm.

"Not so much now I'm home," Bowie said, rubbing Clay's shoulder and flashing a smile at Emiline. "How is the house coming along?"

"You wouldn't imagine it possible," Emiline said, "but we've moved into the lower floors. There's a good deal of carpentry yet to be completed, but the house is so much more pleasant than Mrs. Taylor's boarding establishment."

"Doesn't have a pond," Clay grumbled.

"All the better for your sake," Bowie answered. "Your mama was far from amused by your last adventure at that pond."

Bart laughed, and Clay grinned along with his father. Emiline found no humor in the situation. Instead she lectured on the merits and obligations of civil behavior. Bowie closed his eyes and rested while the carriage took them to Cherry Hill.

Emiline had not understated the progress made on the house. It was finished on the outside, and gardeners had landscaped the approaches and walks with rare art. The banks were sculpted into quiet gardens with a dozen colors splashed across the hillside. The blossoming peach trees and flowering dogwood painted a symphony of pink and white across what otherwise might have been a dull stretch of Texas prairie.

Inside much remained to be done, but Bowie was pleased that the library was finished. Elsewhere bare rooms awaited the arrival of furniture, and many windows remained undraped. All that would come with time.

"I'll take you on a tour," Emiline offered after they'd strolled about the ground floor.

"Later, dear," Bowie replied. "Just now I've grown a little dizzy. It's best I lie down."

Emiline conducted him along to their bedroom, and the boys helped Bowie out of his boots.

"I'll get Cook to make you some dinner, Papa," Clay promised, scampering away.

"Can I get you anything, Mr. Justiss?" Bart asked.

"Do you know where you could locate a writing notebook and a lap desk?" Bart nodded and disappeared immediately.

"You don't intend to work now, do you?" Emiline asked.

"No, just make a few notes," Bowie explained. "Don't worry. My head's pounding, and it's clearly not about to allow me a chance to do anything worthwhile for a few days yet."

Emiline looked a bit skeptical, and Bowie grinned. She did know him, after all.

After eating a bowl of tasty vegetable soup and jotting down some reminders of the meeting with Fitch, Bowie set aside his paper and allowed himself a two hour nap. A doctor arrived soon thereafter to inspect the bandages and drain the wound.

"It appears to me your husband fell into good hands out there in the wilds," the doctor told Emiline. "It's healing rather nicely, and the splints are correctly placed. I'll come again in a week's time."

"Thank you, Dr. Platt," Emiline said, escorting the doctor out of the room. Clay and Bart appeared immediately, and Bowie passed the next hour listening to tales of school pranks and boyish adventures.

"You've gotten taller," Bowie told Clay. "Your birthday's next week. Do you have any special requests?"

"Just one," Clay said, gazing carefully toward the door to make sure his mother wasn't within earshot. "I want a horse, one I can ride this summer when I go to the ranch."

"That's far from certain," Bowie said, frowning.

"Then count that part of the gift," Clay added, poking Bart in the ribs. "Well, go on and say it, Bart."

"Mr. Justiss, I've got a birthday coming, too," Bart said nervously. His ordinarily bright brown eyes seemed suddenly cloudy. The boy was reluctant to speak, but Clay prodded Bart again.

"Go on," Bowie whispered, resting his right hand on the younger boy's shoulder. "Do you want a horse, too?"

Bart nodded, then looked at Clay.

"He wants to come to the ranch as well," Clay said, pleading with his eyes for affirmation. "Please, Papa. This place is like a morgue, and school will be out for summer term."

"I don't know, Clay. There's been trouble out there."

"We'll be all right with Joe and Chris. There are no more Indians, Papa. I don't think I could stand parading around Mama's garden parties all summer, choked by a silk necktie, all scrubbed and stuffed like a prize goose in a butcher's shop. Please?"

"I'll talk to her," Bowie promised. "And you, Bart. When is your birthday? We generally have a celebration of sorts for Clay, and it seems to me we should make like arrangements for you."

"May second," Bart announced proudly.

"Consider it settled then. Now, when do the two of you have to return to Baldwin?" Bowie asked.

The boys exchanged sheepish looks, and Bowie knew their appearance at the station had likely been unauthorized.

"Papa, I had to come," Clay explained. "As for Bart, someone had to keep me from coming to harm."

Bowie laughed loudly. The notion that diminutive Bart Davis could shepherd anyone was too fanciful.

"Better get yourselves back there before the whole cadet corp's mobilized and on the march," Bowie scolded them half-heartedly. "I'm glad you came, boys, and I look forward to seeing you both on Friday."

"Yes, sir," Bart said, shaking Bowie's hand before chasing Clay out the door. Bowie listened to their flying feet resounding on the floorboards. Once they were gone, he closed his eyes and slept peacefully until suppertime.

Bowie rested three days, but he was far from idle. Daily he received reports from Boyd Fitch and exchanged telegrams with Angus Burke. Lafe Freeman's ex-buffalo soldiers kept Rame Polk at bay, but the outlaws raided two small farms in southern Parker County and derailed a supply train by blasting a section of track.

A far more serious problem faced the Fort Worth and Western, though. As Bowie read ledgers and glanced over receipts, it became clear just how spendthrift Henry Thorpe had become. Thorpe's personally appointed directors lived in plush private Pullman cars and enjoyed every luxury while bills for supplies went unpaid. No one seemed to care whether food arrived on time at the work camps, and when the payroll was neglected as well, all work on the railroad ground to a halt.

At the warehouses in Fort Worth open rebellion stirred. Thorpe's cronies had been locked out of their offices, but they'd hired ax-carrying drifters to open the padlocked doors. Boyd Fitch had his crews ready for just that occasion, though, and the would-be axmen scattered. The former warehouse directors, however, were treated to new coats of tar and feathers before being packed into a freight car headed for Shreveport.

None of this went unnoticed by Bowie Justiss. With his head finally cleared of cobwebs left by two weeks of slow recovery, Bowie rode to the station and met with Thorpe in the privacy of the New Yorker's refurbished Pullman.

"This Fitch has lost all control of his senses," Thorpe declared angrily. "Just because the payroll is a trifle late, he's sent armed men to detain the directors of the railroad."

"And just what directors might those be?" Bowie asked.

"Ah, I suppose you haven't received the word. Some of the investors felt we should have a board to run the F W & W."

"What investors are those?"

"Men who have bought an interest in the line. J. L. Barr, the Brent brothers, Tom Coke."

"Don't you think as a partner I should have been consulted?" Bowie asked angrily.

"Keep in mind you are a minority partner. I didn't see how your opinions would alter matters. The others and I still control the majority of the line."

"I see," Bowie grumbled. "Does banker Barr know what his holdings are worth? According to Fitch's ledgers, not very much. You've close to sold every acre of land the state has granted us, and there'll be no more until we lay more track. That won't happen until you pay the work crews."

"We'll pay them in stock then, print a new issue."

"No, you won't," Bowie said. "I know enough law to know you can't print valueless shares. What's more, paper won't feed those men's families or put shoes on their children's feet."

"Then we'll find new crews."

"Thorpe, you're a thief and a liar, and I'll see you dealt with."

"Don't forget, Justiss. I've got friends in high places."

"I have friends, too," Bowie warned. "Some of them are judges and others serve in the state government. I wonder how the state will view your accounts? Not favorably, I'd say. The *Fort Worth Star* might even publish a few reports. How would banker Barr feel if it were known he'd invested in a bankrupt enterprise? I doubt even his daughter's voice would soothe financial ruin."

"You're insane. You don't understand how this business operates!"

"I understand honesty, and I'll wager most of these others do, too. We'll see what happens."

Thorpe turned to block Bowie's exit, but Bowie drew a pocket revolver and grinned.

"Do you really want to make it this easy, Thorpe?" Bowie asked. "I doubt any jury in Texas would fault me for shooting a New York swindler."

"Watch your words!"

"You watch your shadow, Thorpe. It's apt to have company. There are men hereabouts angry and desperate. I hear they're boiling tar over near the warehouses."

Bowie strode past Thorpe and marched on along toward the warehouses. Thorpe remained in the door of his Pullman. An uneasy gaze followed Bowie's departing footsteps.

Bowie wasted no time in meeting with Thorpe's new partners. J. L. Barr, in particular, was astounded to learn Bowie held such a large share of the company.

"I purchased twenty per cent myself, and Coke took another ten. As for the Brents, I thought they'd agreed to buy an additional ten together."

"That accounts for most of the line," Bowie calculated. "I believe it's time we had a meeting with Boyd Fitch and Angus Burke while we still have a railroad."

The meeting was held at Cherry Hill two days later. As the investors read line after line of ledger entries and unpaid accounts, they paled. Barr shook with rage as he figured the lavish sums showered upon his daughter . . . all at company expense.

"What this means, my friends, is that the shares we paid ten dollars for are practically worthless," Coke cried. "We'll all likely to go to jail once all this is revealed."

"By the look of some of those men down at the warehouse, we'll be fortunate if that's all," Barr added. "Now, Captain Justiss, Colonel Burke, what can we do?"

"Sell what we can lay our hands on," Burke declared, "starting with Thorpe's collections of wine and food. Rid ourselves of those Pullmans. That should raise enough funds to meet the payroll."

"Shoot Thorpe," Coke suggested.

"No, we need him awhile yet," Bowie said, sadly shaking his head. "If we lose the public trust, we're doomed. Let him stay on as president of the line—at a reduced salary and without control of the accounts."

"And what about supplies?" Fitch asked. "We'll reach Weatherford with what rails we have on hand, but that will be the end of the line."

"We'll need a loan," Burke said, turning to Barr.

"I only want out," Barr replied.

"I'll find the money elsewhere," Bowie said, "and I'll buy out anyone who feels he hasn't the nerve to play out this hand."

"You're on," Coke said. "Make me an offer."

"Me, too," Barr said.

"And you?" Bowie asked, turning to the Brents.

"We're not bankers," Logan Brent said, grinning. "We made our money driving beeves to Kansas, like you, Justiss. I've made a wager or two at a gaming table, and I know a man who's betting a good hand. You're not bluffing, are you, Justiss? You think you can bring this line in."

"I do," Bowie declared.

"So do I," Burke added, "and I'm willing to put my pocketbook up as well."

"Barr?" Bowie asked.

The banker shook his head, and by the close of the meeting, the F W & W had changed its ownership. Bowie Justiss found himself owning sixty per cent, with ten each in the hands of the Brents and Angus Burke.

When Henry Thorpe called his own directors' meeting, he was surprised to discover that only Bowie Justiss arrived.

"No need to await the others," Bowie said, glaring at Thorpe. "I have their proxies."

"What?"

"I'm the majority owner now, Thorpe. Your dear friend's father found the game's stakes too high and sold out for a song. Coke, too. I believe you have twenty per cent left, which we'll happily take off your hands if you wish. Meanwhile, I have a list of company property which you are to surrender. Boyd Fitch will have some men here this afternoon to take possession."

"This isn't possible."

"For the time being you can continue playing line president. The Brent brothers are arranging a party to celebrate the F W & W's arrival in Weatherford, and we'll expect your witty appearance. The governor will be there, as will two judges of the Texas criminal court."

"You think you've won, do you?"

"I know so."

"You'll never find the funds to continue without my help."

"I wired my brother. On top of that, Weatherford's paid a generous bond to have the tracks pass through its limits. You can keep this Pullman until Weatherford, but the engineers of the locomotives have instructions not to leave this siding before May, and they're to take you only west even then."

"I have friends!"

"I doubt you'll have many once the word of Barr's ruin gets out. What did he pay for those shares, forty-thousand dollars? He sold them for less than five. As for Coke, his brother's in the senate in Washington. I'll bet he's already started an investigation."

"You haven't left me with much of a hand to play."

"You're fortunate I've left you with anything at all. Even that's not out of compassion. We need to keep up appearances while we solidify our position."

"I was wrong about you, Justiss. I thought you'd be a mule to drive like Burke and Fitch. You surprised me. I'll go along with you. I enjoy playing roles, after all, and if you win, I'll at least have something to show for my shares."

"That's right."

"But before you count your winnings, remember this. Life can turn, and the future's often a blur at best."

"I know that all too well, Thorpe. It's you who should have taken those words to heart."

Chapter 8

The funds sent by Charlie Justiss and the $10,000 bond paid by the town of Weatherford allowed the Ft. Worth and Western to continue. Quietly, cautiously, Boyd Fitch disposed of Thorpe's cache of wines, cigars and fine furniture. Word of financial difficulties leaked anyway, and suppliers now demanded cash in advance before they sold flatcars of rails or a quart of milk. Even so, life for Bowie Justiss settled down.

Clay celebrated his fourteenth birthday at Cherry Hill. Young men in tailored uniforms from the Baldwin Academy escorted young ladies from fine Fort Worth and Waco families around the new ballroom while their parents engaged in light conversation or toured Emiline's gardens.

Bowie noted that Clay joined in the dancing with little enthusiasm. Even little Bart, who could barely see the chin of some of his partners, grinned and chatted with the girls.

"Now you see why I want to spend the summer at the ranch, Papa," Clay grumbled. "No one likes me, except maybe Bart, and I'm out of place. I don't care whose family is touring England this summer or why some Russian count is staying with Hilda Runsfield's aunt."

"I know," Bowie said, holding his son still and grinning as Bart waltzed by with an escort a full head taller. "But all those girls aren't going to England. See Sally Brent over there in the corner? Ask her to take a turn around the floor. Her family is in cattle, and I understand she can outride Bedford Forrest."

"Who can't?" Clay muttered. "He must be eighty years old now."

Bowie laughed, and Clay stumbled across to the corner where Sally appeared to be seeking shelter. The two talked briefly, then escaped out the wide twin doors and headed for the backs. An hour later the two of them were riding together atop a sleek roan mare Luis Morales had brought to Ft. Worth only that morning.

"Of course, a city is no place to ride a horse such as she," Luis had declared. "A boy should have the plains at his feet when he rides an Arabian."

Bowie felt a chill as Emiline glared at Luis. Talk of Clay going to the ranch that summer would have to wait.

Clay's birthday was not the only celebration Bowie attended that spring. The Ft. Worth and Western's arrival in Weatherford was greeted with a gala party at the town's new train station. Aside from Parker County's notables, the first train to pull into Weatherford carried two cars of dignitaries from all over the state.

Bowie and Emiline were there. They rode in the second car to Emiline's chagrin. Thorpe and Miss Barbara Barr accompanied the governor's family in the Pullman. In addition seven state senators,

208

ten representatives, a score of judges and most of the ranking military men in the state were on that train.

Emiline, in spite of being irked at riding with common senators and generals, strode about the car, striking up conversations with the notables, sharing tidbits of gossip and in general occupying herself through the short journey from Fort Worth. Bowie spent most of his time with Senator Lawrence Rogers, gazing at maps of proposed detours in the original route which might connect some of West Texas's disparate county seats.

"Such diversions might prove expensive," Bowie mentioned. "I suppose you would support the paying of a bond like the people of Weatherford did."

"Wouldn't the additional land be incentive enough? And don't forget," the senator added, "that these towns will provide riders for your coaches and goods for your boxcars."

"That won't pay the costs of laying the extra track now," Bowie explained.

"I spoke to Thorpe about all this. I thought it was settled."

"He doesn't control the line, Senator. And he doesn't know this country at all. In many places there isn't but one gap in the hills. That will determine the route. As for towns, they'll follow the tracks."

"Palo Pinto County's next," Senator Rogers reminded Bowie. "Your family *is* Palo Pinto County. Will you ask them for a bond as well?"

"I will," Bowie confirmed. "The town's a bit north of the best route, and the terrain is rough at best."

The senator shook his head sadly, and Bowie

moved along to speak to someone else.

When the train arrived, Bowie was surprised to find a band playing at the platform. Girls with flowers decorated each car. Tables of food and drink stood in readiness, and a military honor guard escorted the flags of Texas and the United States.

"Hear, hear for the governor!" a tall, lean rancher cried, and the people cheered.

Governor H. K. Thornton and his auburn-haired wife stepped out of the Pullman accompanied by Henry Thorpe and young Barbara Barr. The crowd closed around them, and Emiline flashed a look of utter disgust toward her husband.

"Never mind them," Bowie said, leading her toward the far end of the platform. "I see someone else."

It didn't ease Emiline's anger one bit when she discovered Charlie and Angela Justiss approaching. With them was their eldest son Ross and his wife, the former Eliza Rogers.

"So, you've made it to Weatherford at least," Charlie said as the brothers linked wrists. "Next comes the Brazos."

"Yes," Bowie said, glancing uneasily at Emiline. "I thank you for your prompt and generous help. Soon I expect to be able to pay you back."

"I'm not worried. You never let anyone down in your whole life, Bowie."

"You men go ahead and have your reunion," Emiline interrupted. "I believe I'll go visit with Jane Thornton. We scarcely had a chance to say hello, what with her riding in the Pullman. Excuse me, won't you?"

Emiline waltzed across the platform, and Bowie

smiled nervously. Em and Angela had never gotten along, and Angela seemed almost as relieved at her sister-in-law's departure.

"Eliza, why don't you introduce Mama to the governor," Ross suggested.

"I'd be pleased to," Eliza said, leading her mother-in-law along. Once the women had left, Ross turned to his uncle.

"I understand the folks in Weatherford posted five thousand dollars to bring the railroad through here," Ross said. "That true?"

"Ten thousand," Bowie told the young man.

"And will you expect that much from Palo Pinto?" Charlie asked.

"Make it seven. Palo Pinto's not quite as large."

"It's on the natural route west," Ross pointed out. "Best gap in the mountains, too."

"Best route west," Bowie agreed. "But we're headed southwest. I'd guess the direct route would pull us a good deal south."

"Towns that get bypassed by the railroad die," Ross complained. "We've helped you, Uncle Bowie. But just now the cattle business isn't at its best. We've had flood and drought of late, and I don't think that much money's to be had from the people."

"Let me ask you something, Ross?" Bowie asked. "Who's going to benefit most from the line cutting through town? You? No, the land there belongs to someone else. The only place you'd benefit is if we kept the tracks along the old Fort Griffin road. That way you'd maybe be able to build your own cattle shipping depot next to the tracks. But if we swung south, we could claim all those state-owned acres down there, build our own town, control the whole length of track. It's

211

easier grade, a more direct route, and it's good range."

"People in town, folks like Art Stanley and Georgia Staves who've invested in their stores and hotels, would take it hard," Charlie pointed out. "We'd have to drive our stock along a narrow road as well. Up in Kansas stock that strayed and romped through fields caused bitterness. I'd hate to see that happen here."

"It will on any account," Bowie said, frowning. "Down south farmers are fencing, and cattlemen are feuding. Outfits that have depended on free range find they've got nowhere for their stock at all."

"Thank God we don't have many of those folks," Charlie said. "It will prove a hardship to old-timers like Joe Nance, and that's bad enough."

"Yes," Ross agreed. "And he'll be farther from a railhead than we will."

The band struck up a tune then, and the men broke off their conversation and went in search of their wives. In no time at all the station filled with music and laughter. Those who chose not to dance sat at tables and enjoyed platters of beef and potatoes. Other sipped wine or fruit punch.

Bowie located Emiline with Governor Thornton's wife, Jane. The two women were discussing Jane Thornton's plans for schools and hospitals in the new towns that would be spawned by the railroad.

"There are so many unfortunate children in our state," Mrs. Thornton said, sighing. "You see them everywhere. We visited the railroad camps last week. With your husband so heavily involved, I'm certain you know how horrible conditions are for the children of the workers. And those poor unfortunate boys! Children, some of them not yet ten, have been horribly mutilated in accidents. One child who spoke with me had three fingers missing from one hand. Imagine starting life with such a handicap, and three out of four couldn't write his own name.

"I spoke with a woman, Rachel Harmer. The angel, those boys call her. She's a miracle worker, for she's introduced those pitiful wretches to books. She's teaching them to read and write. She nurses the injured ones and looks after the orphans. When the work is finished, I'm going to help her build an orphanage for those poor boys. Angus Burke suggested it be a work ranch, like the Harrison Home down in Houston. But, of course, you're aware of the needs of those children. My husband tells me you've taken an orphan into your home, and I've heard wonderful things about the school you helped start in Palo Pinto."

Emiline shook with rage. It hadn't been her idea to shelter Bart Davis, and it was Angela who had started the Palo Pinto school.

"I agree with you these children have dire needs," Emiline said, struggling to mask her true feelings. "It's intolerable that their parents have set them adrift in such hostile country."

"Oh, most have no parents," Mrs. Thornton objected. "Yellow fever down south accounted for many of them, and there have been accidents and hardships. It's a great tragedy, and we'll pay a high price if these children aren't rescued."

"It appears you and the governor have the cause well in hand, though."

"I fear not. H. K. is opposed to using public funds, and with the depression in the cattle industry, many of our usual sources of funds are not available. I pray some benefactor will step forth, but it seems unlikely. Henry Thorpe offered not a penny!"

"I shouldn't be surprised," Emiline said, grinning at what seemed an invitation to boost Bowie's standing. "He's from New York, you know, and the tales we hear of life up there would curl a proper lady's hair. As for the needed funds, let me see what I can do. I know many influential people in Fort Worth, as you know, and we've supported public projects before."

"Bless you, dear."

Bowie drank it all in. It was amazing. He might have talked till doomsday, trying to get Emiline to support the notion of an orphanage, but a few words from Jane Thornton, and suddenly Em was the most generous of women.

"I'm so glad you're taking an interest in those projects," Bowie told his wife. "Mrs. Thornton, you're so right in that we must do something for the unfortunate."

Emiline scowled a bit, but Bowie lifted her chin.

"Then we can count on your support as well, Captain Justiss?" the governor's wife asked.

"Naturally. In fact, I've already spoken to Miss Harmer about the very thing."

"And I understand it was you who provided the schoolbooks," Mrs. Thornton said, smiling brightly. "A marvelous gesture."

"All my wife's idea," Bowie lied. "She's a champion of the people. Her late father was Judge Thayer of Robertson County, a gentleman of great repute."

"I believe I've heard of him," Mrs. Thornton

said, nodding respectfully toward Emiline.

"Now, I really must borrow my wife for a time," Bowie said, bowing to the governor's wife and taking Emiline's hand. "We've scarcely spent five moments together."

"We can't allow that, can we, dear?" Mrs. Thornton asked. "You have to keep a tight rein on a man. I never let H. K. roam far."

Emiline seemed almost grateful at being rescued.

"I wanted to tell her to take her vagabond children and head for Mexico," Emiline confessed. "Another hundred ruffians would hardly be noticed there."

"Emiline!" Bowie exclaimed. "The orphanage is a fine notion. Once we've restored the solvency of the line, I'll do everything I can to see it brought about."

"That's obviously not why you brought me over here, though."

"No," Bowie admitted. "It's because I've been talking to Burke. We've got some difficult days ahead of us, and I will be returning to the work camps. We'll clear out the trouble in Fort Worth first, of course, reorganize the company, but afterward, I'll be leaving again."

"You can't mean to stay out there long. Soon it will be summer. I spoke with Enid Marchand about taking the train to New Orleans. From there we might sail to Europe."

"I can't go anywhere until we connect our line with El Paso."

"Then perhaps I can take Clay. He's eager to see the world."

"He . . . has other plans," Bowie said, nervously shifting his feet.

"Oh?"

"I thought I'd speak to you of it another time, but I've promised him he could pass the summer with his cousins at the ranch. He and Bart both."

"No!" Emiline said, stomping her foot. "I won't have it! I finally freed him from those ragged boys, and here you'd send him out for the entire summer. It will undo all the work I've done. Send the Davis boy if you like, but Clay will go with me."

"He won't like it, Em."

"He doesn't have to. It's time he learned what's expected of a Thayer."

"His name's Justiss. All my life I've worked hard, and never found it a hindrance to anything. He stays up at that school, lonely and unhappy, because he knows you want it so much. I won't have him shut up in a ship's cabin all summer, with no other children about for company, and all that polite talk and high-mannered nonsense that would try Job's patience."

"Bowie, I simply won't have it."

"Em," he said, taking her hand and squeezing it lightly, "I love you. I have from the day we first met. You're the sun in the morning, the brightest and the best thing in the universe. You don't know our son, though. You see your father in him, but it isn't so. Clay's got too much of the Justiss wildness to be the Alexandria gentleman you'd make of him. He's fourteen. In two years he'll be off to college somewhere. After that, he'll be a man with his own dreams and hopes and, yes, his own future."

"I know that. It's why I want him to travel."

"Yes, I know what you want, dear. A mother's wishes should always be respected, especially when her son's small and helpless. But as a boy grows, he develops long legs, a deep voice, and most of all, he comes to have a mind of his own. If he doesn't use it then, he never will."

"He's said nothing about going to a ranch."

"Why do you think he wanted the horse for his birthday? He would have spoken to you about it then, but he feared you wouldn't understand. Maybe you don't know. Perhaps you never will. In another month we'll have the railroad through Palo Pinto. He can come to Fort Worth and visit as often as you like. I think being out in the open, working stock and riding the wind will do him good. He's pale as death, and Luis can teach him more than a little of what it takes to be a man."

"No Mexican can . . ."

"Hush!" Bowie told her. "I've always tolerated such talk in the past, but no longer. Luis Morales is as fine a man as I've ever ridden with, and he's got the touch with horses I never had. Clay wants to go to Fortune Bend and learn how to work the Arabians, and it's fitting he should do so."

"Bowie, no."

"Yes," Bowie told her, glancing off into the distance. "I haven't always taken the tough stands I should have for my son, but I am now. He merits his father's support. And his mother's understanding."

Emiline wrung her hands. Her eyes grew red, and she shed a rare tear.

"I had such plans for my sons," she whispered. "I thought we'd have ten children, bright blond little boys and yellow-haired girls. I never said as much, but I bear a heavy grievance against the God who stole my little ones away. All I have left is Clay. I hoped he would one day step into his grandfather's shoes. Now it seems he's to ride wild horses and chase jackrabbits. It's as if we never left your father's farm. Ten years have passed, but nothing's changed."

He escorted her to the new Parker Hotel where they were to spend the night. Bowie helped her into bed, then took a midnight stroll along the hotel's wide veranda. The music from the party continued to drift through town, and the lights at the station burned brightly. Beyond, on the distant prairie, Rachel Harmer would likely be scrubbing some poor unfortunate with a horsehair brush and hard lye soap. Jay Belton was hobbling around on a crutch, according to Angus Burke, and Lafe Freeman was still patrolling the country in search of Rame Polk.

I'd trade places with any of them, Bowie thought as he sat on the hotel porch and dropped his face into his hands. What was it Em had said. Nothing's changed? That was the worst kind of foolishness. Everything was changing. Cattle would soon graze in fenced pastures, and there'd be no more drives, not even to Fort Worth. The railheads would come to the ranches' doorsteps, and who could know if cowboys would even be needed. Perhaps a boy with a sharp stick would prod the heavy Holsteins about.

Suddenly he envied his brother Charlie. Whenever Charlie grew reflective, he could climb the high cliffs above the Brazos and remember Stands Tall, the Comanche chief who'd fought so long and hard to hold onto a dying culture. Charlie might wage such a fight himself. Hadn't he held out hope even on the morning word had come from General Lee that the army must surrender?

218

I'm no Stands Tall, Bowie told himself. I do what I have to in order to survive. Yesterday I ran a freight outfit. The day before I raised cattle. Now I'm building a railroad. Tomorrow? Who could foretell the future?

He rose to his feet and headed for the upstairs room where Emiline was already sleeping. It was enough, after all, that a man knew his heart, loved his family, and earned his living. To make more of life was folly, and Bowie Justiss, for all that he'd been or would be in the future, had yet to be a fool.

III

Conflict

Chapter 1

The coach rocked along the dusty road toward Palo Pinto, jostling its groggy passengers and groaning as if each new jolt could somehow be felt deep within its iron axles and leather braces. Charlie Justiss stared out the window at the brightening horizon. Angela rested against his shoulder. She slept uneasily as the noisy coach headed homeward.

Yes, Charlie told her silently, we should have waited for morning. Now your dress will be wrinkled beyond repair, and it will take a week to work the kinks out of our bodies. But Charlie couldn't abide the pretentious Parker Hotel, and after all, Weatherford was such a short distance from Palo Pinto. He'd often ridden the thirty or so miles in a single day, and the coach would have them home by breakfast.

Home. It was a comforting word, and the mere thought of it cast away some of Charlie's weariness. Of late he had been too often away from the familiar creeks and hills, away from his beloved Brazos, with its towering cliffs and frothing waters.

It was good to see those eternal cliffs rising above the river. So much was changing. It was reassuring to gaze at rocks that were there when the world began.

As the sun rose, Charlie looked with dismay on the sprawling work camps that even now sped his brother Bowie's railroad across Parker County. Cities of white canvas spread out across acres of what had not long before been buffalo pasture. Ravines which once sheltered maverick longhorns and spotted mustang ponies were filled and leveled for the passage of track. It was as if the wildness of the land was being wrung out of her by the determined hand of some invisible giant. It was.

Civilization, they call it, Charlie told himself. Already the giant had marked Palo Pinto. The little crossroads town had once been a mere huddle of plank buildings. Now three streets spread out from that junction of the Fort Griffin road and the north-south market trace leading from Jacksboro to Art Stanley's old trading post at Village Bend on the Brazos. New farms and ranches spread across the southern half of the county, and each day it seemed some new section of the open range was deeded over to a newcomer.

Once Palo Pinto had been the domain of vast cattle ranches like Charlie's Flying J, Joe Nance's Circle N and the Stokely brothers' Triple S. Well, Brad Stokely was dead, and his brother Ben had sold out and set off for the high peaks of the Rockies. All that remained of the Triple S was a dark scar where the Stokely ranchhouse had once stood, and soon the prairie grasses would erase even that.

The changes unsettled Charlie. When he'd first arrived in the county, life had been a struggle to survive against the hostile climate and marauding bands of Comanches. Later there'd been crooked officials and rustlers to deal with. Each threat had been faced and overcome. But the world of change creeping west on the tracks of the Fort Worth and Western posed a different problem.

"It's progress," Angela told him often. "The trains will bring new settlers. The town will grow and prosper. New churches and schools will be built."

All Charlie saw, though, was that bit by bit the open, unfettered range was being sliced open by plow blades, broken up into small ranches and farms so that the freedom of an endless horizon and an open sky would soon disappear along with the buffalo and the Comanche.

Charlie knew no man could still the hand of progress, but a strong man might temper the changes. Perhaps that is why he had accepted the reins of the county, agreed to serve as judge when the stark wooden walls of his courthouse office seemed more prison than workplace. Often he made the long trip to Austin to argue against the new laws favored by the farmer-dominated legislature.

"It was cattle brought this state out of the

despair of war into the bright sunshine of a new day," Charlie'd orated. "Don't let's carve out our heart, bury our soul. There's land fit for farming, sure, but West Texas is a grassland created for the wandering buffalo. It's the perfect pasture for cattle, good friends, but it will forever scorn the plow!"

Senators had clapped out of respect for the man known as "the Major". Charlie Justiss had bravely led his regiment during the dark days before Appomattox, and he'd staked out an empire in Palo Pinto County when carpetbagger taxes and basement cotton prices had spelled the end for the family farm in Robertson County. Governor Thornton had shaken Charlie's hand out of admiration, but in the end, the farm interests triumphed, and the senators had little heeded Charlie's suggestions.

Charlie Justiss felt like a weary stallion who, after reigning supreme across the prairie, had grown old. He no longer had the heart to face the younger, stronger stallions with their notions of breeding out the longhorn's strength and self-reliance, of stringing the new barbed wire around deeded land so that ranchers long on cattle and short on pasture or water would face ruin. Down south and farther west the free rangers were at war with farmers, and Austin dailies carried tales of murder and massacre. Charlie would spare Palo Pinto such an ordeal.

"Charlie?" Angela whispered as she stirred. "Are we home yet?"

"We've a way to go," he answered, pulling her close. Across the coach their son Ross and his

226

wife Eliza slept soundly.

"Yes," she agreed, gazing out the window at hillsides green with the taste of April rain. May's blankets of bluebonnets and dandelions, daisies and larkspurs splashed blues and yellows and whites across the land. In the golden shadow of the rising sun, the land seemed to change hues each moment.

"Remember how we used to walk out to the river and watch the sun rise in the springtime," Charlie whispered as he clasped her hand.

"It was like we were the first ones to glimpse the world," Angela told him. "It's hard to do that now that we're living in town."

"Maybe we ought to take a morning ride."

"Yes," she agreed.

They both knew it was unlikely. The boys had to be urged toward school, and Angela had taken to caring for her daughter Victoria's little ones. It was a rare moment they could devote to a sunrise or wildflowers.

As the coach topped a hill, though, the glory of spring was marred by an advance camp of the railroad work gangs. Tin pan handlers spread out canvas covers behind ox carts and wagons. A survey party cooked breakfast over a campfire. On beyond, three wide brightly-painted caravan wagons stood together. Clotheslines littered with violet and pink silk undergarments advertised the profession of the wagons' occupants.

Angela scowled.

"Traveling brothels," she muttered. "I thought we'd at least be spared that."

"Likely come out from the Flat," Charlie told

her. "It doesn't take long for those . . . enterprises to locate men with money in their pockets. It was like that on the trail to Kansas. Each river crossing seemed to house its fair share of fancy women, often down by the river in tents or clapboard shelters."

"I always wondered why you paid your crew at trail's end."

"Well, even so, I've known a young cowboy to sell a spare blanket, even a pair of boots for the favors of a lady."

Charlie grinned, but Angela fumed. Under her breath, she uttered a few descriptive phrases and added a Biblical quote or two.

"Don't forget what happened to Sodom," she said. "Fire is a sure cure for such wickedness."

Charlie couldn't help laughing, and that didn't help one bit. Angela's face reddened, and she folded her arms angrily.

They passed the next ten miles in silence. As the sun rose ever higher, Ross and Eliza finally awoke, and the young people soon began conversing about the marvels sure to follow the coming of the railroad to Palo Pinto.

"Surely it will put an end to these long coach rides," Eliza declared, brushing a coating of sand from her dress. "And think of all the fine things which will be at our fingertips? The mercantile shelves will hold the newest, finest milled cloth, and there'll be no waiting a month for a new stovepipe."

"Yes," Ross agreed. "It will certainly mean an increase in population. Cattle shipments will level out. There will be no need of driving a thousand head to Fort Worth. We can ship a few hundred, even fifty at a time."

"That spells hard times for cowboys," Charlie said sadly.

"It means we'll need less at one time," Ross pointed out, "but those we hire on will have steady work throughout the year. As it is now, there are too many seasonal hands. It's hard to make a summer's wages stretch across a whole year. There are those who have families and can't feed the children come winter. It turns others to thieving."

"And worse," Angela added.

"Ryan wrote he's bringing us some more breeding stock," Charlie said, hoping to avoid a renewed discussion of traveling harlots or the fires of perdition.

"The calves we got off that bull he brought last summer are a mark of the future," Ross commented. "They're shorter of leg, and they don't have near the horn. A shoulder roast off a full grown cow ought to provide half again the meat of a longhorn, though."

"The future," Charlie grumbled. "I'll miss the longhorn. He was mighty good to us, son."

"I miss the buffalo, Papa, but there's no going back. Eliza's father says the whole range will be fenced in ten years. I've been thinking we ought to begin sinking posts ourselves."

"What?" Charlie growled.

"Along the south boundary, Papa, where the Fort Griffin road passes alongside our range. We lose a few strays every time there's a thunderstorm. The river keeps stock from straying to the north, and we've got Caddo Creek on the west. Wouldn't hurt to fence along the Jacksboro road, either."

"Jacksboro road?" Charlie asked. A year ago it would still have been called the Ft. Belknap road, but the fort, long deserted, was but a resting place for crows and screech owls now. The farms which had sprung up beyond the Triple S had all played out, and Charlie planned to buy the abandoned acreage from the county for the sum of the unpaid taxes.

"You know I'm right, Papa," Ross continued. "It's only reasonable. Upgrading the herd's only part of the solution. If we don't fence, we'll go on populating half the small ranches in the south half of the county with strays."

"I won't be the first to string wire," Charlie promised.

"You won't have to," Ross replied. "I'll bet Parnell and those farmers have fences up before June's out."

"What? Parnell's no friend of barbed wire."

"Back when he was running cows himself, he wasn't. Now he speaks of little else. You watch. The first time a stray cow tramples a corn plant, they'll be digging fenceposts."

Charlie would have argued, but he knew Ross was probably right. Even Billy, who was born to ride an open range on a rogue stallion, had concluded fencing the southern boundary of the Flying J would be prudent. It was inevitable, but Charlie continued to put it off.

They arrived in Palo Pinto to find the town astir. Alongside the narrow bridge over the

Brazos a miniature canvas city had sprung up. Dry goods, harness, even baked items were for sale. A gunsmith hawked Sharps rifles no doubt sold off by desperate buffalo hunters gone broke.

Charlie was relieved to see no caravans, and Angela grinned with satisfaction. When they reached the town proper, though, they saw that an invasion of newcomers had occurred.

"Speculators," Charlie grumbled, eyeing the men in their St. Louis suits and top hats with suspicion. They were a plague which always crept west with a railroad, buying land cheap on the notion that its value would jump when the rails crossed. Some would find a bonanza of wealth while others would, as all gamblers, go bust.

"What's the word, Charlie?" Art Stanley called when the coach drew to a halt outside the courthouse door. "When will it be here?"

"We're tired just now," Charlie replied as he helped Angela down from the coach. "We'll have a town meeting tonight."

"Why not sooner?" one of the speculators cried. "Now?"

"Because my family's had a rough journey, and I'm hot and tired," Charlie answered. "I need a bath, some breakfast and a shave. If you can't wait for nightfall, though, we can gather around two o'clock at the courthouse."

"That's better," Art said. "I'll have some of my boys spread the word. Parnell's sure to be interested, and Joe Nance should be here."

"Tell them," Charlie said wearily. "We'll meet at

231

two."

Charlie was glad of the all too brief respite. He washed and shaved, then joined Angela for breakfast. Joe and Chris were already on their way to the schoolhouse, and Ross and Eliza had preferred sleep. Vicki's three youngest children were scampering about the parlor, watched over by Enuncia Nunez, the plump woman who had recently arrived to help with the housework. Charlie paused long enough to hug the little ones, then smiled at Enuncia.

"Welcome home, Senor Justiss," she said, lifting two-year-old Thomas in one hand and using the other to caution J. P., three, not to taunt his older sister Hope. Charlie knew Enuncia would be glad of Angela's help with the children.

"I was wondering if you'd gone along back to sleep," Angela told Charlie when he finally entered the kitchen.

"Just having a look at the children," he explained.

"Well, I'll have to excuse you that, Grandpapa. Now sit down and eat. You may need the energy by this afternoon."

A breakfast of ham and eggs and a generous lunch of beef stew helped Charlie muster the courage to face a packed courthouse full of citizens. He'd been no less nervous facing the Texas Senate. Charlie began by describing the Ft. Worth and Western's progress, by telling of the celebration in Weatherford. He saved the hard news for last.

"They say the natural route lies south of town," Charlie declared. Immediately Georgia Staves

232

and Art Stanley cried out in dismay.

"That won't keep them from coming here, will it?" Art asked. "After all, your brother Bowie's got a big interest in that railroad."

"They'll come," Charlie admitted, "but there'll be a price. Weatherford paid a rail bond for passage of the track through there. If we're to bring the tracks here, we'll have to do likewise."

"How much?" Joe Nance asked.

"Five thousand dollars," Charlie announced.

The hall grew deathly quiet. Small farmers who'd never seen that much money in their whole lives exchanged nervous glances. Speculators scowled.

"That isn't so much," Art declared. "We could simply raise it from county funds."

"No, we couldn't," Charlie explained. "There are no such funds in the treasury. You all know the last few years have been hard on the cattle business. We've kept taxes to bare bones. We have to pay Bret and Tut a salary to keep the peace, and we've bridged some roads."

"Too many if you ask me," Joe Nance grumbled.

"Most of those costs have been shouldered by the big ranches," Charlie went on to say. "For myself, I ask no salary, and Ross keeps most of the records. We're sure to have to add a land clerk, what with so many newcomers arriving, and an extra deputy may be needed, even without the railroad coming through. Think hard on this, folks. That bond's bound to come from your pockets and mine."

"What are you saying, Charlie?" Art asked. "Don't you want the railroad here?"

"It's not for me to say," Charlie answered. "It's not my money alone that's involved."

"But what's your feeling?" Georgia Staves asked. "You know I've built onto my hotel. Our town's future rests on the coming of the railroad."

"We've done all right before with no railroad," Joe Nance said, rising to his feet. "Why, back before Charlie Justiss and most of you folks came to Palo Pinto . . ."

"Back before the wheel," someone interrupted.

Nance reddened, and silence settled over the crowd.

"Go on, Joe," Charlie suggested.

"I know you all think I'm an old shoe, worn out and light on sense." Nance continued, "You say I live in the past. Well, the past wasn't such a bad place, providing you forget the Indians and the floods. This railroad's bound to come through the county, and I can't see that it matters so much where. We're talking a lot of money, and it just doesn't seem worth it to keep from going a few miles south to catch a train. Some of you've smelled the cowpens at Fort Worth or even Dodge City. I'd as soon have them a bit away from town myself."

"You wouldn't need cowpens if the station was right here in town," Art Stanley argued. "Some of us have stores and hotels here. We'd be out of business without the stagecoaches coming through with passengers. My freight business will take a blow anyway, but I can still survive by shipping to the outlying farms and ranches. All my money's tied up here in town, though, with warehouses and way stations. I need a station

234

here in Palo Pinto."

"Then you pay for it," Nance complained.

"There's more to this issue than just money," Georgia Staves spoke up. "I've got a financial interest, sure, but more than that, I want our town to prosper. The railroad means we'll grow. We'll have better schools for our children. It would mean doctors and banks and prosperity. I've seen towns die because there was no work for the boys coming of age. A railroad brings new opportunity. Why, we could support a flour mill or maybe a boot factory. That spells a future for our children."

"My children's future is on my farm," J. C. Parnell spoke. "You say a railroad brings progress? I didn't hear one word about churches or law and order. Boom towns bring trouble. Gamblers, drunkards, drifting outlaws, even those harlots on wagon wheels that passed through here yesterday ... they're all bound to arrive. We've got problems enough, I'd say."

Few of the farmers agreed.

"Don't you see, Parnell," Lewis Frost argued, "a railroad could take our vegetables east. Our carrots could be in New York faster than they get to Weatherford now. We could bring in cheap goods, too."

"Yes," others agreed.

"No," Nance and a smaller group grumbled.

"It's clear we need a vote," Charlie called as the meeting broke into a series of shouting duels. "Not everyone is here now. So you'll have time to decide, I say we meet again in one week. Talk it over. Make up your minds. Meeting adjourned!"

As the citizens of Palo Pinto made their way outside, mumbling and grumbling, Charlie shook his head in dismay. Was it possible Parnell was right? Could Palo Pinto fall into such dire straits? Even as Charlie looked on, old friends shoved each other violently, and a fist fight broke out between one of Nance's cowboys and a farmer, Roger Ellis.

"Heaven help us," Charlie said, turning away from the noise. "What have we brought upon ourselves?"

Chapter 2

Palo Pinto soon had a taste of what lay ahead. Scarcely an hour after Charlie Justiss adjourned the town meeting, pistol shots exploded the mid-afternoon quiet. A bullet tore through an upstairs window at the Brazos Hotel, and a woman occupying the room shrieked as a basin atop a wardrobe shattered in a hundred pieces.

Charlie walked to the window of his office and gazed out at the street. A dust-covered cowboy backed his way into the street. A Colt revolver rested in his jittery right hand. Ten yards away a tall moustached man dressed in midnight black followed the cowboy.

"What's all this about?" Bret Pruett called as he trotted out of the sheriff's office. "Hold on there."

"He started it!" the cowboy claimed, raising his pistol as if to point out the dark-clad stranger who continued to approach. The pistol never reached waist level. The man in black fired first, and the cowboy spun around and fell face first into the dusty street.

"Josh!" Joe Nance cried.

By then Bret had been joined by his deputy, Alexander Tuttle. The two of them stepped together toward the street. Charlie made his way outside as well, pausing only to collect a Winchester from its resting place atop the office mantel.

"You saw him, Sheriff," the stranger shouted, pointing to the dead cowboy. "He had a gun. What was I to do?"

"The hammer wasn't even cocked," Nance declared, cradling the head of the slain young man. "He was just celebrating his birthday. Was eighteen today! You baited him, mister!"

"He had a gun," the stranger repeated. "So he was a little drunk. A liquored-up boy can kill as certain as anyone, and I'm telling you, that pistol was aimed at me, friends!"

"And just where was yours aimed, friend?" Bret asked, reaching out his hand for the still smoking weapon.

"A man's got a right to defend himself," the stranger said, turning to face Bret. The people who had collected around the dead cowboy backed their way into the hotel lobby or scattered down the street. Tuttle stepped a few yards to the right, and Charlie hurriedly loaded his rifle.

"I'm not saying it was murder," Bret said, cautiously stepping into the street. "But he was little more'n a boy, and you look as if you're more than just familiar with firearms."

"That might be, but he had a gun!" the stranger objected.

"And I'd have dealt with him as well should he have shot you instead," Bret explained. "Now hand over that pistol."

"And if I don't?"

"I'll likely shoot you," Alex Tuttle said, cocking his pistol as he moved in on the stranger's right side.

"Or I will," Charlie declared from the courthouse steps.

"And if they should miss," Georgia Staves called from the hotel doorway, "I won't. That was my window, and glass doesn't come cheap."

The stranger glanced from side to side. It was clear that the slightest movement of his gun would bring a vicious volley. His eyes turned deadly cold, and for a moment it appeared he would force the issue anyway. Then, in a single instant, the grim gaze parted, and the stranger's lips formed an easy smile. The pistol tumbled into the dusty street.

"That's better," Bret said, marching over and plucking the pistol from the ground. "Now come along. I've got a few questions."

"I only defended myself," the stranger claimed.

"He shot poor Josh Powell!" Joe Nance yelled, scrambling to his feet. "The cold-blooded snake deserves to hang!"

"No, Bret," Jack Duncan said, stepping out from the doorway of the Lone Star Saloon. "They were arguing over a hand of cards. Josh had a bit of whiskey. Anyway, Josh pulled his pistol, and the stranger fired out the door so as to startle the boy."

"Almost killed me, too!" the woman in the hotel

room called from its shattered window.

"Wasn't my intent to kill the kid," the stranger argued. "I could have if I wanted. Then out in the street I had no choice."

"That'd seem to be the truth of it, Bret," Duncan said sadly. "I don't figure Josh intended to shoot, but the stranger couldn't know."

"Even so, you've got the look of a man who's killed before," Bret said. "Got a name?"

"A dozen. Try Luke French."

Bret nodded. "I thought I recognized you, French. You once rode guard for the Overland, right?"

French nodded, then accepted his pistol from Bret.

"You're a fair man after all, Sheriff."

"Am I? Well, that could be. At any rate, what would your business be in Palo Pinto?"

"Just heard the railroad was headed here," French explained. "Thought there might be a game of cards to be had. The Flat's about played out, and there's no money in Jacksboro these days."

"There's none here for you anymore," Bret said, pointing toward the livery. "See the pistol's packed away. Next time you're in town with it, I'll be locking you away. Consider yourself fortunate that Jack here supports your claim. There's to be no more cards, though, nor drinking, either. I heard about the two freighters you shot in Young County. Fair fight or not, I'll not have gunfire in my town."

"As you call it, Sheriff," French said, the smile falling from his lips. "You've got the odds on your

240

side, and I'm too old to draw against a stacked deck. May come another time, though. Nearly always does."

"Maybe," Bret said, shaking his head. "But I seldom allow myself to be put at a disadvantage. And I rarely return a man his gun a second time."

French turned and stalked off toward the livery, and Palo Pinto breathed a collective sigh of relief.

French's departure failed to usher in either peace or quiet. Bret or Tut were busy most of the afternoon separating quarreling neighbors or disarming some drifter wandering into town. Joe Nance and a dozen hands rode into town an hour before sunset in search of Luke French, but fortunately the gunman had already departed.

"Is this how it's to be until the railroad's finished?" Bret asked Charlie. "Lord, a man could tire of this real quick."

That night gunshots disturbed the night. Twice some young vagabond took aim at the moon. Fortunately the wild shooting found no targets, and Bret disarmed the malefactors and locked them in the storeroom which doubled as the county jail.

Little changed by the time the first rays of morning sunlight greeted Charlie Justiss's weary eyes. He'd awakened a dozen times after the last of the shooting. Once a rummaging cat and later a noisy weathervane had disturbed his slumber. He couldn't help worrying about Bret, for the young sheriff was as much a son as Ross or Chris or Joe.

Charlie kept his thoughts to himself, but the anxious look in Victoria's eyes when she dropped off the children on her way to the schoolhouse warned Charlie he was not the only worried soul in Palo Pinto. The fact that Bret and Tut both carried shotguns as they made their morning rounds reflected their concern.

"I've never seen Bret this nervous," fourteen-year-old Joe Justiss told Charlie.

"He was up cleaning that shotgun all night, Papa," Chris added. "Is this all 'cause of the railroad? Can't we just tell Uncle Bowie to send it somewhere else?"

"It's not the railroad exactly," Charlie told them as he led the way outside.

"Then what?" Joe asked, his usually clear blue eyes suddenly clouded with worry. "Papa, I didn't much like the look of that French fellow. He never even flinched after shooting Josh Powell. Josh wasn't but four years older than me."

"And not as smart," Charlie said, gripping Joe's shoulder. "It's pure stupidity to ride into town with a pistol strapped on your belt. It's gotten many a man prematurely buried."

"Sure," Joe said, nodding gravely.

Just then someone whooped loudly from the western edge of Front Street, and a wide-bottomed wagon raced through town. Half rolling out the back end was a woman of generous proportions dressed in a lavender petticoat and waving a pink garter in one hand.

"Papa?" Joe gasped as the woman flipped the garter in the air. Chris jumped to the street and caught it.

242

"Come see me, sonny!" the woman called. Chris returned the lady's smile, but Charlie quickly snatched the garter from the boy's hand.

"Ah, Papa," Chris objected. "I'll be thirteen in another month."

"Not if your mama catches you with this," Charlie declared.

Then two other wagons rolled along. Each was loaded down with scantily-clad girls. A half dozen town boys bound for the schoolhouse followed, whooping and calling for the wagons to halt.

"Can't we chase 'em, too?" Joe asked with wide eyes. "Please, Papa?"

"Not a prayer," Charlie whispered, nodding toward the door where Angela stood, hands on hips, a great scowl painted on her face. "She believes they should all be stoned, you know."

"Those girls?" Chris asked, blushing slightly as he eyed the garter concealed in Charlie's fist.

"I don't see what's so bad about them, Papa," Joe grumbled. "Marty says they're just entertainers."

"He does, eh?" Charlie asked. "And just what sort of entertainment does Marty say they provide?"

"Oh, he says they work the soreness out of a cowboy's muscles," Chris said, grinning. "All his muscles."

"They take the chill out of a winter's night," Joe added. "I wouldn't mind letting 'em try that with me."

"It's not winter," Charlie said, clasping a firm hand on each boy's arm. "I believe I'll have to have a long talk with the both of you tonight.

243

Could be some extra prayers are in order."

"Do you have to ask forgiveness for just thinking about doing something, Papa?" Chris asked.

"Depends on what that something is," Charlie said, trying not to laugh as he gazed at the dreamy look in Chris's eyes. "You boys ought to know this much, though. If your mama hears you even looked toward those girls' camp, she'll skin your backsides raw with a willow switch."

"Yes, sir," Joe mumbled, flinching at the thought. The more adventurous Chris seemed less chilled by the thought.

"Now off to school with the two of you," Charlie said, turning the boys toward their slates and books neatly stacked beside the door. They went inside and grabbed their things, then raced off toward the schoolhouse.

"What's that you have in your hand, Charlie?" Angela asked when he joined her at the door.

"Oh, something Chris found," Charlie said, stuffing the garter in his pocket.

"I believe you'd better take a walk down past the schoolhouse around noon recess," she advised. "You know how the boys like to romp around the river."

"Good idea," Charlie agreed.

"See to it they don't wander too far, Charlie Justiss. They're the same age Billy and Ryan were when you took them to Kansas. They've heard me speak of the wages of sin often enough to know better, but boys have a wide-eyed way of forgetting such things when a petticoat shuffles by."

"I'll speak to the boys tonight," Charlie promised. "Don't hold it against them too much, dear. It's in a boy's nature to wonder at new things."

"Just see to it they don't take it into their heads to go sampling the stew, Charlie."

"Trust me, Angela. I can make a fair fire and brimstone speech when I take it into my head. And besides, I don't believe those gals will find Palo Pinto a very good place for their kind of trade."

"I trust not!"

As it happened, by the time the boys escaped Vicki Pruett's watchful eye at noon recess, the inviting eyes and pink petticoats had moved across the Brazos and along toward the rail camps. Joe kicked a rock across the river in disgust, but the younger boys whispered and imagined a thousand tales of aborted adventure.

"I don't guess a braided lasso or a slate would have bought them much company," Bret said afterward. "Poor Joe. I do believe he had his cap set for the one with the dimpled chin."

"I didn't even see her," Charlie said, laughing at his son-in-law.

"Then your eyes have gone, Charlie. In the old days, you'd never've missed that one."

The next visitor to Palo Pinto came not from the west but from the east. Bowie Justiss and Angus Burke arrived on the paymaster's wagon. Almost immediately Bowie sent Burke out to the Flying J to speak to Billy Justiss about contracting beef to feed the workers. Meanwhile, Bowie led his brother inside the courthouse.

245

"How long before you make a decision on the bond, Charlie?" Bowie asked. "We need to know soon."

"I gave the folks a week from yesterday," Charlie explained. "There's a good deal of mixed emotions."

"I heard about the shooting."

"That's part of it," Charlie admitted. "There are the panhandlers down at the river, too, not to mention the, well, entertainers who roared through town this morning."

"Yes," Bowie said, laughing. "You remember me telling you I hired Lafe Freeman and some of his old cavalry mates to patrol the range. They were out looking for that Polk fellow and caught a pair of boys from town out looking for the harlot camp."

"Not any of mine, I pray."

"Farmers' kids, the both of them. Lafe put the fear of God in them, I think. I don't suppose they'd either of them seen a black man wave a pistol about."

"No, I don't suppose," Charlie said, laughing. "You know that Polk's the one who killed Brad Stokely. We caught him raiding cattle, and he talked his way out of a trial. He's slippery, and he's killed lots of men down in New Mexico."

"We're on our guard. You see to it you are as well. Polk's got a taste for bank money as well as railroad payrolls."

"I'll bear that in mind. So, Thorpe's got you handling supply contracts now, does he?"

"No, not at all," Bowie said, sitting across from Charlie's desk. "Truth is Mr. Henry Thorpe's been

246

called away to New York on business."

"Oh?"

"He near ran the line into bankruptcy, Charlie. He sold most of his shares off to a Fort Worth banker. I bought them up. It's why I needed the money I wired you for. I couldn't explain then."

"So Thorpe's not running the FW & W any more."

"No, you're looking at the new president. I own eighty per cent of the line now that I've bought Thorpe's remaining shares."

"With what?"

"I borrowed some against my new house. It will pay off, Charlie. I figure land holdings alone will be worth a fortune."

"Only if they're sold. There are a lot of speculators in town."

"I've had some generous offers, too. That's why I wanted to know about the bond."

"My guess at present would be that the town will vote the funds. There are too many folks desperate to have the line come this way."

"Nevertheless, I'll hold onto the acreage south of Palo Pinto Creek. It's the only other route that makes sense. It wouldn't be a bad location for a ranch expansion."

"That would leave a lot of land in-between, Bowie."

"You've got a lot of sons. I've got one myself who's got an urge to enter the ranching business."

"Clay? He's awful young yet, isn't he?"

"He writes a lot of letters, especially to his cousins. Luis has offered to take Clay and Joe and Chris on this summer, teach them what he

247

knows of horses."

"That would take more than one summer."

"I'd like him to come, Charlie. He's been in that academy in Fort Worth all year, and it's clearly choking him. He's not got the range in his blood like Billy, but it breaks my heart to see him so pale and thin. A boy can't grow tall on stove food and books. He needs to feel the wind on his face, too."

"Are you sure I'm the one you need to tell this?"

"No," Bowie said, chuckling. "It's Em, of course. She's against it naturally, but just now I don't care. Clay wants it, needs it, and I'll see he gets here. He's got a friend, too, a snip of a boy named Bart Davis. The both of them are to come."

"I'll tell Luis."

"You'll ride out there every so often, won't you? I know it would be best if I keep my distance, but I don't suppose he'd be so suspicious if his uncle kept an eye open."

"I'd find my way out there anyway, Bowie. Truth is, with Joe and Chris gone, life here is a little too tame."

"Then it's settled. I'm glad. The last year I feel we've gone our own ways. It was time, I suppose, but Clay, what with no brothers and all, has need of his cousins."

"And they of him."

The two men grinned and shook hands. Then Bowie set off to speak with Art Stanley, and Charlie devoted himself to tending the county's business.

An hour and a quarter passed without incident, and Charlie managed to get the accounts totaled

248

for the month and post two reports to Austin. He was escorting Bowie and Angus Burke to their wagon when a pair of men tumbled through the doors of the Lone Star, shouting curses and swinging fists like a pair of lunatics.

"Stop that!" Jack Duncan cried, swinging an ax handle against the side of the saloon's twin swinging doors. "Stop or I'll fetch the sheriff!"

"No need," Bret Pruett said, approaching the brawling men with care. They both wore tailored suits, though neither was in the fine shape it had appeared in that morning. The men, too, showed signs of their struggle.

"Break it up, I said!" Duncan shouted.

The men continued, though, and Bret handed the saloonkeeper the shotgun which had become as much a part of the sheriff as the small five-pointed badge of office Bret wore pinned to his vest. Bret then stepped between the brawlers, and other men pulled the two apart.

"What's all this about?" Bret asked the angry men.

"He's moved in on my sections," the first man said. "We had an agreement. I was to buy the southwest corner. He had free rein up north."

"I didn't know one end of this county from the other," the second man pleaded. "Any fool can see I was cheated. Up north's all hills and canyon. No railroad's crossing that country."

"Maybe not," Bret agreed. "But you two won't settle anything this way. I catch either of you in Palo Pinto the rest of the week, I'll lock you up. Understand?"

"You can't do that, Sheriff," the first speculator

249

complained. "We all know the town votes next week on the route. We need to be here, not camped off down the river someplace."

"You can stay," Bret explained, "but you'll get little business conducted locked in my storeroom. And if you're still in town a half hour from now, that's where you'll go. Now get!"

Bret applied a boot to each of the quarrelsome speculators' rumps, and the two stumbled off toward the livery. Neither returned.

Charlie hoped that might be the final disturbance of the day, but it wasn't. A half hour later the street again filled with shouting. Charlie spotted a tall, lean newcomer named Landon Jordan standing on the porch of the mercantile. Ten yards away, seated atop of flatbed wagon, was Ernest Grant. Grant was a farmer who'd once ridden with the cavalry out of Fort Richardson. He was nearing thirty now, and he'd bought a small place south of Buck Creek where he grew vegetables and a few acres of summer corn.

"I don't care how many riders you send to visit me, I won't sell!" Grant shouted. "What's more, if you scare my wife and kids again, I'll place a bullet through your skull!"

Grant was clearly worked up, and when Jordan laughed at the threat, the farmer bounded down from his wagon and headed for the mercantile.

"George, Ben!" Jordan called, and a pair of burly toughs intercepted Ernest Grant. The two had Grant pinned to the side of the mercantile, and Jordan rapped the farmer across the chest with a cane.

"Stop that!" Art Stanley demanded. Jordan

250

urned on the old freighter and caned him across he head. Stanley fell bleeding, and Jordan urned back to Grant.

"That'll be enough of that!" Bret shouted, trotting to the mercantile with shotgun in hand.

"No, Sheriff, it won't!" a familiar voice called rom behind Grant's wagon. Bret froze as Luke 'rench appeared with pistol in hand. Charlie never hesitated. He grabbed his rifle from the mantel and prepared to cover French. But by the ime Charlie reached the courthouse door, a crowd had gathered, blocking the view.

"So, Sheriff, you don't appear to have the odds with you this time," French spoke, watching Jordan continue his caning of the defenseless Ernest Grant. "Your town, you call this place? No, it's my town now."

"No, not yet," Bret said, making a half turn.

"Bret!" Charlie shouted. "Wait!"

The young sheriff fixed French in a sour gaze, and the gunman's grin faded. Good though he was, French had to know if that shotgun discharged, pieces of Luke French would be scattered across half the town.

"Luke, what're you waiting for?" Jordan asked.

French hesitated another moment, though, and a rifle shot tore through the air. French stepped back and stared at the loft of the livery. The big open window appeared empty. Only as the pistol slipped from French's fingers did Joe Nance appear.

"Luke?" Jordan called as French dropped first to his knees, then toppled face first into the street. Bret turned the shotgun, and the men holding the half-conscious Ernest Grant stepped back. Instantly Grant seized the cane and slammed it into Landon Jordan's face.

"Stop it, Grant!" Bret called. The farmer couldn't be restrained, though. His own face bleeding and swollen, Grant aimed to transform Jordan's in like manner.

Charlie finally broke through the milling crowd and rushed to Art Stanley's side. The freighter was recovering his wind, and two boys who worked at the mercantile helped the aging man inside. Grant had finally finished with Jordan by then, and Charlie aided the farmer back to his wagon.

"We'd best get you a doctor," Charlie said as Grant wiped the blood out of his eyes.

"I know you think it best, Judge, but I've got to get back to my family," Grant explained. "No telling what that Jordan's like to do now, and I can't have May and the boys facing it alone."

"Tut can go with you," Bret suggested.

"No, we Grants look after ourselves, Sheriff. Thank you the same, but if you'll look to Jordan and his two friends, we'll likely do just fine."

Grant then whipped his team into motion, and the wagon rolled out of town. Bret was ushering Jordan's henchmen toward jail, and Joe Nance stood over the moaning Landon Jordan.

"An eye for an eye," Joe told Charlie. "I know it's old fashioned, but it has a ring of justice to it. We've seen the likes of that French before, too. The county's better with him dead."

Charlie nodded, but he couldn't help wondering who would appear to take French's place. It al-

252

ways seemed such men were replaced by worse ones, and killing always followed killing.

The shooting of Luke French seemed to ignite a powderkeg of trouble. The farmers south of the Ft. Griffin road had long been angry about roving bands of drifters and marauding cows tramping their cornfields. Now, with the streets of Palo Pinto witnessing daily eruptions of gunfire, it seemed time to act.

"We've always known there was a solution," J. C. Parnell told Charlie. "I've held off because you've done your best to control things, Judge, but now we've got to protect our interests."

The following morning Parnell and others began planting fenceposts. Soon thereafter Parnell's sons were nailing strands of barbed wire in place. Joe Nance had riders pulling down fences as soon as they were in place, and farmers and ranchers squared off in angry shouting matches.

"At least they've kept their guns holsterd so far," Bret said nervously.

"Yes, but for how long?" Charlie wondered.

The twin killings of Josh Powell and Luke French mobilized a new force in Palo Pinto. While the Parnells were stringing barbed wire and the Circle N cowboys were cutting it, a drum beat marked the beginning of a rally in front of the Lone Star Saloon.

"Women for Morality," a large banner read. And leading the twenty-five marchers was Angela Justiss, a white ribbon pinned to her hat and a petition in her right hand.

"It's time we put an end to the evils of strong drink in our town!" Angela shouted. "We've seen men shot down in front of our children. Brazen harlots have tainted our town. We must unite and form a compact against these evils. Close the saloons! Outlaw loose women. Save the morals of our husbands and children!"

Loud cheers followed, and the women paraded from the Lone Star to the Brazos Hotel, then along to the smaller drinking houses – the Bluebonnet, Double P, Lucky Diamond and the Cactus. Women charged into the places, rousing intoxicated cowboys, dragging husbands from the bar, occasionally breaking half-empty whiskey bottles on card tables, all the while decrying the evils of demon rum.

"Lord, save us," Marty Steel cried as he escaped out the back door of the Double P. "We're facing the great evil," he told Charlie.

"Oh?" Charlie asked as he fought to calm his old friend.

"I've seen it elsewhere, Major. These temperance ladies busted a saloon plumb to pieces last year up in Young County. Folks up there had no spirits at all from summer till Christmas. Imagine that!"

Charlie laughed, but some of the saloon patrons were less amused.

"Sheriff, they're breaking my windows!" Emmet Votner of the Double P complained to Bret. "Arrest them!"

Bret turned toward the rampaging women and discovered his mother-in-law leading the parade. There was no hope of locking the whole group in the already crowded courthouse storeroom.

"Build me a bigger jail first," Bret said, shrugging his shoulders.

As if a barbed wire feud and a band of female zealots weren't enough trouble, debate on the pros and cons of the railroad continued to rage. Art Stanley hosted a rally on behalf of the railroad's supporters, and he made the mistake of providing a keg of corn liquor.

"See, friends," the detractors cried. "It's happening already. The accursed railroad will corrupt our young people, spoil our community and bring the lawless ways of Satan into our midst."

The Women for Morality sniffed out the spirits and marched into Art's gathering. Judith Parnell, well past fifty, borrowed a railroad sledge and bashed the keg to pieces. Afterward they began burning Stanley's handbills as the stunned railroad supporters scattered to safety.

Charlie Justiss watched the whole business from the courthouse steps.

"Well, what do I do?" Bret asked. "Arrest them?"

Charlie threw his arms in the air and shook his head. It was worse than fighting Comanches!

Chapter 3

If Charlie Justiss expected to find peace in the days ahead, he was sorely disappointed. Angela and her cohorts continued to march from one saloon to the other, decrying the evils of intoxication, and Parnell's fencing crews hourly tangled with Nance cowboys on the south range.

"It was bound to happen," Ross told his father. "Joe Nance's got his whole life tied up in those steers, and with the markets drying up, he's got little choice but to drive them onto that open range."

Charlie understood all that, just as he knew Parnell would continue erecting fences. It would lead to more violence, even killing, and Charlie Justiss felt powerless to halt it.

Even so, if the battle over barbed wire had been the only problem, Charlie might have found a solution. It wasn't. The women in town were battling the saloons, and Art Stanley's pro-bond group was debating those who opposed not only the raising of the bond but the railroad itself.

In the midst of such myriad trials Raymond Polk reappeared. The outlaw and his men halted a supply train in Parker County and made off with crates of dynamite before blasting the boxcars to high heaven. Two days later Angus Burke's survey party fought off the raiders at the cost of one man dead and most of their equipment destroyed. Thereafter, the work gangs were in constant peril, and Lafe Freeman's scouts must have ridden thirty miles a day in search of the phantom enemy.

Polk's outfit didn't limit its targets to the railroad, though. The small farms along Palo Pinto and Buck creeks received their fair share of attention. Cornfields were set aflame, and midnight raids were staged against farmhouses.

"This has to stop!" Charlie declared angrily after riders slaughtered Ernest Grant's chickens and hogs. "It's madness."

But although Bret Pruett and Alex Tuttle made swings along Buck Creek three nights a week, the elusive Polk continued to work his mischief.

"We all know who's behind this," J. C. Parnell angrily told Charlie. "We're not fools. I've learned a great deal about this Raymond Polk. You caught him thieving cows and set him loose. Then out in New Mexico he rode for the cattlemen, shot down poor Mexican farmers at will. Only left when the governor sent troops after him. But a man who doesn't mind the labors his hands are put to can always find employment, can't he? Tell Nance if this Polk shows up at my house, I'll come to his. And then yours."

"You're wrong," Charlie answered. "I've never known Joe Nance to send men by night. It makes no sense. Why, he's made no secret his men are tearing down your fences. As for me, what have I to gain? I don't run my stock on the open range, Parnell, and I don't hire killers!"

"So you say."

"You know me better than to be pointing fingers my way!"

"I only know what I can plainly see with my own eyes," Parnell growled. "You ranchers have never welcomed us, and now you've made up your mind to run us off. Well, we don't scare that easily. And if it's a fight you're after, you'll get one."

Fresh spools of barbed wire arrived, and armed crews of farmers guarded the fences. When Joe Nance sent cowboys to break the fence line, they were greeted with shotguns. Two cowboys were sprayed with buckshot, and Albert Parnell was hit in the knee with a Winchester slug.

"We're going to need a doctor here in town if this keeps up," Bret complained as Charlie helped carry Albert Parnell from the makeshift surgery Angela had set up in the Brazos Hotel. "That or an undertaker."

"Talk to Nance," J. C. Parnell barked as he comforted Albert's tiny daughters. "I warned you. We'll meet fire with fire."

"If you fellows spent half the time figuring a way out of this mess that you devote to planning raids or ambushes, we'd put an end to this trouble," Charlie argued. "You had a close call tonight. Next time someone's apt to get killed."

"Talk to Nance," Parnell repeated.

Charlie shook his head sadly and sent Bret out to the Circle N. Joe Nance was no less open to compromise than Parnell, though.

While Circle N riders clashed with Parnell's farmers, Rame Polk was busy elsewhere. He made a try at stopping the payroll train, but Bowie Justiss had hired extra guards, and when two raiders were dropped from long range, Polk aborted his raid. Even so, the next morning Polk's gang fell upon the paymaster and three guards as they approached the surveyors' camp. All four men were quickly killed, and close to $2,000 was stolen.

"It's time we brought in the Texas Rangers," Bowie suggested when he personally arrived the next morning to pay for cattle the Flying J had brought to the rail camps. "Lafe's done a fair job, but this Polk's too slippery."

"Help's always welcome," Charlie answered, "but these men were killed in my county, and I don't plan to wait for rangers or anyone else. If need be, I'll go after them myself."

"Charlie, I appreciate your feelings," Bowie said, "but it's been a few years since you rode after Stands Tall. This is a task for younger men."

"Younger men have tried. Maybe it's time we

gray beards take a hand."

So it was that Charlie passed the word around town that he was looking for volunteers to scout out Rame Polk. The mention of the generous reward now offered by the Ft. Worth and Western, coupled with the posters from New Mexico, brought out a considerable crowd. Charlie chose only those he knew as steady, among them Marty Steele, Hector Suarez, Bob Lee Wiley, young Andy Coonce, his son Billy, plus Bret Pruett and Alex Tuttle. They'd scarcely begun riding when Lafe Freeman arrived with two ex-buffalo soldiers, Cyrus North and Malachi Johnson.

"So you decided to come to the dance as well, Mr. Justiss," Lafe said, grinning broadly.

Charlie was struck by the jovial appearance of the usually dour Lafayette Freeman. Lafe then held up a shredded money sack.

"You've found them," Bret cried. "How far?"

"Three, maybe four miles," Johnson replied, waving toward the south. "Ezra's trailin' 'em."

"Ezra?" Charlie asked.

"Best tracker south of the Nations," Lafe explained as he turned his horse southward. "Ezra Walker could find a horned toad in a nest of rattlers, and you'd never hear so much as a whisper."

"Well, then let's get about it," Charlie declared, waving for his companions to follow Lafe's lead.

For a time the riders galloped at breakneck speed. Then Lafe began to slow the pace. Charlie pulled up between Billy and young Andy Coonce.

"Stay close," Charlie warned. This is no time to go charging blindly. "This Polk's no fool, and he knows how to set a snare, I'll bet."

Andy nodded respectfully, but Billy only grinned.

"Papa, you worry too much," Billy said, shaking his head. "We know this country. There aren't that many places to hide."

"No?" Charlie asked. "Just every ravine and hillside. Billy Justiss, you keep to my elbow. You, too, Andy. Or else trail Marty. This is no time to grow venturesome, not if you plan to come back in one piece."

Billy flashed a smile, but the solemn gaze of his father soon erased it. Up ahead Bret and Tut were observing a notch cut in a mesquite tree. Charlie joined them.

"It's Ezra's way of guidin' us along," Johnson said, motioning for the others to follow. Lafe had already ridden a quarter mile ahead. "One notch means he's close behind. We're like as not to see their smoke 'fore long."

If Ezra Walker was close behind, though, the riders from Palo Pinto were clearly a considerable stretch back of Walker. The next notch was a full mile ahead, and another mile after that was crossed before Charlie noticed the first sign of a clear track. Hooves had muddied the banks of the Brazos just above Palo Pinto Creek. A quarter mile upstream a notched pole marked where Polk's riders had completed their crossing.

"You were right about your tracker," Charlie told Lafe. "Some would've lost the trail there. Keep an eye out, though. Polk wouldn't take such precautions to conceal his trail unless he knew he was being followed."

Lafe nodded and cautiously examined the rocky hills overlooking the river. But as it happened, there were no outlaws lying in ambush. Only a startled jackrabbit appeared when Johnson scouted the hillside.

"Papa, I can't see the logic to this," Billy declared as they turned eastward toward the Parker County line. "Why'd they hit the paymaster, cross the river toward town, then double all the way back around like this. It doesn't make sense."

"Could be he meant to throw off pursuit," Charlie suggested. "Or maybe he had someone to meet. This Polk seems to know a lot about the railroad. Maybe he's getting information from somebody."

"I've considered that," Lafe said, joining them. "Would seem more likely than not. How'd he know 'bout that paymaster elsewise."

"Loose talk," Charlie grumbled. "Or maybe somebody in town mentioned they'd soon be paid for their goods. Whenever enough folks know, it's possible somebody will talk too much."

"Well, whoever talked this time got four men killed," Bret pointed out. "So far."

As the riders left the Brazos, they became more cautious. Lafe and Bret scouted ahead. Marty rode a hundred yards to the right while Malachi Johnson did the same on the left. The notion of an ambush was uppermost in everyone's mind, and it wasn't eased a bit when Lafe and Bret came to an abrupt halt at the base of a small hill just ahead.

"Wait here," Charlie told the others as he nudged his horse into a slow trot. "Get your guns ready."

Charlie glanced back but once, gave Billy a nod, then rode on to where Lafe and Bret sat atop their horses. Both men were frozen.

"What's happened?" Charlie asked.

Bret's face paled as he fought to speak. Lafe only pointed to the hillside. There, his bare body nailed upside down to a live oak, was the scout, Ezra Walker. The youthful face of the former buffalo soldier was fixed in a horrific stare.

"Bret, it's best the others don't see this," Charlie said as he dismounted and prepared to approach the grim sight. "I'll cut him down."

"No, I will," Lafe said, rolling off his horse and rushing to Charlie's side. "He was my friend. I sent him on ahead."

"Wasn't your fault," Charlie argued as he followed Lafe up the hill. "This Polk's a demon."

"I'll kill him for what he did to Ezra," Lafe swore, weeping as he reached his murdered comrade. "They didn't have to do it this way. A bullet kills just as sure."

"They likely wanted information," Charlie said, touching Lafe's trembling arm. "By the look of things, they were disappointed."

"What could Ezra tell 'em?" Lafe asked as he pried the nails from the tree. "He didn't know anything! If we'd just been a little closer, we'd stopped this."

We were close enough, Charlie thought as he helped free the scout's body from the tree. The corpse had hardly stiffened. Polk's brutality

served him well, though. No one had the heart to
continue the pursuit.

Chapter 4

They buried Ezra Walker at the base of the live oak. Lafe Freeman carved the scout's name in the tree before leading the way back to Palo Pinto. No one spoke much about that ride, but whenever Rame Polk's name was mentioned, men scowled and children shuddered.

By now the tracks of the Ft. Worth and Western were creeping steadily westward from Weatherford. Palo Pinto had become a giant supply depot of sorts. Spring vegetables filled one of Art Stanley's warehouses, and cattle grazed along the Brazos, ready for the short drive to the rail camps. Butchered chickens and hogs filled wagons headed eastward.

As the crucial bond vote neared, Charlie found less and less time for listening to his quarreling neighbors. The Flying J had previously contracted a thousand head of cattle to a Kansas City slaughterhouse, and the animals had to be delivered to the new railhead at Weatherford.

"Soon we'll be shipping them from our own depot," Ross boasted as he and Charlie signed the bills of sale. Billy and a dozen cowboys would

265

deliver the animals to Weatherford.

"I wouldn't be so certain, son," Charlie said, remembering Art Stanley's failed rally. "Seems to me there are a lot of folks about who'd just as soon that railroad passed Palo Pinto on by."

"I spoke to Joe Nance this morning. He's already changed his mind. Now he's dreaming of building a fine station, of adding a hotel down by the river."

"It's your mother I was thinking about," Charlie said, sighing. "She and her lady friends are up in arms about all the drinking, and those loose women passing through town didn't help matters a bit."

"The women don't vote, Papa," Ross reminded his father.

"Maybe not, but now that you're a married man, you must know they do a fair amount of influencing. If it wasn't for the money, some would surely go along with it, but seven thousand dollars is a fair sum to spend for something you're not sure you want."

"You haven't said much about it yourself."

"No," Charlie admitted. "Maybe that's because I've had other concerns. Partly, though, I don't think I'd care to see what's happening over in Weatherford take place here, especially not with Bret wearing a badge. Weatherford lost one sheriff, you know. They've added three saloons."

Soaring land prices along what most took for the right-of-way posed another problem. A strip along the southern edge of the Ft. Griffin road had long been public land, but one speculator after another had purchased sections, and now

266

the prices seemed to rise daily.

The acreage north of the road belonged to Charlie Justiss, and speculators eager to buy it hovered around the courthouse like horseflies in midsummer. Joe Nance faced a similar plague concerning his land east of town.

Landon Jordan concentrated his efforts on the land between Palo Pinto and Buck creeks in the southern half of the county. Much of that land had belonged to the state, but Bowie had seen to it those acres were included in the sections generously assigned to the F W & W. Small farmers owned the rest, and Jordan continued to press his offers. When the price reached ten dollars an acre, two of the three farmers involved sold out. Only Ernest Grant resisted.

"I'll not sell to a man who sends riders out to scare my family!" Grant vowed. Even when Jordan paid a Jacksboro banker to extend the offer, Grant held out.

"The land's not worth more," Jordon told anyone who would listen. "He's just being stubborn."

"It's his land," most replied. "He doesn't have to sell if he doesn't want to."

Grant's feud with Jordan wasn't the sole conflict raging across the county. Sunday morning while the farmers drove their families to church in town, several hundred longhorns were mysteriously stampeded through the fenced cornfields of Pinkney Cooke and Lewis Frost. Hooves trampled cornstalks until there was scarcely more than powder left.

Cooke's son Bailey was the first to spot the damage. The fourteen-year-old jumped from his father's carriage and ran the quarter mile to the farm's northwest fields. By the time Cooke and the rest of the family appeared, Bailey was lying amidst the shattered stalks muttering curses.

Frost was no less shaken. He returned to find milling longhorns grazing in his wife's vegetable garden. The cornfield he'd planted along the Brazos was laid flat by the rampaging cattle. Frost and his twelve-year-old son Carl spent the next quarter hour shooting longhorns. They killed twenty and might have slaughtered more had they not run low on shells.

"I swear this was none of my doing, Charlie," Joe Nance claimed in spite of the fact that more than half the slain animals bore Circle N brands. "I don't like fences, and I hate this notion of cutting up the free range, but I'd never ruin a man's livelihood. I've got too much respect for the land to lay waste to her fruits!"

The farmers paid little heed to Nance's pleas.

"The next cowboy that sets a foot on my land will get himself shot," Frost warned.

"Not in the foot, either!" Cooke added.

When Vicki complained Monday that the farm children were staying away from school, Charlie did his best to soothe her hurt feelings.

"It's nothing to do with you,' he explained. "It's because they don't dare let the youngsters ride to town alone, and they don't trust whoever stampeded those cattle not to strike again if they lower their guard."

Nevertheless, Charlie and Alex Tuttle took a wagon out to the farms and offered to escort the youngsters into town for school. Charlie found the Cooke place fortified. Trees had been felled to form breastworks, and even tiny Bryant, barely seven, held a Winchester.

"I appreciate you coming out this way, Judge,

Tut, but my Celia wouldn't breathe knowing her boys were in town, at the mercy of Nance's hirelings. Besides, I need 'em out here with me."

"I can't believe Joe Nance was back of this," Charlie declared. "As much as anyone, he built this county. He's a hothead, sure enough, but he'd never do a thing behind your back he wouldn't do to your face."

"Somebody did, Judge. Whoever did wouldn't hesitate putting a bullet through a child."

Charlie read fierce determination in Cooke's eyes, and he shrugged his shoulders. There was no point to arguing. He and Tut did no better at the Frost place.

"I'd like to trust you folks," Frost told them, "but there's too much at stake. Ma's got the little ones at their slates, and they'll catch up with their mates once all this is settled. Carl and Ingrid are both quick with their numbers, you know."

"So Vicki's told me," Charlie said, nodding to the youngsters. "You keep a sharp lookout for trouble, Mr. Frost. If we can help, you just send word."

Frost nodded, but Charlie detected mistrust in the farmer's eyes. That was the saddest part of the spreading violence. A man couldn't even trust his neighbors!

Worse lay ahead. Charlie had barely returned the wagon to the livery when he heard shouts from the Cactus Saloon.

"It's Polk!" a young cowboy named Jurgens cried as he fled the place. "Get the sheriff!"

Charlie grabbed his rifle and stepped to the

courthouse door. Down the street a pair of strutting strangers dressed in cowboy garb cleared the street across from the Cactus. Raymond Polk then stepped through the open door of the saloon, his hat cocked to one side and an arrogant sneer on his lips.

"Well?" Polk called. "Where is this sheriff? I'm not exactly hiding, folks. Isn't there somebody around who'd like to take a shot at Rame Polk? Lord knows you've got my picture tacked to half the trees in the county. Well? I'm here!"

Bret emerged from his office next door, and Charlie yelled a warning.

"It's my job, Charlie," Bret responded as he cradled a shotgun and prepared to challenge the killer.

"At least wait for help," Charlie urged. Tut was likely down at the livery, and Lafe Freeman was somewhere about.

"Well?" Polk screamed, pulling his pistol and firing a shot at the church bell. Children in the schoolhouse next door screamed, and Bret started toward the street. Charlie trotted out of the courthouse and joined the young man.

"Wait up," Charlie urged.

Bret slowed, and the two of them headed for the Cactus. By then the street was virtually deserted. A rifle barrel protruded from the livery loft, and Charlie knew Alex Tuttle was accounted for. Lafe Freeman then appeared behind the corner of the mercantile. Cyrus North crept behind a water trough in front of the Lone Star Saloon.

"You've grown reckless, Polk!" Bret shouted as he hugged the wall on the Cactus and allowed Charlie to enter through the saloon's side window.

"You must be the sheriff," Polk said, bowing in

Bret's direction. "Brave man, ain't he, boys?"

The others joined the laughter. Charlie, meanwhile, crept through the Cactus until he reached the open doorway. Plates and glasses lay all over the place, and Emmet Votner, the owner, was nowhere to be found.

"Rame, there's a rifle over behind that trough!" one of Polk's cohorts warned.

"You should've left when you could," Bret told the outlaw. "You're trapped now."

"Am I?" Polk asked, laughing. "Come try me then, Sheriff! See how trapped I am."

Bret was about to step out when a scream unsettled him. A tall, heavy-set stranger threw open the door of the schoolhouse. He held a pistol to the head of little Gail Hockley. Bret shuddered at the thought of Polk loose among the schoolchildren, and he shouted, "Hold your fire!"

"Now, that's being smart, Sheriff," Polk went on. "I've got three men in that schoolhouse, and they've got all those little kids there to entertain 'em. Why don't you go find your banker? See what he's willing to pay to see those kids live through this."

"Banker's out of town," Charlie answered. "It appears you finally miscalculated, Polk. Makes us even. I let you ride off after you rustled some steers of mine a while back."

"I remember that," Polk said, slapping his knee and laughing loudly. "Felt sorry for me, did you, old man? Well, I've laughed about that more'n once, I can tell you ."

"Laugh while you can," Charlie warned. "Your kind of trail proves itself a short ride at best, with an eternity in hell afterward to consider your mistakes."

271

"Don't preach at me!" Polk screamed, firing wildly in the air. "Now, do we make a deal, or do I have Hank there shoot that little girl?"

The large man at the schoolhouse pushed little Gail out toward the street, then waved his pistol in the air. A single shot split the silent afternoon. A puff of smoke appeared at the loft, and Hank fell back into the schoolhouse. Little Gail scrambled away, and before Polk knew what had happened, two more shots rang out from the school.

"Hank wasn't alone!" Polk cried, retreating to the cover of a nearby freight wagon. "I figure this town just lost two of its young citizens, Sheriff!"

Charlie felt his knees give way. Joe and Chris were in that schoolroom. So was Vicki and her little boy, Charlie's namesake. The thought of two killers loose among those children overpowered him.

"Bill, Cole, you best toss 'em a sample to show we're serious," Polk shouted.

Charlie hid his eyes when the door to the schoolhouse swung wide. But instead of some child, a pair of huge black hands shoved a blood-stained figure dressed in homespun cotton out onto the street. A second figure followed.

"It's all right, Lafe!' the booming voice of Malachi Johnson announced. "I got the both of 'em. Deputy took the third. You was right. It was eeeasy."

Polk's eyes lit with fury, and he opened fire immediately. Bullets shattered the front windows of the Cactus, and Charlie flung himself on the floor. Bret returned the outlaw's fire, as did Alex Tuttle from the livery. Johnson and Lafe pinned the outlaws behind the wagon, but when Cyrus North attempted to circle in behind, Polk shot

272

him dead.

"Well, that's one of those black devils!" Polk shouted.

"Cy?" Lafe called.

"I do enjoy visitin' towns," Polk cried defiantly, "but I fear it's time to leave."

A boy suddenly appeared leading four horses from behind the mercantile, and Polk waved his companions in that direction. The three outlaws raced for the mounts. Lafe Freeman fired frantically, and one of the killers stumbled. All managed to get mounted, though, and the four surviving criminals made their escape southward.

"Everybody all right?" a dazed Bret Pruett called as the smoke began to clear.

Charlie crawled out of the Cactus Saloon, and Malachi escorted Vicki and the children out of the school. Bret raced to his wife, picking up little Charlie along the way. Charlie collected Joe and Chris while Lafe Freeman trotted over beside Cyrus North's prone body and knelt beside it.

"Lafe?" Johnson asked.

"Get your horse, Malachi," Lafe barked. "We've got unfinished business."

"You're in no condition to ride just now," Charlie objected. "Let's get organized. We can raise a posse."

"This is personal, Mr. Justiss," Lafe said with blazing eyes. "That snake's killed two friends of mine, and he'd a shot up a school full of children if Malachi hadn't seen 'em ride in. It's time he was hung, and I'm the man to see it done."

"Others have been wronged as well," Bret declared. "My wife and boy were in that school."

Lafe didn't argue. He carried the body of his friend toward the livery.

"Can you see Cy's put in a nice box?" Lafe asked no one in particular. "I'll gladly pay double the going rate."

"I'll see to it," a groggy Emmet Votner answered from the doorway of the Cactus. "You keep your money. I owe you my life."

Malachi appeared with a pair of horses, and the two black men mounted up.

"Wait for us," Charlie called, but Lafe smelled blood, and he was off that instant.

It took Charlie and Bret half an hour to get the posse organized. When word of what happened spread through town, there was no shortage of volunteers. Half the men in town had children in the schoolhouse, and Bret's chief trouble was sifting through the crowd and selecting those men least likely to get themselves or anyone else killed.

While Bret assembled the posse, Charlie loaded Winchester rifles back at the courthouse. They would be needed by the dozen men Bret chose for the posse since few townsmen kept rifles at the ready anymore. A couple of Joe Nance's cowboys had pistols at the livery, but Charlie knew the peril of closing the range with a killer like Polk.

"Papa, you should've seen Malachi," Joe cried as he and Chris helped Charlie ready the weapons. "When those killers were staring out the windows, he crept in through the back door quiet as a ghost. He slipped along the back of the room. Then when Tut shot the one in front, bam! Bam! Malachi killed the other two before you could say 'whiskers'."

"Thank God he was there," Charlie mumbled.

"It was a sight to see," Joe added, slapping his younger brother on the back. "Chris and I helped drag the second one to the door, us being the oldest there and all. Carl Frost's like to have a fit when he finds out what he missed."

"Carl's got enough worries," Charlie growled. "As for you boys, I won't have you boasting about this, telling tales and such. You saw two men die. I'd spare you that sort of thing if I could."

"We know," Chris whispered, holding onto his father's hand. "I remember that day the rustlers came up Bluff Creek. I was real scared."

"Me, too," Charlie said, pulling both boys close. "I thought maybe we'd find some peace at last, but it doesn't appear to be in the cards."

"You're going after 'em, aren't you, Papa?" Chris asked sadly.

"With a heavy heart," Charlie told them. "It's got to be done, though. They've hurt too many people, and they threatened to ... well, they endangered those I hold dear."

"I love you, too, Papa," Chris said, resting a trembling hand on his father's side.

"Be careful," Joe added.

Charlie nodded, then carried the first two rifles out to the street. Bret had his posse lined up and waiting, so Charlie left Joe and Chris to fetch the other rifles.

"Papa?" Vicki asked as Charlie turned toward his house. Angela stood in the doorway, both hands resting on little Charlie's shoulders.

"I'm glad you're safe, honey," Charlie said, kissing Vicki's forehead. "Now it's best I speak with your mother."

Angela Justiss had seen her husband off to war, had bid him good-bye as he'd headed longhorns north to Kansas a half dozen times, and she'd rubbed the ache from his bones and ban-

275

daged the tears in his body brought about by Comanche raiders and cattle rustlers. Charlie never spoke of death, and she never spoke of partings.

"I'll wait supper on you," she said as he held her tightly.

"We might be out awhile this time, dear. You might ask Vicki over."

Charlie then bent down and picked up his little namesake. Charlie Pruett squealed with delight at his grandfather's antics. Charlie then drew the other grandchildren over and kissed their foreheads.

"Mind your mama, little ones, and don't give your Grandmama cause to complain."

"Yes, Grandpapa," they said solemnly.

Charlie swallowed and gave Angela a final hug. Then he trotted toward the livery to get his horse.

Bret Pruett's posse of fourteen riders joined Lafe Freeman and Malachi Johnson five miles south of town. There was no trail to follow, but Lafe seemed to have a clear idea as to their destination.

"I spotted their camp this mornin'," Malachi explained. "We trailed 'em to town. That's how we knew those three were at the schoolhouse. I got word to Tut, but Cy couldn't get to the sheriff in time."

"Well, he purely did his best," Lafe mumbled. "Now the rest is up to us."

Polk's camp was nestled in the hills between the two forks of Palo Pinto Creek. It offered a fair degree of shelter, and there was wild game and plenty of fish at hand. The posse dismounted and approached the place with caution. Bret and Tut led the left wing. Charlie took charge of the center, and Lafe Freeman headed the right.

Lafe's plan was to encircle the camp and rain lead down on its occupants until they asked quarter. Polk had spread six stolen tents out among the rocks, though, and the horses were farther back still. A single fire blazed beside a cook wagon, and crates of supplies were stacked to form a rampart across one side.

"I thought there were just four of 'em," Josie Nelson whispered to Charlie. There were five gathered around the fire, and harmonica music warned of at least one other in a nearby tent.

Josie wasn't the only one unnerved by the size of Polk's gang. Clearly there were eight or nine men down there. There might be a dozen or more, all of them more accustomed to firing rifles at men than the townfolk of Palo Pinto.

"So there are a few more of them than we thought," Charlie said quietly. "Doesn't matter. Get behind cover and fire. You've got fifteen rounds without reloading. With luck, they'll throw in their cards as soon as we open up."

"And if not?" Josie asked.

"Then we're in for a fight. Don't worry. We've got all the advantages."

Deep down, though, Charlie wondered.

An eternity seemed to pass while Charlie awaited Bret's signal to fire. There would be no talking first. The men below were artists where death was concerned, and Bret was determined not to allow them to practice their craft on his companions.

"Now!" he yelled, and the sky seemed to erupt with gunfire. Winchesters barked, and bullets splintered wagon planks, riddled canvas and whined off rocks. Men stood in dismay and were shot to pieces. Others cried out in wonder as bullets found them in their beds, dozing peacefully while death lowered a curtain on their lives.

"Rame!" one called from the cook fire.

"Help!" another shouted.

"Good Lord, help us!" another cried.

In five minutes the Winchesters emptied their magazines into the camp. Then, as a heavy silence hung over the scene, the posse members frantically reloaded their rifles and prepared to frustrate any attempted escape.

"We've had enough!" a thin-faced young man cried out as he slowly rose from under the shattered wreck of the cook wagon. The young gunman was bleeding from both legs and the left side. One or two others also rose, their arms held skyward. Only back by the horses did anyone attempt to resist. A lone rider made a dash for the open, and Malachi Johnson coldly cut him down.

"Where's Polk?" Bret demanded to know.

No one responded. Charlie motioned for caution, then led the way into the camp. Bodies littered the scene. Shreds of clothings and wood splinters covered corpses. Charlie's stomach turned at the sight of men blown to pieces. Josie Nelson retched violently.

"Where's Polk?" Lafe asked the first of the survivors. "Where is he?" Lafe asked, shaking the outlaw by the neck. "Tell me!"

"Gone," the bleeding captive muttered. "Went to meet somebody at the river."

Lafe refused to believe it. He walked through the camp, turning each corpse over in search of the hated young killer. In all six men had been killed. Two others would certainly never make it

278

back to town, and three others would stand trial. None of them was named Raymond Polk.

"We didn't altogether come up empty, though," Bret said as he held up a small tin box. Inside was most of the railroad payroll. In one of the tents Tut discovered a detailed map of the county with certain properties marked in red.

"That settles one point, Charlie," Bret said, pointing out the twin x's on the Frost and Cooke farms. "I didn't think Joe Nance was behind that stampede."

"I almost wish he was," Charlie mumbled. "Because this isn't over yet."

Chapter 5

Charlie was occasionally prophetic, and that night as he rode back to Palo Pinto, he envisioned a new outbreak of bloodshed. Alex Tuttle waited with Lafe Freeman at the ambushed camp in the hope that Rame Polk would return. The gunfire had obviously warned the outlaw away, though. Meanwhile Bret Pruett rode among the farms and warned each one marked on Polk's map that the danger wasn't over.

"Don't worry about Polk," Lafe said when he gathered with the whole town the following morning to bury Cyrus North. "I'll see him laid low. That's a promise."

Charlie knew it wouldn't be that easy. It wasn't.

Palo Pinto was in an uproar all day. The burial of Cy North and the jailing of Polk's two henchmen stirred a great deal of debate. With the bond vote scheduled for the following day, Art Stanley campaigned loudly for votes, but the Women for Morality drowned the old freighter out with cries of motherhood and temperance.

"What does it matter how big we are if our children can't feel safe in their school?" Angela cried.

Placards reading "BOOKS—NOT BEER, BULLETS OR BONDS" were nailed to storefronts. Schoolchildren sang hymns, and preachers led prayer vigils.

Charlie smiled and did his best to stay out of the way.

"They may persuade a few shopkeepers," Art Stanley declared, "but most of the men in town resent a bunch of women telling 'em what they should do. What's more, Joe Nance will bring his whole crew in off the range, and they'll vote for the bond!"

"Don't underestimate those ladies," Charlie warned. "Polk's raid has a lot of folks up in arms, and a dozen cowboys won't swing much weight if Parnell's farmers go the other way."

Art nodded, then saddled a horse and rode out to speak with the farmers.

If nothing else had happened to stir up the town, Charlie figured the vote would have been close. Around midnight, though, a lone rider galloped into town, fell off his horse and stumbled to the old Padgett place where Bret Pruett lived.

"Sheriff! Sheriff! You've got to come help Papa!" young Ed Grant shouted.

Everyone in town must have heard the commotion. By the time Bret opened his door and caught the exhausted boy in his arms, lamps were lit in half the windows on Front Street. Charlie Justiss was one of the first to scramble into his clothes and step outside. Others appeared in nightshirts, waving candles or oil lamps in the dark, fighting to determine what calamity had now fallen on Palo Pinto.

"It's the Grant place!" Bret shouted as he raced down the street toward the livery. "Polk's back. Anybody who can, grab a rifle and get a horse saddled. Young Ed says they've set the house afire, and his Ma's been shot."

Charlie felt a chill run down his spine as he headed for the courthouse. Chris and Joe had spent the evening cleaning and oiling the Winchesters, and Charlie'd hoped they wouldn't be needed again for years. Instead he passed them out to one man after another before heading for the livery.

"Charlie, be careful," Angela called to him. He gazed up in surprise. It wasn't like her to urge caution, but then perhaps she had seen the fury in his eyes.

Bret led the way toward the Grant farm on Buck Creek. As they rode onward, they collected men from the farms until the posse was more like a small army. Charlie suspected the worst when they splashed their way across Palo Pinto Creek. The glow on the southern horizon surely marked the Grant farmhouse, but not so much as an echo of gunfire disturbed the silent night. The fighting was over, and there could be little hope of survivors.

It was worse than anyone could have imagined, and Charlie was thankful young Ed had been too exhausted to make the return ride. Of the house, only smoldering embers remained. The barn stood empty. Cows and hogs and chickens were slaughtered and strewn about the farmyard.

"Dear God," Alex Tuttle cried as he bent down to pick a discarded hat from the ground. Near the rail corral a pair of corpses lay where they had fallen. Ernest Grant was a fair shot, it seemed.

"He put up a fight, all right," Bret mumbled as he climbed down from his horse. In the woods behind the house May Grant lay propped against a live oak, her heart stopped by an outlaw's bullet. Farther back, rifle in his hands, sat Ernest. His chest showed a half dozen wounds. Leaning against his father was ten-year-old Howard. The boy's soft blond hair fell across his forehead down into round blue eyes that seemed to stare skyward in wonder. The child had been killed by a single shot fired point-blank into his heart.

"They could've let the boy go," Tut said, weeping as he bent over and closed Howard's eyelids. "That's the most brutal kind of murder."

"It's Polk's way of paying us back," Bret said, swallowing. "He's letting us know we've got a war on our hands."

"Some of us have fought before," Charlie growled, staring into the dark emptiness with a hatred he'd never known before. "This isn't Comanches fighting for their land. This isn't even a matter of a desperate man striking out at his enemies. This is cold, heartless brutality, and we've got to end it."

The next morning Charlie held a firm grip on young Ed Grant's wrist at the funeral. Charlie spoke gentle words in the hope that they might comfort the distraught boy.

"We live in a hard land," Charlie spoke, "and it demands a great sacrifice from us sometimes. Some men falter in their struggle. Others hold their heads high and pay a dreadful cost. Ernest Grant was such a man, and our town, our county, our world is poorer for his passing. Rest easy, Ernest, May, little Howard, for you are in our Lord's hands now, and your rest will be a long and peaceful one. Amen."

The others echoed, "Amen."

"Papa told me it's wrong to hate," Ed told Charlie after the burial, "but I can't help myself. I heard some of the men talking about how they shot Howie. He never even hurt an ant. Once I saw him hit Carl Frost for plucking the wings off a dragonfly. So now my folks are dead. My brother, too. I'm all alone, Mr. Justiss! What's to become of me?"

"You stay with us for a time, son," Charlie said, pulling the boy close. "Mr. Parnell says you've got an uncle in Dallas. We've sent word."

"He's got seven kids," Ed said, staring up at Charlie like a small, lost pup. "He sure doesn't need another one."

"Well, there's sure to be a battle of it then. Mr. Parnell says he wants you with him, and Chris won't hear of you not living with us. Alex Tuttle's offered you a place with him as well. Seems you're a mighty popular boy."

"You'll catch that Polk, won't you?"

"Bank on that, Ed. If we have to scour all Texas, we'll find him and bring him to bay."

With the vote due to be held in a few hours, Charlie had pressing business at the courthouse. Just the same, he saw to it Ed Grant was moved into Chris's upstairs bedroom before heading on.

As Charlie crossed Front Street, J. C. Parnell took him in hand.

"The sheriff says we were mistaken about that stampede," Parnell said. "I was wrong to speak as I did. I ask your pardon."

"It wasn't you," Charlie said, shaking the old farmer's hand. "It's the times. You're afraid to trust anybody. I know this, though. It's time to quit fighting each other and concentrate on the real enemy."

"And who'd that be? Not Polk?"

"No, he's too young to have long range plans. He lives from one day to the next. The one who's behind all this has an interest in the southern half of the county."

"Only man I know who's shown much interest in that acreage in over to the hotel. Calls himself Jordan."

"The one who beat Grant that day?"

"One and the same."

"We fined those boys of his a hundred dollars or two months confinement," Charlie said, scratching his head. "Fines were paid the next day."

"If it's him, he's played it smart," Parnell declared. "After last night, the vote's sure to go

285

against the bond. That means the railroad's got to turn south. He's got the critical sections already, and he's in a fair way to buy up Grant's land as well. That uncle in Dallas ought to sell easy enough."

"That's where somebody misfigured, though. The law says the county can appoint a guardian for young Ed. I don't suppose Polk knew there was a second son about."

"You got somebody in mind?"

"I plan to talk to Ed some about it."

"I want him to come stay with us," Parnell reminded Charlie. "You name any guardian you like, but the boy ought to be among farm folk."

"Maybe. Just now I think he's better off around my boys. He needs company. Otherwise his misery's likely to eat his insides out."

"You could be right about that, Judge. Tell him he's welcome, though."

"I have already."

"And what will you do about Jordan?"

"Build a snare," Charlie said, spitting a bitter taste out of his mouth. "I know the bait, and I know the trapper."

Parnell proved right as far as the vote was concerned. After listening to an impassioned recounting of the calamities that had befallen Palo Pinto during the railroad's approach, the people rejected the bond. Even some of Joe Nance's cowboys voted nay.

Art Stanley asked for a recount, but the original polling had been extremely one-sided, and

Stanley was roundly booed.

"So that's it, eh?" Bowie asked when Charlie met with his brother that night at the Brazos Hotel. "It's better for our route, but I hate to think of our leaving the town high and dry."

"I believe the town chooses to be left that way," Charlie said, gazing out the window at the street suddenly grown quiet.

"I spoke with Bret about this Polk business. Do you really think he was hired to raid that farm?"

"Seems likely."

"Then there's something you should know. The F W & W holds claim to most of the public lands that will lie along the route down south. I've had a good deal of attention concerning that acreage."

"From anybody in particular."

"One man."

"Landon Jordan?"

"The very same. He's even purchased stock in the railroad to gain leverage. I don't suppose he knew I held eighty per cent."

"Not so long ago you offered me that land, Bowie. Does the offer still stand?"

"You hold my note, Charlie. That would be more than a fair settlement."

"Then let Jordan know he must deal with me."

"You're planning something, Charlie, and I don't like it. You're too old to lead cavalry charges. If you've got yourself in mind as a target, that's crazy."

"No, I've got something else in mind," Charlie promised, but Bowie remained unconvinced.

Bret and Charlie made their plans, then brought Lafe Freeman in as well.

"I don't know that I like this," Lafe said. "Mr. Justiss, you might as well paint a bull's eye on your forehead!"

"It will never get that far if we're lucky," Charlie declared. "You'll have Polk buried before he can harm anyone."

"Yeah, we thought so last time, too," Lafe grumbled. "He's slippery, that one. And he's deadlier than a rattler."

Chapter 6

The Ft. Worth and Western swung southward, making a gentle arc around the town of Palo Pinto and heading into the largely unsettled southern section of the county. As the work crews laid track toward the Brazos and farther west below Palo Pinto Creek, bands of riders spread out in a dozen directions searching for Rame Polk's raiders. But as the days passed into late spring, no sign of the outlaw could be detected.

"Suits me just fine," Angus Burke growled. "That son of Satan's likely found new hunting grounds elsewhere."

Charlie Justiss would have liked to believe that, but wolves rarely departed such fertile hunting grounds, and deep down he knew Polk would reappear, probably at the least convenient moment.

The railroad's swing southwest brought great

changes to the town of Palo Pinto. The army of speculators and idlers departed for the new depot town that was springing up below Palo Pinto Creek. A clapboard sign over a makeshift loading platform bore the title *Justiss Junction.* Most people called the place Wallowville on account of the boggy ground once used as a bathing ground by buffalo.

"All that will change," Bowie boasted as he put men to work constructing warehouses and cattle pens. "Before long the ground will dry out, and this place will be a regular boomtown."

Charlie had a hard time explaining it was that very thought that brought a scowl to his face and a heaviness to his heart. It was essential to ship the stock from somewhere, but the daily arrival of everything from saloonkeepers and freighters to card dealers and women of easy virtue warned that progress was never bought cheap.

The land in and around Justiss Junction belonged to the Justiss brothers, but soaring prices made disposal of small plots too profitable to resist. Speculators and enterprising businessmen scrambled to buy lots near the new depot. Bowie sold his plots shrewdly, waiting on rising prices and then selling off chunks of land a bit at a time. Charlie first dealt with small cafes and boarding houses, but when a widow named Garnett sold her cafe to a bawdy house operator named Snake-eyed Betty Harper, Charlie abandoned all hope. He did, however, turn a good deal of the profits over to Angela so that a section south of Buck Creek could be set aside for a school and an orphanage.

The orphanage itself was planned by Rachel Harmer. Three bunkhouses would be flanked by two barns, and fields for growing corn and vegetables were planted. Bowie donated two hundred acres pasture for cattle and horses.

"Of course, we'll have few customers for the place before the tracks reach El Paso," Rachel said, sighing. "Afterward, I fear we'll be packing them in like cordwood."

The little town at Justiss Junction sprang up seemingly overnight. Angus Burke faced a far more perilous construction task fifteen miles to the east where the F W & W route crossed the surging Brazos. If bridging the Trinity had been a challenge, then constructing a trestle across the Brazos was pure murder. In times of rain, Palo Pinto and Buck creeks drained half the county, it seemed, and those waters poured into the Brazos near the very spot where surveyors had located the Brazos bridge. What was worse, the riverbed was all sand and loose clay. Piers were sunk deep into the base rock, causing great delays and frustration. Often just when it seemed the foundation would at last allow the crew to begin assembling a trestle, some beam would crack.

Bridging the Brazos might have undone Burke's crew had it not been for the tireless efforts of a newcomer. In late May Ryan Justiss appeared in Burke's camp, eager to apply the new training he had received at agricultural and mechanical college.

"That boy's a wonder," Burke told Charlie. "He's

not afraid to strip his shirt and muddy his hands with the boys. He's got an eye for structure faults, and he's quicker with figures than anyone I've known. I thought he'd learn from me, but I'm hanged if I don't daily pick up some new notion that speeds the work."

Ryan's innovations were noticed by others as well. Rachel Harmer had enlisted his efforts digging wells for her camp, and the young woman spent many an afternoon observing the construction of the bridge. In the evening they walked together alongside the river, and Charlie suspected Ryan was the latest of many to fall under Rachel's bewitching charms.

"I wouldn't be surprised to learn they've pledged their affections by midsummer," Angela told Charlie. "I've never seen Ryan so struck by anyone."

"Do I detect a mother's approval?" Charlie asked.

"You do. Ryan's in need of a firm and settling hand. What's more, Rachel's as fine a person as a mother could wish her son to find."

Charlie grinned. Angela was surely plotting now, and the two unsuspecting youngsters were clearly headed for the spider's web.

Summer brought about the first Justiss family gathering in what seemed a decade. Although Emiline would have wished it held in her turreted house in Ft. Worth, Bowie and Charlie settled instead on the new Spur Hotel at Justiss Junction. To no one's surprise, Ryan escorted Rachel

292

Harmer. Ross and Eliza ruled the dance floor, but the belle of the ball was certainly Emiline, dressed as she was in a New Orleans gown of fine silk with Belgian lace cuffs and French petticoats.

Bret and Vicki ushered their little army of youngsters along, and Angela devoted the better part of her time to tending the little ones. She found an eager helper in little Bart Davis, who of late was never far from his erstwhile brother Clay.

While the elders danced and chatted away the evening, Clay himself joined forces with his cousins Joe and Chris to set off firecrackers and in general torment anyone within reach. It wasn't until Luis Morales hogtied the troublesome trio that peace descended on the Spur.

"It seems like we've ridden a far ways since leaving Robertson County," Charlie remarked to Bowie when the brothers freed their hooligan sons. "These three were barely old enough to keep their britches dry at night."

"Well, times do change," Bowie lamented. "We've done our own fair bit of fashioning it so."

"Yes," Charlie agreed as he removed a wad of cloth from Joe's mouth. "And these boys will finish the job, I fear."

Maybe it was that notion of a world slipping away from him that prompted Charlie to visit Luis's mustang camp later that week. Clay and young Bart were there, as were Joe and Chris. The Justiss boys had grown up with half-wild horses, but range mustangs never ran short on

293

new twists and foul tricks that sent teenage riders flying. As for Bart Davis, the splinter of boy seemed destined to spend half of June sleeping on his belly.

"Best fasten a mattress to your hindquarters, son," Marty Steele advised. But Bart was nothing if not game, and Charlie admired the manner in which the little orphan kept at each task.

"Puts me in mind of Bret Pruett," Bowie said, laughing as Bart took yet another spill. "When his uncle all but abandoned the lad, I couldn't help taking him in. Must be in the blood, this tendency to adopt strays. Ryan's taken to Rachel, and Angela's determined to house and feed half the urchins in Texas."

"There are worse vices," Charlie remarked. "I suppose it's on account of knowing the pain of want. A man who knows another's need is faster to help salve it."

"I imagine that's so."

"Sometimes I wonder how much longer boys will be able to run down range mustangs out here," Charlie said, gazing off into the distance. "Wasn't it just yesterday we were heading up the trail to Kansas, Bowie. Now the railroad's practically at our door. I pass my days in an office at the courthouse and you . . ."

"Shuffle papers and send telegrams. I miss the old times, too, Charlie."

"Emiline doesn't."

"No, she's taken to city life. Her one sadness is that Clay never has. Ag college has worked a miracle with Ryan, though, and it might do the same for Clay. If not, there are worse futures than ranching."

"I can think of a hundred."

"It seems odd we should be standing here, watching the youngsters work horses and talking about their futures. I don't feel so old, Charlie. They sneak up on you, these boys of ours. One day you've got 'em on your knee, listening to yarns. The next they're spinning their own."

"Well, there's grandfathering to do, too."

"Now you really do make me feel my years."

"It happens. Range gets fenced, and towns grow. Men turn gray and their bones turn weary. That's progress, or so I'm told."

"Progress," Bowie mumbled. "If you really want to see progress, come down to the river day after tomorrow. The bridge will be finished, and Angus plans to run the work train into Justiss Junction. Would you care to come along on the first run west of the Brazos?"

"Boys might like to come along as well."

"No, they've got their horses. It's for old men to mark the passage of time while young ones concentrate on the use of those same minutes."

"I suppose. I would like to come along, though. I'll see if Angela can come."

"It might be better if you bring your rifle instead. Lafe's seen signs of riders."

"Polk?"

"Was bound to be around come payroll."

"Then it'd be best if Bret came, too. I'll have Billy send some men out from the ranch as well."

"Might be wise."

As with the Trinity bridge, Angus Burke had the construction crew initial the completed structure. By ten o'clock the work train was inching its way across the trestle. Charlie wished the train would speed along and have done with the crossing, but he knew it was wise to proceed gingerly on the odd chance that some rail or beam might be flawed.

"There's no need to worry, Papa," Ryan assured his father. "Angus and I looked it all over ourselves. Sound as a dollar."

"Paper or silver?" Charlie asked.

"Well, not Confederate. That's for sure," Burke said, laughing loudly.

The engine picked up speed as it neared the far side of the bridge, and the workers gathered along the river banks cheered and threw their hats in the air. The passengers inside answered in kind. The engineer blew his whistle, then shoved the throttle forward. The massive gears turned, and the train roared westward.

Charlie sat back in his cushioned chair and watched the countryside roll past his window. Armed railroaders appeared from time to time, obviously guarding the flanks of the track. In the mail car Alex Tuttle stood guard over two large chests. With Tut sat Marty Steele, Bob Lee Wiley and young Andy Coonce.

In Justiss Junction the depot platform was lined with merchants and vendors. Farmers brought their whole families to witness the arrival of the first train. Women held infants in their arms, and dogs howled in dismay at the thundering, smoke-breathing monster.

Gazing out the window, Charlie couldn't help feeling a twinge of regret that Palo Pinto would never witness such a spectacle. Even the loose women who haunted the far end of the tracks and the gambling tents along Buck Creek might have been tolerated for a time.

He had no time for further reflection, though.

"This is it!" Angus Burke cried. "Ladies and gentlemen, we're in Justiss Junction, final stop of the line."

Some of the passengers who'd ridden from Marshall clapped their hands. The long journey in the June heat had taken a toll. Exhausted and sweat-streaked, most of the travelers prepared to exit the car quietly, for Justiss Station was but the starting point on a longer journey via stagecoach.

"Well, what do you think of our railroad, Major?" Burke asked Charlie as the two followed Bowie out onto the platform.

"Truly a marvel," Charlie remarked.

Burke then turned to supervise the unloading of the mail pouches. After the mailbags had been dispatched on a stagecoach, a pair of broad-backed railroaders began lugging the two heavy chests from the mail car.

"That's far enough!" a voice suddenly shouted.

Charlie turned in time to see Rame Polk and a trio of men emerge from the crowd. Each held a cocked Colt, and Bowie motioned for his guards to lay down their weapons.

"It was as easy as you said, Rame," one of the outlaws said, racing to where the chests lay. When he opened the chest, though, the smile fell from his face.

297

"It's just paper!" Polk gasped as his bewildered comrade held up scraps of newsprint. "Where's the payroll."

"Delivered yesterday," Bowie explained. "By the same men who've got their guns on you right now, Polk. Give it up. There's no chance of escape."

"Give it up?" Polk said, laughing. "I'll see you all in hell first."

A rifle fired from atop the mailcar, and the outlaw standing beside the chest clutched his forehead and collapsed. Another fell from a second shot. Polk and the remaining gunman withdrew toward the edge of the platform, firing wildly. Charlie scrambled to safety as the platform quickly turned into a madhouse. Stampeding onlookers sought to escape the fusillade. Lafe Freeman and a dozen railroad guards kept up a hot fire on Polk, but the outlaw continued to return fire. Rushing passengers and terrified visitors masked Polk's withdrawal.

"There'll be another day!" Polk shouted as he smashed a lantern into the ticket office and set the depot alight. "I'll be back!"

As flames licked at the walls of the ticket office, railroaders abandoned their pursuit of Polk in order to douse the fire. Lafe appeared vexed at having again missed the killer, but the youthful faces of the dead raiders attested to the fact that Rame Polk was no longer able to be selective in choosing companions.

"He's on the run. That's clear," Bowie observed as the fire was extinguished.

"That one can run a hundred ways in as many

days," Lafe grumbled. "Slippery as a watersnake, he is. We'll be settling accounts soon, though."

"I hope you're right," Bowie told Lafe. "It's time."

Chapter 7

In Palo Pinto word of Polk's raid spread through town in a grim whisper. Men whose familiarity with weapons was limited to hunting rifles and fowling pieces purchased Winchesters from Art Stanley. Farmers kept their wives and children close to home, and range crews kept a sharp watch. When the stagecoach from Jacksboro was ambushed, Bret Pruett sent out a call for a posse.

"Leave it to the rail detectives," Charlie Justiss urged.

"No, this was done in my county," Bret declared. "It's my duty to deal with it."

"There are duties and duties," Charlie argued. "I know all about honor. I fought a war for what some called honor. In the end, survival was more important. Don't forget that there are those who depend on you."

"I can never forget that," Bret said somberly. The young sheriff's eyes blazed as he glanced toward the schoolhouse.

"You could get yourself killed, son."

"I know that, Charlie, but what kind of man could I call myself if I backed away from this? I sure couldn't pin that badge on my chest. You had responsibilities when you took on Stands Tall. There are things you have to do, even though there are risks involved."

"But Polk . . ."

"You heard what the stage passengers said. There were but three outlaws, and two of those appeared reluctant to fire their pistols."

"A single man can kill as sure as twenty, Bret, and Polk has the devil's way of eluding capture. There's a viciousness to the way he strikes out at anyone and anything in his way."

"All the more reason for bringing him in."

"You'll never do that," Charlie grumbled. "His kind won't throw even a bad hand in. He'll fight it out. And, Bret, don't you give him a hair of a chance. He'll kill you. Or others."

"I'll keep that in mind, Charlie," Bret said, shaking his father-in-law's hand.

An hour later Alex Tuttle assembled a posse on the courthouse steps. A few who were too old or too young to ride after the likes of Rame Polk were sprinkled through town to guard the bank and the freight office. Billy Justiss rode in with Marty Steele and Bob Lee Wiley and Andy Coonce from the Flying J. Lafe Freeman and Malachi Johnson appeared with a pair of railroaders. The remainder of the posse was composed of townsmen and a pair of farmers.

While Tut organized the men and equipped those not armed with Winchesters, Bret walked to the schoolhouse. The children were at recess, and Bret wrapped a weary arm around little Charlie, then sent the boy back to his playmates.

"I've been expecting you," Vicki said when Bret entered the silent classroom. An odor of chalk and damp clothing clung to the place, and he

301

paused long enough to replace a discarded slate on a nearby bench.

"Then I guess you know I'll be gone for a time," Bret told her. "Don't wait supper."

"Talk to Papa. I'm sure he'd rather you stay in town and let Tut handle the posse."

"That's my decision to make, Vee," he said, taking her hand and pressing it to his chest. "Don't worry. I can take care of myself."

"Don't worry?" she gasped. "This Polk's killed men. Don't I know? I witnessed his raid first-hand, remember? He sent his men into my school. Why, he'd think less of shooting you than a normal man would think of squashing an ant. Bret, this is a task for Texas Rangers."

"No, it's for me to do. Please, Vee, don't let's spend this time quarreling. The children will be stampeding back here in a moment, and I can't ride off knowing we're at odds."

"Then don't."

"Vee, you know I have to go."

She frowned. Such an admission was not forthcoming, but she rested her chin on his shoulder, and Bret knew she would speak no more against his going.

"Have you said good-bye to the little ones?" she whispered. "I saw you with Charlie. Hope and the boys are with Mama. If anything were to happen . . ."

"It won't!"

"Of course not," Vicki said, nervously shuffling her feet. "But if it did, they'd want to remember you kissed them good-bye. You always do."

"Yes," he mumbled.

"Ask Mama if she and Papa will join us for supper. They haven't been over in a while, and I'd welcome their company."

"I'll tell her."

"Bret, you'll take care, won't you? I remember how foolhardy you were as a boy, always climbing the tallest trees or running down angry bulls. Don't get yourself killed! I need you."

"I wasn't planning on giving Polk a chance to kill anybody. I'd like to think we'll put an end to all that."

"Just don't let him put an end to you, Bret Pruett," she said, holding him tightly. "I rather love you."

"I love you, Vee," he said, closing his eyes and clutching her with all his strength. "And I'll be back."

After stopping by Angela's house for a brief chat and a farewell kiss from the little ones, Bret trotted over to the courthouse. Tut had a horse saddled and waiting. Bret mounted and led the way out of town.

"We'll see that Polk strung up to a white oak!" Clancy Parnell boasted. "He can't be far!"

"Yeah, and you keep hollerin', he'll be even closer," Marty said angrily. "Keep quiet or Polk'll be the least of your worries, friend."

"Good advice for us all," Bret declared. "Now, let's see what trace of a trail we can find."

The posse rode northeastward toward the river, crossing upstream of the stagecoach route to Jacksboro. Before long they reached the scene of the stage holdup. From there tracks of fleeing ponies could be spotted in the sandy soil.

All too soon the trail played out. Polk wasn't foolish enough to leave a trail, not with the reward on his hide mounting daily. The horses headed into the rocky hills above the river, and

Bret called a momentary halt.

"Thing to do is fan out, see what we can spot," Bret told the others. "My guess is that he's circling around, headed for the south. There are too many folks up here in the north part of the county for anyone to remain unseen for long."

"Who'd notice a drifter down south, though?" Clancy Parnell asked. "We get a dozen no-accounts passing by our farm every week. And down below the railroad tracks, there's nothing at all."

"Used to be," Clancy said, frowning. "The Grants had their farm there."

"Polk'd know that country," Tut pointed out. "We hit his camp down that way, remember?"

"He wouldn't go back to the same spot," Bret argued. "It would be inviting trouble."

"Oh?" Billy said, shaking his head. "This is the same fellow who raided Palo Pinto in broad daylight, who hit the train depot on the busiest day of its history. He hasn't shown a lot of good sense that I've seen."

"Well, arguing's getting us nowhere," Bret announced. "Pick a partner and fan out. Everyone ride in twos or threes. I want nobody by himself. That's an invitation to get killed, and I'd as soon bring you all back. We'll meet for supper on Buck Creek if not before. Understood?"

The others voiced their agreement, and Tut paired off the men. Soon they were headed out across the county, twenty solemn, cold-hearted riders in search of an elusive quarry.

Bret and Tut rode along the Brazos. It was an unlikely route, but Bret held out hope of picking up the trail if Polk made a crossing south of the Weatherford market road bridge. Few riders muddied the water thereabouts, and if Polk had, indeed, turned south, perhaps the outlaws hadn't hidden their trail too carefully.

Most of the afternoon the two lawmen wandered the Brazos. They found nothing, not even so much as a disturbed cattail. Bret was thoroughly frustrated. As he munched a cold biscuit from his provision bag, he imagined the fine supper Angela Justiss would oversee back in Palo Pinto. A bowl of soup seemed fine fare compared to the cold meal the posse would sup that night.

By late afternoon half the posse had given up the chase. Farmers like the Parnells had families waiting. Others wearied of the chase. Those who stayed collected near a small spring and ate jerked beef and cold bread. At dusk Billy Justiss heard horses splashing through Buck Creek a mile or so away. He and Andy Coonce set off to investigate.

"You disappointed we didn't scare up their trail?" Tut asked Bret after the two riders left.

"If you mean am I looking forward to squaring off with Rame Polk, no, I am not." Bret mumbled to himself, then stared southward. "I am determined to see those outlaws brought to task. I'll do whatever has to be done to see it happen."

"And the rest of us? That Coonce boy's hardly begun to shave."

"Polk isn't a lot older himself. The two that were shot at the depot were young, too. Texas grows her sons up quick."

Their conversation was interrupted by the reappearance of Billy Justiss.

"I don't know that it's them, Bret," the young

rancher explained, "but we followed that Jordan fellow and somebody else better'n a mile to a fork in the creek. They appear to be waiting for somebody."

"That'd be a fair wager," Bret said as he grimly waved the others to assemble. "Well, Billy, lead the way."

"Sure," Billy agreed.

For a mile or so Billy led the way along a clear trail following Buck Creek. Then Bret spotted Andy Coonce watching from horseback perhaps a hundred yards ahead.

"It's like Billy said," Andy explained. "They're clearly waiting for somebody. I never trusted that snake, Jordan."

"I've been a little surprised he hasn't had anyone chasing Charlie," Bret whispered. "We expected it when the title to the Grant farm was transferred. Maybe he was up to something else, though."

"The railroad," Lafe suggested. "There's been talk of a new partner."

Nice way to buy into a railroad, Bret thought as he dismounted. Rob the payrolls, burn a few camps, a station maybe, and watch the schedule fall behind. And who better to do the job than a renegade killer like Rame Polk?

The only thing Bret couldn't figure was the stage robbery. Why bother with such a trifle? But then men like Polk were often hard to control.

Bret formed the posse in a crescent. Tut took the right, and Bret assigned Marty and young Andy Coonce to help. Lafe and his three companions formed the left. Bret kept Billy Justiss, a Circle N hand named Kilpatrick and Bob Lee Wiley in the center.

"Hold your fire till Polk shows," Bret instructed the others. "Follow my lead, and shoot for effect."

"Don't you plan to warn 'em?" Andy asked.

"What I don't plan is to get any of us killed," Bret answered. "Polk's slipped away more than once. If he gets loose, more people will likely die."

"He's right," Lafe agreed.

Tut nodded his head, and the others followed. Soon the posse fanned out so that they encircled Jordan. The speculator's companion built a small fire and soon had a pot of coffee brewing. The aroma of the coffee drifted through the cool, damp air, speaking to Bret of home and comfort. It was a stark contrast to the cold grip that was even now seizing his insides.

What was it Charlie Justiss had said when a rustler's bullet laid Bret low that first trail drive into Kansas? Nobody lives forever. It's not the time a man has but how he spends it. Those were old man's words, comforting to gray heads and wrinkled foreheads. They were lost on the young.

Bret had too many dreams yet to fulfill. There were Vee and the children back home. The horse ranch Luis was turning toward prosperity was only now bringing in income. Little Charlie would need a father's stern hand, and who would escort Hope to the altar if something were to happen to Bret?

No, he voiced silently. I'm not ready to end my life as of yet. There's too much still to be done.

The icy chill seemed to pass. In its place came a fierce determination. Bret Pruett was, above all else, a survivor. Charlie had spoken of survival that morning, but what did he know of burying a family, fighting winter's chill at twelve with little more than rags to wear, nothing but turnips and sweet corn to eat?

I've been through worse, Bret told himself. And so he ran his fingers along the cold barrel of the Winchester and readied himself to fight.

Most of the night Landon Jordan and his companion sat beside the fire and waited. Bret allowed some of his men to sleep while others watched. It was a wise idea, for the sun was creeping over the horizon before the sound of hooves on the rocky ground warned of approaching riders. Jordan pulled a revolver and rose to his feet. Anxiety was sketched on his brow. Then Raymond Polk and two youthful riders appeared, each cradling a rifle and smiling sourly.

"About time," Jordan declared, holstering his gun and waiting for Polk to dismount. "I thought maybe you forgot."

"I don't forget anything that's got to do with money," Polk snapped as he jumped to the ground. "You recall you promised me five hundred dollars for jumping that payroll."

"You missed it, though," Jordan pointed out. "To make matters worse, you hit that stage on the Jacksboro road. What manner of foolishness was that? Half the county's out looking for you."

"A man's got to eat," Polk said, spitting tobacco juice at the fire. "That payroll wasn't on the train. Besides, it does our enterprise good for those sheriffs not to get too certain as to my plans. After we hit the Grant farm, I had to ride a hundred miles. Lost some good men to a posse, too. You should've had someone in town deal with that other Grant boy. I shot his kid brother for nothing."

"I'll bet you stayed up nights worrying over that," Jordan said, laughing. "Anyway, I brought the money. What's more, Potts here says the next payroll will be carried by those darky guards of Justiss's."

"Be my pleasure to meet them, yes, sir," Polk boasted. "I got a fine way of handling 'em."

"You just see you get the money. Unless they're broke, the railroad isn't about to part with shares, and Justiss and his brother own that prime land along the right-of-way."

"That'd be your business," Polk said, taking a leather pouch and counting the greenbacks inside. "I'll tend to my part of the arrangement."

"See you do."

"And is that supposed to be a threat?" Polk asked, turning angrily toward Jordan. "What do you think you can do to me, turn me over to the sheriff? How long you suppose he'd stay alive drawing down on me? Then you'd have a first-hand demonstration of how a man's skin gets peeled from his bones."

"I've got friends, Polk," Jordan warned.

"All your friends put together wouldn't fill a privy, Jordan. You see you don't run crosswise of me, hear?"

Jordan shuddered, but Polk merely laughed and passed out shares of the money to the grinning boys still sitting atop their horses.

"Long as he's got coffee on that fire, can we have a cup?" a sandy-haired youngster of seventeen or so asked. "Eh, Rame?"

"Why not?" Polk said, waving his cohorts toward the fire. "I'm sure Mr. Jordan here meant for us to share in his good fortune. Night's peculiarly chilly for June."

"Sure is," the second boy, a sullen-faced youth of perhaps twenty, added. "Rame, should I tie off the horses?"

"Leave 'em," Polk said. "Do 'em good to graze awhile."

As the outlaws gathered with Jordan around the small fire, Bret readied himself.

"Pass the word," he whispered to Billy. "Close in and be ready."

Billy nodded, then set off to tell the others. By the time he returned, Bret had a rifle trained on Polk's forehead. The two brothers-in-law said nothing, just nodded in the faint light cast by an orange sun. Bret counted silently, then aimed and fired.

Polk was less than a hundred feet away, and if all had gone as expected, the Winchester's first shot would have torn the outlaw apart. At the instant Bret fired, though, the sullen-faced outlaw turned and intercepted the bullet.

"Rame!" the twenty-year-old gasped when the bullet tore through his heart. The young outlaw's bloody corpse fell across Polk's knees.

"Scatter!" Polk shouted as the woods exploded with gunfire. Jordan was still holding a tin cup to his lips when three shots smashed his chest. The man Jordan had called Potts never even looked up. A Sharps ball slammed into the back of his head. Only Polk and the younger of his outlaw companions escaped that first volley.

"Rame, hold up!" the boy cried desperately as rifle fire tore apart the camp and stampeded the horses. "Rame, I'm hit!"

"So's the pity, Nevins," Polk called as he

310

threaded his way into a pile of boulders. "You're on your own!"

For a time the fury of the fighting ebbed. Nevins fought from behind a fallen oak, keeping the posse at bay for a moment. Malachi Johnson slipped around from behind and shot the youngster dead, though.

Now the noose around Polk began to tighten. But Rame Polk had learned a few tricks in his year riding the lawless trail, and he fought back stubbornly and with great effect.

Andy Coonce was the first to feel the sting of Polk's rifle. The young cowhand was creeping through the rocks when Polk suddenly popped up and fired. Andy gazed up in surprise, then rolled off into the brush like a fallen sparrow.

"Andy!" Billy Justiss cried, rushing through the underbrush like a man possessed. Bret and Tut opened up a withering fire on the rocks, and Polk was forced to take cover.

"How many you got left out there, Sheriff?" Polk called when the firing abated.

"More'n you," Bret answered.

Billy dragged a stricken Andy Coonce to cover, and Alex Tuttle made a move from the right. Again Polk sensed it coming and fired to deadly effect. Tut staggered, then fell, moaning.

"You all right?" Bret yelled.

"Leg's shot," Tut answered, "but I can still shoot."

"Your turn, Sheriff!" Polk shouted. The outlaw laughed so loudly so that the trees seem to ring with the haunting words. Bret reloaded his rifle and paused a moment.

"You've got family," Marty said, appearing suddenly at Bret's side. "I've popped weasels out of

311

their dens before."

"No," Bret said, holding his old friend back. "I've got the badge."

"You've got young ones waitin' for you to come home, too," Marty reminded him. "This isn't like rounding up rustlers."

"Maybe not," Bret agreed, "but whatever it is, it's for me to do. The war's fifteen years over, Marty, and I'm younger and quicker."

"Maybe," Marty said, stepping back. "You've that on your side at least."

"Then let's hope it's enough. Cover me."

Bret waited as the others opened up a furious volley on the rocks. He then made a mad dash toward Polk's position. One of Lafe Freeman's railroaders made a like charge. Polk rose from the rocks and aimed his rifle right at Bret, but his attention was drawn away by the railroader's charge. The bullet that might have smothered Bret's dreams knocked the railroader from the rocks instead. By the time Polk turned back, Marty, Bob Lee and Kilpatrick has resumed their covering fire.

"Come on, Sheriff," Polk taunted as he recovered his breath. "I saw you down there. Isn't much farther. I'll make it quick and easy for you, not like with those buffalo heads the railroad sent. Come on. I'm waiting."

Bret swallowed a surge of fear and bit his lip. Blood seeped into his mouth, and he forced the numbness out of his feet. Fear gnawed at him like a hundred cold, silent daggers. He finally hugged his rifle and moved along. Polk fired twice, and Bret answered. For fully five minutes the two of them exchanged shots as Bret crept ever deeper into the tangle of boulders and briars. Then a bit of cloth waved through the gunsmoke ahead, and Bret fired.

"An old trick," a haunting voice called from Bret's left. A barechested Rame Polk fired, and Bret only barely dodged the fatal shot. Even so Bret found himself pinned by what soon became a murderously close pattern of shells.

"Hold on, Bret!" Billy called, starting out from the trees.

A shot from Polk sent Billy diving for cover.

"Stay put!" Bret ordered. "He's up in the trees, and he's got too clear a field of fire."

Even in the faint light, shrouded by the acrid smoke of gunpowder, Bret could tell he faced a desperate struggle. Each time he tried to move, Polk would open fire.

"How does it feel?" the outlaw taunted. "Ready to die, are you?"

"Are you?" Bret answered. "I'm far from dead."

"You sure? How many shots you got left for that rifle? Five? Six? Won't be long 'fore your friends turn to their own business. I'll have the whole day to finish with you. Ever tasted the blade of a Bowie knife?"

Bret recalled the awful spectacle of Ezra Walker and again bit his lip. Courage often flowed from anger, and it was fury that sent Bret forward again. He'd managed to crawl fifty feet when an uneasy feeling settled over him. He heard a hammer click and froze.

"A bit careless, Sheriff," Polk said, his feet snapping twigs as he approached Bret's back. "Turn around, won't you? I want to read the look on your face when I kill you."

"Why bother?" Bret asked, feeling his knees wobble.

"Call it a courtesy. Do drop that rifle first, though. A man lives longer when he doesn't press the odds."

Bret felt the Winchester slip from his fingers. He envisioned little Hope's bright eyes, the frown that would take possession of little Charlie's small face as the news reached Palo Pinto. He turned slowly, hoping to prolong life as long as he could. When he finally glared up at Raymond Polk's laughing eyes, he felt a huge weight press down on his chest.

"So, Sheriff, you didn't snare me after all," Polk said, rocking on his knees. He started to speak again, but the dense undergrowth exploded. The outlaw's chest seemed to surge ahead of the rest of his body. Blood poured out of his bare flesh, and Polk's hands lost their grip on his rifle.

Lafe Freeman stepped out of the trees as Polk slumped to his knees and pitched forward.

"He should've stayed put," Lafe declared as he kicked the outlaw's corpse with his boot. "He was good, but he made a mistake. He forgot about me."

"Yes," Bret said, leaning against a tree for support. "And he wanted to see my face.'

"Lucky for you. I'd allow him no such edge. In this game, it doesn't figure to give a man many chances to kill you. They catch up with you."

"I owe you my life," Bret mumbled.

"No, Polk was overdue for the graveyard. Malachi and I were close to him last week, and he could've got shot at the depot."

"Thank you just the same."

"Well, could be when this railroad's built, I could wind up needin' a job, Mr. Bret Pruett, sir. You keep me in mind, will you?"

314

"Anything that's mine to give is yours."

"Fair enough," Lafe said, kicking Polk's corpse a final time as if suspecting the demon might rise from the dead. "Now let's see about gettin' these shot up boys of yours back home."

Chapter 8

Raymond Polk was buried with his unknown companions on the lonely, forlorn hillside where they'd fought and lost their final battle. A sister claimed Landon Jordan's body, and the speculator was carried east on a Ft. Worth and Western supply train.

The town of Palo Pinto welcomed the returning posse as heroes, and although Bret Pruett insisted Lafe Freeman accept most of the credit, the reward money was split among the men who'd stayed and dealt with Polk.

Within a week all the survivors save Andy Coonce were up and about. Alex Tuttle walked with a limp which Angela Justiss claimed worsened at the approach of any female above the age of sixteen. And if complaining was an indication of recovery, Charlie judged Andy would soon be riding the range once more.

"What range there is to ride," Joe Nance grumbled when Charlie passed on the word. "More wire strung every day it seems, and I'll bet young Ross hasn't had a day this month when he hasn't issued title to some stretch along Buck Creek or up north along the Jacksboro road."

"Bound to happen," Charlie said, shaking his

head sadly. "Once the Comanches were gone, the population was bound to start west again. Too many young men eager to try their hand with cattle. Now the railroad's through, there's little risk to the business. So long as the price holds."

"And how long will that be? You know yourself, Charlie, we're flooding the markets."

"Oh, I don't know. I hear there's a new wave of settlement hitting the midwest. Prosperity's come to the cities. Hungry mouths have to be fed."

"I hope you're right. You know yourself that some of the big outfits in Young County pulled up stakes and headed out onto the Llano. I heard there are some ranches up in the Panhandle that cover three counties. A man that's got that kind of acreage has no need of open range."

"Thinking of selling your place, moving along?"

"Oh, I spoke to Randolph on it," Nance mumbled. "He's of an age to try new things, and it would be a chance to leave his father's shadow. As for me, I'm too old to go anywhere else. My roots are here. I've buried pieces of my life in this county, and it's where I plan to lay my bones when the time comes."

"That's a ways off."

"Is it? You know I feel every horse I ever rode on winter mornings, and the breaks in my hip warn of storms. Much as I'd like to think I'll live forever, it's not likely to happen."

To hear a man like Joe Nance talk of dying turned Charlie Justiss to thinking again of the changes that had come to his beloved valley. The Comanches were gone. There were fewer traces of them every year. Ryan had sent more Herefords out, and the cross-breeding was already taking its toll of the doughty longhorns. A few more shipments would leave but a few hundred of the ungainly twisted-horned creatures. The shorter legged, round-shouldered offspring would soon dominate the Flying J.

"Had to happen, Papa," Ryan remarked as he packed his gear in preparation for continuing southwest with Bowie's construction crews. Ryan planned to pass the remainder of summer aiding Angus Burke and learning firsthand the skills of an engineer.

"Well, I feel like I'm losing another old friend," Charlie grumbled.

"Do what some of the folks down south are then. Save back a hundred head or so for old times sake. Fence 'em off from the rest, though. Otherwise those longhorn bulls will be no end of trouble."

"Sounds fair. I'll speak to Billy about it."

"You really ought to fence the boundaries, too, Papa. That stretch north of the Ft. Griffin road is wide open to rustlers, and it's too tempting by half. There's no other range still open to 'em from the Flat."

Charlie nodded. The Flat? The town was practically deserted. Rumor had it the post at Ft. Griffin was to be abandoned soon. Soon the road westward would be called the Albany road after the new county seat of Shackleford County.

Charlie recalled the first time he'd ridden toward the Flat, how buffalo still grazed in their hundreds and Comanches remained master of the plains.

"Papa?" Ryan whispered, breaking Charlie from

318

his recollection.

"Just thinking back," Charlie confessed. "We'd best get you along to your train. Burke won't wait forever, you know."

"He'll wait a bit. Isn't every day he finds an engineer to help who'll do the work of five for free."

"I'd say you're getting your fair share in the bargain, son. How many of your ag college friends have a chance to ply their trade on the Ft. Worth and Western?"

Ryan smiled, and Charlie pulled his son close for a moment. It seemed that sandy-haired scamp of a boy had grown up overnight.

"Best say your good-byes to your mama," Charlie said, swallowing his own sadness and urging Ryan toward the house. "Don't be too long."

"No, sir."

That afternoon Charlie had gripped Angela's hand as Ryan boarded the work train at Justiss Junction and headed on to the construction camps. Afterward Charlie led the way toward the new cattle pens.

"When will you start shipping from here?" Angela asked.

"Next week," Charlie responded. "A thousand head. Another five hundred come September, and again in October. Bowie's railroad's apt to make us rich."

"We already are," she told him. "In all that really matters."

"I've thought so for a long time. Vicki's done fine for herself, and the boys are gaining ground. Ross's about taken over the courthouse, and Billy's done well with the ranch. I worried about Ryan, but after the work he did on the Brazos

319

bridge, I couldn't be prouder."

"I believe Rachel Harmer will be keeping him out of trouble from now on."

"He's still got some schooling to complete. Don't forget that. As for Rachel, she seems too even-headed to take on a wild mustang of a Justiss."

"Oh, we women have our way of breaking a bronco, Charlie."

"Do you now?"

"Yes, indeed."

They laughed at each other. As Charlie took her hand and headed them back to where a carriage awaited, Angela rested her head on his shoulder.

"It will be quite an event, won't it?" she asked.

"What?"

"The shipping. I've never seen it before. Why don't you bring the little ones? It's something they should see, the first shipment of Flying J beeves from Justiss Junction. Don't you think?"

"That's a fine idea, Angela. Luis can bring that wild bunch of his along, too."

"Do you mean his family or ours? Teresa rides herd on her children like Luis guards those Arabians."

"I meant Chris and Joe, though from what I hear, young Clay and that Davis boy are as good at making mischief as our pair of scalawags."

"Maybe when it's all over, you can take the four of them up to the cliffs, tell them about Stands Tall."

"Oh, there's not much up there anymore, Angela."

"Memories," she said, holding him tightly. "They're as much a legacy of this place as any longhorn steer."

He nodded, and they turned toward the carriage.

So it was that Charlie gathered the four young mustangers, together with Vicki's brood, and watched the Flying J crew herd cattle into the waiting pens at Justiss Junction. Little James Patrick and Thomas probably understood little of it, but Charlie knew it might well be important to them one day. Hope and little Charlie coughed away the dust and listened to their grandfather's tales of the wild days of driving longhorns north to Kansas.

Was it only ten years ago that we started that first drive? Charlie asked himself as he witnessed the children's amazement at a world now altogether foreign.

"Oh, well," Bret said, laughing when the youngsters abandoned Charlie to chase each other around a berry patch. "It's a day to remember, and as such, it's lost on the young."

Charlie nodded his agreement.

That night he and Luis took Chris, Joe, Clay and Bart Davis to the cliffs. Charlie himself had not been to the heights in weeks, and he discovered the place profoundly changed. Few signs remained of the old Comanche burial ground, but even so, the wind seemed to whistle a haunting refrain across the summit. The boys appeared especially uneasy, and when Charlie gathered them together and began spinning his tales, they grew quite fretful.

"None of that really happened, did it?" Bart

asked.

"All of it," Luis said, waving his hand at the land below. "Many was the time we felt death hanging over us like a cloud, but we always found the strength to continue, to prevail."

"It's like that day when we were chasing the horses along Rock Creek," Clay said solemnly. "We were all tired, ready to roll off our saddles and die. But Luis said to reach inside and pull together what was left. We had to go on or be prepared to fail ourselves and our friends. We went on."

"I thought for sure I'd die," Bart added. "I think my legs about did. I was so chafed I thought I'd never be able to walk natural again."

"You get through things," Charlie said, pulling Chris and Joe nearer. "That's the legacy I'd leave you boys. The knowledge that you're strong enough to do what's required, that you'll stand for what's right and be true to your beliefs."

"Yes, sir," Chris said, giving his father a rare pat on the shoulder. "And you don't mind too much if we have a bit of fun along the way, eh, Papa?"

"No," Charlie said, grinning.

They shared the midnight sky atop the cliffs, and they watched the sun break bright and golden across the eastern horizon. It was a special, magical moment, and Charlie read in the eyes of those four youngsters the same awe and wonderment that he'd once felt in watching the marvels of life unfold.

"It's a new day," Luis declared, urging the boys to roll their blankets and prepare for the ride back to Fortune Bend and a hard day's work with the horses.

"Yes, a new dawn," Charlie agreed. A new beginning of sorts. Perhaps it would be a finer, brighter day that awaited those boys. And if there were no Indians or buffalo, Charlie knew other challenges would take their place. For the Brazos country was a hard land, and it grew only the best of men.

These'll do, Charlie told himself, grinning at the youngsters. They'll carry on.

IV

THE CRUSADE

Chapter 1

With Rame Polk dead, the railroad surging westward, and hundreds of cattle being shipped from the station at Justiss Junction, life in Palo Pinto should have returned to normal. Memories of Polk's raiders died hard, though, particularly when Alex Tuttle limped around town on a bad leg and young Andy Coonce passed two full weeks on his back at Charlie Justiss's house.

There were daily calls for changes. Some suggested hiring a second deputy, perhaps a man familiar with firearms who would be able to stand up to the likes of Polk.

"Bret was up to the task this time," Art Stanley said, "but what about next week or next year?"

"It doesn't do us much good to have a sheriff who's going to get his head blown off by some cowboy eager to test a reputation," Charlie argued.

"If I had my way," Angela added, "I'd see all the guns in town mounted on walls or stored in trunks."

"Yes," several town ladies agreed.

"That's what they did in Abilene," Alice Hart declared. "Wes wrote me a letter from there about it years ago. From one end of town to the other, only the sheriff and his deputies could wear a pistol. Isn't that right, Charlie?"

Charlie suddenly found himself encircled by a crowd of townspeople.

"That's what they did," he admitted. "It would be hard to enforce out here. We get cowboys in and out of town who need their guns to shoot wolves or snakes. Art Stanley's freighters have to guard against thieves."

"It would be a start," Angela argued. "But the real trouble is the whiskey."

The women grumbled in unison, and Charlie retreated immediately. Within minutes Angela and others were arguing for a law closing down every saloon in the county.

"Well, at least we're safe on that account," Marty Steele told Charlie from the doorway of the Lone Star Saloon. "So long as men do the voting, you won't get whiskey outlawed in Texas."

"Look there, Marty," Charlie said, pointing to the demonstrative ladies up the street. "I wouldn't etch anything in stone if I were you. Those females may not have a vote, but they've sure as thunder got a say."

That became even clearer the final sweltering weeks of summer. Angela took the opportunity to argue temperance at least once a day, usually at dinner. With Joe and Chris still off breaking mustang ponies at Luis Morales's ranch at Fortune Bend, Angela was less than shy about arguing. Poor Andy Coonce, barely on his feet, was subjected to all manner of examples of the evil of strong drink.

328

"Now Miz Justiss," Andy said, "you know I'm only eighteen. I've not been alive long enough to've done half the things you're warnin' me against. I've tasted a drop of spirits, I confess, and I've shot at men. Mostly they were already shootin' at me, of course. If you ask me, we've got a pretty calm town here, and there isn't half the cause for worry that you think."

Charlie grinned, but Angela only bided her time. When a pair of drunken cowboys shot the cross off the church steeple the next Friday night, Angela and her female friends marched up and down Front Street, demanding the culprits spend a month in jail.

"They've paid for the damage," Charlie explained. "We've got no place in the courthouse fit to keep grown men for four days much less four weeks."

"Then it's time we built a regular jail," Angela suggested.

"And who's to pay for it?" Charlie asked. "Who would pay for the food your prisoners would eat? The county does well to buy a few new books for the school."

"There are those who would help with the work, and others could buy lumber."

"Others?" Charlie asked. "You mean me?"

"I know the Parnells would gladly contribute money for a jail if that would quiet some of Joe Nance's lawless cowboys. Lew Frost is a fair carpenter, and the Parnell boys are handy enough with a hammer."

Charlie didn't respond. He'd argued personally for a jail and sheriff's office ever since taking office as county judge, but no one else had seen the need.

The jail was only part of Angela's plan for Palo Pinto. She envisioned a new courthouse, too, and she'd spoken for adding onto the school ever since it had been moved out of the Methodist church. Palo Pinto's growing population had need of more room, and some suggested relocating the school south of town where it was closer to the many farm children who attended.

"A thriving county needs an appropriate seat of government," Angela told Charlie. "Your office is so full of deeds and papers that you can scarcely breathe. It's time we moved into the nineteenth century. If we don't do it soon, we'll have missed it. We'll find ourselves in 1901 with no hope of ever catching up."

Charlie understood her wish to improve the town, but building cost money, and the ranches had struggled lately. There hadn't been a particularly good year for corn since the war, so the farmers were hard-pressed as well.

By late summer the talk had gathered force, and every Sunday after services the women collected to argue for temperance and a new school and against the wearing of firearms within the town limits.

Summer's close brought Chris and Joe back to the house. Andy Coonce was well enough to return to his duties at the Flying J, and Charlie complimented Angela on the ease with which she replaced her boarder with the two boys. Bart Davis and Clay passed two nights in town as well prior to their departure on the eastbound train to Ft. Worth.

Ryan spent two days in Palo Pinto preparatory

to his return to college. His tales of wild country to the west reminded Charlie of his long journey from Robertson County to Palo Pinto back in 1870. Ryan spoke of more than the country and Bowie's railroad, though.

"I've grown really fond of Rachel Harmer," he explained. "She's the finest person I've ever met. Her tireless efforts on behalf of those orphans put me to shame. Mama, the railroad will soon be finished. It wasn't long ago you and Rachel made plans for an orphanage. I wish you'd put your mind to making the place come into being. Poor Rachel's got enough to do just seeing to the needs of all those urchins. There must be a hundred now, and by winter they'll have no place to be at all."

"They will have," Angela promised, and Charlie started considering when the ranch could best spare men to construct the barns and bunkhouses.

By the time Ryan left, the county began to feel the full weight of progress. Trains stopping at Justiss Junction dropped farmers eager for new land. Merchants came as well, hoping to ply their wares at the junction or its growing neighbor town to the north. For the first time Palo Pinto had its own doctor. Soon a barber appeared, followed by a saddlemaker and a tailor.

In September the growing population of the two towns attracted the attentions of less desirable elements. Three caravans made camp just south of the bridge across the Brazos east of town. By the following morning, bright tents sprang up. "Miss Molly's Palace of Delight" was brightly painted across the front of one, and the others featured faro and roulette, poker tables and cheap beer.

Nightly, cowboys made their way to "Mollyville" to sample the hospitality of the Brazos belles. Other frequent visitors to the camp included Art Stanley's drivers and guards. Once a week a gang from the Justiss Junction cattle pens would pile in the bed of a wagon and follow the river to Miss Molly's tents.

"This is the devil's doing," Celia Cooke cried out in church. "We should put those harlots on the first train east! Do you know my boy Bailey was out there yesterday watching 'em bathe? Naked, in full view of the innocents, they were. Why, Judith Parnell says they even waved to Albert!"

Charlie held back a notion to speak. Albert was married with daughters, and Bailey Cooke, at fourteen, was as old as Joe and probably every bit as innocent.

Following Celia Cooke's speech, the women met for nearly an hour in the schoolhouse, arguing bitterly about what was to be done. Thereafter Mollyville was known as "Deviltown" and spoken of daily.

Charlie hoped the storm would blow over. Harlots had been a constant presence on the Texas frontier ever since San Jacinto. According to some accounts, the true hero of the Texas Revolution was a well-endowed woman of easy virtue who distracted Santa Anna from more pressing matters and allowed the Texans to strike the Mexican camp by surprise.

Charlie knew better than to mention that to his wife. Angela had made it her personal crusade to rid the county of Deviltown, and no argument known to man would deter her.

Angela's attitude grew more intense the next week when she accompanied Celia Cooke to the river. Charlie was afraid to let them go alone for fear they might set upon Miss Molly with sticks. He was not surprised to discover Molly's maidens bathing in the shallows, but he was not prepared to find Chris and Joe among the dozen or so youngsters observing the event from the nearby bridge.

"Lord, help us!" Bailey Cooke cried as when his mother yanked him to his feet.

"Papa?" Chris gasped as Angela appeared.

"I think you boys best come along home," Charlie said as their mother's face changed from pink to scarlet. The other boys scrambled in panic toward the far side of the bridge, covering their faces and praying no one had recognized them.

"I see you, Jasper Grimmitt!" Celia shouted. "You, too, Tom Ingram and Phillip Rivers. You boys will pay for surrendering to the devil's temptation!"

"That's right!" one of the girls in the river called. "Best learn early, boys. You always pay!"

The other girls laughed loudly, and Celia turned toward the river, shook her fist and began quoting scripture. If she had been a prophet loosing bolts of lightning she couldn't have painted a more fearful picture of the fate awaiting the female sinners. Charlie escorted his sheepish sons back up the road and tried to keep from laughing at the guilt-etched faces. Angela followed closely, muttering as she searched the nearby peach trees for an appropriate switch.

Once back home, Charlie marched the boys to their room, then led Angela into the kitchen and tried to soothe her ruffled feathers.

"It was harmless enough, dear," he whispered, holding her tightly and mopping her fevered brow. "Boys are just bound to be curious, and all they did was watch. I used to steal a glance at the Lambert girls once in a while when I was their age."

"Charlie, I won't have it," she stormed. "Harlots bathing in full view of schoolboys. Why, it's just as that other group. We sent them on their way, and we'd best do the same with this batch."

"They'll only move downriver to the railroad bridge," Charlie declared. "You can't build a fence around our town and keep out everything you don't like."

"I can keep my boys from visiting Deviltown."

"How long? Another year, two, maybe five? They're good enough boys, you know. They're probably mortified that you caught them on that bridge."

"They should be."

"Let me have a talk with them. I'll see they don't return there."

"I suppose you think a good talking will suffice?"

"If you'd like, I'll nail them to the privy."

Charlie grinned and lifted her chin. She wasn't about to be coaxed out of her anger, though.

"Charlie?"

"Well, the church is in need of a fresh coat of paint. I'll see they volunteer for the task."

"That's better. It still wouldn't hurt them to feel

the touch of a switch to the seats of their pants."

"Oh, I think the painting's enough. Besides, they're likely scared half to death just waiting in their rooms all this time."

"They should be."

Charlie lifted Angela's chin again and kissed her forehead. Finally she cracked a smile, and he kissed her again.

"It wouldn't be natural for them not to take a look," he whispered. "I'll see to it that's as far as it gets."

"Do that, Charlie. And scare 'em halfway to Kansas, too."

He nodded, then headed out the door with a grin on his face.

"Papa, you know we only went on account of what Mrs. Cooke said in church last week," Chris pleaded when Charlie confronted the boys. "We seen girls before, you know. Wasn't so long ago that other batch was taking baths there, too. Must be a good spot, huh?"

"Yeah," Joe added with a smile.

"Then I'd judge it a place you should avoid like a pit of rattlers," Charlie warned. " 'Cause if your mama ever catches sight of either of you doing any such thing again, you'll wish you were a yearling calf at branding time."

"Yes, sir," the youngsters said in unison.

Charlie then explained about the punishment and further assigned a pair of Angela's favorite Bible verses for reading. Satisfied the boys were as penitent as could be expected from lads of thirteen and fourteen, Charlie rejoined Angela.

Sunday after worship Angela and the other ladies suddenly vanished. They reappeared shortly, however, wearing white bonnets and carrying a banner reading "Women for Morality". Mary Grimmitt began pounding a drum, and before Charlie realized it, the women were singing hymns and heading for the river.

"Oh, Lord," George Grimmitt gasped as he hurried after his wife. Other men collected their children and herded them back inside the church. Charlie sent Chris and Joe to help Vicki get her young ones home, then grabbed Bret Pruett and headed after the marchers.

"Ladies, please!" Bret shouted, but the marchers were intent on continuing. Charlie waved his son-in-law along, and fortunately the two men were able to head off the rampaging ladies halfway to the river.

"Of all people to stop us!" Angela complained. "Bret, you ought to be down there arresting those harlots. As for you, Charlie Justiss, I hope you like eating tinned beans!"

The others grumbled their own objections to the march's premature halt.

"Tell you what," Charlie said, turning toward the tents. "I'll go have a talk with Miss Molly. Maybe she'll move along of her own accord. You don't really want a fight, do you?"

"We mean to chastise the wicked!" Celia Cooke replied, raising a Bible in one hand and a hammer in the other.

"You've got ten minutes," Bret said, nudging Charlie toward the mobile brothel. "I don't think I

336

can hold 'em off longer'n that."

The ladies nodded and began singing again. Charlie turned back but once, staring in disbelief as the entire hillside seemed to fill with angry hymn singers. He could only pray Miss Molly would listen to reason.

"So, the old crows are gathering," Molly Sharpe said when Charlie appeared in the open doorway of her tent. "I heard how they ran Hanna Spring's bunch out of here in the spring. I don't run, you know."

"I'm Charlie Justiss," Charlie said, introducing himself.

"I know who you are," Molly answered. "In my business, it pays to learn who the judge is. So, do you mean to throw us in jail? Fine us? Isn't that how it works? We help your road fund or something, and you let us stay?"

"No, that's not how it works," Charlie said, refusing the handful of bills she extended toward him. "Trouble's brewing. I came to warn you."

"Thanks, Judge, but we can take care of ourselves. Me, I've been through three sour marriages, two labors and had myself run across half of Texas by Comanches and bluecoats. I've got a shotgun that's real handy for keepin' wolves at bay. Ought to work on crows, too."

"You wouldn't want to do that. Right now this is a matter of some difference of opinion. You raise a gun, and the law takes sides. You're smart enough to know which side of the line the sheriff will be on."

"I don't scare!" Molly shouted.

"You ought to. You may have run across Comanches, but that's my wife out there. The reason the Comanches don't still camp here is that she chased them off. You haven't dreamed of the kind of tempest she's going to raise over your heads."

"We've got to live, Judge!"

"Sure, and I hold no great grudge against you doing it in Palo Pinto. But your girls didn't exactly keep to the shadows. Taking your baths beside the main road in broad daylight where half the little boys in the county . . ."

"Not all those boys were little," Molly objected. "A few of 'em came to call on my girls."

"Please, keep that to yourself," Charlie said, wiping the sweat from his forehead. "Stoning hasn't been in fashion for a long time, and I'd hate to see it start up here. Can't you pull up stakes and move across the river, maybe head downstream a few miles?"

"Cross the river? There's hardly enough business here as it is. We could, I suppose, follow the river south a mile or so. It's not as good a spot. Here we catch all the road traffic, and word gets around the junction that we're in business."

"It'd be a start," Charlie told them. "And if you'd take your baths in the evening or early morn . . ."

"Sure, Judge. Anything to keep the courthouse quiet. Want me to have my girls wear sackcloth, too?"

"Have them wear something," Charlie told them. "Just remember this. If those ladies down there took it into their heads, they could storm down here and chase you all clear to Weatherford.

338

Some among them know how to apply tar and feathers, too."

For the first time Molly cringed. Charlie knew her fingers longed for the aforementioned shotgun. He turned toward the door and headed for Angela's brigade.

"Well?" she asked when he arrived.

"They've agreed to move, and they promise not to take their baths in the daylight near the bridge."

"They should be run off a cliff!" Celia shouted. "Corrupting the morals of our children!"

"Yes, Celia," Charlie said. "But this way maybe they'll have a chance to consider the evil nature of their ways. Perhaps they'll repent."

"You're sure they'll move, Charlie?" Angela asked.

"I'm sure of nothing other than the fact that I'm tired and hungry," he told them. "Bret, you coming? Let's go see if that pretty wife of yours has Sunday supper cooking."

"All men are the same," Celia lamented. "They think all a woman can do is cook and clean. We'll have Victoria with us next time, Sheriff. Wait and see."

Bret shook his head in dismay and started back toward town. Charlie followed, thinking Celia was probably right.

By midafternoon Deviltown had pulled up stakes and relocated two miles to the south. The new camp was half-hidden by a grove of willows, and Charlie hoped it would be at least a week before the boys discovered the belles' time and

339

place of bathing.

Meanwhile Angela's crusade gathered force. The women, elated over their victory over the harlots of Deviltown, were more determined than ever to close the saloons, inspire the men to sign the temperance pledge and bring peace and quiet to Palo Pinto.

Chapter 2

With the Women for Morality marching and singing and passing some new petition around almost daily, Charlie Justiss was more than a little relieved when his son Ross suggested they ride out and explore the new acreage acquired from the Ft. Worth and Western. The new range sprawled across the southern quarter of the county, offering good grass and plentiful water for stock. The trouble was nearly eight miles of open range and small farms split the newly acquired land from the rest of the Flying J.

"With land prices as they are, there's little profit to selling it off," Ross lamented as he led the way on horseback south from Justiss Junction. "Just now there must be half a dozen outfits running longhorns out here. And we don't even have a man looking after our interests."

"Interests?" Charlie asked, laughing. "The only use we've had for this country as of yet is to water the stock we're readying for shipment. Ryan's putting us out of the longhorn business,

341

and the new breed's building slowly."

"Papa, you know what should be done," Ross said, scratching his chin. "We ought to bring in a couple of hundred Hereford cows, breed them with a premium bull, and generate a pure Hereford strain out here. It would give you a chance to compare them with your cross-bred longhorns."

"And who's going to keep two hundred Hereford cows from mixing with the range cattle?"

"You know the answer to that," Ross said, frowning. "Barbed wire fences. I'll bet Marty Steele could have a crew out here tomorrow, and they'd have fences up in two weeks. Uncle Bowie had the boundary surveyed. There'd be nothing to it."

"Except Marty just might knock your front teeth out. He's not high on fences, you know."

"Oh, he's smart enough to know it's going to happen sooner or later. What's more, if he was put in charge down here, he'd grow downright possessive of this country."

"You know your Mama's picked out that hill where the railroad crosses Buck Creek for Rachel Harmer's orphanage. Bowie's set aside the nearby fields and some range for cows. I'd like for us to contribute a like section of range."

"I thought about that. Truth is, I figured when Ryan gets through with his schooling, he might want to supervise the new acreage."

Charlie scratched his head. Already Ryan was writing letters about new notions for improving the breed and expanding the ranch.

"So, that would provide for Ryan," Charlie concluded. "Billy has the main ranch to tend. Chris and Joe are a little young to worry over yet. What about you, son?"

"I'll have my law practice. I've saved some money, and I've considered building a small house and office on the outskirts of town. The ranch has a lot of land along the Jacksboro road, and Eliza's spoken of raising chickens. And maybe some kids."

"Even with you helping out at the courthouse, there's scant work for a lawyer in Palo Pinto, Ross."

"There will be. Besides, I'll have the ranch accounts to manage, and in time, Senator Rogers thinks I have a fair chance to get myself elected to Congress."

"Providing your mama doesn't petition the place out of existence."

Ross barely grinned, and Charlie gazed in surprise.

"Papa, I'm proud of what she's doing," the young man explained. "She's fighting for what she believes, for the welfare of her family just like you fought the Yankees and later the Comanches. I can't claim to be as bothered by Miss Molly's camp girls, but the drinking and fighting in town have been growing worse. Most of what the ladies are proposing would benefit the whole county."

"Sure, son. Nobody argues that. You have to understand, though, that writing laws that limit a man's freedom can get to be a bad habit. You take range cowboys like Marty Steele. Marty's got no notion of drawing a pistol and shooting anybody, but he carries his Colt because it gives him a feeling of independence. As for the whiskey, half the farmers whose wives march with Angela make their own out of the leavings of the corn crop. I'm not much of a drinker of hard spirits, Ross, but it doesn't mean I consider myself fit to judge the actions of everybody else."

"I know you mean well, Papa," Ross said sourly, "but Palo Pinto's growing into a town. There are little kids around the streets, and so long as Circle N cowboys keep shooting off their pistols, somebody's bound to get hurt. Then you and the other men will vote in Mama's law, only it will be too late for the one who got shot."

"And what happens when a cowboy rides in and refuses to hand over his gun, Ross? Will Bret shoot? Maybe that cowboy will shoot Bret. Is that going to help anybody?"

Ross frowned, and Charlie turned his horse so that the animal splashed into the shallow waters of Buck Creek. Charlie rode perhaps a mile and a half before Ross rejoined him.

"Papa," Ross spoke, "there's no need our arguing. Palo Pinto has little to do with any decisions made about this southern range. Should I order wire? Do we have Marty bring a crew here?"

"Don't you think first we should ask Billy his opinion? He's supposed to run things, remember?"

"Supposed to," Ross said, grinning.

"Well, I don't make all the decisions, do I?" Ross didn't respond, and Charlie went on to say, "I won't make this one."

The two of them spent the afternoon wandering the range. Charlie rescued a derelict longhorn from a bog and shot a prowling wolf just south of the cattle pens. For the briefest of times, he felt as if ten years had been swept away, and he was riding along Bluff Creek. He could almost glimpse Stands Tall frowning down from a nearby outcropping, and bawling calves brought back memories of the first long and exhausting drive to Kansas.

"Papa?" Ross called at last.

"Son?"

"It's turned late," Ross said, pointing to where a dying sun dipped toward the western horizon. "We'd best turn homeward."

Charlie nodded, then nudged his horse northward.

The next morning Charlie rode out to the ranch. He cornered Billy at the horse corral. They spoke of routine business at first. Luis Morales had offered a pair of Arabian colts for sale, and Wes Tyler wished to hire a couple of new hands to help with cutting winter feed. Charlie quickly agreed to both proposals. He then turned the conversation to fencing the south acreage. Billy responded quickly.

"Papa, you know how we all feel about barbed wire!" Billy shouted. "It's bad enough these farmers wrap that devil thread around their places. Papa, they're slicing the range into little pieces. You can hardly ride across the county anymore!"

"We don't own the county," Charlie pointed out. "You know what's running across that south range? A good thousand longhorns, and nary a one's wearing our brand."

"Sure, and we lose a lot of strays from the ranch, too. But that's the way it's always been, Papa. It's not just a matter of fencing in the cows, you know. It's fencing in the cowboys, too."

"It'll happen soon anyway."

"Maybe," Billy said, pacing back and forth beside the rails of the corral. "Things have a way of changing, don't they? Ryan's determined to get rid of the longhorns, and those farmers mean to fence the whole county. You remember how it was when we first came here? I was twelve years old, my leg swollen from snakebite. There were no fences then. Few enough houses. The longhorns were running free, and they saved us, let us build this place. I won't turn my back on them, Papa. And I won't fence 'em in, either. If it happens, then I'll learn to live with it. But I won't add my hand to those who'd hasten it along."

"I'm older than you, son. I've learned you can't halt progress."

"Progress?" Billy asked, spitting the bad taste from his mouth. "It's not progress, Papa. It won't make anything better."

"Maybe not," Charlie mumbled. "But the thing about progress is that it comes whether you want it or not. The trick is to be one step ahead."

"Like with Uncle Bowie and the railroad?"

"Exactly. We'll wait on the fencing until you're ready, son. You're the one running the Flying J now, and it should be your call. When you're ready, holler at Ross, have him order the fool wire. Then let me know, and we'll ride off to the cliffs and sing about the old days."

"I always wondered why you climbed those cliffs?"

"My way of looking over the world, so to speak. And of bidding the old ways good-bye."

"As good a way as any, I suppose."

"Better than most."

Billy Justiss ordered no wire and set no crews to work marking the Flying J boundaries or enclosing southern acreage. And yet fences did come. Once the corn crops had been harvested, it seemed as though every farm in Palo Pinto County began stringing wire. Scrub juniper and mesquite trees by the dozens were felled for posts, and boys Bailey Cooke's age passed whole days nailing the treacherous wire in place. J. C. Parnell vowed that by Christmas he'd have every acre of field and wood free of roving longhorns, and Charlie knew Parnell was no man to boast idly.

Billy Justiss muttered a few curses, and Marty Steele and others complained openly. Charlie insisted the Flying J hands be kept on a short rope, though, and most confrontations with farmers consisted of taunts and insults. Joe Nance's Circle N boys observed no such restraint.

Randolph Nance had of late hired a South Texas drover named Griffin Spence, and Spence was well-acquainted with barbed wire. In no time at all Spence managed to burn one of Pinkney Cooke's wagons, and when a stampeding herd of range longhorns demolished a quarter mile of Parnell's fence, Spence was immediately suspected.

"Do we have law here?" Parnell cried aloud to Charlie on the courthouse steps. "I want Spence arrested!"

Charlie immediately escorted the farmer to Bret Pruett's dingy office. No one had spotted Spence, though, and a half dozen Circle N hands swore he was miles away rounding up strays.

"You knew they wouldn't accept this without a fight," Charlie told Parnell. "Your fields are idle. Wait to finish your fences. There'll be time before planting in the spring. Meanwhile maybe Joe can sell off his extra steers."

"I knew?" Parnell responded. "Let me tell you

what I was told. This is cattle country! If you break the sod, we will break your necks. These things I was told. Your wife speaks of law and order, rules to make us safe in our beds. Let me tell you this, Judge. The next cowboy who rides down my fence will have need of friends. Someone will have to bury him!"

Charlie immediately set off for the Circle N. Joe Nance invited him inside, and the two veteran cattlemen sat together in Nance's parlor and talked. Though polite enough, Nance proved less than helpful.

"We need that range, Charlie. I've got no brother who can find me a few thousand acres of spare range down south. I know you think the open range is doomed, and maybe it is. All I know is that the price of beef is rising again, and if Parnell's boys will hold their horses, I'll sell off my excess and drive what's left onto my own land."

"I spoke of that, Joe," Charlie explained, "but Parnell's got his dander up. Even so, I figure he'll let it ride a bit. If you need some help . . ."

"We'll manage," Nance said, turning away. "I've run steers across this range close on twenty-five years now. I think I can herd a thousand to the railhead."

"Sure," Charlie said, taking his hat and rising to his feet. "Never thought otherwise."

"Then it seems to me you've gone out of your way to meddle in my business. You and your wife! Pretty soon we'll all be riding sheep and sipping lemonade."

Charlie laughed to himself, then stepped to the door.

"You're old enough to know you can't hold back

a flood with your bare hands, Joe," Charlie called. "Change is rising fast, old friend. Don't let it swamp you."

Joe Nance might storm and stomp about a thing, but he was smart enough to read the roll of the dice and act accordingly. Within the week Circle N drovers collected the last 800 of their animals from the open range and started them toward the stockyards at Justiss Junction. The day the cattle were shipped to market, Griff Spence and the rest of the trail crew rode into Palo Pinto at a gallop, firing pistols in the air and shouting to high heaven.

"Charlie, stop them!" Angela demanded.

"No, let them get it out of their craws, dear. They know their day's about done. Let them have this one last time."

"And if somebody gets killed?"

"Then we'll have to build a gallows, I suppose. Till then, leave Bret to manage the town."

If Spence and his companions had been left to themselves, the noise might have died a swift death. As it was, though, the shooting aroused the resentment of a number of townspeople. Worse, Judith Parnell and Celia Cooke happened to have ridden into town for their monthly visit to the mercantile. In no time at all, a dozen women had collected outside the door of the Lone Star Saloon.

"Lord, help us now," Charlie grumbled as he heard the first notes of a hymn drift through town. Instantly he was on his feet and headed for the door. Angela rushed after him.

"Repent, sinners!" Celia called over the clamor

349

of boasting cowboys. "Repent. Demon rum will lead you away from the path to salvation. Repent. Turn aside from your evil ways and fall upon your knees."

Griff Spence charged through the Lone Star's twin doors and confronted the women.

"Be gone, you old crows!" he shouted. "Meddling bunch of women! Go pester your husbands and run your kids off from Miss Molly's. The better part of 'em's likely down there right now, havin' a look at a real female. Can't tell by the look of you old nags that a woman's different from an old mama longhorn!"

"Heathens!" Celia replied angrily. "God will surely punish you!"

"Looks like he's already finished with you, woman!" Spence retorted.

A crowd began to gather, and the fuming women threatened to engulf Spence and his companions. It was then that the cowboys drew pistols and fired.

"They'll kill us all!" someone shrieked, and Judith Parnell clubbed Spence across the forehead with a placard. Spence fell to his knees, and the women attacked him with a passion. The other cowboys beat a hasty retreat.

"That's enough!" Charlie pleaded, but even when Angela called for restraint, the mob refused to calm down. Finally Bret Pruett arrived with shotgun in hand. The sheriff fired one barrel in the air, and the stunned ladies stepped back.

"You all right, Spence?" Bret asked, bending down beside the fallen cowboy.

"Damned women," the cowboy muttered as he fought to get to his feet. His face was cut and bleeding, and he held his left arm gingerly.

"Best get him to Doc Garnett," Charlie suggested.

"I'll take him," Jack Duncan volunteered, stepping through the door and helping Spence down the street.

"Now the rest of you go along home," Bret urged. "There's been enough excitement here tonight."

The crowd grumbled, and Celia Cooke yelled, "Mend your ways, sinner!" But in the end, the mob disbanded, and all returned to more peaceful pursuits.

The so-called battle at the Lone Star ignited a fuse of sorts. Thereafter a day rarely passed when the Women for Morality didn't march or sing or tack petitions to the doors of the saloons. Jack Duncan at the Lone Star paid little attention, but the Double P was sold to new owners, and the hotel scratched spirits from its bill of fare. The Lucky Diamond suffered a mysterious fire and thereafter became a saddle shop. The Cactus and Bluebonnet owners took the hint and closed their doors.

"It's a sad day indeed when a man can't sip a shot of whiskey in peace," Marty Steele complained to Charlie. "You know a poor honest cowboy can't walk into the Lone Star or the Double P without some woman calling him a dozen names, half of 'em beyond his understanding. My ma read me the Bible when I was a tadpole, but I never remembered all these things Miz Cooke's forever shoutin' at us. Her boy Bailey's the wildest kid in seven counties, but to hear her talk, you'd guess he was a preacher."

"I know," Charlie said, grinning, "You know Pinkney caught the boy down at Molly's again. I'll bet that youngster doesn't sit for a month."

"Charlie, this is worse'n Abilene. If it keeps up, I'm bound to saddle my horse and head for the far range. I always held Angela was a fair woman, but she's taken after this temperance nonsense like a coyote after a hen. She means to shake this town dry!"

"There's merit to some of her ideas."

"I'll not argue that, Charlie. But she's got to leave a man something. I feel like she's roped and tied me, and now she's ready to do even more."

Charlie broke out laughing, but Marty was plainly not amused. He kicked up a spiral of dust, then charged down the street toward the Double P, mumbling to himself all the while.

Chapter 3

Charlie Justiss soon sought out any reason he could find for staying clear of Palo Pinto. Angry females and frustrated cowboys often exchanged insults or threatened violence, and more often than not, Charlie found himself in the middle of it all. The only men in town more uncomfortable were Bret Pruett and Alex Tuttle, but they had no choice but to stay and try to keep the peace.

Charlie, on the other hand, found plenty to keep him out of town. First, he and Ross began laying out a new road south from Justiss Junction to the new settlements in Erath County. Once the route was marked, Charlie set a crew from the Flying J to work clearing scrub trees from the trace. By October they'd carved a fair wagon road through the hills and ravines.

With the south road finished, Charlie turned his attentions to the final cattle delivery of the year. A thousand head had been promised to Kansas City, and for the Flying J it was suddenly old times.

Marty Steele and Wes Tyler headed roundup crews, and the whole drive was placed in Billy Justiss's hands. The most active cowboy on the ranch, though, was an aging Charlie Justiss.

"Just like the old days, huh, Charlie?" Marty asked as the two of them rounded up strays from the tangled brush along Ioni Creek. "Wasn't so long ago you and I were chasing rustlers through here."

"Seems a long time now."

"That's because you've passed too many days in that fool town. I don't see how you stomach it. A man who's chased Yanks and Comanches ought to spend his autumns chasing wild mustangs."

"Well, the spirit might be willing, but the bones have grown weary."

"Mine, too," Marty said, laughing.

When the cattle were collected in two large camps, a thousand longhorn steers were cut out and readied for the road. Charlie watched with a degree of sadness, for each drive reduced the number of tough old longhorns. The new mixed breed was destined to take over, and each departing longhorn seemed like another old friend leaving the ranch.

Well, old boys, we're fading fast, we oldtimers, Charlie thought as he headed a pair of drifting steers back toward the herd. He wondered how many more autumns would pass before Ryan's Herefords would dominate the Texas range. He was still thinking of that when he rode into town and invited Chris and Joe to join the brief drive from the Flying J to Justiss Junction.

"Can we go, Mama?" Chris begged. "It's only a single day away from school, and we'll catch up our lessons."

"Please?" Joe added. "We've been cooped up here in town most all the fall."

Angela was reluctant to let the renegade schoolboys escape her watchful eye, and she said as much.

"I'll watch 'em like a hawk," Charlie promised, "and we'll ride well clear of Molly Sharpe's place."

Angela frowned, but she finally agreed. An hour before daybreak Charlie and his younger boys joined the herd on the road. Billy and Ross were mounted as well, and it was like a family reunion for a time. Then the cattle began to stray, and everyone went to work.

Some might have found the dust and turmoil of the drive a nuisance. It was hot for October, and sweat soon mixed with sand to coat every man with a pasty grit. Charlie recalled the long treks through the Nations when the entire outfit prayed they'd reach the next river crossing.

"I don't see how you put up with these mangy cows for whole weeks," Joe grumbled when Charlie rode by to inspect the fourteen-year-old's work on the left flank.

"Well, to begin with these aren't cows," Charlie said, laughing. "They're steers. As for the mange, we never trailed a Justiss steer to market that wasn't healthy."

"Papa, you miss the old times?"

"Often," Charlie confessed. "Most of all I miss chasing you boys through the barnyard, rocking you on my knee. You grow taller every day it seems, and I get older."

"Little Charlie and Hope like to sit on your lap," Joe reminded his father.

"Yes, and grandkids are a blessing to be sure. It's not the same thing, though."

"I kind of like you, too, Papa," Joe said, grinning from under the brim of an oversized hat. "You figure Mama'd forgive us if we rode by Miss Molly's and just took a peek inside?"

"You'd be worse off than these steers headed for the slaughterhouse. And you, Joe, why we couldn't even make a fair-sized boot out of what'd be left of your hide."

Joe laughed at his father, then headed off a wandering steer. Charlie nudged his horse into a trot and visited Chris farther forward.

"I remember how I used to dream about going to Kansas with these longhorns," Chris said as Charlie drew alongside. "I suppose nothing's ever what you imagine when you're little."

"Guess you heard too many stories from your brothers."

"Could be," Chris admitted. "The best parts of those stories were always about Dodge City and Abilene. Billy and Ryan'd never tell us everything that happened, though."

"Oh?"

"Said we were too young. We weren't. I guess we pretty much filled in the left-out parts by the time we were twelve."

"And now that you're thirteen, you know everything, I suppose."

"Close to it," Chris said, grinning. "We had ourselves a pretty fair look down at the river when Miss Molly had her tents there."

"There's a whale of a lot more to life than a feather in a cap and pink drawers, son."

"I know that, Papa. Still, that Miss Velvet had about the finest look to her of anybody I've ever seen."

"See your mama doesn't hear such talk."

"Oh, I'm smart enough to know that, Papa. You should've seen what Bailey's backside looked like after his papa caught him sneaking back from the river. My, he was just about peeled raw, and that was just for asking . . ."

"Asking what?"

"Oh, I don't know," Chris said, suddenly growing pinkish about the face. "I'm no expert on such things, you know."

"You'd better not be," Charlie warned.

The best parts of the brief drive to the railhead were those talks Charlie had with the boys. There was something about sharing a journey that bonded men to each other, and Charlie'd missed that with Joe and Chris. Soon they'd be too old for easy bonding. A boy of fifteen had a way of straining his harness, breaking loose, and Joe had always been a little less tame than the others.

Toward late afternoon, Marty and Bob Lee Wiley headed the lead steers into the cattle pens. The F W & W, unusually prompt, had boxcars ready and waiting. Longhorn after longhorn threaded its way through the maze of chutes and then plodded up a gangway into a car.

"It seems like we hardly even got started," Chris grumbled to his father as the cowboys nudged the increasingly reluctant creatures into the network of pens. "Maybe we should make camp around here tonight, bed down beside the river."

"Your mama'd fry us for even considering it," Charlie answered. "But maybe if the weather holds, we'll go up into the hills for a night or two later. Maybe we can shoot a deer."

"I'd like a buckskin jacket. Think I could make one?"

"Marty can show you how. He's got a talent for working hides."

Chris scurried off to locate Marty, and Charlie busied himself with the final 200 beeves. By the time all the animals were loaded in the cars, the entire outfit was exhausted. Charlie hosted a celebration of sorts back of the hotel. Juicy steaks and mounds of vegetables were brought out from the kitchen, and the cowboys joined in singing and a friendly game or two of cards.

"I miss the singing," Wes told Charlie. "I could do without the dust and the rustlers and the stale coffee, but I do miss the company you share on the trail."

"Yes," Charlie agreed as he accepted a cup of steaming coffee from his old friend.

"I heard Cactus Jack Howard was hung up in Albany last week."

"Oh? I always thought him a good man."

"Best hand with a rope I ever saw, 'cept maybe Marty and young Billy. Cactus fell in with bad company, it seems. Took up with a farmer's wife, then had the bad sense to talk about it. Husband caught 'em together, and Cactus shot the farmer stone cold dead. Sheriff was sorry enough about takin' Cactus in, but wasn't much else to do. I heard the farmer's widow cried when they dropped the trap."

"Colby Jimerson's gone, too," Charlie mumbled. "Tried to fill an inside straight with a doctored nine. Was shot for his trouble."

"I hadn't heard that. Colby never did have much luck with cards, though."

"He was what, sixteen, the year we first took him to Dodge?"

"That or thereabouts."

"Cowboys come and go. I deem myself lucky that you and Marty have stayed on. It helps to have men around you can rely on."

"Marty? Never let him hear that. He prides

himself on bein' a loner, you know. Truth is he's as attached to this country as somebody born here. Takes a pride in your boys, too."

"Well, you've both had a hand in raising them."

"No son of Charlie Justiss ever needed anybody else's hand. You've done just fine by those youngsters. I marvel that Billy's settled, and what's this we hear about Ryan keepin' company with that gal who looked after the railroad orphans?"

"I believe they're set on each other."

"Looks like the family's apt to get bigger in a hurry."

"Could be," Charlie said, laughing. "I don't expect Ryan will be taking 'em all in."

"Lord, no. I heard there was a hundred of 'em."

"Maybe more."

Charlie went on to talk to Wes about Joe and Chris, about Bret and Vicki's little ones, about the baby Ross hoped would come before too long.

"I've got my four, Charlie," Wes said proudly, "not counting Alice's brother Toby, who's close to a son to me as well. I don't know that I could winter without 'em now. There's no feelin' on earth like the touch of those little hands on your face."

"No feeling on earth," Charlie agreed. For a moment he stared over at where Joe and Chris sat singing to the tune of Hector Suarez's guitar. Their voices were deepening. The childlike sweetness was gone. In its place had come a more solemn tone like the toll of a churchbell. It was but another sign that they were children no longer.

Toward dusk Charlie collected his crew and led them back to Palo Pinto. Billy and Wes headed back to the ranch with four or five others. Ross rode home alone. Charlie directed Joe and Chris to the livery, and after they'd tended their horses, the three Justiss men went home.

Angela was waiting with a peach pie. The boys devoured their share, and their mother then ushered them into the kitchen and instructed Enuncia to prepare a bath.

"We can take our own bath, don't you think?" Joe complained.

"Then do so with as little argument as is possible," Angela told them. "Do it before the stench overpowers the wallpaper."

Charlie laughed, then led her out onto the porch. Across the street a pair of cowboys were singing a trail song. The noise of laughter drifted down from the Lone Star Saloon.

"I wish you'd support our petition," Angela said, gripping Charlie's wrist and pointing to the lights shining brightly from the saloon. "They'll be at it half the night."

"Only till nightfall. Bret will quiet them down then."

"I can't abide the wickedness of it."

"You're beginning to sound like Celia Cooke," Charlie grumbled. "They're just boys, little older than Chris and Joe. They're eager to show they've grown tall, and playing a hand of poker and sipping whiskey is the way they do it."

"Drinking liquor never made anyone a man."

"I know that. So will they in time. There's no harm to it."

"Did you know Griffin Spence was in there. Dr. Garnett splinted his arm. He's been boasting all day how he'll even things with the ladies who broke that arm."

"It's just talk, dear."

"I warned Bret to keep his eyes open. Spence has a dark eye, Charlie. I know you don't believe in such things, but I've seen it before. We Spanish know things."

"Bret can handle it."

An hour and a half later Charlie was resting peacefully in the bathtub in the kitchen, humming softly an old trail tune when Angela drew his attention to a loud commotion up the street.

"I think you should get dressed," she said. "I believe it's more than just a couple of cowboys arguing over a poker hand."

"Bret and Tut will deal with it," Charlie said. "I'm weary. All I want to do is soak a bit longer."

There was a knock at the front door then, and Angela set off to investigate. Chris got there ahead of her and led little Roger Monday into the kitchen.

"Sorry to disturb your bath, Judge," the twelve-year-old said, "but Sheriff Pruett asked if I'd find you. There's trouble at the Lone Star."

Charlie nodded, and Angela handed him a towel. The arguing had grown worse, and now Bret's voice had joined in.

"I'll fetch your rifle, Papa," Chris said, darting out of the room. Roger followed. Charlie meanwhile dried himself and scrambled into some clothes. He was pulling on his boots when a shotgun blast shattered the night.

"Charlie?" Angela cried in alarm as her husband pulled on his boots, took the rifle from Chris and dashed out the back door. It took less than a minute for Charlie to race across the street to the Lone Star. As he entered, a dozen young cowboys stumbled outside.

"Bret?" Charlie asked, staring at his son-in-law.

Alex Tuttle was back of the bar helping a dazed Jack Duncan recover his senses. Griff Spence stood on one side of a poker table holding a loaded Colt. Young Andy Coonce stood opposite, shaking slightly as he gazed wide-eyed at the pistol in Spence's hand.

"Put the gun down, Spence," Bret ordered. "I won't be firing at the ceiling next time."

"You'll be dead afore that," Spence muttered angrily. "I've shot men before, plenty of 'em down south. A sheriff and a cheat of a card-playing cowboy won't bear too heavy on my conscience."

"I didn't cheat you, mister," Andy declared. "I drew that other king fair as day. You keep the pot, though. I mean you no trouble."

"Let him go, Spence," Bret said, steadying his grip on the shotgun. "He's a kid. We can settle this."

"Sure, we can," Spence said, slurring his speech slightly as he turned toward the sheriff. "I'll kill you quick and simple. You won't even feel it."

"That's enough!" Charlie interrupted. "Put that pistol in its holster or be prepared to meet your maker. We'll have no such foolishness in Palo Pinto."

"I killed a judge once before," Spence boasted. He then lowered the barrel of the pistol, and Bret breathed a sign of relief. Spence turned toward the wall as if to leave, but Andy cried out an alarm.

"Bret, look out!"

Spence turned in a single motion, but Andy Coonce caught the gunman's hand before the Colt could take aim on the sheriff. The pistol exploded, and young Andy reeled back, his belly torn apart.

"Help me," the boy mumbled as he fell.

Bret swung his shotgun over and fired. The blast lifted Spence off the floor and drove him against the far wall. Powder smoke filled the air, stinging Charlie's eyes. Nevertheless he raced over beside Andy Coonce and tried to comfort the young man.

"I, uh, I did what . . . what . . . I . . ."

"What you could," Charlie said, finishing the thought. Andy glanced up, smiled, then died. The boy didn't moan or mutter. His eyes just went blank, and there was a rush of air from his pierced lungs as the life flowed out of him.

"Spence!" Charlie shouted as he rested young Andy's head softly on the floor.

"He's dead," Jack Duncan declared. "Sheriff's shotgun flat took him apart."

Charlie didn't examine Spence's body. Instead he cradled Andy Coonce in his arms and placed the boy's still body on a nearby table. Andy'd never been very tall, and it seemed to Charlie the boy was scarce as heavy as Chris or Joe.

"I'll tend to him," Tut offered, prying Charlie's hands from the corpse. "I'll see he's taken to the church."

"And him?" Charlie asked, pointing to the swirl of smoke that marked the resting place of Griffin Spence.

"I'll get my boy to dig a hole tonight," Duncan spoke up. "I can't see the reverend wishing to bless his burying."

"No," Charlie agreed. "He's best put in the ground in darkness, for that's what he's apt to find from now on."

Charlie didn't say much about the shooting.

Angela readied a second bath, for Charlie returned with blood on his arms and shirt. After bathing, Charlie took to his bed, but he remained awake the better part of the night.

"It was the drinking," Angela declared. "And carrying guns. Maybe folks will listen to us now."

Early the next morning most of the town gathered at the church to pray for Andy Coonce. The new preacher, Douglas Fairchild, spoke of how the bright promise of youth had been so suddenly cut short. Bret told of Andy's sacrifice. But it was Angela who spoke most eloquently.

"We're burying this boy today," she began. "I knew Andy. I doctored him the first time he rolled off his horse into a stand of pencil cactus, and I once set a broken arm of his. He ate my biscuits and shared his prayers. Now I'm helping to put him in the ground.

"He was a fine youngster, as good a boy as any we've known, and the crime of it is that he's dead when he ought to be just starting his life. That could be your son there, Celia Cooke, or mine. It could be young Homer Welles or Jasper Grimmitt. So long as strong drink is allowed in Palo Pinto, so long as men carry pistols on our streets, so long as our children remain in peril, this crime will continue to happen.

"I feel grave sorrow today, but perhaps some good may yet come of this tragic death. Don't let Andy Coonce have died in vain. Let's band together and put an end to the influence of this demon that has too long cast a shadow over our community. Help me shut the doors of saloons in Palo Pinto forever. Let's ban handguns from our streets. And let's build a town where we can all be safe."

364

"Amen!" the ladies spoke as one. Charlie noticed many of the men joined in this time, and when the Women for Morality gathered on the church steps at noon to sign a temperance pledge, many a husband and son signed as well.

By moonlight an effigy titled "Demon Whiskey" burned in the center of Front Street. Gathered around it in a circle, forty women and children sang a hymn about everlasting life.

"Help us end this plague, friends!" Angela appealed to those who watched. "Ban guns and whiskey from our town. Give our children a future, not an early grave."

Chapter 4

The Women for Morality found a powerful ally in the young Methodist minister, Douglas Fairchild. Reverend Fairchild combined youthful enthusiasm with that rare energy found in those men who devoted years to preaching on the circuit – traveling from town to town, sermonizing to cowboys from the back of a chuck wagon or conducting baptisms at creeks and river crossings.

"He speaks with passion," Angela told Charlie. "He's seen the ravages of whiskey on men and women alike, and he won't let Palo Pinto shut its ears to our cause."

Charlie nodded, though in truth he found it difficult to believe anyone twenty-five years of age could know all that much about anything. To make matters worse, there was a wild, rebellious nature to Fairchild's hair, and his clothes seemed in need of repair. He flayed his hands wildly when speaking, but Charlie reasoned that habit, combined with a voice that boomed across whole rooms, had the advantage of keeping the congregation attentive and the children and old men awake.

Reverend Fairchild did no marching, though he occasionally joined in a few hymns when passing the lady marchers near the Double P or Lone Star. Stirred by what he called the Gospel of Temperance, though, he ranted against the evil of strong drink and summoned the entire town to the river twice the week after Andy Coonce's burial.

"Here is water, brought to us by the hand of God," Fairchild bellowed. "Gather with me, brothers and sisters. And if there are those among you who have not washed away the sins of the world and forsworn the temptation of demon whiskey, may you step with me into the waters and cleanse yourselves of evil."

Charlie gazed with amazement as women nudged husbands and children into the shallows. Shiftless cowboys joined profane freighters at the reverend's side. Fairchild dunked each in the river, calling out in his best voice how the spirit of temperance would bring rebirth.

"I never knew a Methodist to be such a dunker," Bret remarked. "Thought sprinkling satisfied 'em."

"Dive in, brother!" Fairchild cried as if hearing Bret. "Let the deep waters wash from you a mountain of sin."

"I guess Reverend Fairchild feels a good sprinkle wouldn't get the job done," Charlie said, grinning as the preacher grabbed a good hunk of Bailey Cooke's auburn hair and pushed the boy's face into the Brazos. "Could be he's right."

"And how about you, Brother Steele?" Fairchild suddenly boomed out.

Marty, who'd been watching from the bridge, retreated immediately. Unfortunately, Celia Cooke was at hand, and she quickly had help. A handful of females captured Marty and pulled him along the shore. Marty Steele had fought Yankees and Indians, had wrestled longhorns and bested rustlers, but he was wholly unprepared for Celia Cooke's zealots. The women herded Marty and a pair of young Circle N hands to the river, and Reverend Fairchild took each in hand.

"Do you repent of your sins?" the preacher asked as he pushed each head in turn beneath the surface. "Will you be saved?"

"Yes!" Marty cried. "Hopefuly from you!"

Afterward a soggy Marty led Charlie aside.

"I told you, Charlie," the cowboy muttered. "Didn't I say it? They aim to geld us next! It's not safe to ride into this town anymore."

The dunkings were only the beginning, though. Charlie was awakened the next morning by a loud pounding outside. He raised his head and searched the room for Angela. She was nowhere to be found.

"What's happening, Papa?" Chris asked, appearing at the door in an oversized nightshirt. The boy's blond hair was as disheveled as Reverend Fairchild's, and Charlie grew alarmed. The clatter outside sounded like the fire gong, and he suddenly leaped to his feet and hurried to the

368

window. Was the town burning? What mischief was afoot?

Charlie soon had his answer. Forty women marched in a circle in the center of Front Street. Each carried a copper pot and banged it with a ladle. The clatter had even the soundest sleeper at his window, and as other marchers joined the parade, Charlie wondered what purpose could bring so many farm wives to town so early.

"Papa?" Chris asked again. "What are they up to?"

"I don't know," Charlie confessed as he hurriedly got dressed. "I plan to find out, though."

By the time Charlie got to the door of the house, close to sixty marchers stood in a column of twos. Charlie was astounded to see level-headed folk like Alice Tyler and Georgia Staves. His own family was well represented. Ross's wife Eliza marched beside Angela near the head of the column, and Vicki brought along Hope and little Charlie. Children ran in and out of the line of stern-faced marchers, and it reminded Charlie of a wartime parade.

"Angela?" Charlie called. She didn't respond. Instead she followed Celia Cooke and Judith Parnell as the leaders suddenly turned their company to the east, then a bit south.

Charlie relaxed. There were no saloons in that direction. Art Stanley's warehouse was safe as well.

"Oh, no," Chris suddenly cried, stepping barefooted to his father's side. Joe followed. The two boys, bare save for their nightshirts, had looks of utter horror etched onto their faces.

"Pull your britches on, boys!" Charlie shouted.

369

"You can't walk down Front Street in your bed-clothes."

"Papa, you don't understand," Joe gasped as Charlie ushered them back into the house. "They're headed for the river."

"So they're bound to dunk some poor farmer," Charlie said, shaking his head. "Get dressed and we'll go see what it's all about."

"I know what it's about," Joe said as he started toward the stairway. "They've gone to visit Miss Molly."

"What?" Charlie asked.

"He's right," Chris agreed. "Papa, they're headed right for Miss Molly's tents."

"And how would you know?" Charlie asked as he angrily nudged the boys up the stairs.

"We passed by her tents when we went out to visit Bailey Cooke," Chris explained. "Miz Cooke's mightily upset about Bailey and Barrett paying a call there. Feathers are sure to fly, Papa."

Charlie nodded. He then left the boys to dress while he hurried back downstairs. It took only a minute to locate Bret Pruett. The two then saddled horses and rode out in hopes of barring a confrontation.

Charlie had known troops to march fast during the war, and Comanches were famous for feats of wonder. No one ever rivaled the Women for Morality, though, as they set off to do battle with Molly Sharpe's Brazos belles.

By the time Charlie and Bret arrived at the camp, Celia Cooke had already torched every stitch of canvas in the place. The harlots were herded together behind some trees near the river, and Charlie could only wonder what ordeal lay in store for them there. The children, meanwhile, stood on a hill overlooking the river. Celia Cooke lectured them on the wicked ways of fallen women, but the little ones seemed more interested in the blazing tents.

"Let the fires of hell consume this sinful place!" Celia cried out.

Then Miss Molly and her companions reappeared. Their lace girdles and fancy hats were gone. The women stared horror-stricken as flames devoured their camp. Molly Sharpe was draped in a canvas sack that pinned her arms to her sides, and the belles were likewise restrained. They walked barefoot to a waiting wagon driven by Ilse Frost, and their hair was wet and matted. Charlie guessed a special dunking had been conducted.

"Sheriff, arrest these hags!" Molly cried. Bret turned to Charlie, then gazed at the sixty fiery-eyed females.

"What right have you to do this to us?" Molly screamed. Tears rolled down her face, and Charlie's heart opened.

"Miz Cooke, can you explain what you're about?" Bret asked.

"Evictin' squatters," Celia explained. "They have no title to this land, but my husband Pinkney does."

"Couldn't you just ask 'em to move?" Bret asked.

"We thought they needed some help," Judith Parnell answered.

Charlie heard a cry from the woods then. He turned in time to gaze upon little Carl Frost, Bailey and Barrett Cooke, and Homer Welles all tied to trees and forced to watch their mothers' handiwork.

"I never plied my trade with them boys, Sheriff!" Molly protested. "I got rules, you know."

"Be gone, sinners!" Celia shouted then, and the others clanged their pots as Molly and her companions were piled into the back of the waiting wagon. Ilse then whipped the horses into motion, and the Brazos belles were rumbling south toward Justiss Junction.

A less determined group might have left it at that, but the Women for Morality bore a strong grudge toward Molly Sharpe. They not only drove the wagonload of sinners to the railhead, they kept a careful watch lest any escape. Angela bought tickets to Ft. Worth personally, and not until Molly promised to head east and not return did the Celia Cooke's alert guards relax their vigilance.

As for Molly, once the initial shock wore off, she regained her sense of humor.

"I've been run out of places before," Molly explained to Charlie. "One bunch even clipped my hair. Give us an hour, and we'll be fine."

Sure enough, by the time the eastbound train pulled up at the depot, Molly and her girls had managed to acquire simple poplin dresses and shoes. Molly even had sufficient funds left over to tip the porter who carried her hat box.

"Don't worry, boys!" Molly shouted from the window of her coach. "We may be a little worse for the wear, but we'll soon be back in business elsewhere. If you ever get to Ft. Worth, look us up."

The men at the stockyards cheered as the train

372

pulled out, and Charlie laughed. What else was there to do?

The departure of Molly Sharpe didn't end the episode, though. Marty Steele met with Charlie and Bret the following day. In his hand was a petition of complaint signed by most every cowboy riding Palo Pinto range.

"Those women ought to be arrested," Marty argued. "First they kidnap me and dump me in the river. Now they've burned Molly's camp and done heaven knows what manner of crimes to those girls. It's time something was done, and the others agree."

"What would you suggest?" Bret asked. "We couldn't fit all those women into the courthouse, much less my storeroom of a jail."

"You can't just look the other way, Bret!" Marty shouted.

"You weren't there, Marty," Bret said, staring at the floor. "My own wife and kids were marching. Shoot, every wife and mother in the county was there, I'll bet. Some grandmothers even. They had us treed, and what's worse, they knew it."

"The tents were on Celia's property," Charlie added. "I checked the records. I wish they'd come to me, let me talk Molly into moving south of Buck Creek, but I don't know that it wasn't bound to happen. Molly's not done much business lately. Times have changed."

"I guess so," Marty said, clearly disappointed. "Time was when you two would have sided with me on this. And what about the saloons?" They'll chose them next."

"Then you'll find Jack Duncan sets up a cantina

373

on the Albany road," Charlie said, sighing. "After what happened to Andy, I'm not convinced the ban on guns is all that bad an idea."

"Charlie!"

"I don't like the notion of men pulling pistols on anybody they lose a bit of money to at cards. And I shudder every time I think of Griff Spence pointing that pistol at Bret."

"Well, I won't argue that," Marty said, calming slightly. "I just want you to think about the future of Palo Pinto. Look what these meddlers have brought already. The railroad's down south. All that money rolling through the streets at the junction would've bought a lot of new school-books. It may turn quiet here at night, but there's purely little here to draw anyone to town. I don't expect Reverend Fairchild's dunkings will bring much cash into Art's mercantile."

"No," Charlie grumbled.

"There's been talk on the range of headin' for the Panhandle, Charlie. Some of the Circle N boys are rolling their blankets right now. You're going to need help come winter. Billy and Wes can't do it all."

"I know," Charlie admitted. "Stick around, Marty. I do need you. And all this ruckus will pass."

"Will it?" Marty asked. "I wouldn't bet my last dime on that."

Charlie was shaken by Marty's petition, and when a dozen Circle N cowboys rode west later in the week, Charlie sat down with Angela and tried to work out a compromise solution to the question of banning saloons from Palo Pinto.

"Be patient," he urged.

374

"I have been," Angela answered angrily. "For ten years I've waited for civilization to come to Palo Pinto. I've seen harlots parade down Front Street. Gunmen have held pistols to my children's heads! A boy I nursed back to life was shot over a fool game of cards. I've got no more patience, Charlie Justiss. None of us have. We want a better world for our children, and if we have to fight for it, we will!"

Chapter 5

With Molly Sharpe's tents gone, the Women for Morality turned their attention next to the saloons. Each afternoon Celia Cooke or Angela formed a circle of friends outside the doors of the Lone Star or Double P. Soon the women began singing. When Vicki excused the children from the schoolhouse, several would join their mothers, and the noise would grow louder.

Mostly the men inside ignored the hymns. Celia quoted scripture and lectured on the evils of drink, but no one responded. Only when the braver of the ladies stepped inside the saloons and chastised one of the gamblers or drinkers did real trouble begin. Often serious shouting would follow. Once or twice an angry cowboy showered his persecuters with whiskey or tossed a bottle at them. For his trouble, he was usually mobbed and hauled outside.

Bret Pruett did his best to intervene before matters grew any worse, but three cowboys were dunked in a watering trough the same day, and

Bowie Nichols, a Circle N cowboy, was brained with a chair. Even so, the saloons continued to do a flourishing business. Friday and Saturday nights cowboys streamed into town to enjoy a game of cards and a few drinks.

"You could put a stop to that, Charlie!" Angela stormed. "Tell Billy to keep the men on the ranch."

"Cowboys aren't longhorns to be fenced in or hogtied," Charlie answered. "They're independent minded, and they aren't about to work for a man who shackles them at night."

But when the Circle N and Flying J outfits came charging into town together, Charlie acted quickly.

"You boys may consider this to be your town," he told the boisterous cowboys. "It isn't. It belongs to those ladies over there and to their children. Towns are for folks who build. We old saddle bandits may own the range, but here we're guests. We should act that way."

"To them?" Bowie Nichols asked. "Why, one of those old crows near bashed my head in the other day. We can do what we want, can't we, Joe?"

Joe Nance emerged from the others. The white-haired cattleman stared angrily at the crowd gathering across the street.

"No Circle N hand ever needed an invitation to spend Friday night in Palo Pinto," Nance declared. "This was my town before it was anybody's, and if you'd keep those meddling women out of our way, everybody would get along just fine!"

Such words were akin to waving a red flag in front of a Mexican bull. In minutes open warfare broke out. Cowboys shouted insults, and the townspeople responded. Reverend Fairchild soon arrived, and his booming voice rang through town.

"Beware, brothers, for the sins of today will weigh heavily upon you come Judgment Day."

"Amen," the ladies cried. Then they broke out in song, and the cowboys retreated inside the Lone Star or the Double P. For nearly two hours the town was serenaded with hymns before Bret convinced the saloons to close for the night. Even then, most of the cowboys gathered outside town and emptied two final bottles.

Thereafter a pair of ladies kept vigil beside the saloon doors. Each time someone, anyone, entered, the women would begin ringing handbells. The noise was deafening, and the saloon patrons reacted angrily. Jack Duncan at the Lone Star threatened violence.

"If you don't stop that clanging," Duncan warned, "you'll learn all about Judgment Day firsthand!" When that didn't halt the bell ringing, Duncan emptied the contents of a spittoon on the ringers.

Such actions only served to make things worse, though. Soon Celia Cooke arranged a wall of children around the Lone Star and demanded an apology from Jack Duncan.

Duncan laughed at the youngsters blocking the doorway, but when customers, wary of confronting Celia Cooke and a dozen little ones, turned instead to the Double P, Duncan finally surrendered.

"I give up," the weary saloonkeeper cried. "Ring your fool bells. Sing your hymns. Just leave me some hope of makin' a livin'."

It was shortly thereafter that Marty Steele pleaded with Charlie to put an end to the saloon war.

"I've got nothin' against Miz Cooke and those ladies," Marty said. "We all feel the same. I've even gotten to like the singin'. But it's not fair puttin' those little kids up in front of Jack Duncan's place. All that preachin' gets to you, too."

"I guess it does," Charlie said, grinning. Marty was clearly past the point of being amused, though.

"Charlie, there's been talk of stormin' in here and settin' a fire in the center of Front Street. You know I'm against it, but things are turnin' ugly. You know some of those farmers even offered to drop their fences and help us chase Miz Cooke into the river?"

"I don't think they'd have much luck doing that."

"Nobody's goin' to have any luck dealin' with the farm women. Angela, though, knows how a man gets a thirst come winter. When he rides the range with that north wind howlin' down his neck, he needs somethin' to brace him against the cold."

"I hate to disappoint you, Marty, but Angela's dead set against those saloons. She's been passing temperance pledges from house to house lately. She's got near everyone in town to sign them."

"You?"

Charlie glanced at the corner of his desk. The pledge lay in the same place it had since Angela had set it there two days earlier.

"Not yet," Charlie said, "but I believe it's the only hope I've got of restoring order to my household. Sooner or later we'll sign those pledges, I'd guess."

"I feel like we're back at Petersburg, watchin' the whole army wither away," Marty lamented. "Just don't have any fight left to us, eh?"

"Oh, a little," Charlie said, grinning. "Towns up and down the river are closing their saloons, though. It's just a matter of time now here."

"I sure never thought I'd live to see the day.

But though Charlie signed his pledge, and others did likewise, neither surviving saloon was ready to bolt its doors. In truth the Douple P was doing record business as many of the county's men flocked to the bar to prove they weren't ruled by their wives.

Celia Cooke continued to ring her bell, but Angela turned her attentions to a difference tack. She observed how Art Stanley's freight wagons brought in case after case of whiskey as well as kegs of beer.

"There's an easy way to put a halt to that," Angela vowed. The next morning she and Ilse Frost began spreading word that no one would shop in the Stanley mercantile as long as Art's freighters carried whiskey.

"It's not fair!" Art complained. "My boys and I've signed the pledge. We're regulars in church. If there was somebody else hauling freight from the depot, I'd refuse the cargo. As it is, it wouldn't be right not to haul goods a man depends on to make his living."

The words had little effect on Angela. And when the loss of business failed to change old

Art's mind, the ladies gathered together and decided on another course of action.

The first hint Charlie had of trouble was when Angela left before dawn to ride out to the Parnell place.

"J. C.'s got a fever," she had explained, "and Judith asked me to take a look."

"Why not send for Doc Garnett?" Charlie argued.

"J. C.'s got little use for doctors, you know, and a great deal of dread."

Charlie nodded and helped her prepare for the ride to the Parnell farm. Angela left shortly thereafter, but a half hour later J. C. Parnell appeared in person to ask about his wife.

"She said she was coming into town to help your wife make curtains," Parnell said. "And they're neither of them here?"

"No," Charlie said, suspecting serious trouble. He walked to the livery and saddled a horse. No sooner did he climb aboard the animal than the sound of distant rifle fire echoed through town.

"Road agents!" Art Stanley shouted. "They've gone to raid my wagons. Hurry!"

Bret Pruett and Alex Tuttle immediately headed for the livery. Charlie and Parnell, already mounted as they were, headed out first.

Stanley's freight wagons were rolling up the Jacksboro road three miles due south of Palo Pinto when two dozen masked riders suddenly swooped down upon them. The lead riders fired warning shots, and all seven wagons drew to an immediate halt.

"Drop those guns!" a smallish, round-shouldered figure commanded. The guards sitting alongside the drivers of the front and rear wagons complied. "Check the cargo," the leader then instructed the others. Instantly riders dismounted and rummaged through the wagons.

"Here it is!" one of the searchers cried. "Last wagon!"

"Lord, help us!" Walter Joplin, the driver of the whiskey wagon, called out. "It's those blamed women."

The other drivers muttered curses as they realized their attackers included wives and sisters.

"Let the others go," the leader ordered, and the riders waved the front wagons along. "You, too," she added, pointing to Joplin and Gordon Slate, the lanky guard seated alongside. The two scrambled down from the seat and raced after the departing wagons. With the freighters gone, the female raiders set upon the remaining wagon with a passion.

Charlie Justiss met the other six wagons on the outskirts of town.

"What's happened?" Parnell asked.

"We've been robbed by those fool women," Joplin explained. "Best round up some help. They're sure to burn the cargo."

Charlie turned and led the way back into Palo Pinto, collecting Bret and Tut along the way. Soon the angry freighters were telling their story to half the town.

"They wouldn't destroy it all, would they?" Jack Duncan asked.

"Every drop they can lay hold of," Charlie answered.

The Women for Morality had another solution, though. Rather than burn the sinful goods, they drove the wagon across the Cooke farm to the river. There they had a real Brazos Temperance Baptism.

By the time Charlie and Parnell arrived with Bret Pruett, the Brazos was already dotted with floating bottles. Smashed barrel staves marked the demise of the beer kegs.

The bandits, no longer masked, sat atop their horses along the banks, laughing and decrying the influence of spirits upon the young. A great deal of singing and dancing followed the destruction of the cargo. The mood turned less friendly when Alex Tuttle appeared with Art Stanley and a gang of freighters.

"Which ones stopped the wagons?" Bret asked the freighters.

"They wore masks. They all looked pretty much the same to me," Joplin replied. "I guess it was all of 'em."

Bret gazed at the defiant faces of the culprits. His mother-in-law and wife were among them.

"Arrest them, Bret!" Art demanded. "There's such a thing as justice, isn't there?"

"I can't very well lock 'em all up," Bret protested. "I'm sure we can come to terms on the cargo."

"No, we can't!" Angela cried. "Lock us up. We're eager for a trial."

"Angela," Charlie said, riding into the midst of the miscreants. "Stealing freight's bad enough."

"We were doing the Lord's bidding!" Celia protested. "He'll stand at our side."

Charlie looked at Bret, and the two men sighed. Bret nodded to Tut, and the deputy waved Angela, Celia Cooke and Judith Parnell along.

The three women were escorted back to the courthouse and locked in the storeroom.

"I guess now we'll really see the fur fly," Bret grumbled.

"Yes," Charlie agreed, "and I'd rather be facing the whole Yankee cavalry at Five Forks than deal with your prisoners."

Chapter 6

Art Stanley was for chaining the raid's ring-leaders to the courthouse wall and leaving them there to rot. Jack Duncan proposed taking after the women with a barrel stave. As it happened, though, not a single witness appeared to support the charges.

"We can't very well lock up our own wives and mothers," Walt Joplin explained. "Sometimes it's best to know when you're licked."

"I can't charge anyone unless somebody swears to what happened," Bret then told Art Stanley.

"You mean you think those ladies just happened by the river about the time my cargo was dumped in the river?" Art cried in disbelief. "You sure you wouldn't press the matter a bit harder if your own wife and her meddling mother weren't back of this whole thing?"

"I am," Bret replied. "I guess what you have to decide is whether you want to join in the prank or declare war on every female in Palo Pinto. You can't tell me they're not hurting your trade at the mercantile."

"So you'd just fold the hand, eh, Bret?"

"And I'd suggest to Jack Duncan at the Lone Star and Oliver Clayton at the Double P that they find another source for their whiskey."

"They'll enjoy hearing that."

"Doesn't much matter. To tell the truth, I figure those ladies'll have every man over the age of seven signing one of their pledges soon."

"Probably right. I never thought I'd find myself signing one of those papers, but a man'll do close to anything to dodge fifty preaching females."

Bret laughed at Art's scowling face. At one time or another everyone had to swallow bitter news. It was best taken with an ounce of humor.

The Women for Morality celebrated their victory with a bonfire at the edge of town. Douglas Fairchild gave a loud and passionate oration on the wisdom of temperance and afterward led a torchlit parade from one end of Front Street to the other.

The next day Eliza Justiss appeared at the courthouse an hour after breakfast. With Ross working two days a week on the county's business, Eliza's arrival was no great surprise. But when she began tacking papers to the courthouse doors, Ross, Bret Pruett and Charlie Justiss trotted out to see what was amiss.

"Eliza?" Ross called out in surprise.

"This is a petition calling for a special election," she explained. "Half the town's voters signed."

"And when do we call for this vote?" Charlie asked.

"Two weeks," Eliza answered. "That's plenty of time for us to spread the word and discuss the issues."

"Which are?"

"Listed right here," she said, handing a neatly printed poster to each of the men. "By noon I'll have them tacked up all over town."

Charlie nodded, then read the list of proposed new laws as Ross ushered Eliza down the street for a talk.

The poster was entitled "A Campaign for Decency". First and foremost was a law forbidding the sale of alcoholic beverages within the town limits of Palo Pinto. A ban on the carrying of sidearms was next. The final proposal addressed houses of entertainment, though clearly its target was not the houses but the entertainers.

"Well," Bret said, grinning, "they've about accomplished number three, and the first one's well on its way. As for the other, we're in for another storm from Marty, not to mention Joe Nance."

"Before young Andy Coonce got shot, you'd had a tough time of it," Charlie said, "but now, well, I wouldn't be near as sure. I understand they're passing such laws elsewhere, and I'd not be surprised if these are voted onto the books here."

"After that raid on Stanley's wagons, nothing's going to surprise me ever again," Bret remarked.

Charlie nodded his agreement, and the two returned to their labors inside the courthouse.

Eliza's posters were soon spread all over town. Some were even nailed up on bunkhouse doors at the nearby ranches. As expected, the cowboys were less than pleased with the idea of closing the saloons. Joe Nance led the Circle N outfit into town nearly every night to protest the unfairness of laws aimed at poor cowboys and travelers.

"This town couldn't survive without our trade!"

Joe told the townspeople. "We buy our flour and coffee, our shirts and stockings, and yes, our whiskey here in Palo Pinto. Could be if we have to turn elsewhere for our liquor, we might buy supplies there as well."

"He's right," Art Stanley spoke up. "Think about it. The railroad's already sent the better part of the county's commerce down south. If the cowboys take their money to Justiss Junction, what will happen to Georgia's hotel? Will Doc Garnett stay? Why, I've even seen county seats change. Is that what you want, friends? Will you kill this town?"

The crowd muttered a dozen different answers before Angela stepped forward to reply.

"What we won't kill is our children," she thundered. "Have you forgotten so soon that we buried Andy Coonce? Wasn't it just yesterday I was feeding him broth after he was shot by Raymond Polk? We've grown weary of burying boys. It's time men holstered their guns and took the pledge."

"Amen!" the ladies in the crowd added.

"And what will we do for business? Art asked.

"Oh, Art," Angela grumbled. "How many pairs of breeches do you sell to cowboys? How many of them stay at the hotel? Families buy cloth and flour, and they'll come by the score to a town that offers them a good life and a real future for their children. Towns may be built by ranchers, Joe Nance, but they're peopled by families.

Each night thereafter the bonfire was rekindled, and soon it became apparent to Charlie that persuasive speakers like Angela and Reverend Fairchild were having an effect on the election. It would be up to the men of Palo Pinto to decide the issue, but the women seemed set in their minds to control the outcome.

Joe Nance was no less determined to defeat the new laws, but his cowboys worked hard all day on the range. They began to tire of arguing with ladies armed with Bibles and bells.

Marty Steele tried to rouse the feelings of the Flying J hands, but with Angela Justiss speaking fiery words and urging especially the younger ones to sign temperance pledges, it was a hopeless cause.

"I believe two of every three's bound to vote for those new laws," a frustrated Marty told Charlie. "It'll prove hard on 'em later. The junction's a mightly long way to go for a drink."

"Oh, I expect Jack Duncan'll just move his place outside the town limits," Charlie said.

"Won't be there for long. Those ladies'll see to that."

"Well, there are parcels of land all over the place. And besides, I figure Angela will have you signing a pledge inside six weeks."

"Not me," Marty declared. "I'll never let myself be shackled by anybody."

Charlie grinned. He'd not long before thought that about himself.

Two days before the election the Women for Morality played their final ace. It was simple really. Those ladies who had been unable to convince their husbands to vote for the new statutes left home and children to set up camp outside the church.

"We will not live under a Godless roof!" they bellowed. And as farmers and shopkeepers tried to deal with anxious children, with washing and cooking and mending, not to mention their usual chores, many soon changed their minds.

Even before the vote was taken, it was clear the odds favored the temperance ladies. Sunday's sermon was a feverish plea to support the new laws, and the enthusiastic response of the congregation hinted at the outcome.

Early Monday morning Bret and Ross passed ballots out to a long line of townsmen and farmers. Across the street banners urging a yes vote filled shop windows. Bell-ringing women walked back and forth, and small children sat in the backs of farm wagons as a reminder that the new laws were intended to better those youngsters' lives.

The cowboys appeared around noon. Joe Nance led his outfit up the courthouse steps. The Flying J hands trickled in later.

"I know we're hard-pressed," Nance admitted to Charlie, "but who's to say what a man will do when he marks his ballot. Even some of those farmers may change their minds when there's nobody clanging a bell in their ears."

The voting lasted until suppertime, but there were few ballots cast after two o'clock. Charlie waited until six to begin the count, and he called Art Stanley and Eliza in to observe. Bret was there as well, and Joe Nance was invited.

At first the totals favored the new laws three to one, but that began to change. Charlie had figured the cowboys would vote nay, but clearly others, as Joe Nance had said, were changing their feeling once liberated from the watchful eyes of wives.

"I don't understand," Eliza cried in dismay

when the nays caught and passed the yea votes. "It's treachery, pure and simple. We've been betrayed."

In contrast, Art Stanley could hardly conceal his joy. It proved short-lived. The final twenty ballots were overwhelmingly in favor of the new proposals, and Charlie Justiss, after recounting the tally twice, announced it to a crowd gathered outside despite a chill wind and falling temperatures.

"Saints be praised!" Celia Cooke cried. "We've done it!"

The bonfire was relit, and hymns resounded across the town most of the night.

After a brief supper, Bret and Charlie returned to the courthouse to begin making placards explaining the new statutes. They lettered each sign carefully, then went on to the next one. Around nine Angela brought over a pitcher of mint tea.

"I guess it wouldn't be proper to drink anything stronger this night," Bret muttered as he sipped a cup of tea. "If the law's obeyed, it should make life a little easier for me and Tut."

"I pray that's how it will work," Charlie said. "I'll never forget that gun hand Joe Nance brought along on our first drive to Abilene. He just had to test the law, and he was shot for his trouble."

"I don't even remember his name."

"Nor I. That's the way it is with fools. It does seem a man ought to be remembered a little, though."

"That's what families are for. It's the saddest part of Andy's getting shot. He had nobody."

"From Ryan's wires, I'd say we're going to be knee deep in orphans pretty soon. Rachel Harmer's bringing her rail rats."

"It'll do the town some good. Maybe we can take our minds off quarreling and lend a hand."

"Maybe. I don't know anymore. I only thought this was my town. The way things happen nowadays, I feel mostly a stranger. If you want to know what's going to happen, ask Angela or Celia Cooke."

"Marty's threatened to leave. Did Billy tell you that?"

"Marty makes rumblings every so often. It's his way of showing he's not tied to this place. He is, though. It's home and family, past and present. He loves those accursed rocks and blasted cactus more than anybody."

"Not more than you," Bret said, smiling. "Nobody could."

"Maybe not," Charlie admitted.

The signs were nailed up on the outskirts of town early the next morning. Bret and Tut passed the rest of the day collecting sidearms or helping Jack Duncan load his remaining stock into a wagon. Oliver Clayton had moved to Justiss Junction the night before, and the Double P, a mainstay on Front Street for fourteen years, ironically became a sewing shop.

"Where will you go, Jack?" Charlie asked when Duncan filled his wagonbed with the final crate of bottles.

"For now, I'll set up a tent saloon up north where the Jacksboro road crosses the Brazos. We'll see how that works. If I'm not attacked by masked riders, I'll build a real place, maybe make it a trading post."

The closing of the saloons brought celebration aplenty. Others brooded and grumbled. Charlie was surprised, however, to discover Chris and Joe so affected, though.

"First the buffalo were all shot off," Chris complained. "Then the railroad came, and the days of driving cattle up the trail to Kansas disappeared. Now the range is mostly fenced, and we're getting rid of the longhorns. These new cows Ryan favors raising look like overgrown prairie dogs. There's no trick to turning them with a good horse."

"The excitement's all gone," Joe pointed out. "What kind of life is a cowboy going to have? We can't . . . oh, you know, Papa. Pretty soon it'll get so you can't be a real Texan anymore."

"No," Charlie objected. "That's not it at all. A real Texan's a man who stands by his faith, who tends his work and cares for his family. It doesn't take killing buffalo or drinking whiskey to make a man strong. The strongest ones are like your mama. They know who they are and where they're going. They build for the future. They study a question, decide what's right and then stick to their guns."

"You weren't much in favor of all these new laws, were you, Papa?" Chris asked.

"I was in favor of your mama. They made sense to her, and that was good enough for me."

"Marty says we'll be wearing skirts next," Joe grumbled. "We men didn't exactly stand our ground."

"Maybe that's because deep down we knew who was in the right this time," Charlie said, drawing the boys to his side. "It may hurt our pride some to admit, but we don't always do what's best unless somebody gives us a pretty fair nudge in the right direction."

"Yeah?" Joe asked. "Like an hornery old longhorn?"

"Exactly," Charlie said, resting a weary hand on each of the boys' shoulders. "Now, what would you think about taking a ride out to the range? I haven't been there in two weeks."

"Sure, Papa," Chris responded, and the two boys raced out of the house toward the livery as if reborn.

Chapter 7

With the Double P converted to a sewing shop and the Lone Star boarded up and awaiting sale, peace reigned over Palo Pinto come nightfall. The first breath of winter was upon the land, and evening's chill had the effect of drawing families together around fireplaces. After the turmoil of October, it was a time of mending fences, of bringing old friends over for Sunday dinner and holding socials at the schoolhouse.

For Angela Justiss it was a time, also, to look back in triumph. But even as Charlie and Bret were posting the new laws, she was envisioning other changes for Palo Pinto. From its huddle of wooden buildings and humble houses a real community would blossom. There would be a new courthouse, perhaps of stone, and a real jailhouse. Vicki would have a school away from the distractions of the center of town.

When Charlie had finished collecting fall's taxes, Angela spoke of her plans. It wasn't the first time, of course, that she'd brought up the subject, but this time she laid out sets of building plans she'd received from Eliza's father, Senator Lawrence Rogers.

"I can't see where we'd get the funds for all this," Charlie said, shaking his head. "Stone? Even the lumber for the beams is beyond the county's budget."

"Charlie, you know as well as I do there are trees that warrant cutting up in the hills. We can quarry the stone ourselves."

"We can? Who's going to do that? We had a struggle just building the old house on Bluff Creek. We'd have to hire stonecutters and masons."

"Well, there are men to be hired, especially in late autumn."

"And the money?"

"What the county lacks can be raised."

"Oh?" Charlie said, folding his arms. "Just how would that be done?"

"Listen to me, Charlie Justiss, when I say it can be done. It wasn't so long ago no one in Palo Pinto would have believed we could rid the town of saloons. We did. Now, are you still such a nonbeliever?"

"No, go ahead and see what you can do. I'll bring the people together, and we'll have ourselves a vote. I'd delay the courthouse myself, for there's high sentiment for building a real jail. As for the school, it could wait for spring."

"It can if it has to," Angela grumbled. "But there will be cattle to brand and roofs to patch. If we build now, Billy can send some men from the ranch. Joe Nance can spare others, and there will be men among the farmers who can join in. J. C. Parnell has a fine eye for framing barns. I'll bet he could set the beams in place."

"You've done a fair amount of planning. I suppose I have no choice, do I?"

"Would you want it otherwise?"

"No," Charlie said, pulling her to his side. "I'd be a fool not to trust your judgment by now. So when do we begin?"

"When can you gather the people for a vote?"

They smiled and laughed, then sat a table and examined Senator Rogers's plans.

Surprisingly, there was little argument when Charlie proposed the courthouse and the school. As for the jail, young Chris had a ready solution.

"Why not use the old schoolhouse?" the boy suggested. "It's been a ready enough prison for us boys these past years."

Charlie rocked with laughter, then countered.

"That schoolhouse stands beside the church, Chris, and though there'd be those who'd say a jail and a church resting one alongside the other would prompt repentance, I'd judge the ladies might feel better with the jail more distant from their children."

"I guess so," Chris admitted.

It wasn't long thereafter that Palo Pinto became a beehive of activity. Stonecutters from Austin arrived to begin carving building material out of the nearby hills. Billy Justiss had the whole Flying J outfit driving wagons laden with lumber from Justiss Junction. Bars for the new jail arrived as well, and J. C. Parnell had the handier of the farmers busy framing the jail.

Even before the foundation stones for the new buildings were set in place, other changes came to Palo Pinto. New enterprises came to town, and old ones painted their walls and placed new signs over their doors. Stanley & Sons Mercantile replaced the fading Stanley Trading Post sign which Art had brought from the old place down at Village Bend. Albert Parnell opened a farm supply store on the west end of Front Street.

"It puts me in mind of that first autumn when we were building the ranch," Charlie told Angela. "There's something about the smell of raw lumber, the sound of children running across rough floorboards, the sight of a building rising from empty space that makes a man quit reflecting on his past and start looking to his future."

"I know," Angela said as she gripped Charlie's arm. "It's a fine thing, looking at our grandchildren running around town, watching Ross and Eliza put up their house on the Jacksboro road. We've done all right by them, Charlie. And they'll do just fine by us."

"You don't miss the old days much, do you?"

"Not much. There were a lot of lonely hours for me, Charlie. First the war and then those long cattle drives. I do miss them some. I wonder if I'm needed now. My legs don't let me move as fast when there's a chill to the air."

"We're getting old."

"Oh, it's scarcely time to bury you yet. There are still mountains to climb. It'll take a firm hand to keep Joe and Chris on the right path."

"Oh, Billy and Ryan have turned out fine, and they were twice as wild. Ryan says there are boys of sixteen at ag college now. That leaves Joe but a year and a half left at home."

"That's when we're going to feel the years," Angela said, clutching Charlie's hands. "As long as there are boys at home to vex their mother, she'll not turn gray. But when there's only silence . . ."

"Silence?" Charlie asked, laughing. "You'll have a dozen grandkids by then. Or else you'll build another town or maybe reform the state. I can't see you ever sitting in a rocker darning socks like some patient old granny."

"I never learned patience."

"No, and I've always thought that your strongest suit, Angela Justiss. It's made the world a better place."

They held each other tightly, and Charlie wondered that so many autumns could have passed since that first time they'd walked together in the Brazos moonlight.

In the days that followed, Charlie and Angela toured the skeletons that would soon become jail and school and courthouse. The masons arrived to shape the rough stone into walls, and by mid-November the first floor of the courthouse began to rise. By then the jail was completed, and only the windows and roof remained to be completed at the school.

By then another challenge lay at hand. Cowboys from the Flying J and stockyard men from Justiss Junction worked to complete a barn and a large bunkhouse above Buck Creek. Any day a train would pull up and deposit a hundred ragged urchins who'd only lately helped construct a railroad from Ft. Worth to El Paso.

"This has always been good land for growing things," Charlie remarked to Marty Steele as the two old friends nailed planks into place. "It's no gentle place, and that's fitting, for the youngsters Rachel Harmer will bring are far from gentle themselves. They've known hard times, and the hardships have fashioned them well."

"Was much the same with me," Marty said. "I wasn't eighteen when I shouldered a rifle and marched to war. I was powerful ignorant, but I recall a man who gave me a hand up when I fell, who taught me the straight way to look at a thing, who got me through the worst times. Even if he's got a hymn-singer of a wife, I guess I'll always know him for a friend."

"I take that as high praise," Charlie said, hammering a nail and laughing loudly.

"You ever miss ridin' the range?"

"Sometimes, but I don't miss the loneliness or the cold. I do recall the singing and the company, though. I regret Chris and Joe haven't spent more time in the company of the stars. Maybe this summer I'll take them out for a week or so."

"Luis will have them mustangin' again."

"I suspect. They came back taller and tanned for their labor."

"I envy you them," Marty said, suddenly turning away and staring off into the distant horizon. "It's the price a man pays for independence, I suppose, not havin' boys to leave his name."

"There are those who'd say it wasn't too late."

400

"Can you see me helpin' some female hang her laundry?"

"Wes has adapted."

"Well, there aren't many Alice Harts about."

"Some."

"Think maybe I should take a look around?"

"You have to do a lot more than look, Marty. You pass enough hours at the junction nowadays. Open your eyes."

"I do," Marty said, grinning. "And I've seen a few I wouldn't mind winterin' with."

"Next time try telling them."

"Sure. So long as they don't ask me to temper my drinkin' or curb my language." Marty went on to list a dozen other faults that should be overlooked.

Charlie shook his head and laughed. Marty was hopeless.

The first barn and a long bunkhouse were complete when the train carrying Rachel Harmer's homeless charges pulled to a halt at Buck Creek. The doors of two cattle cars swung open, and the first ragged, weary youngsters jumped to the sandy ground below.

"Oh, Lord," Angela Justiss gasped as the threadbare children wandered alongside the tracks, their bare feet jabbed by sharp bits of rock or the wicked spines of pencil cactus.

"Come along," Rachel called as she climbed down from the musty boxcar. "We're finally here. This is our new home."

As the children continued to pour from the cars, they gazed skeptically at the bunkhouse. Years of pain and broken promises had taught them to be wary of strange places and new people. Even so there were some who looked with hope at the buildings, and others danced toward the longhorns grazing near the barn.

"Are we truly home?" little Jay Belton asked Rachel as she hurried toward Angela and Charlie.

"Jay, we are," Rachel said, taking the boy by the arm and leading him along. When they reached the Justisses, Angela stepped back. She beheld young Jay's maimed hand and grew pale. Though she'd heard Bowie's tales of mutilated shakers, it was her first encounter with one firsthand.

The boy saw Angela's face and immediately stuffed his hand in a pocket. Rachel frowned, but Charlie bent down, snatched the boy in firm hands and lifted him onto one shoulder.

"Welcome to Buck Creek, son," Charlie said. And Angela, seeing the grin return to the child's face, brightened as well.

"Shall we have a look at the place?" Angela asked.

"If we don't, I'm afraid I'll have a rebellion on my hands," Rachel said, grinning as hardened cowboys like Marty Steele led hesitant urchins toward the house. Oldtimers like Joe Nance and Art Stanley greeted others. Celia Cooke set aside her welcoming speech and instead wrapped an arm around a girl of ten.

"We'll have to get a second house up quickly," Charlie said as orphans continued to pour from the cattle cars. "I never realized how much space a hundred children could occupy."

"I'm afraid it's not a hundred," Rachel whispered. "We picked up twenty-five more along the

402

way. Word spread rather rapidly. There are fifteen girls now, too."

"I'm glad," Angela declared. "They'll have a softening effect."

"Some would," Rachel said, frowning. "I'm afraid there's little soft about these children. They're painfully self-reliant, and they are suspect of kindness."

"Then we'll just have to show them there's good about as well as bad," Angela countered.

A miracle of sorts occurred along Buck Creek. In no time word of the orphans' needs spread throughout the county. Shoes and clothing began arriving. Farmers and ranchers who'd just months before fired rifles at each other across barbed wire fences banded together to finish the buildings. The older orphans joined in the labor, and soon three bunkhouses stood in a line above Buck Creek.

Ash slats were cut for beds, and mattresses were stuffed. Wood was cut for fending off winter chills. Daily some ranch offered steers or pigs, and wagons of vegetables appeared as if by magic. No call was sent out. People witnessed need and responded.

The little community of orphans was transformed. Boys caked with grime and thin as fence rails began to grow. Buck Creek washed away the dirt, and Eliza Rogers helped Rachel clip hair. Trousers torn by abuse and paper thin from wear were exchanged for woolen breeches fit for keeping out the winter draft. Shirts of plain cotton were sewn by Celia Cooke's quilting circle, and a boxcar full of woolen coats and army blankets arrived from Ft. Worth, provided through the generosity of Emiline Justiss.

The entire county opened its heart to the unfortunates. Any hours the masons and carpenters were not devoting to finishing the courthouse in Palo Pinto would be turned to improving the wooden barracks of the orphanage. Cowboys and farmers and even schoolchildren like Joe and Chris would offer their help showing the orphans how to tend stock or caulk the insides of the buildings.

Some did even more. Celia Cooke was the first to open her door.

"I've got three boys," she told Rachel, "and little Thalia and her sister Violet would be a blessing upon our house. They'd fit right in the middle, my Bryant being seven, Violet, eight, and Thalia, ten."

Rachel turned to the girls, and they brightened like blooming roses.

Within days families invited others. The girls went quickly, followed by the older boys. There was work on a farm fit even for children with one hand, it seemed, and perhaps those least blessed by fate were more beloved for their misfortune. Joe Nance hired ten of the oldest, and three others joined the Flying J crew.

By Christmas Rachel had delivered into other hands all but sixty of her charges. Some who remained had been offered work or homes, but they stayed to help Rachel with the others. A few remained distrustful. And many had given their hearts to Rachel Harmer and would in no case desert her side.

Christmas Eve a special visitor arrived at Buck Creek. Clad in red wool and sporting a beard of South Texas cotton, Ryan Justiss brought rare laughter to the smaller of the orphanage's residents and jests from the oldest.

"Welcome, Mr. Ryan," Clark Channning, Rachel's unofficial assistant, cried when they all gathered for supper. "Miz Rachel's missed you some."

"I see you've taken good care of her, boys," Ryan responded. "You'll manage winter just fine. And come spring, you'll grow to be cowboys, the all of you."

When the boys were safely bedded down and the last prayers had been witnessed, Rachel and Ryan walked alone beside the creek and gazed overhead at a sky alive with stars.

"It's your family's doing, this place," Rachel exclaimed. "Nobody else could have prompted so many to give so much."

"No, it's you and the young ones," Ryan objected. "There've been grave quarrels hereabouts, but one thing I've learned about good people. When a common trial appears, they band together and face it. Texans are always at their best when it's most needed. I learned that early."

"You'll return to school soon."

"I will, but in May, I'll be finished. I thought maybe with cattle to market you might need somebody with experience to help out around here. Think I should apply for the job?"

"What about your training? Shouldn't you go to

405

work for your uncle?"

"I can still build bridges when there's need, but I could never be happy far from you."

"You'll have to share me with sixty boys."

"I planned to share you with children. Most people have to wait years for a family. I'll have my chance straight away."

"Think you can wait until June for the wedding? I always dreamed of being a summer bride."

"It will seem an eternity, but I suppose it's worth it."

"I think so," she said, falling into Ryan's arms.

"I know so," he replied.

Chapter 8

1881 found Palo Pinto changed. As winter gave way to spring, a new prosperity settled over the county. The Ft. Worth and Western's coaches brought new settlers, and its boxcars bore cattle to hungry stockyards in return for the cash which built new fortunes.

By April the new courthouse stood complete. The old structure became a town hall of sorts, playing host to dancing and gatherings instead of trials and debates. The jail occasionally housed a rebellious cowboy who refused to surrender his Colt or an idler who picked a pocket or borrowed a horse. Only the school had heavy use, for almost every family in town had grown a new son or daughter thanks to Rachel Harmer.

After long argument, Ross Justiss supervised the fencing of the new south range. Another 500 acres were enclosed for the use of the orphanage. Circle N and Flying J hands joined together in a roundup, and all mavericks were driven to Buck Creek and marked with a new BC brand thought appropriate for the orphans. In addition, each ranch contributed another hundred head.

In late May Ryan returned from college. He brought with him an engineering degree and a thousand young Hereford cows for the south range. Two impressive bulls arrived the following week.

"They're the future," Ryan pronounced when he and Charlie rode together along Buck Creek the first of June. "Just look at the shoulders on those bulls. You'll find half again as much meat as on a longhorn, and it won't be long before buyers take note."

"I'll miss the longhorns, though," Charlie growled.

"Me, too," Ryan admitted. "I ate a lot of their dust when I was Chris's age. Pretty soon you'll have to look far and wide to see those mangy beasts, all hoof and horn and contrary as a mule. They'll go the way of the buffalo, and we'll find ourselves singing about them around a campfire."

"Most likely."

"You remember when we first got here, Papa?"

"Often," Charlie confessed. "You?"

"I was only eleven, but it's never far from my mind. Those were hard times. I've got reminders, though," Ryan added, opening his shirt and running his fingers along the jagged scar left there by Stands Tall's hatchet in '71. "I worry what the future will hold for me, for Rachel, for those boys at the orphanage and the kids Rachel will bear later on."

"Does no good," Charlie declared. "Worrying. The future comes whether we want it or not. We never choose what changes will come or when. We do our best to tend those dear to us, and we trust the Lord will take care of everything else."

"Even so, I can't help worrying whether I'll be a good husband. Sometimes I think Rachel's a hundred years older than me. I know so little."

"You'll learn. What's important is that you love her, that you care. Everything else will come along if you give it time."

"I try to believe that, but . . ."

"Listen, son," Charlie said, drawing his horse to a halt and motioning Ryan closer. "Everyone gets cold feet now and then. I don't think the groom was born who didn't wonder. Only ask yourself this. Can you live without her?"

"No, sir."

"Then there's but one course open to you. Wed her and pray. You'll do fine."

Ryan did just that, and when Charlie and Angela bid the newlyweds farewell at the Justiss Junction depot, neither bride nor groom seemed to have a doubt that only the best lay ahead. Sixty well-scrubbed boys lined the track and shouted encouragement. Wes and Alice Tyler, having volunteered to stand in for Rachel, stood nearby.

"There's just Billy left to marry off now," Angela said as Charlie drove her back to town in an open carriage.

"For now. Chris and Joe are around, too. Forget?"

"Wish I could," she confessed. "Joe's grown a foot, it seems. He's burst out of all his clothes here lately, and Chris is not far behind. They're boys no more, Charlie."

"It happens."

"Pretty soon we'll be a pair of hobbled old grandparents. Little Charlie leaves me behind already, and Hope exhausts me. The little ones scamper around like squirrels."

"I haven't noticed you giving them much ground."

"I do, though. Thank goodness Enuncia's around to lend a hand."

"Ah, enough of this old age nonsense. What do you say we race this buggy back to town?"

"Charlie!"

"Hang on."

He prodded the horses into motion, then whipped them into a gallop. The carriage raced along the road, throwing up a tail of dust a quarter mile long. For a moment Charlie was twenty again, showing off his lady on a Sunday afternoon to the best of Robertson County. Too soon they arrived at Palo Pinto, though, and Charlie drew the weary horses to a halt. County judges were expected to show some restraint.

"Act your age," Angela chastised him.

Charlie only grinned and started to goad the horses into a trot. Angela laughed and surrendered. Age, after all, was relative.

Even so, their talk prompted Charlie to pay a rare evening visit to the small room Chris and Joe shared. The boys lay sleeping in their beds. Joe's lanky legs sprawled out past the bedposts and Chris curled in a crescent. Moonlight streamed in through an open window, and Chris's golden hair seemed to sparkle as it had when the boys had rested on Charlie's lap at five.

Joe turned uneasily, as if the weight of being fifteen rested uncomfortably on his thin shoulders. Already the boy talked of following Ryan to A & M College, perhaps to study medicine.

Charlie sighed. It would be hard letting go of the youngest. He then felt a hand intertwine itself with his own. Angela rested her head on his shoulder, and Charlie smiled.

"They're growing tall, and we're getting old,"

she whispered. He nodded, then led her away from the open door and down the hall.

"We've been very lucky," he said as he opened the door to their bedroom. "Life's been kind to us."

"We have Vicki and the little ones," Angela told him. "Ross and Eliza, Ryan and Rachel, Billy, Joe and Chris."

"And each other," Charlie added, drawing her close. They continued inside then, allowing the silent darkness to swallow them.

THE UNTAMED WEST
brought to you by Zebra Books

THE LAST MOUNTAIN MAN   (1480, $2.25)
by William W. Johnstone
He rode out West looking for the men who murdered his father
and brother. When an old mountain man taught him how to kill a
man a hundred different ways from Sunday, he knew he'd make
sure they all remembered . . . THE LAST MOUNTAIN MAN.

SAN LOMAH SHOOTOUT   (1853, $2.50)
by Doyle Trent
Jim Kinslow didn't even own a gun, but a group of hardcases
tried to turn him into buzzard meat. There was only one way to
find out why anybody would want to stretch his hide out to dry,
and that was to strap on a borrowed six-gun and ride to death or
glory.

TOMBSTONE LODE   (1915, $2.95)
by Doyle Trent
When the Josey mine caved in on Buckshot Dobbs, he left behind
a rich vein of Colorado gold—but no will. James Alexander,
hired to investigate Buckshot's self-proclaimed blood relations
learns too soon that he has one more chance to solve the mystery
and save his skin or become another victim of TOMBSTONE
LODE.

GALLOWS RIDERS   (1934, $2.50)
by Mark K. Roberts
When Stark and his killer-dogs reached Colby, all it took was a
little muscle and some well-placed slugs to run roughshod over
the small town—until the avenging stranger stepped out of the
shadows for one last bloody showdown.

DEVIL WIRE   (1937, $2.50)
by Cameron Judd
They came by night, striking terror into the hearts of the settlers.
The message was clear: Get rid of the devil wire or the land would
turn red with fencestringer blood. It was the beginning of a brutal
range war.

*Available wherever paperbacks are sold, or order direct from the
Publisher. Send cover price plus 50¢ per copy for mailing and
handling to Zebra Books, Dept. 2164, 475 Park Avenue South,
New York, N.Y. 10016. Residents of New York, New Jersey and
Pennsylvania must include sales tax. DO NOT SEND CASH.*

BEST OF THE WEST
from Zebra Books

BROTHER WOLF   (1728, $2.95)
by Dan Parkinson
Only two men could help Lattimer run down the sheriff's killers—a stranger named Stillwell and an Apache who was as deadly with a Colt as he was with a knife. One of them would see justice done—from the muzzle of a six-gun.

THUNDERLAND   (1991, $3.50)
by Dan Parkinson
Men were suddenly dying all around Jonathan, and he needed to know why—before he became the next bloody victim of the ancient sword that would shape the future of the Texas frontier.

APACHE GOLD   (1899, $2.95)
by Mark K. Roberts & Patrick E. Andrews
Chief Halcon burned with a fierce hatred for the pony soldiers that rode from Fort Dawson, and vowed to take the scalp of every round-eye in the territory. Sergeant O'Callan must ride to glory or death for peace on the new frontier.

OKLAHOMA SHOWDOWN   (1961, $2.25)
by Patrick E. Andrews
When Dace chose the code of lawman over an old friendship, he knew he might have to use his Colt .45 to back up his choice. Because a meeting between good friends who'd ended up on different sides of the law as sure to be one blazing hellfire.

Available wherever paperbacks are sold, or order direct from the Publisher. Send cover price plus 50¢ per copy for mailing and handling to Zebra Books, Dept. 2164, 475 Park Avenue South, New York, N.Y. 10016. Residents of New York, New Jersey and Pennsylvania must include sales tax. DO NOT SEND CASH.

YOUR FAVORITE CELEBRITIES
From Zebra Books

STRANGER IN TWO WORLDS (2112, $4.50)
by Jean Harris
For the first time, the woman convicted in the shooting death of Scarsdale Diet Doctor Herman Tarnower tells her own story. Here is the powerful and compelling truth of the love affair and its shocking aftermath.

STOCKMAN: THE MAN, THE MYTH,
THE FUTURE (2005, $4.50)
by Owen Ullmann
As director of the Office of Management & Budget, Stockman was the youngest man to sit at the Cabinet in more than 160 years. Here is the first full-scale, objective, no-holds-barred story of Ronald Reagan's most controversial advisor, David Stockman.

DUKE: THE LIFE AND TIMES OF
JOHN WAYNE (1935, $3.95)
by Donald Shepherd & Robert Slatzer with Dave Grayson
From his childhood as the son of a failed druggist to his gallant battle against cancer, here's what the "Duke" was really like — with all the faults that made him human and all the courage and honesty that made him one of Hollywood's greatest and most endearing stars.

IACOCCA (1700, $3.95)
by David Abodaher
As president of Ford and father of the Mustang, Iacocca's been a force to be reckoned with in the car industry for two decades. But it was due to his inexplicable fall from grace with Henry Ford that Iacocca took on the Chrysler challenge. By turning that dying corporation around through sheer will power and pull in the biggest profits in Chrysler's hisotry, the respected business leader became a modern-day folk hero.

Available wherever paperbacks are sold, or order direct from the Publisher. Send cover price plus 50¢ per copy for mailing and handling to Zebra Books, Dept. 2164, 475 Park Avenue South, New York, N.Y. 10016. Residents of New York, New Jersey and Pennsylvania must include sales tax. DO NOT SEND CASH.